F

Crow, Donna Fletcher

AUTHOR

Where Love Calls

TITLE

DATE DUE	BORROWER'S NAME

Where Love Calls

Donna Fletcher Crow

CROSSWAY BOOKS • WHEATON, ILLINOIS
A DIVISION OF GOOD NEWS PUBLISHERS

Where Love Calls

Published by Crossway Books
a division of Good News Publishers
1300 Crescent Street
Wheaton, Illinois 60187

Cover illustration: Chris Cocozza

First printing, 1998

Printed in the United States of America

Library of Congress Cataloging-in-Publication Data
Crow, Donna Fletcher.
  Where love calls / Donna Fletcher Crow.
      p.   cm.
  ISBN 0-89107-988-X
  I. Title.
PS3553.R5872W485 1998
813'.54—dc21   98-9951

11	10	09	08	07	06	05	04	03	02	01	00	99	98
15	14	13	12	11	10	9	8	7	6	5	4	3	2	1

To Anne and John Pollock
for their encouragement and guidance
on paths they blazed with far greater light

THE BEAUCHAMP AND STUDD FAMILIES

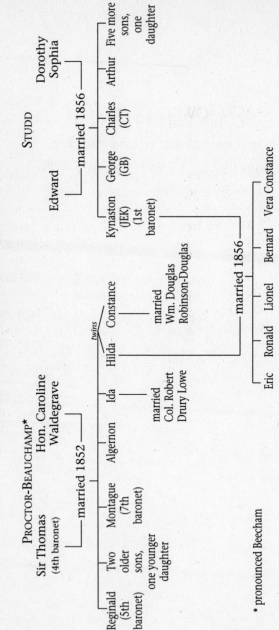

* pronounced Beecham

ACKNOWLEDGMENTS

My grateful appreciation for encouragement and help on this project to: The Reverend John Charles Pollock, biographer; Sir Christopher R. Proctor-Beauchamp; Mrs. Audrey Young, formerly of Langley School; retired missionaries of the China Inland Mission at Lammermuir House, especially Marguerite G. Owen, Grace Frey, Helen Cox, and Sadie Custer; Donald L. Crawford, Director of Public Ministries, Overseas Missionary Fellowship; The Association of Cricket Statisticians and Historians, Nottingham; and my friend and hostess in Norwich, Hazel Flavell.

Prologue

T'ai-yuen Fu, capital of the province of Shansi, North China, was four hundred miles inland from the nearest port—twenty days' travel by foot and pony cart, then six weeks by sea to England. But tonight Harold Schofield's heart was in England as he poured out his deepest longing to God.

One of the most brilliant medical students of his generation, winner of scholarships, prizes, and honors in Oxford, London, Vienna, and Prague, Harold had ignored the protests of all who argued that it would be a waste to abandon his brilliant career and bury himself in far-off China. He never considered forsaking his spiritual call. Harold and his young wife had served for the past three years with the China Inland Mission.

Now, after a day that began before the sun rose—starting with a prayer meeting for their 35 inpatients, then preaching to the 150 outpatients who had come to the dispensary that day, and ended with an evening of street preaching alongside a fellow missionary—Harold could leave the sounds and smells of China behind him and focus on his vision for God to raise up young men in England to preach His Word. "Give us the very best, Lord. Call the best for Your kingdom, the brightest to bear the torch of Your truth."

Harold dropped his broad, smooth forehead into his hands and then ran his fingers over the fair hair that fell to his shoulder in a pigtail. His mind filled with images of the men of talent and leadership he longed for God to send to China. "Oh, God, move in the universities of England. Across the land call out the most able to be Your servants through whom You will show Your glory. Make these, Your chosen ones, glorious in Your sight that people may be brought to You."

Time passed. Had he been praying for an hour? Two hours? He was vaguely aware of the fading light in his room and of the fact that dinnertime was long past. Yet the urgency of his burden would not lift. He pictured the universities in his mind as if a great map hung on the wall in front of him: Glasgow, Edinburgh, Oxford, Cambridge… "Oh, God, work among the students there. Pour out Your Spirit. Call young men from the universities. Call them to You. Send them forth in Your power. Send them to China. Be their strength. Make them a light to the nations that Your salvation might reach the ends of the earth."

One

T he late April sunshine glinted off the slow-flowing waters of the Cam. Hilda Beauchamp adjusted her parasol to shade her eyes better and tried to identify the men sitting in the long, slim shell of the Trinity boat, each holding his oar just above the surface of the water. Her brother Montague was easy enough to pick out, with his smooth, dark hair and dramatically drooping mustache. *That must be his friend William Hoste behind him.* She hadn't met Hoste but had heard Monty mention that William wore his sideburns long and full, in the fashion of the Royal Artillery. *But where is Stanley Smith?*

She scanned the length of the boat and back again. None of the eight heads bent over their oars gleamed with the familiar pale gold. And none of the bodies seemed built on his somewhat slighter lines, although most seemed slender compared to her brother's vigorous build. Had Stanley's lungs worsened? Had his wracking cough returned? Or worse, had the illness recurred that had made him leave Repton early and spend a year convalescing before coming up to Cambridge? She knew he overworked, spending long hours training on the cold, damp river when he would have been much better off reading before a fire in his rooms in Market Passage.

"Are you ready?" The starter, standing in his box with upraised flag, called Hilda's attention back to the race. There was no reply to the starter's question from the six Cambridge crews, all sitting with raised oars.

"Go." The flag snapped down.

The four oars on each side of the Trinity boat cut into the water, and it shot forward. As the rowers pulled against the oars, their seats slid backward, adding leg drive to the thrust of the arms. Hilda well understood this as she had heard her brother talk endlessly about the strong back and stomach muscles required to achieve the all-important body swing.

The smooth motion propelled the scull swiftly up its lane. But apparently not swiftly enough, for the Jesus boat in the lane next to Trinity was pulling steadily ahead of all the others. Impossible. Their technique was terrible. Even an untrained eye like Hilda's could see that the body swing of the Jesus team was almost nonexistent, and their stroke, while smooth, lacked form. Yet they held, even increased, their speed.

The boats skimmed on up the straight stretch of the river above Ely where the Cambridge crews rowed because the river was too curved closer to the university. *How will Monty bear it if he loses his place for the university races?* Hilda worried. *Worse, how will those around him bear it if Monty loses his temper?*

Hilda felt as if she had held her breath for the full time it took the boats to cover the 6,600-foot course. And the Jesus crew held their lead the whole way. At least Trinity came in next. Would that be enough for them to qualify for the University Eights? And if so, would Monty be on the final crew? And where on earth was Stanley?

Hilda turned at the pressure of her mother's hand on her arm. "Pity they didn't win. But Montague was quite magnificent—don't you think? I'm certain he'll make the Eights."

Hilda smiled. As usual, Lady Beauchamp was indomitable. "Yes, Mother, I do hope so. Let's go ask him." She lifted the skirt of her blue and green striped dress just enough to allow her to walk down the riverbank toward the spot where the crews were bringing their shells ashore.

Halfway there she stopped. Was Monty upbraiding the captain of the Jesus boat for his team's bad form? Surely her brother would not display such bad manners. And yet when his temper got the upper hand...

Lady Beauchamp was as cool as her son was heated. "I am sorry, my dear. I would love to speak to Montague, too. But he appears to be quite involved at the moment. And we really mustn't miss the next train to Norwich. I'm chairing the meeting of the Seamen's Relief Society this afternoon."

Hilda sighed. She wanted to know the results of the race, and yet she must return to Langley Hall. Her mother would not be home until dinnertime, and Hilda must see to the preparations for their weekend guests. They had been lucky that Lady Beauchamp's morning meeting with the dean of Ely Cathedral had given them just enough time to watch Monty row. Hilda turned with a final look around for Stanley Smith.

"Hilda, where are your manners, dear? Acknowledge those young men. I'm sure their bows are for you and not for me." Lady Beauchamp dipped her parasol in gracious recognition of three varsity men. "Aren't those the cricketing brothers Montague introduced us to at Christmas?"

Hilda tipped her head their direction. "Oh, yes, the three Studd brothers." Then she offered her most gracious smile to the one on the left side. "The eldest one—Kynaston—would make a fine beau for Ida. Don't you think so, Mama?"

"I'm certain any friend of Montague's would be most respectable."

"Yes. I rather fancy Kynaston is somewhat more than respectable. I have asked Monty to bring him to Langley." Hilda moved on, still hoping to catch sight of the slim, blond, fine-featured young man that she had settled on as a most respectable beau for herself.

Two hours later Hilda sighed with satisfaction. Surely in all of God's green earth there wasn't a lovelier spot than Langley Park at daffodil time. And in all Hilda's twenty-one years, there had never been a more beautiful spring than this of 1881. Everything was perfect. As perfect, at least, as it could be in view of her worry over her temperamental brother and his erratic friend. Her satisfaction faded, and her high, usually smooth brow wrinkled with a scowl. And where was her sister?

"Ida!" Her voice took on an impatient edge—not at all the way Lady Beauchamp, the daughter of Baron Radstock, had so carefully trained her daughters to speak, but it was Hilda.

She tugged up the flounce of the white cotton dress she had changed into for afternoon, pulling it backward to add to the fashionable bustle effect. *Thank goodness for dress reforms.* Ladies' dresses now allowed for more flexibility at the waist and in the shoulders. Hilda disliked being restricted in her movements, especially when there was so much to see to. She had left precise orders with Beeson, but she must see that tea was laid out properly to welcome Monty and his friends. Whatever the outcome of the trials, her brother's appetite would be unflagging. And if Stanley were unwell, he would need all the nourishment he could be encouraged to take. Perhaps she could add cheese to the tea menu. Or egg sandwiches. Cook's heavy, dark currant cake was strengthening; she would give orders that it be cut extra thick.

Hilda had taken only a few steps along the daffodil-bordered gravel path leading from the conservatory across the northeast lawn, when she heard the crunch of carriage wheels approaching from the wooded drive. She was torn between welcoming their guests or finding her sister to make certain Ida's hair was properly arranged in case Kynaston Studd had joined the party.

Hilda hesitated only a moment. In spite of her desire to see Stanley Smith, she knew her duty. Which Ida obviously did not. Although it was nearly teatime, the eldest Beauchamp daughter would doubtless still be wearing a loose-fitting morning dress, sunk deep in reading a meditation by Donne or a volume of sermons.

Hilda hurried into the house and flung open the study's high, dark oak doors. "Just as I suspected. Ida, you really are hopeless." Hilda crossed the deep pile of the maroon carpet to the high-backed plush chair where Ida sat bent over a leather-bound volume. "Who is it—Rowland Hill or Mr. Spurgeon?" She plucked the book from Ida's hands.

Ida looked up, blinking her round blue eyes in the soft light filtering through the stained-glass window. "Oh. No, no. This is a new volume Mother had sent down from Edinburgh. The Rev. George MacDonald." She reached for the book. "Here, let me read a passage to you, Hilda. It's most instructive."

"I've no doubt that it is." Hilda firmly placed the book on a table far from Ida's reach. "But Monty and his friends have just arrived, and Mama is still at her meeting. As the eldest daughter, you must see to serving the tea. But not in that dress. And have Violet fix your hair."

"Oh, Hilda, can't you and Tottie..."

Hilda didn't even bother to answer as she ushered her sister from the room. She sighed. As usual, it was all up to her. In the dressing room the sisters shared, she stepped to the wall and gave two sharp tugs at the bell cord, issuing her call in the depths of the house. The third yank pulled the gold silk rope from the wall and left it limp in her hand. Ellen, the parlor maid, her dark hair topped with a crisp lace cap, hurried in and bobbed a curtsy.

"Ellen, send someone to the stables to inform Miss Constance that our guests are arriving." Not that Hilda expected such information would prod her twin sister into cutting short her ride in the park to see to her duty.

Life would have been so much easier for Hilda if she could have been the perfect submissive lady, like Ida, or concerned only about her own activities, like Tottie. But then who would have seen to the interests of the family while their mother was about her evangelical work? Of course, it should be Ida's place, but she was the most hopeless of all. Reading sermons and poetry from morning till night. Well, at least she did take an interest in her policemen's charity, but she would have to stir herself more forcefully if she were to become the wife of Kynaston Studd. Or Hilda would stir herself on her sister's behalf.

Perhaps it would be different if their father were still living, but since his death seven years ago, Lady Beauchamp had become ever more spiritually minded. Hilda made her way down the polished parquet floor of the circular passage toward the grand entrance. She paused before an oval gilt-framed mirror in the anteroom just long enough to smooth a few strands of hair back into their swirling cluster atop her head and run a dampened fingertip over the heavy brows that framed her wide, dark eyes. At the sound of Beeson moving to open the main door, Hilda squared her unfashionably broad shoulders and stepped between the cut velvet curtains draping the archway.

"Monty, welcome home." She lifted her cheek to her brother, and he gave her an offhanded kiss, tickling her cheek with his sharply angled mustache. She turned to his companion. "How nice to see you again, Mr. Studd." She offered her hand for their guest to bow over.

Kynaston Studd brushed her hand with his mustache, which was smaller and more finely trimmed than Montague's—in perfect keeping with Kynaston's sharp aristocratic features. Yes, he and Ida would make a striking couple.

Hilda frowned in puzzlement as Beeson closed the door. "Oh, Mr. Studd, didn't your brothers come, too?" Stanley Smith was the one she wanted to know about, but it would seem forward to ask.

"Won't you call me Kynaston, Miss Hilda? My brothers were sadly disappointed not to be able to speak to you and Lady Beauchamp at Ely. Unfortunately, George won't be able to come, but C. T. will be coming later with Smith and Hoste."

Ah, that was good news. At least Stanley wasn't too ill to travel.

Monty's explanation put Hilda's mind at rest. "Smith's boat raced last. Came on ahead—Kinny and I."

"Yes, that's fine. Monty, you rowed superbly, but…" Concern for his feelings stopped her question.

Monty gave a roll of his hearty laughter. As always his earlier temper outburst had been short-lived. "Ah, that Aussie on the Jesus crew, you mean? Strange notions of style. Nuisance of a fellow. Told him so."

"But, Monty, did you make the Eight?"

"Hope so. Know soon." He gave an expansive bound that carried him past the fireplace and onto the first step of the dark oak stairway. "Need more than your cucumber sandwiches for tea, Hilda. Kinny and I are hungry. Won't have to wait on Tottie, will we? Saw her chasing through the park on that long-legged chestnut of hers when we came up the drive."

Hilda smiled at her brother's disappearing back. At least her augmented tea menu wouldn't go to waste. She followed Monty up the stairs. Her twin could look after herself. It was Ida who needed her help—whether she appreciated the fact or not.

Hilda found her sister in the Ladies' Boudoir sitting beneath the exquisitely painted rococo ceiling, reading an essay by John Bunyan. Hilda surveyed her sister's ivory lace afternoon dress.

"Yes, that will do very well. But why didn't you have Violet dress your hair with ribbons? I'm certain Mr. Studd is a man who would like ribbons in a lady's hair. He has exquisite taste in his own dress. He's wearing the most perfectly cut frock coat—unlike that odious sack coat of Monty's." She shuddered.

Ida sighed and laid her book aside. "Sister, if Kynaston Studd is such a fine catch, why don't you have him yourself? I'm sure he far preferred your company when we all met last Christmas."

Hilda plumped the pillow in the velvet chair Ida rose from. "Don't be silly, Ida. You and Kynaston suit perfectly. Now Stanley Smith—there's a man I could make something of. Such great spirit and determination. Look what he's accomplished with the Trinity Boat Club."

"Then why does he need you?" In spite of her normal complaisance, Ida seemed bent on being difficult today.

"Precisely because of his enormous potential. When I think of all the time he spends in the damp at Cambridge with his lungs..." She shook her head. "And then all his high spiritual goals that end in such discouragement."

"Hilda, how do you know such things?" Ida sounded shocked.

"Why, Monty tells me of his concern for his friends. Which is a very good sign in Monty. His own convictions are casual enough. He even spoke of the possibility of a Bible study for the boat club—and I encouraged him, of course."

As she spoke, Hilda removed the amber and topaz necklace from Ida's neck and replaced it with a triple strand of delicate pearls. "There. That's much better." She tipped her head to one side to regard her sister. "But I didn't come to discuss Mr. Smith. I want you to promise to pay attention to Kynaston Studd."

Ida started to protest, but Hilda rushed on. "Of all the Studd brothers, he's the best. He's a fine Christian and the only one who thinks of anything besides cricket and horses as far as I can see. Of course, he's had to see to the business since his father died three years ago. That's why he went up to Cambridge later than his two younger brothers." Hilda paused, considering. "Ida, you must take a little more interest in sport. Ask Mr. Studd about his cricketing."

Hilda ignored Ida's firmly shaking head. "And you should ride out for a little exercise while he's here. Tottie always garners admiring looks when she's on Admiral."

Now Ida laughed. "Hilda, you're the one who should be riding Admiral. You take after Grandfather."

The wall above the high, dark wainscoting of Lady Beauchamp's sitting room was surrounded with the sea paintings collected by her father—George Granville Waldegrave, the second Baron Radstock, who had risen to the position of vice-admiral.

Hilda shooed her sister out of the room in front of her. "I'm perfectly convinced that being a commander in the Mediterranean couldn't have been any more difficult than trying to see to the best interests of this family."

Ida saluted and made her way with her sister to the tea table set beside the gently splashing fountain on the northeast lawn. Their brother and his guest were already there. The men stood at the ladies' approach, and Hilda frowned when Monty seated Ida while Kynaston held a chair for herself.

"Mr. Studd," Hilda urged, "tell us about the prospects for the Cambridge Eleven this season. My sister was just saying how much she enjoys cricket."

He turned to Ida. "I am happy to hear that, Miss Beauchamp. You must come to one of our matches sometime."

Ida acknowledged the invitation, and Hilda was certain Kynaston would have gone on if only Ida had asked. Instead the infuriating girl turned to their brother. "Oh, Monty, I received a letter from Alice Polhill-Turner. She mentioned that her brother Arthur is at Cambridge. Do you know him?"

"P.T.?" Monty nodded. "Trinity Hall. Sporting fellow. Very lively. Drives the smartest dog cart around."

Ida frowned. "I wonder if that's the same man? Alice said her brother is studying for ordination."

Kynaston wrinkled his fine brow. "That's the one. Cricket, dramatics club, hunting—but no time for the Christian Union."

The two varsity men continued talking of university activities while Hilda's irritation increased. Even with Monty and Kynaston doing full justice to all the cake and sandwiches, the others had not arrived by the time they were finished.

Kynaston looked at the smooth green lawn spreading before them down to the daffodil-bordered park. "I see the fame of Langley's gardens is well deserved."

"Yes. They were laid out by Capability Brown in the time of the first baronet. And our brother Granville has added some most interesting specimens to the arboretum. He was taken with the magnificent redwood trees he saw on his visit to California a few years ago. We have several seedlings sprouting in the park now. Ida, I'm sure our guest would like..." With one of her quick gestures, Hilda waved toward the path in a hint that Ida should offer to accompany their guest on a stroll.

But as with so many of her hasty movements, this one ended in disaster. She bumped Ida's half-full teacup, sending it into her sister's lap.

Hilda jumped up, dabbing at Ida's lace gown with a linen napkin. "Oh, Ida, I'm so sorry. Why do I do these things? I simply hate being so clumsy. And you were just about to set out on such a lovely stroll. But I'm sure Mr. Studd won't mind waiting while you change."

"No, no, think nothing of it, Hilda," Ida insisted. "I'm sure our guest would rather have you for escort. Besides, Monty was just telling me of a new book he brought from Cambridge."

Hilda bit her lip as Monty escorted his elder sister toward the house. All her careful planning, all her hard work—ruined by one careless dash of her hand. Why couldn't she be soft and contemplative like Ida or carefree and open like Constance? It seemed that her only admirable quality was her desire to help people. Too bad they had no desire to be helped by her.

Two

W ell..." Hilda covered her irritation with brightness.
"Would you care for a stroll in the park, sir? Our daffodils are quite famous."

"It's Kynaston, please—remember?" He helped her with her
chair.

"Then you must call me Hilda." As she took his offered arm,
she reconsidered her reluctant attitude. This could be a golden
opportunity. She would talk to him about Ida.

They walked along a graveled path to the forge where the
ring of the blacksmith's hammer told them that one of the thor-
oughbreds was getting a new pair of shoes. Hilda chatted about
their surroundings and waited for her companion to take the lead
in serious conversation. Kynaston, however, was showing a surprising reticence. Hilda had not noticed his being so quiet before.
Her two attempts to bring her sister into the conversation had
failed to spark an interest, so instead she said, "I believe you keep
a large stable at Tedworth?"

"Yes, we still keep horses for pleasure, but we've had no
racehorses since Father's conversion. He gave racing up immediately. You probably know—he once won the Grand National. He
gave a racehorse each to C. T., George, and myself to ride as
hunters and then sold the remainder."

With the blacksmith's hammer ringing on the anvil behind
them, they turned up a curving tree-shaded lane. "How admirable
of your father. I hadn't heard that story. Do tell me more."

Now that she had hit on a topic of interest, her guest lost

his disinclination to talk. He told her of his father's friend who had gone to Dublin for a horse race and missed his return boat. Seeking entertainment that evening, he went to hear the Americans Moody and Sankey at a theater in Dublin. "I don't suppose he even realized they were evangelists. Probably thought they were a vaudeville team."

Hilda laughed. "That must have been quite a surprise. I understand their fervor can be rather alarming. Have you heard them?"

"No." He shook his head. "But fervent was definitely the word for Father's friend. He came home and all but abducted Father to the Drury Lane Theater in London where Moody was then preaching. They had seats on the platform—practically under the shadow of Mr. Moody, Father said."

Gravel crunched under their feet as they passed the carpenter shop. At the orchard they paused to savor the sight and scent of apple trees just approaching full bloom. A few early bees buzzed around the sun-tipped branches. With a smug air Hilda reflected on how useful this conversation could be. It was just the sort of topic to interest her sermon-reading sister. She would repeat everything to Ida. As they resumed their stroll, she urged, "Please continue. I'm most interested."

Kynaston gave her a long, level look. "Thank you. I think most young ladies would not find this an engrossing tale."

She shrugged. "I am not like most young ladies, sir."

He smiled. "Yes, I do realize that." He paused. "Well, I recall Father telling how he went again and again to the meetings. He said he felt Moody was speaking to him personally all the time—not to him as a businessman or social leader—but to him as a sinner. The change in Father really was amazing. Conversion was the only word for it. He had the same skin, but there was a different man inside.

"C. T., George, and I were all up at Eaton together that year. In the middle of the term Father wrote and told us that he had arranged for us to come meet him in town. We thought he was going to reward us for all being on the cricket eleven that year—take us to a theater or the Christy Minstrels. We got a shock when we found out it was a God-talk!" Kynaston laughed and shook his head.

Hilda noticed what a gentle, faraway look his dark brown eyes took on when he spoke of his father. "You miss him terribly, don't you?" She brushed his arm with her free hand. If only Ida could see him now.

"Yes, I do. He died just two years later—three years ago it was. But not until he had brought the three of us to the same experience he had found." Again Kynaston shook his head. "I can't say I was altogether pleased with him at the time. Everyone in the house had a dog's life of it until each was converted. He used to come into my room at night and ask if I was converted. After a time I feigned sleep when I saw the door open, and in the day I'd creep around to the other side of the house when I saw him coming.

"I'd never met a real Christian before. I used to think that religion was a once-a-week thing, like Sunday clothes, to be put away on Monday morning. Oh, we were brought up to go to church regularly. We had a kind of religion, but it didn't amount to much. It was just like having a toothache. We were always sorry to have Sunday come and glad when it was Monday morning. The Sabbath was the dullest day of the whole week—all because we had got hold of the wrong end of religion."

Just past the walled kitchen garden they paused again before the gardener's tidy cottage. Grapevines grew over its brick walls, and peach trees flowered in the warm south corner.

Hilda smiled. This really was a remarkable account. She must remember every word for Ida. Of course, if Ida had paid an ounce of attention to her, she could be hearing it all for herself. Why was it people required so much managing?

With renewed vigor she set out walking again and asked, "But when did you come to real faith?"

Again Kynaston gave her a deep look and then shook his head slowly. "Miss Beauchamp—Hilda, I can't tell you how flattered—that is, how I appreciate your interest in serious things. But I have no wish to bore you."

"I am never bored by deeper things. A frivolous conversation would bore me."

"Remarkable. Delightful." He smiled, then continued. "It was the next year—summer holidays. We always had a number of cricket matches arranged. Father built a cricket pitch at Tedworth House and engaged a professional coach. As usual, several of Father's London friends were staying at the house for the matches. I blush to tell you that we boys made terrible sport of one of them—Mr. Wilson—because we considered him a milksop. We discovered that, although he said he could ride, he was no good at it. So Saturday morning we invited him to go for a ride with Father and us. We three boys rode behind and then suddenly spurred our mounts to a canter and passed Father and Wilson, riding like the wind. Of course, nothing could hold the other horses."

Hilda's eyes sparkled. "And was he unhorsed?"

"No. Fortunately Wilson had more mettle than we gave him credit for. He kept his seat. We even repeated the game several times, and even Father couldn't rebuke us because he was bursting with laughter himself.

"But that afternoon Wilson had his revenge. He caught me as I was going out to play cricket. He just took me totally unawares, came straight out, and said, 'Are you a Christian?' I made the best answer I could: 'Not what *you'd* call a Christian, but I have believed on Jesus Christ since I was knee high, and, of course, I believe in the church, too.' I thought if I came close enough, he'd leave me alone. But he didn't. I had to make a decision.

"I didn't know until we were all back at Eaton that he had cornered C. T. and George the same way that very day. We received a joint letter from Father saying how glad he was to hear the good news that we had given our lives to Christ. We got quite a surprise as we passed the letter from one to the other."

Hilda nodded enthusiastically. "Remarkable indeed."

They had put the last of the estate buildings behind them and entered the wooded park. Songbirds chirped overhead, and clumps of daffodils spread a golden riot at their feet. Hilda spoke again. "How thoroughly gratifying."

But to her surprise her companion didn't seem to share her satisfaction. "If only it were that simple."

"What do you mean?"

"Charlie is one of those persons who goes all out for the thing he loves. And it seems he can only have one love at a time."

"Yes? I have trouble finding fault with single-mindedness. Energetic concentration is the key to success. How else may one reach difficult goals?"

"Well, I fear C. T.'s love for cricket has replaced his love for Christ. I suppose he could be called a 'proper' Christian, but there's no obedience, no sacrifice—no fire."

"Oh. Yes, I see the problem. What about George?"

"George is equally mad about cricket, but he can manage more than one love in his life." He grinned. "His Wild West books, for example—we all tease him about that enthusiasm. But as to his spiritual life, Hoste is a great influence on G. B."

"Hoste?" Then she remembered. "Oh, yes. We saw him row today."

Kynaston nodded. "Fine fellow, Willie. Family lives near Brighton. Has a brother in the Royal Artillery. When he finishes at Trinity, he plans to study for orders at Ridley Hall."

But the conversation had strayed entirely too far from the point. Hilda steered them to a path curving around a particularly sunny patch of daffodils and increased her pace back toward the house. "We've been gone far too long, Mr. St—er—Kynaston. I've been remiss keeping you so long when I know you'd prefer my sister's company. Ida is longing to hear about your studies. A medical degree—I'm sure Monty mentioned that's what you're reading for. How splendid. There is such a need for well-qualified medical men in England. You must tell Ida all about your plans."

"Oh. Er—tell Ida? Well, you see, it's rather complicated. I've told almost no one, but..." He paused, staring intently at the gravel walk. "You've been so very kind—shown such interest—I would like to tell you." He paused again and then announced in a rush, "I'm taking the degree with a view to becoming a missionary." His voice took on a new intensity. "Perhaps you've heard of Harold Schofield, the medical man who went out to China with Hudson Taylor. I want to go to China as he did."

Hilda stopped so abruptly she kicked up a spurt of pebbles

with her high-laced shoes. "Medical missionary! You can't be serious. People of wealth, education, and position don't do that."

"Harold Schofield was one of the best-educated men in England."

"Perhaps. But he hasn't the responsibility of a family estate. It simply isn't done." This would never do. She couldn't marry Ida to a man who was planning to spend the rest of his life behind the Great Wall of China. "Surely you have family responsibilities. Your mother is a widow. You have three younger brothers yet at home." She had never heard of such nonsense. What a fortunate thing he had mentioned the scheme to her so she could straighten him out.

But her good advice seemed only to depress him. "Yes. I fear you have gone straight to the heart of the matter. That is why I told you—I felt certain you would understand." He turned abruptly and grasped both her hands. "Hilda, might I presume to ask—to beg the great favor—would you be so good as to join me in prayer that God would somehow open the way for me to go to China in spite of the very great obstacles you have pointed out?"

If Hilda had been less self-possessed, she would have gasped aloud. As it was, he quite mistook the pressure that, in her agitation, she returned to his handclasp.

"Oh, thank you. I have long admired your firm resolution. And I didn't know whom I could tell without risk of it getting back to my family."

"Indeed, you can count on my discretion and my prayers, sir—er, Kynaston. Yes, most assuredly, I shall pray for you daily." *I shall pray that you will speedily come to your senses and give up all notion of going to China.*

Three

When they emerged from the park, Hilda saw that Tottie had returned from her ride and was organizing a croquet match on the front lawn just inside its border of copper beech trees.

Constance hailed them. "There you are, you two. And just in time. You can play a side. Take the red and yellow balls there. Monty and I have the blue and black."

Hilda looked sharply around. Where could Ida have gotten to now? "I trust you had a nice ride, Tot. I'll just go fetch Ida. She can partner our guest. I've monopolized him far too long."

Tottie strode toward them with her hands full of croquet equipment and plunked a ball down on the balk line. "No hope. Ida has her nose in that book of Charles Simeon's sermons Monty brought her. But I shall be delighted to partner Mr. Studd." She gave Kynaston a wide smile and thrust a mallet toward him. Constance Beauchamp was never one to stand around while young men bowed over her hand.

Hilda knew better than to try to rein in her twin. She turned to her brother and attempted to give her best effort to the game. But she was no match for her sister's athletic ability. Even before she and Monty were through the second wicket, Tottie had roqueted Hilda's ball and sent it perilously near the boundary line. And, as if that weren't enough, Tot continued by peeling Kynaston's ball through the wicket ahead of her own.

"Well played, Miss Constance. I'm afraid I'm not up to your skill with a mallet." Kynaston grinned at his partner.

"Oh, you must call me Tot. Everyone does." She aimed a straight shot that left her ball in line for the next hoop, but since there was no other ball to roquet, she was forced to stop. She turned back to Kynaston. "You're too modest, Mr. Studd. I know your skill with a cricket bat far exceeds any poor play you'll see here today. And Monty tells me you ride one of the finest hunters in all Wiltshire."

"Ah, I fear Donegal no longer gets the exercise he deserves. Of course, the grooms are good about keeping the stable up, but it's not what it was in my father's day."

"What a pity. I believe Tedworth is quite famous for the sport it offers."

Monty's play was soon over, and Kynaston aimed a long shot carefully at the next wicket with his long-handled mallet. There was a solid clank of hardwood, and the ball skimmed across the closely cropped turf straight through the hoop.

"As I said, far too modest, sir." Constance was quiet while he continued his play and then returned to her subject. "So you've hunted all your life?"

Kynaston wrinkled his high brow beneath his sleek, dark hair. "Quite literally. When I turned six, I was strapped to my saddle and sent to the hunting field in my little red coat. I was blooded at eight."

Tottie clapped her hands. "How marvelous!" She dashed her fingers across her forehead as if they were a fox brush. "I can imagine how proud you must have been when the fox blood was brushed across your forehead."

Kynaston winced and took a step backward. "As a matter of fact, it was a grueling experience."

The shift of the play ended the conversation. A lucky placement of the balls combined with well-aimed strokes enabled Tottie to make a break that took her through two hoops.

It was some time later when Hilda was standing by the next to the last arch in the center of the court that she looked to the sun lowering toward the west and frowned. "Surely the trials have been over for hours. The others should have been here long ago."

Could they have had an accident en route? Hilda worried. She had instructed Beeson to have every train from Ely met at the Norwich station. There was only one more this evening. *Maybe Stanley's crew failed to qualify. If he had won his place, he would have hurried to tell the good news.* Hilda felt growing disappointment.

"I do hope they haven't stopped for a drink," she fretted.

Kynaston turned from watching Tottie make the rover loop and knock her ball against the peg with a triumphant thud. He gave Hilda a kind smile. "I don't think you need worry on that score. Not when Willie Hoste is with them."

Kynaston's comment said little as to his faith in Stanley Smith's resolve. It was Hilda's turn to play so she didn't reply.

Tottie and Kynaston were just shaking hands in celebration of their victorious finish when the delinquents arrived. They had indeed caught the last train down from Cambridge. William Hoste, C. T. Studd, and Stanley Smith strode across the lawn with jubilant strides. Smith and Hoste wore their yellow and midnight blue Trinity Boat Club ties, which were a match for Monty's.

"The Trinity Eight will row at Henley," C. T. announced.

Loud congratulations went around. But Hilda noticed that something had not been voiced. Which eight men would be on the crew?

Tottie, who always ran straight at all her fences, spoke up. "Well done, all of you. But who has the places?"

Smith and Hoste looked at the ground, leaving C. T. to answer. He placed a strong hand on Monty's shoulder. "Sorry, old fellow. Bad luck having to row against that Jesus boat."

Hilda held her breath, dreading an embarrassing outburst from her brother. But no hot words came. Instead, Montague turned almost as white as his collar, and his dramatic mustache worked furiously. At last he dipped his head. "Right. Not surprised. Well, I'll have more time to recruit for the club while you fellows are slogging it out down on the river."

"I say, Beauchamp, you're taking it well." Stanley Smith gave him an encouraging smile.

Then everyone looked at the ground again.

"We had expected you earlier." Hilda spoke into the awkward pause.

"Figured we couldn't start too soon preparing to beat Oxford," Stanley said. "I cornered Fairbairn and got the lowdown on his eccentric style."

"Fairbairn? The Australian on the Jesus Eight?" Hilda had to admit he *was* fast.

"Right. His theory is that smooth blade work is more important than exaggerated body work."

Hilda deftly moved the group toward the house while encouraging Smith to continue talking. He did. "I got a close look at the Jesus boat. That's why we didn't catch an earlier train. I'm convinced we ought to consider some of Fairbairn's adaptations. Maybe replace our fixed pins with swivel rowlocks."

Once inside the entrance hall, the group dispersed to dress for dinner. Hilda cornered Ida once again in their dressing room. After one look at the dark green gown Ida was holding, Hilda took it and placed it back in the armoire. "No, no, Ida. Tot is wearing her dark chocolate crepe de chine—just the thing to set off the red highlights in her hair—and I shall wear my midnight blue trimmed with gold. You must wear your lavender lace with the velvet bodice. It will make you stand out far more."

"But I don't wish to stand out," Ida protested.

Hilda ignored her. "And pink roses on your shoulder and in your hair." Hilda was too impatient to wait for Violet to help her with her gown. Three tugs should have left her afternoon dress in a heap at her feet, but the back drape caught on the wire frame of her bustle. The sound of ripping fabric made her stop with her head still somewhere inside the lace flounces.

Tottie turned with a shake of her head. "Hilda, you should know better than to cram your jumps." She extricated her twin from the folds of fabric and placed the dress aside to be mended.

But the single-minded Hilda continued with her main theme. "Ida, I'm absolutely certain that Kynaston Studd admires you. I don't know why you insist on resisting. You're perfectly suited."

Ida held up her arms for Violet to slip the pale lavender dinner dress over her head. "I'm not sure I shall marry at all. I've noticed that even though Mama misses dear Papa dreadfully, she has been able to accomplish so much more charity work in recent years."

"What nonsense you do talk, Ida. Of course we shall all marry. It's our duty. And Kynaston is such a gentleman—so dignified and gentle." She paused to find the right word. "You know, *sweet* is really the only word. If you could have heard him this afternoon—I can't wait to tell you all he said, but there isn't time now. I must get downstairs to see that all is arranged properly."

Hilda crossed the room to pick up her gold brocade fan, requiring Violet to scurry behind her to complete the fasteners on the back of her silk gown. "And be sure Miss Ida wears the pink cameo with that dress," she instructed the maid over her shoulder. At the door she turned. "Do be careful of Kynaston's feelings, Ida. I'm convinced he could be very easily hurt."

A short time later the party assembled around the enormous circular oak table in the dining room. Since Reginald, who had succeeded to the baronetcy on their father's death, was on the continent, Monty sat at the head of the table under the imposing portraits of the first baronet and his wife. Tottie sat on her brother's right, and William Hoste on his left.

Lady Beauchamp, who had returned from her compassionate meeting just in time to don her black silk dinner dress, looked stunning at the foot of the table. Behind her the rich red walls were hung with smaller gold-framed portraits. Kynaston sat in the place of honor to his hostess's right, with Ida beside him. Stanley Smith sat on Lady Beauchamp's left with Hilda between him and C. T. Hilda smiled as she looked around the candlelit, flower-decked table. Arranging the nine place cards had not been easy. Each of the round dining tables seated eight more comfortably than nine, and there was the added challenge of having an uneven number of men and women. But she felt satisfied she had accomplished matters most satisfactorily. If only Ida would bestir herself to engage Kynaston in conversation.

But, to be fair, her sister was doing an admirable job drawing out the quieter William Hoste, and Kynaston seemed absorbed in Lady Beauchamp's account of Hudson Taylor's visits to Langley Hall.

"Montague was only five years old at the time and, believe it or not, very small for his age." Lady Beauchamp smiled at her son. "He was absolutely fascinated with the chopsticks and other curiosities Mr. Taylor showed the children."

"S'right," Monty affirmed. "Vivid memories of playing with his pigtail—detached, of course. I kept holding it up to my head and sneaking looks in the mirror. No good, though—couldn't see the back of my head." He paused. "Still wonder how I'd look in such a thing—with one of those little round black caps."

"It would not suit you at all, Monty. Don't talk such nonsense." Hilda spoke more sharply than she intended, but all this talk of China made her distinctly uneasy. She did not want Kynaston Studd encouraged in his nonsensical scheme.

"I believe the key to much of the success of Mr. Taylor's mission has been his insistence that they wear Chinese dress—no matter how disgusting other Westerners there find it." Lady Beauchamp leaned forward as she warmed to her topic. "What splendid work the China Inland Mission does. Such brave, self-sacrificing men and women."

Hilda grew alarmed, but she could hardly contradict her mother openly. "Certainly, Mama. It's a fine thing to be a minister. England needs good vicars. But China? Why must people be running off to the end of beyond when there's such need at home? Think of all the good that could be accomplished here if they would just give up this mad idea of foreign fields."

Lady Beauchamp took a bite of her curried fowl with a look that told Hilda she was speaking with far too much passion for the dinner table. Then her mother turned her gaze across to her eldest daughter. "Ida, dear, how is your society for the aid and evangelism of London policemen progressing?"

At least Hilda was gratified with Ida's answer and the admiring way Kynaston followed her account.

As candlelight played on the crystal and silver around the table, Lady Beauchamp kept up the smooth flow of conversation. "And how is your father, Mr. Smith?"

"Happy to say he was in excellent health the last time I was in London. Thank you, Lady Beauchamp."

"Remember me to him and your mother. Fine people. You must be proud of your heritage."

"Yes, ma'am. I am."

"Not every young person today had the advantage of such a godly upbringing."

"Yes, ma'am." Stanley's fair skin colored slightly.

"Have you thought of following your father's course and becoming a surgeon?"

"I think not, Lady Beauchamp, but my eldest brother Ernest has. He's in practice at Twickenham."

The main course was replaced with an apple charlotte, and the conversation turned back to the day's rowing events. Hilda's earlier concern returned. In spite of his victory, something was bothering Stanley. She looked at his blue-gray eyes and finely drawn mouth. Yes, something was not as it should be.

Hilda was still worrying some time later when Beeson directed the clearing of the cheese board, but then she joined in the general enthusiasm for Tottie's suggestion that they should retire to the drawing room for a Sankey.

Chattering and laughing, the company crossed the long entrance hall and continued down the circular passage leading to the elegant room with its baroque plaster ceiling and matching red and gold scrolled carpet. Tottie thrust a songbook at Monty and C. T. sitting on the padded circular ottoman in the center of the room. "Now, sing out, you two, or we shall make you move closer to the piano."

Hilda found herself being ushered toward the piano. "No, Ida plays far better than I do," she protested. But her retiring sister had already seated herself on the silk and gilt sofa beside Willie Hoste.

"Nonsense, dear." Lady Beauchamp opened the hymnal to her favorite Sankey song and placed it on the music rack. Hilda sat down on the piano stool.

"O safe to the Rock that is higher than I..." Hilda heard Kynaston and Tottie singing strongly behind her. Monty's rich baritone reached from the center of the large room. But where was Stanley Smith? "My soul in its conflicts and sorrows..." She glanced briefly over her left shoulder. There he was, holding a book for her mother, but even as she listened, she couldn't hear his distinctive high tenor.

From the music of the popular American hymn writer, they turned to the beloved familiar works of Charles Wesley and Isaac Watts. Then Kynaston produced a sheet from the stack of music he had been looking through. "Here, let's do this one next."

Hilda blinked. The hymn writer's words made her distinctly uncomfortable. "Ready to go..." Her fingers stumbled over a note. "...Ready my place to fill; Ready for service, lowly or great; Ready to do His will."

When at last the fourth verse came to an end, she swiveled around on the stool so abruptly that several sheets of music fell off the piano. As she grabbed for the pages, she glimpsed Stanley Smith slipping through the side door into the conservatory. "I'm getting tired. Ida, you must spell me." Hilda thrust the music at her sister.

Ida sat at the piano, her slim white fingers feathering the keys with a light touch. Hilda moved toward the garden room. Apparently Stanley had gone on outside because the conservatory appeared to be empty. She walked along the brick path between planters of ferns and palms and statuary on stone pedestals.

At the far end was the mermaid grotto. At first she thought the figure standing so still to one side was one of the statues. Then he moved. "Oh, Mr. Smith..." Hilda started forward.

He turned, and she stopped. In the dim light the red glow of the cigarette between his fingers flared like a torch. "Miss Hilda, I do apologize. You mustn't think the worst." His protest was interrupted by a hacking cough. He shook his head. "Oh, you might as well. It is the worst."

Four

onday morning back at Cambridge Kynaston began the
day with compulsory prayers in the Trinity chapel.
Then, adjusting his short black academic robe more
firmly on his shoulders, he strode to his biology lecture. But he
had more trouble than usual keeping his mind on his lecturer's
droning voice. He had put off for far too long now his determination to start a prayer meeting in his rooms. Encouraging his
brothers' spiritual growth had been one of his goals in coming
up to Cambridge, but he had been here most of a year now and
had accomplished little. Of course, his work as one of the leaders
of the Christian Union counted for something, but there was so
much more he would do. How could he ever hope to be a missionary if he did so little among those nearest to him?

"Mr. Studd, would you be so good as to define venous gangrene?" The instructor's voice interrupted his thoughts.

Fortunately Kynaston had been following with half his
mind. "Sir." He rose to his feet. "Static or venous gangrene
includes those cases in which stagnation of blood is caused by the
mechanical arrest of the circulation through the veins." His
answer was somewhat elementary but better than most, so the
master let it pass. Kynaston resumed his seat and returned to his
thoughts.

As soon as this lecture was over, he would see his brothers
on the cricket ground. They were probably already there now.
Smith, Beauchamp, and Hoste would be at the river beyond
Midsummer Common. It would be a fine thing, indeed, if all

those closest to him could be gathered, but he realized the unlike-lihood of prying these devoted sportsmen from their game. Kynaston felt the need for someone more deeply grounded than himself with whom to share his burden. He went over the list of CU members, but, while all were at least nominal Christians, no one came to mind.

"...one of those anomalous, fatal instances in which the medulla has been found apparently free from static disease..." A gownsman on the far side of the room gave a creditable recita-tion, and Kynaston's finger moved across the page of his text in case he would be called on again. He had to admit that if it weren't for his desire to be a medical missionary, he certainly would not have chosen this course of study. Nothing in the sub-ject fitted his natural inclinations.

His mind would not stay focused on kinetic diseases in the higher primates. Instead, it had the most disconcerting tendency to stray to a green park strewn riotously with daffodils and to a young woman in a white gown matching his own long-legged stride along a gravel path. A young woman whose emphatic eye-brows had risen alarmingly when he spoke of going to China, but who had promised to pray for him. He would like to think of her as his friend, and yet it seemed as though she had spent the week-end trying to escape his company except when she wished to argue a point with him. But those snapping dark eyes were a fine thing when roused in disputation.

At last the droning recitation came to an end, and he was freed to the alternating gentle rain and weak sunshine of a late April morning. Kynaston strode across Trinity Great Court just as the clock in the tower behind him struck the hour. He stopped only briefly to dump his books and gown in his upstairs rooms in the small passage off Market Street and pick up his cricket bat. C. T. would be none too happy to hear that he proposed to post-pone after-hall practice for a prayer meeting.

He smiled as he thought of Charlie's intense single-mind-edness. He recalled how, as a young lad, Charlie would spend hours practicing in his room at Tedworth. The long looking glass on his wardrobe reflected the center carpet seam. Hundreds upon hundreds of times young C. T. practiced holding his cricket bat straight with that seam, reasoning that if a man put a dead straight bat every time in front of the ball, it must be impossible for the ball to hit the wicket. His brothers ragged him mercilessly for taking things so seriously, but he stuck to it.

Kynaston was in excellent form for today's practice, scoring twenty wickets before he was bowled down. Charlie was almost pleased enough with the prospects of the Cambridge Eleven to consider attending his brother's God-talk. And George would have come if C. T. had. In the end, however, Charlie gave Kynaston a hearty slap on the back. "Prayer in your rooms? Great. Fine thing. You do that, Kinny. You're much better at that sort of thing than the rest of us. God listens best to you."

Kynaston had just turned from the pitch when three schoolboys from the town ran toward the wicket where C. T. still stood. The youngsters waved their bats excitedly. "I say, aren't you Studd?" exclaimed one.

"*All* of you!" The eyes of the short, chubby one grew wide.

"What luck—the three Studd brothers all together!" The tallest of the three yanked his cap off in reverence and then thrust his cricket bat toward C. T. "Do you have a pencil, sir? Could you—would you sign my bat? Please, sir?" His companions likewise thrust theirs at George and Kynaston.

Kynaston dug deeply in his pocket and produced a fat, stubby pencil which all three brothers used to sign the bats. Kynaston wished he could be leaving the ground with as much satisfaction as the schoolboys, who ran off, shouting their thanks.

Kynaston slung his broad, flat bat over his shoulder and headed toward the river. If he timed it right, the Trinity rowers would just be taking their boats from the water before returning to their rooms to dress for hall. This should be the perfect time to approach them.

He saluted Arthur Polhill-Turner heading toward Trinity Hall with cricketers from his college and caught up with Beauchamp and Hoste as they crossed the common with their oars over their shoulders. It seemed from their demeanor that their practice session had not gone its best this afternoon. Monty, who in spite of losing his place on the crew was still practicing with the Trinity club, shook his head. "This new style is fine for the Jesus crew, but we'll have a dog's life of it trying to switch over in time for the Mays."

Hoste lowered his oar and leaned against it. "Swivel oarlocks are very well, but now Smith wants to increase the slide of our seats for more leg pull."

Monty shrugged. "'Course, doesn't matter for me. Won't be rowing against Oxford myself."

Kynaston took advantage of the slight pause to invite the two up to his rooms later that evening.

Beauchamp looked doubtful. "Do my best. But don't wait on me. Need to see a recruit. May be late." He moved on.

At least Hoste was more supportive. "Great idea. Chance to pray for our friends here and for my brother. Concerned for Dick. He doesn't find much place for God in his regiment. Trouble is, my tutor's been at me for weeks—this being my last term. If I fail my exams, I won't be able to go on to Ridley for ordination." He shouldered his oar and started on to catch up with Beauchamp. "Maybe I can drop by later. Be there in spirit at least," he called over his shoulder.

Kynaston squared his shoulders and turned toward the river. For some reason the image of Hilda bearing down determinedly on one of her sisters crossed his mind, and he smiled. A few refusals wouldn't have dampened Hilda's spirit.

He found Stanley Smith kneeling by the first Trinity boat explaining his new idea to their coach. The older man sat astride his bicycle on the tow path, his megaphone dangling from the handlebars. His red hair glistened in the rain falling through the low-slanting rays of late afternoon sunshine. He shook his head to clear the gathering moisture as much as to answer. "Try it on yer single scull, man. I'll no' be changing the whole boat just because it works for that daft Aussie."

Smith laughed and wiped the rain from his face with a pass of his arm. "Right, Sandy. No daft Aussies on the Trinity boat— just daft Scots." He looked up and saw Kynaston. "Ah, Studd, just the man. Now look—as it is, our seat slides extend only about half the length of our legs. Therefore on every pull, we lose that much thrust. Now if we lengthened the slides just four inches..."

Sandy shook his head and rode on up the path.

Kynaston dropped to his knees. "Yes, I see what you mean. Where's your scull? Do you have an extra spanner? I'll give you a hand with it."

"Thanks. When I beat every other single on the river tomorrow, Robert the Bruce here will see I'm right."

They had been working for well over an hour, removing the old slide rail and securing a longer one, then waxing the slide for smooth, easy movement. Suddenly Kynaston recalled what had brought him to the river in the first place.

He couldn't have been more surprised by Stanley Smith's response. "A little prayer gathering in your rooms? I say, that sounds just the thing. Brilliant idea. I'll just try out this new adjustment first." He stooped to slip his oars into the locks. "Just to Fen Ditton and back, no further. Plenty of time."

Kynaston started to protest that his friend would miss hall and then realized the futility of such an objection. Once S. P. S. was on the river, he would lose all track of time, forget to eat, and take a chill in the rain. There was certainly no chance of his taking any thought for an evening prayer gathering. After all the months Kynaston had delayed trying to launch his prayer scheme, here it was—failed before he started.

"I say, J. E. K. Hullo there."

Kynaston stopped at the pleasant, gentle greeting and turned to see William Cassels, who had taken his B.A. last year and was now reading for his deacon's examinations. Cassels still rowed with St. John's Boat Club. "Ah, Cassels, getting in some extra practice for the Mays?"

William ducked his head, and a little trickle of rain ran off his head and landed on the tip of his light brown mustache. He readjusted his rowing cap. "I fear my skill with an oar is moderate at best. Don't want to let the side down, you know."

Kynaston sighed. He thought that was exactly what he had done with his failed prayer group. The two walked on some distance. William was as quiet as would be expected from one nick-named "William the Silent," but Kynaston felt a warm companionship in his company and soon found himself speaking freely. He told Cassels about his desire to see his friends and brothers deepen their spiritual lives. That had been one of his major goals in working so energetically to get the Christian Union going at Cambridge. "They're all members, of course, but they seemed to make no progress. So I thought to start a little prayer group." He shook his head. "I can't seem to get it off the ground though."

Cassels's silence continued as he ran his fingertips over his bristly mustache. At last he said, almost to himself, "'Where two or three are gathered together...' I'd be honored to make a second member."

A short time later the two gownsmen knelt in Kynaston's rooms. The sounds of the bustling market in the street below made a humming background to their prayers, giving them the feeling that they were a larger gathering than just two men.

And indeed they were. More than 6,000 miles away, Harold Schofield knelt in his small room with sounds of bargaining in a far different tongue in an awakening marketplace floating through his window. But his heart was focused on the same goal. "Oh, Lord, our God, send Your Holy Spirit to move on the universities of Great Britain. Call out young men and make them a light to the nations that Thy great salvation might reach to the ends of the earth."

One in spirit with the medical missionary, Kynaston Studd prayed, "Show me, Lord, what I can do to help my brothers in Christ. Help them to catch the vision."

The two men were just finishing their prayers when a clatter on the stairs announced a newcomer. Kynaston's spirits soared. Which one had decided to accept his invitation after all? Still on his knees, he called, "Come in."

"Oh, hello. What's this? You fellows lose something? Here,

let me help you." Before Kynaston could stop him, the visitor dropped to his knees and began looking under the plush-covered sofa. "What is it? Cricket ball roll under here?"

"Er...P.T., glad to see you. You took us by surprise. Thought it was someone else." Kynaston scrambled to his feet and dusted off his pants. "No, no, get up, man—nothing lost under there. Thanks just the same."

The stocky Arthur Polhill-Turner bounded to his feet with surprising grace. "Oh, well. Just thought I'd pop by and ask if you'd care to drive over to Newmarket with me tomorrow. Got a new dog cart, sprung higher than my old one. Should make a good go of it. Know you're from a racing family, Studd, so thought I'd ask you along. Hooper going too, of course. He lives for Newmarket."

"Good of you to think of me, P. T. Truth is, though, I don't go in for that sort of thing much anymore."

Arthur ran his fingers through his springy blond curls as he looked from the standing gownsmen back to the places where they had been kneeling a few moments before. "Oh, I say, I didn't burst in on one of those Christian Union things, did I? Awfully sorry. Not quite my line, you know. My sister Alice now—she'd go for all that just fine. Quite the talk of the Bedford Hunt, she is—gave up horses and parties to rescue fallen women—and I don't mean ones who've fallen off their horses." The ebullient Polhill-Turner ended with a jolly laugh.

Kynaston smiled. "Here, have a seat by the fire." He reached for the kettle bubbling on the hob. "I was just going to pour up. You'll join us? You know Cassels—St. John's Boat, reading for ordination?"

Arthur bounded across the room to shake hands before taking the chair Kynaston offered him. "Pleased to meet you, Cassels. I'm at Trinity Hall. Taking orders myself. Family living, you know. I'm the third son, so that means ordination."

"Then I'm surprised I haven't met you at the CU." Cassels accepted the steaming cup their host held out to him.

"Oh, I've nothing against CU. Fine fellows and all that. Bit enthusiastic though, don't you think? No offense." He gestured to the two in the room. "Your muscular Christianity is just the thing."

Kynaston offered him a hot drink. "Glad you see it that way. What are your own views?"

"On racing or on Christianity?" Arthur laughed and took a gulp of Kynaston's strong, sweet tea. "For the racing I've got several hot tips. As to Christianity, I guess you could say my views are vague enough to be safe."

Before Kynaston could reply, he heard two more voices outside his door. There was a cursory knock, and the door opened before Kynaston could respond.

"Not too late am I?" Stanley Smith looked around apologetically. "Sorry. Found the scull needed just a bit more adjustment, so took her on up to Green End. Smooth as a peach now." He looked just a bit sheepish. "I didn't forget you, Studd."

Kynaston gave him and Hoste a warm smile and hot cups of tea. "Don't worry. We didn't forget you either."

Hoste turned to Arthur. "P.T., surprised to see you here. Delighted, actually. I didn't know you went in for this sort of thing. Welcome."

Arthur gave a rather confused answer, so Hoste went on. "What do you hear from your brother? Enjoying his regiment, is he?"

"Brilliant, apparently. Not that he's much at writing letters—we leave that to our sister Alice. But she sent word that Cecil's gone to Ireland with the Queen's Bays." The two gownsmen began comparing notes on their military brothers, Dixon Hoste recently having been posted to the Isle of Wight with the Royal Artillery.

Kynaston was just reaching to refill Cassels's cup when his quiet friend gave an uncharacteristic outburst. "Oh, no! Boat club meeting. Started half an hour ago. I'll do well to get there before it's over." He set his cup down with a clatter. "Must run."

"Wait." Stanley Smith followed him to the door. "I've a better idea. Parked my penny-farthing just inside the gate down there. Take it."

Cassels pulled back. "Er—no thanks, I don't think so."

Smith grabbed his arm and pulled him toward the stairs.

"Of course, you must. It's great. Get you there in a fraction of the time. Here, I'll help you. Meeting at the Blue Boar?"

Cassels nodded.

"Fine. You'll be there in five minutes. Less if the market traffic's cleared out."

In the absence of a mounting block, Stanley cupped his hands for Cassels's foot and lifted him to the high seat of the large-wheeled bicycle. "There now—grand up there, isn't it? Straight up Sidney Street. Just pedal straight ahead."

Cassels gripped the handlebars and pressed forward. The enormous front wheel wobbled.

"Faster. Just pedal faster. It'll straighten out." Stanley Smith cheered him on.

Kynaston stood on the sidewalk and watched his friend disappear around the corner. *What a stalwart fellow. For all his silence Cassels has real staying power.*

Stanley Smith turned to join the party upstairs, but Kynaston stood in the gathering dusk, thinking, as the sound of laughter floated down the stairs. *Such fine fellows, all of them. But living so shallowly.* If only he could find some way to bring them to real commitment. What could the Christian Union do? Sponsor a series of meetings? A debate maybe? An attention-getting speaker? That might work, but who?

He shook his head. At least he had Cassels. He could count on William the Silent to be a faithful prayer partner. They had agreed to meet for a quarter of an hour every evening after hall. He turned toward the door.

The sound of running feet made him stop. "Mister! Yoo-hoo, mister! Are you Studd?" The scruffy youngster yanked the cloth cap off his head and pointed toward Sidney Street. "There's been a turrible accident outside the Blue Boar. Fellow on one of those penny-farthings tangled with a market cart. He gave your name 'afore 'e went out."

Five

Hilda plumped the ruffled chintz cushions in the wicker chairs on the deck of the rented houseboat. The boat rocked in easy rhythm as she placed a basket of daisies and roses in the center of the Battenburg lace tablecloth.

"You don't think that will block the view, do you?" She turned to Kynaston Studd standing at the top of the stairs with his arms full of hampers from the cabin below.

"Ones on the table should be fine. Hanging baskets may require a bit of ducking around."

The flags on the poles at each end of the pink and white striped canopy fluttered overhead, and the banks of potted flowers bordering the railing gave off a sweet scent as a breeze lapped the waters of the Thames against the boat's flat bottom. Hilda considered the pink and purple fuchsias hanging beneath the scalloped edge of the canopy. "If you taller men can watch the race from this end, our flowers shouldn't block your view. We really mustn't appear less festive than the other boats. I understand that the Prince and Princess of Wales, Prince George, and the Princesses Louise and Victoria are to be on Lord Camoy's yacht."

Kynaston laughed as he placed the hampers behind the chairs. "By all means, we mustn't let our side down. Especially when we're cheering for the boat that's sure to win the Challenge Cup."

Hilda smoothed the skirt of her deep rose silk dress. "Trinity will win, won't they? Monty has told me how much the crew have put into this race."

Kynaston removed his white straw boater to smooth his dark hair and then replaced it before answering. "I fear far more has been sacrificed for the Trinity boat than one could guess."

"What do you mean?"

Kynaston shook his head. "Smith has given up all pretense of his half-hour Bible time. He's in a precarious state spiritually—and deeply unhappy. Rowing is now his all in all, and that's not enough for one who has known better."

"Well, then," Hilda said turning to the first hamper with vigor, "the matter should be simple enough. After they win today, he will have plenty of time to return to other matters for the long vacation. We shall engage him to address the children's mission. He could never resist a chance to speak."

Her hands full of lemonade glasses, she called over the railing, "Ida, put that book away and come help Mr. Studd and me." The matter was very clear in her mind. Once the racing season ended, she could engage Kynaston Studd to help Ida with the policemen's charity and Stanley Smith to preach to slum children and flower girls. That should get matters back on track.

But, of course, they must win the race first.

That left only Monty to be sorted out. He had said nothing since that first night, but she knew that losing his place on the crew still troubled him deeply. Actually her brother's uncharacteristic silence had shown how much it bothered him.

She did hope he would come today. Missing the Royal Regatta was unthinkable. And yet he had been noncommittal when last they talked. What harm might he come to if he stayed away in a temper? Or would it be too painful for him to stand by and watch the others win? If she could just know where he was.

"Ida, hurry up," Hilda urged.

Ida obediently followed her summons, and Tot was close behind with Lady Beauchamp and several of her guests, including Lady Beauchamp's brother, the Baron Radstock, and his son Granville Waldegrave. They made as colorful a group as any on the river that day—the women in their bright silk dresses and wide-brimmed flowered hats, the men all in white flannels, multicolored striped blazers, and straw boaters.

The Buckinghamshire side of the Thames was lined with houseboats decorated with flags, flowers, and canopies. The river beyond them was choked with small craft—rowboats and punts—filled with men in white flannels and blazers and ladies with parasols shading their delicate complexions from the sunlight that glittered on the water—in those few spots where one could see water between the closely packed boats.

"Something ought to be done." Tottie leaned over the rail to get a closer look at three wooden boats that had collided just below them with a loud scraping and scrunching of wood on wood. "Pretty soon the river will be so full of boaters observing the race there'll be no room to race."

Her Uncle Radstock considered the crush. "Yes. Something could be done. A series of pilings and booms to hold the crowds back perhaps. Looks rather like the Volga. Only this lot's better dressed."

This reference to the baron's recent evangelistic mission to Russian aristocrats caught Kynaston's immediate interest. He began to ply Lord Radstock with questions.

"Of course, what opened the door to everything was having letters of recommendation to the court at St. Petersburg from Russian royalty here. Prince Lieven is an old friend of Lord Shaftesbury, you know." Lord Radstock grinned and looked at Hilda. "Matter of fact, Shaftesbury was on his way to call on Princess Lieven when he proposed to his Emily—before you were born, of course, my dear."

Hilda smiled vaguely at her uncle and wished Kynaston would talk about something besides missionary work. Then she had to suppress a giggle as she pictured her meticulously groomed friend with a long black queue hanging underneath his boater.

She turned back to the river and looked far to her left toward Temple Island where the race would begin. She could just see the top of the Etruscan temple-style summerhouse on the island, but in her mind she could picture the teams in their white pants, colorful shirts, and matching caps as they prepared their sculls.

To her right were the graceful arches of the stone bridge

lined solid with spectators. Behind that rose the distinctive square flint and stone tower of the parish church of St. Mary. And beyond she could see the trees and red-tiled roofs of the town with flags flying everywhere. The sound of a band drifted up to them from the lawn of the Red Lion Inn.

A loud whistle from the bank made her turn so sharply she struck one of the hanging flowers with her hat brim, breaking off several delicate blossoms. She hardly noticed, however, as she returned a wave from the broad-shouldered young man in a red, white, and blue striped blazer. "Monty! I'm so glad to see you!" She ran to the top of the stairs.

"Permission to come aboard?" He cupped his hands as if calling through a megaphone.

Even as she noted with relief the return of his ebullient spirits, she saw his companion. The young man in the green and yellow striped blazer leaned awkwardly on crutches with his leg in heavy plaster from foot to knee. "Mr. Cassels, isn't it? I heard about your accident. Do you need help to come up?" She darted down three steps.

But Monty stopped her. "No, no. Back up with you, Hilda. In the way." He held his friend's crutches while William Cassels toiled clumsily upward. When he reached the top deck, small beads of perspiration stood out on his high, round forehead.

Kynaston met him with a steadying hand. "Glad you could make it today, old man, so glad." Even when Cassels was ensconced in one of the deep wicker chairs with his foot on a rush basket, Kynaston kept a hand on his friend's shoulder.

William the Silent nodded. Monty spoke for him. "Not as glad as I am. Had a little talk—the boat thing, you know."

Cassels gave a shy smile. "Glad I could be of help." He ducked his head. "It's experience, you see. Lost my football blue with a broken leg last year. Team won though."

Kynaston nodded. Hilda recalled his telling her that William Cassels was a man who knew what was important. And he didn't mean his football team winning.

The sound of shouting from the spectators below drew their attention back to the river. The first race had begun. The small craft had cleared a path for the racing course as far as the lawn of the Red Lion Inn where the race would end. And already Hilda could see the first of the four-oared sculls competing for the Town Challenge Cup skimming toward them.

She turned to Kynaston but stopped as she saw him bend toward Ida and say something close to her ear. Ida blushed prettily. Hilda felt a swell of satisfaction. She had been right to insist that Ida wear her sea green gown with lemon silk fringe around the yoke and sleeves. The birdcage bustle under the ruffled skirt perfectly emphasized Ida's fragile looks. This would be the day when all her plans took root.

Down the river the large silver Town Challenge Cup, one of the two original cups of the Henley Regatta, was being presented to the winning local team. But on Lady Beauchamp's boat interest was turning back upriver toward Temple Island where the crews would be entering the water for the most historic of the races. The whole Henley rowing festival had its origin in the first University Boat Race, which had taken place there in 1829. That race had demonstrated to the people of Henley that they possessed the finest stretch of river for boat racing in the entire country.

Ten years later the local landed gentry established two cups: the Town Challenge, and the Grand Challenge for eight-oared boats. That first Henley Regatta had seen four eights compete— three from Oxford and one from Cambridge. And the event had been won by none other than Trinity College, Cambridge. Hilda twisted her lace-edged handkerchief. Surely, with such a tradition they could do it again.

She blinked against eyestrain as she scanned the river intently for the first scull. *Let them be wearing the Trinity blue and yellow— with Stanley Smith sitting in the position of stroke, setting the pace.*

The Beauchamp party was nearly a mile from the island, much too far to hear the starter's orders. But surely the sculls would be skimming toward them any minute, the crews' backs bending together, their muscles rippling as the oar blades sliced into the water and they pulled against it for the length of the stroke. Stroke. Stroke. Stroke. In perfect unison.

And then there they were. Six boats raced almost side by

side, but to Hilda's eyes there was only the one with the blue and yellow clad crew that seemed take a bit more lead each time the eight oars, silver-tipped in the sun, flashed in and out of the water like a shoal of leaping salmon.

Hilda leaned so far out to see the finish she was almost bent over the rail. "Do be careful, Hilda." She felt her mother's restraining hand at her waist.

Then she was jumping and clapping and hugging her sisters. "Oh, well done. They did it! They did it!"

Lady Beauchamp shook her head at her daughter's unlady-like exuberance, but she, too, was smiling broadly.

"Come." Hilda grabbed Tottie's hand as it was the closest to her. "Let's go congratulate them." She turned toward the stairs, pulling her sister. She started to enlist her Cousin Granville also but saw that he and his father were deep in conversation with William Cassels. Surely they hadn't talked about evangelism in Russia the whole time and missed the race. She turned to Monty, who was looking sullen again. Apparently the good done by Cassels's talk had been short-lived. Well, she would talk to him later. "You'll escort us, Monty."

Her brother would have been her obedient servant, but Kynaston Studd stopped them. "Er, I don't think that's a good idea." He seemed to be looking around for an excuse. He gestured toward the servants emerging from the cabin with trays of salmon sandwiches and lobster salad. "I believe our hostess means for us to eat lunch now."

Hilda laughed. "Nonsense. Mother won't mind. We must bring Stanley Smith and Mr. Hoste up to eat with us. They're sure to be starved after that race."

Still Kynaston held back. "I'm not sure it's a good idea just now, Hilda. The towpath is blocked solid with people." He gestured toward the narrow path along the bank that had been used by tow horses in the days before the railroad replaced the barge traffic on the river. "It could take us an hour to go there and back. Best to let them come to us."

"Silly." Hilda laughed. "They don't know where we are. I

don't understand you. Come on, Monty." She started down the stairs without looking back.

Tot laughed and followed after her. "Mr. Studd, don't you know better than to try to stop Hilda when she has the bit in her mouth? It's much easier just to let her have her head."

"And follow along to pick up the pieces?" He handed Constance her parasol.

Kynaston had not overstated the difficulty of making their way along the crowded towpath, but many who had been watching from the riverbank were moving now to spread their hampers on the sloping green grass, clearing the path a bit.

Then a long, sleek craft flying royal flags glided past on the river. The gentle strains of a string quartet serenaded those in the launch as well as all the boaters in the small craft cluttering the waterway. The spectators on the bank pushed forward to get a closer look at the princes and princesses aboard Lord Camoy's yacht, giving Hilda room to lengthen her stride.

On the green lawn below the high, white, ornately draped official stand, she saw her goal. "Oh, look! There they are."

"Hilda, wait! I must warn—"

But Kynaston's words came too late. She darted forward. And then stopped.

She had arrived just in time to see the captain of the Trinity boat uncork a bottle of champagne and empty its bubbling contents into the large silver loving cup. She stood as the cup made its rounds of the jubilant crew. William Hoste made only a gesture of raising it to his lips, but when it came to Stanley Smith, last in line as stroke, he grasped the cup with both hands and emptied its contents.

Hilda felt sick, as if she'd received a blow in the chest. She stumbled backward against Kynaston and felt his hands on her arms steadying her. "I'm sorry, Hilda. I tried to warn you."

"You did, but I wouldn't listen. You told me he was unstable, but I didn't realize..."

"Shall I talk to him?"

Hilda raised her chin. The wavering had been only momentary. "Certainly. Inform Mr. Smith that Lady Beauchamp will take no answer but an acceptance of her luncheon invitation. And Mr. Hoste also. My brother will want to see them."

It was sometime later, when they had changed from their rowing uniforms to the traditional white flannels and blazers with the Trinity blue and yellow striped ties, that the victorious rowers joined Lady Beauchamp's party. Large crystal bowls of strawberries and jugs of cream were going around the tables when Stanley Smith took the seat Hilda had managed to save for him.

For all his triumph and gracious acceptance of the party's congratulations, Hilda could tell by the tension in his blue-gray eyes and at the corners of his small, firm mouth that Stanley Smith was a troubled man.

"Miss Hilda, I am so sorry you witnessed that scene by the stands."

"My witnessing it is not the thing to be sorry for. Nor am I the person to apologize to." Hilda's words were severe, but she smiled as she handed him a double-tiered plate of small cakes iced with colorful marzipan.

"You're quite right, of course." He ate one of the cakes in a single bite. "But I do have good intentions. I had determined to celebrate if we won—"

"It appeared to me you celebrated quite fully."

"No, you don't understand. I had quite different aspirations. I was going to buy a painting." He spread his red callused hands.

Hilda raised her heavy eyebrows. "A painting? I don't understand."

"Yes. It's quite wonderful—*The Light of the World* by Holman Hunt, one of those pre-Raphaelite fellows. I thought to hang it in my room as an aid to evangelism."

"Why, that's wonderful! Why shouldn't you do that very thing?"

"Yes, of course, I still can. I expect I will. But it seems so hypocritical. I don't know." He shook his head and turned to take a salmon and cucumber sandwich.

Attention moved back to the river for the rowing of the Stewards Challenge Cup for coxswainless fours. It was sometime later that Hilda felt their party was becoming impossibly languid. Her ever-vigorous brother was showing signs of boredom, and Stanley Smith simply would not be jarred out of his doldrums. Ida, in spite of Kynaston's earlier attentions, had returned to her book of poetry.

"Punting," Hilda announced setting her rose-patterned teacup down with a clatter that made Lady Beauchamp wince.

"What's that?" Montague frowned at her, the long ends of his mustache sticking out like wings. "You taken leave of your senses, Hilda? No punting races at Henley."

"Not races, Monty. A party. We'll rent a punt at Hobbs. It will be the perfect conclusion for our day on the river." She looked at her sister standing beside the rail. A fine figure. Perfect posture and always graceful—unlike herself. "Yes, and Ida shall punt."

Once again they made their way along the crowded river-bank to the public slipway at the bottom of New Street. There had, of course, been no question of William Cassels joining them, and Willie Hoste had been anxious to spend more time with Granville Waldegrave, so the remaining six young people made a perfect punting party. If she could just maneuver every-one into the proper places and keep anything from sparking Monty's temper.

The deck of the gingerbread-gabled boathouse was filled with regatta viewers, but the youngest of the Hobbs sons came down to attend to them. Fortunately a punt had just been returned, as most of their craft were out for the day. Monty took the long pole and knelt to hold the rectangular, flat-bottomed boat steady to the dock. Stanley Smith held out a hand to help Tot to the bench at the front and then turned to assist Ida to a seat.

"Oh, no. Ida is punting." Hilda took the pole Monty was balancing across his knees and exchanged it for the parasol in Ida's hand.

"Oh, no—really, I—"

"Nonsense, Ida. You punt the best of any of us. And I shall sit right here below you."

Smith moved to the rear of the boat and steadied Ida as she stepped onto the flat platform. Since their party was from Cambridge, they would punt from the back. Hilda took Stanley's hand gingerly, wincing at the blisters his triumphant row had cost him. When the ladies were settled, Monty sat forward beside Tottie, swatting at her parasol as if it were a mosquito until she moved it to her left shoulder. Stanley and Kynaston took the middle bench, facing Hilda.

"Ah, a rare treat to be on the water and not propelling oneself, I must say." Stanley leaned over and dangled his fingers in the water.

But not for long, as the crush of punts, launches, skiffs, dinghies, and canoes made extending one's arm over the side a dangerous activity. Ida's skill with a punt pole, however, was quite as good as Hilda had proclaimed it. With steady strokes, she inserted the pole into the river bottom and pushed the boat forward, then lifted and reinserted the pole for another thrust, moving the boat toward the center arch of the bridge.

Once they were onto the stretch of the river beyond the bridge, the crowd thinned out somewhat. The party relaxed into idle chatter. Here ducks quacked by in long lines, and disdainful swans floated along as if they owned the river. They passed Marsh Meadow where long purple spikes of buddleia lined the river attracting yellow butterflies.

Hilda turned to Stanley. "What are your plans for the vacation?"

"Visit my brother Ernest at Twickenham first. Famous for their lawn tennis."

Hilda twirled Ida's silk-fringed parasol loosely over her shoulder. "But surely you don't intend to spend your whole vacation so casually? By all means, take a little relaxation. But then you must take on something worthwhile. My sisters and I always need help with the slum children's mission."

The lines showed at the corners of Stanley's eyes again. "Er, I'm not certain—that is, mission work..."

"Of course, you must. I've heard so much of your speaking talent."

Monty laughed. "Don't badger him, Hilda. Smith would rather tennis than tracts this summer."

Even with all her concern for Stanley Smith, Hilda wasn't about to forget that the purpose of this outing was to focus attention on Ida's charms. Perhaps she had been wrong to separate Ida from the party, no matter how attractive she looked standing there. Would it have been better to have maneuvered her sister into sitting next to Kynaston? Perhaps if they moved to a quieter bit of the river, Ida would join in the general conversation.

The approach of two large launches gave her an excuse. She folded her parasol so it wouldn't block Kynaston's view of Ida and turned to her sister. "Ida, the meadow is so delightful up here. Just move us closer to the bank where we'll be out of the line of such busy traffic."

Then perhaps she should offer to punt. Ida could have her seat. That would place her directly across from Kynaston.

Ida deftly moved the punt close in to the smooth green riverbank. Hilda started to remark on her sister's excellent job, but Stanley looked alarmed. "Not so close to the bank. Those launches are coming too fast. Here, let me help you." He stood up and reached for the pole. "The rebound wash of a launch is—"

He got no further as the first launch sped by. The punt rocked in the wake of the direct wash, then rolled astonishingly in the rebound from the bank.

Even with the fast approach of the wash from the second launch, they would likely have ridden the whole thing out with nothing worse than a mild splashing, but Hilda, rushing to offer her sister a hand, swung around abruptly, the folded parasol still over her shoulder.

The parasol caught Ida just behind the knees. "Oh!" With a startled cry and a splash, Ida landed in the Thames.

Stanley Smith flung off his hat and blazer and was over the side in a flash. Ida floundered in the water, the second rebound wash almost swamping her. Her flowered, beribboned hat slipped over her eyes. Stanley, a strong swimmer, reached her in a few strokes and pulled her to the edge of the punt.

Kynaston lifted the sputtering, dripping girl aboard while Smith struck out to regain the dropped punt pole.

Now Monty had an excuse to take his renewed frustration out on his sister. "You've really topped it, Hilda. Stupidest trick you ever pulled." His face got redder. "How could you—"

Kynaston put a hand on his arm. "No one seriously hurt, Beauchamp. No broken bones."

In a few minutes all were aboard again, Monty poling them furiously toward the houseboat. Ida snuggled in Kynaston Studd's coat while Hilda groped for words. "Oh, Ida, I'm so sorry. It's all my fault. I'm so awkward." She took a deep breath. "I'm so sorry," she started again.

Ida shook her head, a few drops from her dripping hair landing on Kynaston. "No, never mind, Hilda. There's no real harm done. And it's my own fault." She grinned weakly. "I do know better than to listen to you."

The breeze freshened, blowing a cool wind off the river. Ida sneezed.

"Would you permit me?" Kynaston put his arm around Ida to warm her.

Hilda blinked at the scene in front of her. This was better than she had planned. Far more than she could have hoped for. Ida even managed to look rather charming with her soft brown hair drying into ringlets around her face.

Hilda blinked again and frowned. So why was she not happy? Then from the forward bench Stanley Smith gave an alarmingly deep cough, and her worries increased.

Six

A little more to the right, I think." Stanley Smith stood back and observed the picture in its heavy gold frame. Kynaston moved it closer to the window. "Yes, exactly there. That's perfect. Look how the light shines in right on it."

Kynaston set the painting on the floor, picked up a hammer from the table by the sofa, and pounded the nail into the wall. When the picture was firmly on its hook, he stood beside his friend. "Yes, that is good. What an inspiration. *The Light of the World*. We should pray that that light would shine from this room just as the light of salvation shines from Christ's face."

Smith blinked and frowned. "Is that what you see?" He considered. "Yes, of course you do, but I'm afraid what I see is the light from the lantern—red and fierce—the light of conscience."

Kynaston looked sideways at his complicated, confused friend. He knew Smith had spent his summer alternating between rounds of mission work and retreats to casual country house parties, between bouts of serious Bible study and bursts of spiritual despair. Stanley's sensitive conscience was a tremendous boon that could be used for God's highest. But it could also drag him down to discouragement and depression.

Perhaps the best approach would be indirect. "Why don't we form a prayer group here, right under this picture. We could pray for a different gownsman each week." When Smith didn't answer, Kynaston forged ahead. "I was thinking we might start with Beauchamp. Such a cold, stilted spirit—when one thinks of the warmth of the faith he's been raised with."

Stanley laughed and shook his head. "And when one thinks of the heat of his temper when he loses it." Then Smith turned away. "What a hypocrite I am talking about anyone else. My soul is in a wretchedly poor state."

"Is that a reason we shouldn't pray or that we should?"

Smith shrugged and walked toward the door. "By all means—pray. I bought the picture to be a good influence. Someone might as well put it to its intended use."

He left the door ajar behind him. A few moments later Kynaston smelled the acrid scent of burning tobacco. Kynaston slumped into the nearest chair. He hated to see his friend so unhappy. He had known Smith when his life was going well. *What can I do? Smith, Beauchamp, C. T., Polhill-Turner—such outstandingly fine men. But such vacillation. This group could set the world on fire for Christ if they could just commit themselves to Him.*

Surely as leader of the Christian Union, it was Kynaston's responsibility to help its members stabilize their spiritual lives. Yet his own life seemed to be going nowhere. He had found no encouragement and no hint of an open door to go to China. His summer spent working in the family firm had clearly shown the truth of his mother's argument that he was needed here. Someone had to do the work, and it was certain that neither C. T. nor George would leave the cricket pitch long enough to take an interest in such matters.

If only he could talk to Hilda again. Perhaps at the Christmas break. She had asked him to help with her mission work in London sometime. If he couldn't go to China, at least there was plenty to be done here. His mind lingered on thoughts of Langley Hall and its inhabitants.

And with those thoughts his own doubts fled. The world was so full of goodness and beauty. Kynaston's heart turned from his friend's troubles as his own happiness—far deeper and more sure than his uncertainties about the future—welled up within him. This was what he wanted to share with the world, wanted his Cambridge friends to experience, wanted to take to China.

Underneath all the daily confusions was the peace of knowing God. If only more could know this—the best life had to offer. He looked at the painting. Christ, shining in a dark world, asking admittance at the door as He does at each person's heart—it was a portrayal of the moment when human destiny hangs in the balance, divine love waiting upon human reluctance—the choice each person must make.

The artist's mastery of color and blended light and shade called to Kynaston's desire that the Light of the world shine on his own land, that England in its national life and in the lives of its people would proclaim the glory of the true God to all the pagan nations of the world.

And that he would be part of it.

For a moment he knew a sharp intensity of joy that was like pain. Then a whiff of cigarette smoke brought him back to the needs around him. He had no answer, but there had to be one. He would not give up.

Nor would Harold Schofield give up. The dispensary had just closed for the day. He stood and tugged at his long blue Makwa gown with the little standup collar. His wife came toward him, clad likewise in native blue and black pajamas. He put his hand on her stomach. It still felt flat under the padded jacket. "And how is Little Harold today?"

Libby laughed and kissed his cheek. "Your son is very well, honorable husband. Do you have time to go for a walk before the street preaching?"

"Absolutely. Wonderful idea." Harold's enthusiasm was always unbounded, especially for getting out into the beauties of the world he loved so much.

They crossed the courtyard with the dispensary, operating room, and men's waiting room on one side and the women's room on the other. Crossing the garden, they paused to inspect their grapevines, fruit trees, potatoes, and beans—all producing healthy crops. At the little lodge by the one entrance in the high wall that surrounded the house, Harold waved to Lao Yang, the porter. Yang's job was to keep out disreputable characters and admit patients to the dispensary at proper hours.

Tonight Harold and Libby turned toward their favorite

path. Strolling atop the city wall, they moved slowly, enjoying the view of the city below them on one side and on the other, open green countryside running to a gleaming river at the foot of a steep mountain range.

"What are you thinking, Harold?" Libby slipped her hand into his.

His face lit with his characteristic sweet smile. "I was thinking of the 40,000 souls inside that wall—and wondering if those who urged me to stay in England would feel differently if they could see the need here."

"No regrets then?"

"Only that I didn't come sooner. Oh, Libby, if only Christians would pray in one accord for a great outpouring of the Holy Spirit. A multitude of missionaries for home and foreign work could speedily be raised up—and people to support them."

Libby nodded. "It would be wonderful to see."

"Yes! Just think what would happen with an outpouring of the Holy Spirit upon Oxford—Cambridge—all the universities—just think..." He took a deep breath. "And we must pray harder here."

Two days later a partial answer to both men's prayers arrived from an unexpected source, for Monty Beauchamp came up to Cambridge bubbling with joy. "Incredible. Can't imagine how I missed it before. Been there all along—didn't see it."

After morning chapel Monty and Kynaston walked along the green Backs sloping to the Cam behind Trinity. Trees in the park beyond were a bright gold and rust. The ivy growing over the mellow stone of the college buildings was a bright October red. There were no boats out this early, so ducks, geese, and assorted waterfowl commandeered the smooth, slow waters, bobbing for early fish.

Kynaston turned to his friend. "Beauchamp, what are you talking about?"

"Not sure. Can't be salvation—already had that. Jesus in my heart since I was a nipper. But I feel reborn." He ran his fingers through his straight black hair.

Kynaston grabbed his friend's arm. "That's wonderful. How did it come about?"

"Started with Cassels. Made me see how unimportant losing my place on the boat was compared to losing my place in heaven." He grinned sheepishly. "And the stupidity of losing my temper. Hard on Cassels, having to break his leg for an object lesson. Never saw anyone bear anything so well. I didn't have what it took."

"So you talked to Cassels?"

"When? He around, is he?"

"No, I mean he gave you spiritual counsel. What did he say?"

"No, no. Nothing of the sort. Haven't seen him since Henley. He just sat there and smiled in his quiet, peaceful way that I remembered later in contrast to my fuming about, wanting to be on the river. Blew off steam when I got home. Poor old Hilda took the brunt."

Kynaston laughed. "I expect she was equal to it."

"Didn't phase her. She's always telling people what they should do. Just looked at me with those fierce brown eyes of hers and said, 'Monty, you need to commit your life to the Lord.' I laughed at that. Hilda's a fine one to talk about commitment. Knew she was right though."

Kynaston was still shaking his head a few moments later when Stanley Smith joined them. "Welcome back, Beauchamp. See you on the river this afternoon? You'll get your summons to the varsity boat this year."

"S. P. S., the very man. Had an idea. Let's start a Bible reading club for the boat. You and me."

Smith blinked. "Er—a Bible reading group for the Trinity Boat Club?" He wrinkled his forehead and then shrugged. "Why not?"

Kynaston smiled. Why not, indeed? This could be the very thing. Smith would undoubtedly be chosen to captain the first Trinity boat this year. He could have tremendous influence on his fellow crew. And crew members like Beauchamp and Willie Hoste would have a much-needed influence on him. If Monty's enormous energy were now to be used for good and not wasted on flights of temper, there were few limits to what he could accomplish.

And then his smile broadened as he thought of Hilda. First

his mind summoned up her strong, striking features with dark hair and eyebrows and flashing eyes that made every woman around her pale by comparison. Then he thought of the force of her personality—steadfast, determined, spirited. A woman might not consider the comparison much of a compliment, but she did remind him of his favorite thoroughbred hunter.

And there went her equally energetic brother now, striding ahead, ambitious for the good he could accomplish—and all because Hilda was faithful to her commission. He did look forward to seeing her in London at Christmas. For a moment his mind filled with pleasant pictures of Hilda gliding across the frozen Serpentine on ice skates, her long, fur-trimmed coat swaying with the motion.

But the bubble burst with Montague Beauchamp's next words. "I say, Smith. Almost forgot. Old Hilda sends her love. Not what she said, of course. 'Greetings' was her word, but knew what she meant." He gave his friend a lopsided grin. "Don't know what she sees in you."

The ice-skating scene suddenly seemed as chilling as if Kynaston had stepped in a snowbank.

Seven

During Christmas of 1881, however, there was no skating on the Serpentine for Hilda or doing charity work among London's flower girls either. The Beauchamps did not even open their house at 3 Cromwell Road. Instead, they crossed the Channel to spend the holiday with their Waldegrave cousins in Honfleur.

"I know your disappointment at not getting to see Kynaston Studd, Ida." Hilda breezed into the bright sunroom of the villa Baron Radstock had rented on the coast of Normandy. She stopped and smiled as she observed her sister in the act of writing a letter. "Oh, well done. That's just what I'd come to suggest you do. Write Kynaston a nice New Year's letter. I'm sure it will mean so much to him." Then she frowned at her sister's choice of stationery. "That is very pretty, Ida, but do you think it's quite proper to write to Mr. Studd on paper so covered with hearts and flowers?"

Ida blinked at her nearsightedly. "I'm sure I have no idea, sister. But Alice will think it very nice."

"Alice?"

"Polhill-Turner. You remember her? Tottie introduced us at the hunt breakfast in Bedford two years ago."

"Oh, yes. One of those sporting families—three girls and three boys. All hunted, didn't they?"

"Yes. Alice is the oldest, and the poor dear is having a hard time of it. This will be their first Christmas without their father. He died last summer."

"Oh." Hilda looked out the window of their villa situated on the side of the high wooded hill. Beneath her she saw the steep slate roofs of the tall buildings clustered around the harbor with the masts of the fishing fleet rocking gently just beyond. In her mind she was seeing her own family seven years ago at their first Christmas without her father. Christmas in black crepe was a solemn affair. "I'm so sorry. It must be dreadful for her. Does she have spiritual comfort?"

"Yes, that's what she wrote to me about. In a way, it makes it harder for her—apart from her personal consolation, of course."

"Harder? How can that be?"

"She's the only real Christian in her family. She turned to Bible reading on her own and then found Christ at a mission meeting in Bedford. She is quite determined to follow Christ even to the extent of giving up hunting and parties. But her family considers her a fearful disturbance."

"Oh, I wouldn't say that." Both sisters turned at the boisterous entrance of their brother and Stanley Smith. "Old Hilda can be a bit of a nuisance but not fearful."

Hilda laughed. "I thank you for that character, I'm sure, Monty. But Ida is telling me about a friend of hers. Her family disapproves of her decision to follow Christ."

Monty nodded. "Don't appreciate it enough—our family. Always supportive." He grinned at his sister. "Bossy, but supportive."

"True. Too true," commented Stanley.

Hilda gasped.

Then Stanley's face broke into amused embarrassment. "Sorry. I didn't mean that the way it sounded."

"'Course not. Too polite," Monty muttered.

Smith, who had come to Normandy for the holidays with Monty, shook his head. "I was agreeing with the first part of what you said. Supportive families. We don't appreciate them enough. I couldn't have better, and I let them down so often. I remember when my father first took me up to Cambridge. Last thing he did before leaving was kneel and pray with me in my rooms."

"Pity your friend doesn't have encouragement like that, Ida," Hilda observed. "Is there no one there for her?"

Ida picked up the letter lying beside the one she was writing. "Their old nurse, Nanny Redshaw, who raised the children on Bible stories is still there but very frail. Remarkably, since Alice began charity visiting, she has discovered an old woman in a cottage in the village who told her she had been praying for the children at the manor house for years. It gave Alice great joy to think of all that going on unbeknownst to her, and that at least part of the woman's prayer had been answered."

Monty looked at the signature on the letter his sister held. "Polhill-Turner? Must be a sister of P.T. at Trinity Hall."

Stanley Smith shook his head. "Hard to understand. He's reading for holy orders."

Their tall, lanky cousin Granville Waldegrave entered in a dark tweed sack coat piped in dark brown leather. "Can't find my blotting paper anywhere, Ida. May I borrow some of yours?"

Ida handed her cousin a rocker-shaped leather-clad blotter. "Catching up on your correspondence, too, Granville?"

Granville shook his head, emphasizing the brown hair and generous sideburns and mustache, which he still wore in the long, full style he had adopted while at the Russian court. "I'm trying but without much luck. Need to write advice to J. E. K. Interesting note he sent me—after one deciphers his scrawl. The Australians are asking for a cricket match with Cambridge. Stirred up considerable controversy, it seems. President of the club says the university will get a sound beating and disgrace themselves."

"So what will you advise Kynaston, Cousin?"

"Oh, no—no advice on that. It's G. B.'s decision anyway. Georgie is captain this year. No, point I want to help Kinny on is his request for suggestions for a speaker or activity to spark the CU. Goodness knows it needs it. But I haven't thought of a thing to suggest. Any ideas?" He looked hopefully around the room.

"Certainly we must help." Hilda was the first to speak. "Tell him Ida will make an eye-catching poster for their booth for Freshers week."

The suggestion elicited only a mild response, but no one

had anything better to offer. They were still mulling over half-hearted suggestions when Baron Radstock, shorter and stockier than his son, joined them. His son put the question to him.

The baron brushed his fingers through his dark brown hair, which he wore in a similar Russian style. "Get attention for the Christian Union? Don't need more attention—just need more Christians. Same problem in the whole country. That's why I'm heading a committee to bring Moody back."

Stanley turned quietly to Hilda. "Mr. Moody was the cause of my coming to Christ."

"Oh? I didn't know." She leaned closer to him across the arm of her white wicker chair and spoke under the general conversational buzz in the room. "Tell me about it."

"Seven years ago, in London. Lived around Christians all my life, but listening to Moody, I suddenly realized that Christ had died on the cross for *me*, and that every man was called to give a personal response to the risen Savior. One must choose to open one's heart to His Spirit. That's why I like the Hunt painting so much—that's the door of my heart Christ is standing outside of, and the handle is on the inside. I'm the only one who can open it."

Smith's natural fluency caught Hilda's imagination. She could see Moody's fiery preaching igniting the image of *The Light of the World* in the heart of every gownsman at Cambridge. "That's marvelous." She turned back to the others. "Granville, we have the answer! The Christian Union must sponsor Moody at Cambridge. Uncle Radstock, you can arrange it in his schedule. It's all perfectly simple."

She rose in a quick motion that knocked two flowered cushions to the tile floor of the solarium. "I shall write to Kynaston Studd myself. If you can wait, Granville, I'll have my letter ready to be posted with yours." Without apology to her sister, she took the pen from in front of Ida and dipped the nib in the inkwell.

But a short time later, her task completed, she felt the letdown she so often experienced when her duty had been discharged. She sighed and picked up her paisley shawl. For all her seeming assurance, there were so many things she didn't under-

stand. The wind whipped at her skirt as she stepped onto the terrace. In spite of the soft yellow sunshine of the Normandy skies,
the day was sharply chilly. Their fortnight here had passed so
quickly, and they had made so little progress on evangelizing the
villagers, artists, and fishermen that they had hoped to reach
when they came.

She had been so pleased when Monty had suggested inviting Stanley Smith along. She had so hoped that an evangelistic
activity would help him grow spiritually. But so far she couldn't
see that any of them had accomplished much. And Stanley's testimony of having surrendered all his life to Christ as a boy of thirteen made his having taken much of it back now all the sadder.

Tomorrow, though, was a village festival. This was certain to
be the opportunity they had come for. Hilda and her family had
crossed the Channel with determination to do more than have a
pleasant holiday—although the time had been pleasant enough.
Hilda smiled as she leaned on the low terrace wall of white Caen
limestone. Bells chimed from the tall-steepled, all-wooden belfry
of St. Catherine's church beside the Old Dock. The lowering sun
reflected a golden path across the Seine estuary as it sank beneath
an apricot sky, highlighting the boats clustered there.

Perhaps some of these very boats were ones she or her
cousins had approached with their tracts during the past two
weeks. They had come with such high hopes of winning people
to Christ in this charming village. But so far the only achieve-
ment had been an increase in her fluency with the French
language.

But, Hilda vowed, tomorrow would be the day—a great day
for evangelizing in Honfleur and a new start for Stanley Smith. It
must be, for the day following would see them back on the ship
sailing from Le Havre to Portsmouth.

Hilda awoke the next morning to the gentle sounds of the
Normandy coast: seabirds called overhead; the waters of the
English Channel slapped gently against the long, sandy beach;
and a band of sheep grazing in the salty marsh meadow along the

shore beyond the villa baaed softly. What a perfect ending to their holiday—the fulfillment of all they had come for.

. They breakfasted on thickly buttered slabs of fresh, crisp-crusted bread and small cups of strong, black coffee flavored with the rich Norman cream of which Bessin, chef for the villa, was so proud. One-fourth of all French cows lived in Normandy, he told them—good brown and white cows brought over by the Vikings. They gave the world's richest cream. And then he plied them with wedges of the local Camembert cheese.

Hilda and her sisters wrapped themselves in warm black woolen mantelets, secured their felt hats with long hatpins, and gathered their tracts. As usual Hilda strode out ahead, Tottie close behind. The men followed more slowly, discussing a final outreach to the fishermen after seeing what might be done in the village.

Stone stairs formed a steep path through the woods and down the hillside to the village where narrow medieval cobbled streets took them to the waterfront. Tall, thin, gray stone buildings stood, a tight row of sentinels, around the broad cobbled dock.

But Constance had spotted a cart horse that appeared to be limping, and she was off across the quay. Hilda looked around for the rest of their party. Tottie, in stumbling French, was advising the cart owner on the proper trimming and cleaning of a horse's hoof, apparently much to the man's bemusement. Ida was cooing at a baby on a swaddling board. The men were nowhere to be seen, so Hilda made her way through the crowd of merrymakers. She strode determinedly back down the street toward the shale-covered beach beyond the walled harbor where Monty and her cousins were probably contacting the fishermen.

There was not much activity in the estuary this morning. Although there was some fishing done year-round, one of the main reasons such festivals were popular in January was the fact that neither fieldwork nor fisheries were in full swing yet. Not far from Hilda a group of fishermen sat against upturned boats, repairing the nets draped over their hulls. Most of the men wore smocks, but one fellow who stood with his back to her was dressed in the puffy pantaloons and floppy-brimmed hat the villagers wore on festival days.

Since she could see none of the men of her party, Hilda

thought she might as well approach this group. They appeared to be chatting idly with one another and were accomplishing little enough work on their nets. So far as she could see, they were giving most of their attention to the clay pipes they puffed on with such intensity.

"*Bonjour, Monsieur.*" The man in festival dress with his back to her blew a small cloud from his pipe. "*Je vous donne—*" Hilda stopped in midsentence as the man turned. "Stanley Smith!" In her confusion she thrust a handful of tracts at him and fled up the beach, kicking small pebbles against the flounced hem of her skirt with every step.

She was almost to the path to the village when a pair of strong hands gripped her shoulders. "Steady on, old thing. What is it?"

Hilda looked up into her brother's dark eyes. "Oh, Monty. It's Stanley. He's—he's gone native." She gestured weakly toward the beach behind her.

Monty threw back his head with a shout of laughter. "That all? Nothing to get in a duster about. Thought they might listen to him better if he looked less strange."

"*Less* strange? In that—that monkey suit?"

Granville came down the path behind Monty. "Blame me, Hilda. I suggested it. Hudson Taylor believes dressing like a native is the key to much of his success."

Hilda stiffened. "In China perhaps. But France is a civilized country. Supposedly. And surely even Mr. Taylor wouldn't go so far as to suggest that his missionaries take up smoking with the natives."

Now Monty's jovial face turned serious. "Oh, I say. Bad news. My fault, I fear."

"What!" This really was too much for Hilda. "You suggested—"

"No, no. Summons to the varsity boat. Mine came today. Smith's didn't. Shouldn't have told him."

"Well, someone needs to tell him how ridiculous—" Hilda turned toward the beach, but her brother pulled her back.

"I'll talk to him." She had never seen Monty look more concerned as he headed for his friend on the beach.

Hilda smiled as she looked at her brother's broad-shouldered back. Even from the back Monty was different now—more erect, freer. He was her same, lovable, energetic brother, and yet there was something shining new about him. It wasn't just an absence of temper but a new presence. Not just sins forgiven but an emptiness filled. Never fluent at the best of times, Monty had been particularly nonverbal about his new commitment. But there was no need to communicate the experience in words. His life glowed.

Then her smile faded. Monty's brightness made Stanley's gloom seem all the darker. And what about herself? There was certainly no vacillation in her life and no gloom. But neither was there the glow nor the commitment she saw in her brother.

Strange. She had certainly never considered submission and compliance to be attractive qualities before. And yet...

She looked once more at the distant figure of Stanley Smith and then turned toward the hillside path leading up to the villa, taking out her frustration in her long stride. How could their entire venture have been such a failure? It was bad enough they'd had so little success in evangelizing the Normans. Now they needed to evangelize their own party. Native dress indeed. Well, she had to admit that Chinese pajamas and pigtails would be worse. At least she needn't worry about any of this group becoming foreign missionaries. Kynaston Studd's wild notion in that direction was quite enough.

And thank goodness, he'll have plenty of other things to occupy his mind as soon as he receives my letter advising him to sponsor that Mr. Moody in a campaign at Cambridge. And there will be the excitement of a cricket match against Australia—if George accepts the challenge for Cambridge. She paused to consider, then smiled. *Yes. That could be another way to bring Ida and Kynaston together.*

Eight

Hilda frowned at her sister. "Ida, please stop fidgeting. You almost knocked that man's hat off with your parasol."

"Oh, I am sorry." Ida batted her soft blue eyes at the bowler-clad man to her left. They were sitting in the small grandstand at the side of Fenner's Cricket Ground in Cambridge.

"Think nothing of it, young lady. Nothing of it. A great day for Cambridge, this is. Bit nervous myself, if the truth's to be told."

"Think they can sustain yesterday's play?" Monty asked him.

"Got to. No question about it. Honor of the university and all that." The man twirled the end of his handlebar mustache with a gray-gloved hand.

"Do you think Studd was right to accept the Australian challenge?" Stanley Smith, sitting just below the man, turned to ask.

"Right? Quite right. Only thing to do. As he said, since everybody expected the university to be beaten, there could be no disgrace in it. 'Course, truth is, that will make the win all the sweeter."

"Held up fine yesterday. Brilliant play," Monty said.

Hilda looked around her and across the round green field. She couldn't remember ever having finer weather at the end of May. And everyone said this was the largest attendance in the history of the university cricket ground. Yesterday the weather and the Cambridge Eleven had both been brilliant. And today they appeared to be in for even better. Word of yesterday's play

71

had spread, and excursion trains had been run down from London for the continuation of the match.

Hilda had been worried when Murdoch, the Australian captain, won the toss. And at first the Australians had put on runs at a great pace, the first two batsmen scoring 87 against the fast bowling of C. T. and Ramsay, his fellow bowler. But then the Australian collapse came as quickly as the gleam faded on the shiny red cricket ball.

The Australians had 139 runs at the end of their first innings. J. E. K. and G. B. had led off the Cambridge innings and scored 48 runs together. Now Hilda felt herself tensing again just as she had yesterday when C. T. began his remarkable innings. She could still hear the cheers and applause when the Cambridge 100 went up. Then C. T. put on a splendid on-drive, and there was a roar of applause when Cambridge passed the Australian total. Hilda closed her eyes and smiled, clasping her gloved hands so tightly her fingers hurt.

"What an unusual set of shirt studs." Tottie's forward remark to the man beside them jerked Hilda from her reverie.

But it was obvious the man, whose rotund profile made the gold studs in his stiffly starched shirt protrude like gleaming lights, was delighted with Tot's comment.

"Ah, you like these, do you?" He polished them with the velour of his gloves. "Fine idea, what? Mighty fine. Devilishly clever, if I do say so myself."

Hilda was startled at the man's language but couldn't resist leaning forward to get a closer look at the engraving on the studs. Ida, squinting nearsightedly, was the first to make out the letters. "Oh! C. T.; G. B., J. E. K. You've a stud for each brother."

"Have to admit, it was *Punch* that gave me the idea—called them 'The set of Studds.' Thought I'd go one better. Whichever brother makes top score goes on top in the shirt. What-ho?"

Three university men making their way to higher seats in the grandstand paused to look at the proudly displayed shirt studs. "I say, what a fine thing. Could have used those myself at Eton."

"P.T. Good to see you." Monty introduced Arthur Polhill-Turner and his friends Lander and Hooper to the Beauchamp party.

"Your sister—," Hilda began.

"I remember the match," P.T. interrupted, "when they beat Winchester by an inning. J. E. K. made 52, C. T. 53, and G. B. 54. You'd have had your studs right in a row there." The effusive gentleman slapped his knee in appreciation at the joke as Arthur Polhill-Turner went on. "Received my blue from C. T. at Eton. Great honor."

The three made their way on up. Hilda felt her nervousness return as play resumed on the field below. Cambridge had been brilliant yesterday, but could they hold up against the undefeated Australian team? The visiting eleven in their spotless white flannels, shirts, and caps took their positions on the field as their captain directed. C. T. stood a little to the side of his wicket, holding his specially made bat. Its handle was a full inch longer than most, his wrists being so strong that he could manage the extra weight. Bather, his partner, stood at the opposite wicket, bat in hand also.

With a lightning movement, Spofforth, the Australian bowler, took a startling long run forward and let fly his famous fast ball. It bounced just in front of C. T.

C. T.'s bat never wavered from the absolutely straight batting line he had perfected in meticulous practice years ago. While the spectators applauded, the batsmen ran to the opposite wickets, adding two to the score. C. T.'s partners, Bather and then Spencer, were bowled out. Henery joined him.

With one eye on the score card, Hilda told herself she must breathe. How could her sisters chat in such a relaxed manner? Didn't they realize what was taking place on the pitch in front of them? She glanced at the man behind her and saw that he was gnawing on his umbrella handle. If only C. T. could score two more runs. But how could anyone continue to hold up to bowling that was entirely new to him? Spofforth, called the "Demon Bowler," was thought by many to be the greatest bowler who ever lived. And C. T. faced him now, as apparently unruffled as if back on the practice ground his father had built at Tedworth.

Just down two rows and a little to her right, Hilda spotted Mrs. Studd, surrounded by her daughter and younger sons. Then

Hilda's attention snapped back to the pitch. In the second she had looked away, Spofforth had dashed forward and bowled a shooter, fast and low.

With equal speed, C. T. dropped to one knee and hit the ball deep into the field. As the batsmen ran back and forth between the wickets, touching their bats down over the popping creases each time, Hilda applauded until her hands stung through her gloves. When at last the ball was returned by the fielders, Hilda looked at the scorecard and joined in another round of applause. C. T. had scored his century.

Finally, after scoring 118, C. T.'s ball was caught by Murdoch, the Australian captain. At the end of the first inning the Australians had 139, Cambridge 266. But could the university hold its lead? In spite of the superior bowling of Studd and Ramsay, Australia scored 290 in their second inning. When all went out to refresh themselves during the luncheon interval, it indeed looked as though victory might be snatched from the Cambridge men.

Amidst much nervousness and high spirits, the Beauchamp group spread the contents of a picnic hamper on a blanket under a leafy oak tree just beyond the cricket ground. "See *The Times* today?" Monty took a generous slab of ham and veal pie and then surrounded it with pickled onions, deviled eggs, and sweet jerkin salad. "Australians worried about Studds."

Stanley set down his bottle of lemonade. "Right they should be. I saw the lead article. They quote the Australian Horan as saying, 'We shall win if we can get the Studds out.'"

"Oh, but they won't, will they?" Ida sounded so distressed Monty gave her an awkward brotherly hug that knocked French roll crumbs all over her pale blue skirt.

"Good old Ida. Don't worry. G. B. and Kinny bat next. Show those Australians a thing or two."

Hilda smiled. Ida's manner was understated as always, but her feelings were clear. Ida was beginning to see what a true prize Kynaston was. It wouldn't be long now before Hilda would see her planning bear fruit. And yet even with the thought her smile faded.

Certainly, though, if brilliant play could further Hilda's

schemes, Cambridge's second inning left nothing to be desired. J. E. K. and G. B. were the first pair of batsmen, and G. B. had his captain's innings. Together the two brothers put on 106 runs before the Australians knocked the first peg off the wicket.

"Great performance....That will be long remembered by lovers of cricket—practically won the match for Cambridge." The gray-suited man with the elegant mustache held out his umbrella. He had chewed the handle clear in two. But now he began polishing his studs with vigor.

His confidence was justified, for a short time later C. T. made the winning hit. Cambridge had beaten Australia by six wickets. All around them were applauding, chatting happily, and beginning to move forward, but Hilda held her breath in concern as she watched her stud-shirted neighbor check the totals on the score card, looking back and forth from the figures to the line of initials on his chest.

Quite unable to believe such a thing could be taking place in public, Hilda turned away in confusion. But when a satisfied sigh followed an approving grunt, she couldn't resist looking again at the man. As she suspected, the golden studs had been moved into proper order. The man tipped his hat to her and moved off, his chest puffed out further than even before, J. E. K. gleaming from the top position, followed by C. T. and G. B.

Hilda found herself unaccountably quiet as her mother and sisters filled their train compartment with bubbling chatter about the match all the way back to Norwich. They were halfway across the entrance hall of Langley when Ida grabbed her arm. "Oh, Hilda, wasn't it just too wonderful? All this time you've been telling me how wonderful Kynaston Studd is, and I didn't realize. How could I not have seen—"

"Yes, Ida. Wonderful—as you say." Hilda turned to the stairs so abruptly she sent one of the barrel-backed claw-footed chairs skimming across the polished parquet floor.

Ida stood blinking at her. "Hilda? I thought you'd be pleased."

Hilda stopped on the third step, still gripping the cut velvet curtain she had pushed aside so hard it almost came off the rings.

"I am. Of course I am. How silly of you to think me displeased, Ida. I just have a very bad headache."

What had she rushed into—and pushed others into—so heedlessly? And now how was she going to live with the results of her heedlessness?

In her room she turned up the gaslights in their wall brackets on either side of her gilt-framed mirror, took a deep breath, squared her shoulders, and forced herself to face the looking glass. She saw nothing she hadn't seen before—eyes too large, eyebrows too dark, mouth too expressive. Everything wrong with her features, but no fault in her veracity. She would always cling to the truth—even when it came too late.

And the truth was that she wanted Kynaston Studd for herself.

Nine

"Buy a flower, miss?" The flower girl plucked a small bunch of violets from the basket hanging by a strap around her shoulders and held them out to Hilda with a thin hand. Although recently washed, the hand, which shook slightly, had ground-in grime in its creases.

Hilda extended her hand to the girl. "Yes, I'd very much like a posy."

The eyes that had been looking at Hilda from dark-rimmed hollows grew round with surprise when the hand that formerly held the flowers suddenly found itself grasping a shilling. Then the girl dropped her head so that all Hilda could see of her was the flat brim of the battered black straw hat with a few wisps of limp brown hair hanging around it. "Garn, lady. I ain't got change."

Hilda took the girl's hand and curled the grimy fingers around the coin. "No, it's all for you. But see that you don't spend it on drink."

"No, I won't. Truth, I won't. This'll buy bread for Jackie— my brother—enough for a whole week. Oh, thank you, Miss."

"Yes, and tonight you must come to the mission in Maiden Lane. What's your name?"

"Lizzie, miss."

"Well, they'll have a nice bowl of soup for you, Lizzie. And you'll hear a message that will do you much good. Bring your friends."

"I'll come, I will."

"And your friends. Fresh bread and soup for all."

"Yes, miss. Thank you." The flower girl, who could have been eighteen or twenty-eight, bobbed her head and then wiped her nose on the sleeve of her ragged jacket.

Hilda gathered her skirts and stepped gingerly over the squashed cabbage leaves and tomatoes on the cobblestones of Covent Garden Market. A colorful motley array of vendors haggled with buyers of all ages and classes. Well-stocked fruit, vegetable, and herb carts and stalls filled the large square between the arcade and the church. The sweet, heady scent of fruits and flowers covered the sharper tang of human bodies.

If only the mission could reach these people, Hilda thought. *There's so much good to be done. It seems that for every one we reach, ten must be missed. If only the girls could read, we could give them tracts.* She sighed.

"Come, Ida." Hilda made for the Beauchamp carriage waiting beside the portico of the church. "Mother expects us home for tea before we return for the evening service. Monty is speaking tonight, so we must lend him all our support."

A top-hatted driver handed the young women into the Victoria. Then he climbed aboard the coachman's seat in front. Ida settled herself on the seat beside Hilda and sighed. "Yes, dear Monty isn't the most fluent of speakers, but I do think the true goodness of his heart shines through, don't you?"

"Indeed, it does. And he does so well in leading the songs."

Ida raised her parasol as the open carriage made its way toward Piccadilly. "What a pity Kynaston can't be here to help with the work. He's the finest speaker of all."

Hilda smoothed her skirt and raised her chin. "Not so fine as Stanley Smith, sister. But it is most unlikely we shall see any of our friends for quite some time. We must carry on with our duty the best we can." As so many times in the past two months, Hilda tried to soothe herself with assurances that it would be weeks—months even—before they saw Monty's friends again. And who knew how feelings might change in that time—Ida's or hers?

As so many times since that celebrated cricket match Hilda asked herself if she should tell Ida about Kynaston's desire to go to China. Every time Ida mentioned Kynaston's name—which seemed to be more frequent in the weeks since she had suddenly fallen under the spell of his considerable charms—Hilda renewed the question. Kynaston had spoken to her of his missionary zeal in confidence. Would it be a betrayal to share the information with her sister under the circumstances? After all, Kynaston's concern was that his desires not distress his mother. Telling Ida could hardly cause the word to spread to Mrs. Studd.

What effect would the information have on Ida's feelings if Hilda did speak? *Knowing Ida, it would probably increase her romantic notion of Kynaston's perfection.*

It was really confusion over her motives that held Hilda's tongue. Would she be divulging the confidence to Ida merely in hopes that her sister would lose interest in Kynaston? Hilda had to admit that if that were the case, it would be a despicable act.

And yet she asked herself what effect the knowledge had on her own feelings for Kynaston. She had known of his desire to go to China long before she felt attracted to him. And now, although the prospects of life in a distant foreign village hardly seemed appealing, she could not say it in any way deterred her feelings for the man who had set this for his life's goal.

"And what about Mr. Smith, sister? Don't you long to see him?"

Hilda started and blinked. It was as if Ida had given voice to the question next in her mind before the words formed. Indeed, what of her feelings for Stanley Smith? There was no denying his fine appearance, his captivating brilliance as a speaker and as an athlete. There was no question that she shared her brother's concern for their friend's spiritual growth. But had the attraction she thought she felt ever been anything more than concern? She shook her head in answer to her own question, not to Ida's.

"Indeed, I would be most happy to have Mr. Smith accompany us. He is one of the most magnetic speakers I've ever heard. Although his fame as an oarsman would likely be lost on a mission audience."

Ida smiled. "They did do so well, didn't they—Mr. Smith and Monty—working so hard to Christianize the Trinity boat that it became known as the 'Teapot Eight'…even if Oxford did win the university race."

"Indeed, Stanley Smith being nicknamed 'Hallelujah Stroke' is a fine indication of the growth he's made this past year. But I believe he is fully engaged this summer."

"Oh, what is that?"

"Monty said something about Stanley's accepting a holiday tutorship. I believe he has a Winchester boy for a pupil—a cousin or something of Willie Hoste's."

Ida shook her head. "It's hard to believe time flies so quickly. To think Mr. Smith has graduated already."

Hilda agreed. She couldn't help wondering what effect such changes would have on the delightful camaraderie of their circle of friends. "Yes. He'll be teaching at a school his brother-in-law runs in South London. That will make quite a change for him. He'll certainly be missed on the Trinity boat."

"And is that the only place he'll be missed?" Ida gave her a saucy grin that was quite unlike her shy sister.

"I'm sure I have no notion of what you're hinting at, Ida. Mr. Smith's athletic abilities are certain to make him most popular with the schoolboys. That should be adequate for the success of his career."

"I'm sure you're right, Hilda. It seems you always are. But it would be pleasant to see them again." Ida subsided into a dreamy half-smile.

The precise meaning of Ida's "them" was left undefined, but Hilda's pronouncement was all the more decided because her own feelings were so confused. "Well, I'm certain I'm quite right that we shall be required to make do without the company of either Mr. Studd or Mr. Smith for a considerable time to come. And we shall do very well without them, I'm sure."

Ida gave an abstracted answer that left Hilda in doubt as to whether her sister had even heard her.

The shiny black Victoria, pulled by a pair of perfectly matched high-stepping chestnuts, stopped before the sand-colored Georgian house on Cromwell Road. A heavy black wrought-iron fence ran the length of the house from the square

Corinthian columns of the portico, while black and white marble steps led up to the arched wooden door. Talley, their London butler, opened the door and informed the ladies that Her Ladyship had asked that they join her in the drawing room as soon as they arrived.

Hilda was still thinking so hard about whether or not to tell Ida about Kynaston's plans that she didn't even blink at finding that very handsome young man, properly clad in frock coat and high collar, seated next to Lady Beauchamp on the rose damask sofa with a Wedgwood teacup in his hand. It was as if he were a projection of her own mind.

"Oh, Kynaston. I have a matter to discuss with you." Hilda handed her gloves to the parlor maid and turned to select a sliver of almond cake to accompany her tea.

Tottie, sitting in a floral brocade chair near the lace-curtained window, gave a gasp of exasperated laughter. "I must say, that's direct even for you, Hilda. You might greet our guests first."

Then Hilda saw that her recent pronouncement had been doubly wrong, for Stanley Smith was also there with her brother. She set her teacup down to give full attention to offering both gentlemen her welcome.

"Prettily done, Hilda," Monty boomed at her. "But needn't bother hitting Smith up to preach at your mission. Already did that. Better speaker than I am. No argument."

"Oh. Well, that's fine. Thank you, Mr. Smith." Hilda was exceedingly pleased but carefully kept any note of relief out of her voice for fear of offending her brother. "So," she looked around the room, "we shall be a fine delegation tonight. This shall be a considerable boost to our little mission. Ida, don't forget your reticule."

Ida turned obediently to get her small net bag lying on the table, but Constance shook her head. "I'm sure you shall do very well without me. I'm to go riding in the park with the Douglas ladies and their brother."

Hilda gave her twin a frown, which Tot ignored. Hilda did not approve of her sister going off with that wild Scottish group from Castle Douglas, but if their mother had given her permission, there was nothing more to be said.

As it was, even with the addition of the two men to their party, Tottie's services could have been used. Mr. Groom, who ran the Maiden Lane Mission, met them at the door with an expression virtually funereal. Hilda felt alarm as the stocky missioner shook his head, his sandy-gray beard swaying like a brush. "And I'm sure I don't know what we'll do. I'm that concerned."

"Mr. Groom, what has happened? Has there been some sort of accident?" Hilda pushed her way inside the abandoned counting house that had been transformed into a soup kitchen and meeting hall with a sleeping room upstairs for flower girls.

"No, no accident. It's just there's sae many—"

And Hilda saw the problem. But it could hardly be called a problem. It was much more a blessing. The supper queue stretched to the end of the room and curled back on itself. At least half again as many as the mission was accustomed to ministering to in an evening—especially in the summer when fewer were driven indoors in search of warmth.

"Hullo, miss. I did like you said. Hope it's arlright." Lizzie bobbed a curtsy and looked up at Hilda shyly from under the brim of her hat.

"Indeed, Lizzie, you did extremely well. I just didn't realize you had quite so many friends." She turned to their party, but they needed little direction. Monty was already striding toward the back of the kitchen where the frail little Mrs. Bernard was struggling with a soup kettle that seemed as big as herself.

"There's a bakery in Bedford Street. I'll see what they have left of today's rolls." Kynaston turned toward the door.

And Stanley moved to the dilapidated but reasonably in tune upright piano standing against the far wall. "I know you've spent the day using your voices calling your wares at the market. Now I invite you to use your voices to sing to the God who made the fruits and flowers you sell and who loves us all."

Hilda smiled in admiration at Stanley's quickness and smoothness. His whole manner seemed to change when he was in front of an audience. He took on a special shine and liveliness that she hadn't seen in him even when he was rowing, although the intensity and ability to focus on the challenge at hand were the same.

"I am so glad that our Father in heav'n/Tells of His love in the book He has giv'n…" The song filled the mission hall as Ida and Hilda tied large white aprons over their dresses and began ladling up bowls of the soup. Mrs. Groom hastily added tomatoes and other vegetables to the pot.

"It's a rare blessing to be so close to the market, that it is. Proof that the good Lord knows our needs before we've an inkling, and that's the way of it. Would you be knowing that lettuce makes a fine flavoring for soup? I do wish I'd more lentils cooked though. They're that nourishing, and these poor bairns are in such need of a mite of flesh on their bones." Little Mrs. Bernard fluttered about her kitchen adding seasoning to her extended soup.

Then, just as Hilda cut the last loaf of bread from Mrs. Bernard's ovens, a wave of warm, yeast-scented air announced Kynaston's entrance with a basket of fresh rolls. And all ate, if not exactly their fill, at least enough nourishing food to warm their stomachs.

When all the tin plates and spoons had been gathered, Hilda and Ida rolled their sleeves a turn higher and helped Mrs. Groom with the washing up, moving as quietly as they could so as to be able to hear the service at the far end of the room. After several more songs, which Monty led with great gusto, Stanley Smith gave a beautifully simple, clear explanation of the Gospel to those who labored in the streets of London since before sunup every morning and then had only the poorest of corners to rest their heads in at night.

"'Come unto me, all ye that labour and are heavy laden, and I will give you rest,' the Master invites you—each one of you individually just as you received a personal invitation to come to this mission tonight.

"'Take my yoke upon you and learn of me,' the Lord Jesus says, for He is meek and lowly in heart and He promises that in Him you shall find rest for your souls. The yokes and burdens of this world are heavy. But the Lord promises a yoke that is easy and a burden that is light."

Hilda moved her hands around in the soapy water and ran the scrub brush over another tin plate as she marveled at the conviction of Stanley's words. She knew how he vacillated in his own faith, how easily he became discouraged as he failed to maintain the high standard he set for himself. But tonight as he spoke, there was no doubt in his voice or on the faces of his rapt listeners.

When Monty led them in the familiar "Almost Persuaded" and Stanley invited any who wanted to accept Christ to step forward to a seekers' bench, Lizzie was one of the first to make her way forward, wiping her nose on her sleeve. Hilda rejoiced that her small efforts should bear such fruit.

The long shadows of a summer's evening stretched across London when the group left the mission some time later. "Oh, what a lovely, warm evening. What a beautiful world." If Hilda had been at Langley, she would have flung her arms out and whirled across the lawn. The proprieties of being in a London street restricted her, however. "That was the best mission service we've ever had. I'm so pleased that Lizzie responded."

She accepted Stanley's hand to help her into the carriage awaiting them at the end of Maiden Lane. As the evening was still young, Monty directed the coachman to drive them to Regent's Park and then sprang onto the bench beside the driver as there was only room for four on the seat of the Victoria.

Stanley continued talking to Hilda as soon as they were settled. "Yes, there really is nothing to equal the thrill of Christian service, is there? I discovered that last summer when I went with Edward Clifford—the portrait painter, you know—to the temperance mission Charrington started outside his family's brewery in Stepney."

Hilda laughed. "Oh, yes, I've heard Uncle Radstock speak of that—the brewer's son who turned teetotal."

Smith nodded. "Charrington is quite my hero. Working with him, I turned teetotal myself. I felt certain then that my vocation lay in working with such as those poor, ragged drunkards. I felt quite certain for a time that God was calling me to the mission field. Even fancied I might follow up on some of Beauchamp's tales of Hudson Taylor and inquire about his China mission."

Hilda caught her breath. She snatched a sideways glance across the carriage to see that Ida had Kynaston fully engaged in conversation. It would not be helpful for him to hear encouragement of his harebrained scheme from one of his friends. And the last thing she wanted to hear about was another of their group taking up the notion of going to China. Surely just one night of such excellent mission work as this should demonstrate that there was more than enough to do on their very doorsteps.

"I assume, sir, that we can take comfort in the fact that you spoke of such ideas in the past tense?"

Hilda regretted her satisfied tone when she saw the abashed look on Stanley's face. He was quiet for several moments as the clopping of their horses' hooves rang on the paving of Regent Street. "For a time I was completely consumed with the passion for winning souls. I asked the Lord for at least 25,000. I thought to quit Cambridge and go full time into mission work."

"Your parents must have been horrified."

"They were wise. Didn't forbid it—just advised caution. Fortunately, I was keeping up with my daily half-hour then." He grimaced. "Wish I could always say the same. Anyway, my allotted chapter was Ezekiel 3. The Lord said, 'Thou art not sent to a people of a strange speech.' I took that to mean full-time missions here as well as China."

"Yes, an excellent Scripture indeed." Hilda leaned around Ida in hopes this time that Kynaston might have heard Stanley's quotation, but he was observing the buildings they passed.

"What a fine, old building that is. It appears empty. Do you know what it is, Smith?"

"What? Oh, the old Polytechnic Institution. Closed last year. I have heard Mr. Quinten Hogg, the philanthropist, bought it."

Smith, whose home was only about a mile away in John Street, continued in a reminiscing tone. "Pity to see it closed. The arts, practical sciences, agriculture, mining—they covered everything. My father used to bring me here to lectures illustrated by dissolving views. Lecture hall seated over a thousand. They did musical entertainments, too. They had an incredibly miscellaneous collection. I remember being fascinated by the diving bell in the Great Hall. Wonder what became of it?"

They were now well past the fine facade with its pillared portico, but Kynaston turned backward in his seat, still looking at it. "Wonder what Hogg has in mind? Something could be done there. That should be put to a good use. Maybe something for young men like your splendid work with the flower girls." He turned back to Ida as the carriage approached Crescent Park.

Monty directed the driver to take them through to the Inner Circle drive that surrounded the botanical gardens. They descended from the carriage and joined the many couples strolling along the ornamental water as a sprightly air rang from the Grenadier Guards playing in the bandstand. They stood for a few moments observing two boys in short pants and sailor hats floating a large model sailboat at the edge of the water.

Stanley shook his head. "Fearful accident here when I was just six years old. I remember my nanny keeping me away from the water for years with dire warnings. The ice broke that winter with some 200 people on it. Forty lost their lives. My father's surgery was full of pneumonia cases. Fortunately they reduced the depth of the water so it won't happen again—about four feet now."

Hilda couldn't suppress a shiver.

"Some tea for the ladies, I should think." Kynaston offered his arm to Ida who was closest to him and led the way through the circular garden to the tea pavilion. The strains of the military band playing a popular march reached them over the chatter of the lively parties seated around the white iron tables. Kynaston went off to order tea and cakes.

Hilda turned back to Stanley Smith. "I'm certain you were quite right to reject the notion of going to China. An evening such as this one should clearly demonstrate to you the good you can do right here."

Stanley did not seem encouraged. His shoulders slumped, and his fine mouth tightened at the corners. "Oh, yes, it's quite easy really to stifle one's own uncertainties in unstinting activity. Especially spiritual activity. Open-air preaching, mission work, hospital visits, country house conferences for the deepening of spiritual life…the list is quite endless.

"The trouble is, when the activity is over, I always feel a worse hypocrite than before. I truly believe what I'm saying when I say it—like tonight. And I have every intention of living true and victorious. I set all manner of goals for Bible reading and prayer—but it's like St. Paul said, that which I mean to do, I leave undone, and that which I mean not to do, I do." He shook his head. "The spirit is willing, but the flesh, indeed, is weak."

Hilda tried to make an answer, but he went on. "Sometimes I think I must have missed something in the whole gospel message. There must be something more. Something beyond salvation. But then when I think of what Christ paid for our salvation, I feel a worse heel than ever."

Kynaston returned leading a waiter bearing a tray, and suddenly the party discovered they were ravenous, having eaten nothing themselves since they left Lady Beauchamp's drawing room. Halfway through his third cake, Monty gestured across the table at his friend. "Looks like you need cheering up, Smith. Your charge getting you down? Needed a break from the young scalawag."

"No, not at all. The family was doing some visiting today, so I thought I'd just run up to town, but the position is quite delightful. Burroughs is an excellent lad. They're a fine family. Position couldn't be better—tennis, sailing, duck-shooting. And the Burroughses are thoroughgoing Christians—cottage meetings, open-air hymn-sings. They do a regular work amongst the navies building the docks at Lowestoft."

When the others turned their attentions back to the food and music, Hilda said softly to Stanley, "So more of the unstinting activity you referred to. Is that the problem?"

Stanley took a long sip of tea and then set his cup down. "If I knew what the problem was, perhaps I could find the answer. I just feel so shallow. So out of touch."

Stanley fell silent. On the other side of the table Ida and Monty were talking. Kynaston turned to Hilda. "Would you care to see the zoological gardens?"

Hilda blinked at the abruptness of his suggestion. She wasn't certain it would be quite proper to leave their party, yet here was the perfect opportunity to talk to Kynaston about the whole China matter. She could even quote the Scripture Stanley had mentioned and perhaps persuade Kynaston the guidance was for him as well. Or perhaps he had given the whole thing up on his own. He hadn't spoken of it for a long time. "Why, thank you." She started to hold her hand out to him when she caught Ida's hurt look. Did her sister really feel so deeply over sharing Kynaston Studd's company? If so, Ida's feelings must run deeper than she already feared.

In that case, there was nothing to do but refuse, in spite of the good she might accomplish. Then she was aware of Stanley coming to his feet beside her. She looked his direction and saw that he had risen to greet two uniformed officers. One was in the brilliant gold-braided red jacket over black trousers of the Grenadier Guards who had just finished their concert. The other was in the long sashed coat over white trousers of the Royal Artillery.

"You're Hoste, aren't you?" Stanley asked the artillery officer.

"Yes, indeed." He removed his tall, black hat.

Stanley presented Willie Hoste's brother Dixon to the ladies. Dixon Hoste then introduced his friend from the band, "Captain Robert Henry Curzon Drury Lowe of her Majesty's Grenadier Guards."

Captain Lowe bowed to all the party and immediately engaged Ida in conversation while Stanley and Monty conversed with their friend's brother.

Hilda smiled at Kynaston. "I think we might take just a brief stroll."

In the last glow of sunset they took the broad walk toward the top of the park. The avenue was lined with trees, and everywhere on each side of them the greensward was intersected by footpaths along which couples wandered. Here and there a few boys romped with their dogs or continued tossing a ball in spite of the dimming light. The vibrant colors from the flower beds still glowed as if illuminated, however. Hilda paused before one particularly lovely red, gold, and purple planting of geraniums, marigolds, and petunias. "Isn't it wonderful? The flowers are the same colors as the sunset. One always thinks early morning the best time in the garden, but it couldn't be lovelier than now."

"Yes. I am afraid we will be rather late for seeing the animals though."

"Oh, I don't care about the animals. I rather think they close the zoological gardens at sunset anyway." Hilda had resumed walking at her usual rapid pace toward their stated goal. Now she slowed to a leisurely stroll. "I really wanted to talk to you."

Kynaston's rather tense expression relaxed into a lively smile, and he directed their steps off the broad avenue to one of the footpaths winding through a planting of ornamental shrubbery. "I was hoping you wouldn't mind. Actually, the zoo was just an excuse for me, too. I wanted to thank you for the letter you wrote from France. I'm tardy in my reply, but I wanted you to know that I have followed your advice. Just last week Lord Radstock informed me that the arrangements are confirmed. Mr. Moody will be speaking in Cambridge at the invitation of the Christian Union."

Hilda clapped her hands. "Excellent! That's certain to produce the interest you hope for. I know you won't be sorry. Is that what brings you to town?"

"No, I came to make inquiries at Mildmay."

"Mildmay?"

"The headquarters of the China Inland Mission—in north London."

Hilda stiffened at the words but forced herself to keep moving along the path. "Indeed? That is precisely what I wished to talk to you about."

"Yes, I thought it might be." Now Kynaston stopped walking and turned to her. "Oh, Hilda, I can't tell you how much it's meant to me in the past months, knowing you were praying for me. That's why I was so anxious to show you this." He pulled a thin magazine from the inside pocket of his frock coat. "Mr. Broomhall, Mr. Taylor's brother-in-law, gave it to me. He runs the office."

"*China's Millions*." Hilda read the title scrolled across the cover.

"Here, read it. It's so exciting."

Hilda shook her head. She felt she would as soon have taken a toad in her hand. "It's too dark." It wasn't really, but the excuse served.

"Oh, yes. Sorry. But let me tell you. There's an article here by Harold Schofield. Remember, he's the medical missionary I told you about?"

Hilda nodded. She could hardly have forgotten.

"Just listen to this." The fading sunset glow was no hindrance to Kynaston's reading. "'Of heathen nations the Chinese are the most prejudiced against foreign missionaries. To overcome this prejudice against the missionary and the Gospel which he brings, nothing can be better fitted than medical work.'"

"Perhaps we should be getting back. Ida will be worried."

But Hilda might as well not have spoken. Kynaston continued, the fervor in his voice increasing, "'...the vast and crying need for more labourers constrains me most earnestly to beg every Christian reader possessed of competent medical knowledge, or who has the means of acquiring it, to pray constantly for a blessing on medical mission work in this land...'"

"Well, certainly," Hilda spoke with a rush of relief that here was something she could agree to unhesitatingly. "Of course, we must pray. I'm certain all Christians pray for missionaries."

Kynaston held up a finger to silence her. "Yes, but listen. It gets better: 'and further to consider whether God is calling him to devote his medical knowledge and skill to the relief of the sick and suffering in China, with the avowed object of bringing the light of the Gospel to those who sit in darkness and the shadow of death.'" Then Kynaston did the most shocking thing of all.

He tucked the magazine under his arm, grasped both of Hilda's hands in his, and looked straight at her with his dark, brilliant eyes. "Hilda, he adds an especially fervent appeal for lady missionaries. Will you pray?"

She withdrew her hands in considerable confusion. "I already told you I would."

"Yes, yes, I know. And I'm most grateful. But I mean more, er—specifically. 'That God may speedily call some who read this appeal to work for China is my earnest prayer,' Schofield concludes. I can do no better."

Hilda stared, speechless.

"I realize I've pushed this on you dreadfully. Forgive me. But the time seems so short. Do consider all we've talked about, won't you?" Fortunately Hilda was not required to give an answer as he concluded, "We'll talk on the matter again soon, I hope."

In the face of such enthusiasm Hilda could find no way to

present to Kynaston the argument that he had not been "sent to a people of a strange speech and of a hard language, but to the house of Israel." A trumpet fanfare followed by a lively oom-pa-pa announced the beginning of the final numbers by the Grenadiers. Hilda welcomed the excuse to turn back to their party.

They found their friends among those sitting on park benches arranged around the bandstand. Hilda approached with some trepidation over how Ida would react to her truancy with Kynaston Studd, but Ida sat on one of the long benches next to Monty, so intent on the lilting Strauss waltz she didn't even note their approach. The space to Ida's right was occupied by a neatly dressed woman in a gray cape, who sat stiffly erect throughout the number. Hilda would have thought her most likely a nanny on her night out except that the woman kept both her hands folded inside an ivory satin muff that was too elegant for a governess. And yet it seemed strange that a woman of higher class would be out so late unescorted.

The puzzle was solved when a man in a checked suit and brown bowler hat approached at the end of the number. The woman nodded her head and rose to leave with him. Hilda took her place on the bench, happy to escape Kynaston's disturbing company. Stanley Smith sauntered over and stood by Kynaston as the band began their final set of numbers. Hilda reflected on her conversations that evening with each of those young men.

Hilda, who always knew what she was doing and what other people should do, who never hesitated toward her own goals or to inform others what their goals should be, was at a loss. She had no answers for Stanley Smith, and she even felt fearful of asking questions of Kynaston Studd. Her only consolation was that she wouldn't have to wrestle with the situation until they were together again. And since Mr. Smith would be returning to his tutoring in the morning and Kynaston would soon be back in Tedworth, she could be certain of a two months' reprieve or better.

The applause for the finale had barely died away when Kynaston stepped forward to the three of them on the bench. "I can't imagine how I could have forgotten to tell you. C. T. has been chosen for the All-England Eleven. He'll be playing in the test match at the Oval next week. Mother has taken a block of tickets. You'll be in the party, of course."

Monty and Ida accepted enthusiastically. Hilda gave a brave smile. Even in the excitement of an international cricket match, Kynaston would certainly find a way for them to talk privately. She had only a few days to consider her approach to bring Kynaston to his senses.

"Oh, where is it?" Ida's sharp cry jerked Hilda from her thoughts.

"What? Your parasol? You didn't have it with you, Ida." Hilda let her irritation with her sister's muddle show in her voice.

"No, I know I didn't. But I had my bag. The ivory net one with the bugle beads. I would have forgotten, but you reminded me. I had three crowns in it. I was going to give them to the mission, but I forgot."

Monty searched the ground under the bench to no avail. "Left it at the tea pavilion. Certain to have." He strode off toward the enclosed circle of the garden while the others continued looking around the bandstand area.

"Not unless one of the waiters filched it." Monty returned shaking his head.

"No, I'm certain I had it with me here," Ida insisted. "I only set it down when they began 'The Blue Danube.' It was so lovely... "

"Good old Ida. Left it in the carriage. You'll see." Monty ignored her protests. But the small beaded bag was not in the Beauchamps' victoria either. "Don't fret. I'll make it up. Quarter allowance due soon. Mission won't suffer. Buy you a new bag, too."

Ida smiled. "Monty, you're so good."

Hilda agreed. Monty certainly was good—and so changed. Before last winter he would have been raging with impatience at his sister's incompetence and at the loss of money. It was really a miracle that there was simply no trace of the former temper that had so often left his sisters in tears.

But what of Ida's bag? She thought of the woman in the gray cape, but Hilda had noticed her so specifically. She was absolutely certain the woman's hands had never left her muff.

Ten

While in London seemingly every mind was turned to the upcoming test match between England and Australia, in T'ai-yuen Fu, provincial capitol of Shansi, China, Harold Schofield sat in his office off the surgery room of his hospital/home with his mind on quite different matters. That morning he had tended to the physical and spiritual needs of 135 outpatients who had come to his dispensary—including four opium addicts. Then he had spent an hour preaching on the street under the projecting roofs of the shop fronts.

It was so good to have gained sufficient fluency in the language that he could now take full part in preaching the Gospel. Today the people had been jovial and friendly—none of the ill-feeling against foreigners one often encountered. And none had been dead drunk, although a good many had smelled strongly of drink.

Harold's arms were so tired that even the task of dipping his pen was difficult, yet he poured out his heart in his journal: "We cannot expect successfully to imitate Christ unless we contemplate His person; any more than a painter can reproduce a landscape without studying it and drinking in the spirit that pervades the whole. We must take time to sit at His feet, studying His character as revealed to us in the Gospels, and being transformed unconsciously into His image."

Harold dropped his pen and looked out his unshuttered window to the wall surrounding their garden. In his mind he could see the vast plateau that covered most of this northern province, the mountains that bounded it on three sides, and the Yellow River that flowed from the northern mountains along its western border. He saw the land dotted with tiny agricultural villages with their flocks of sheep and chickens and herds of pigs beside the fields of wheat, oats, and sesame.

But mostly he saw the people locked in the darkness of their devotion to Buddha, the women kept in submission with their doll-sized bound feet, the children growing up without hope of a better life. And Harold Schofield's heart went out to them in love, a reflection of the love he knew Christ bore for them. He turned again to his journal with his heart full of the needs around him: "What we want is not more knowledge of truth, but more practical carrying it out. Christ must be our one object in everything. We need an intense, abiding desire to do His will. None but abiding desires will God fulfill."

And then he turned from his writing table as the weight of his constant prayer burden drove him to his knees. "Oh, God, give us more laborers for the carrying out of Your work here. God, move in the hearts and minds of the educated men and women of England. Move in the universities. Send Your finest to carry Your light to those who sit in darkness."

"Of course, we shall win, Ida. What nonsense you talk. England made 71 runs to Australia's 63 yesterday, and we haven't even finished our innings." Hilda adjusted the small brim of her flower-decked peach straw hat as the carriage rolled across Vauxhall Bridge toward the Oval on the south side of the Thames. "Besides, England has never lost to Australia." And in Hilda's mind that settled the matter.

If only different matters could be as easily settled in other minds. In a few minutes they would be meeting the Studd party. This was certain to be the last time she and Kynaston would be together for a considerable period. She would not let the time pass without speaking to him directly on the China issue. She must do her best to dissuade him of his medical missionary notion or, failing that, obtain his permission to tell her sister.

Hilda had to admit that she had gotten herself into this predicament by not being more direct with Kynaston when he first broached the topic to her and by pushing Ida to care for him. Ironic that she of all people should be in a muddle due to lack of directness. And how could she possibly have been so wrong about that when she had been so sure at the time? But then, how could she have foreseen the turn her own feelings would take—she who had always known her own head and heart so well?

The crush of vehicles crossing the bridge made their progress slow, and they moved no more rapidly once across the river. It seemed that the whole world was converging on the cricket ground to see England beat Australia. The *Sporting Times* that morning had declared that this team, captained by A. N. Hornby and including W. G. Grace, A. G. Steel, and Hon. A. Lyttelton, as well as C. T. Studd, was as good as any England had ever put in the field. And it looked as though the predictions that a crowd of over 20,000 would attend were not an overstatement. The Beauchamp victoria barely missed being scraped by the rear wheel of a landau that was forced to veer sharply to avoid two hansom cabs jockeying for position at the entrance to the ground.

At last they alighted beside the clubhouse of the Surrey Cricket Club. Hilda saw with relief that Kynaston was waiting for them. He stepped forward to offer his escort to the Beauchamp daughters while Montague offered his arm to his mother.

"A flower for your lady, mister? Buy a flower."

Hilda turned at the sound of the cockney voice and smiled. She hadn't seen Lizzie since the night at the mission when the girl had responded to Stanley's message. "How nice to see you, Lizzie. I trust you are continuing to attend the mission."

"Oh, yes, miss. It's right fine. I like the songs they sing."

"Yes, and I hope you are taking Mr. Groom's instruction to heart. It will do you much good."

Lizzie bobbed a curtsy. "Yes, miss." Then she turned to the gentlemen, holding out a bright posy of pink and purple asters from her basket. Kynaston bought one of the tiny bouquets for each of the Beauchamp ladies, and they proceeded to the covered seats Mrs. Studd had taken just down from the clubhouse.

Hilda observed Mrs. Studd, a fine-looking woman in her forties, clad in the black appropriate to widows. Her thick chestnut hair was done in a heavy braid looping the back and top of her head, almost making her small black hat superfluous. Her lively younger sons, Herbert, twelve, and Reginald, nine, argued over whether their brother or W. G. Grace would be the first to score a century against Australia. Even Grace had scored only four runs and Studd nothing in yesterday's play. Their fifteen-year-old sister Dora Sophia was clearly losing the struggle to keep her brothers in order.

Nineteen-year-old Arthur studied his scorecard with a serious face as G. B., who was himself considered by many to be the finest mid-off fielder of his day, explained the science of arranging the batting and bowling order to his brother. Because of their father's death, none of the younger Studds had received the same rigorous training in cricket as the three older sons.

"The captain usually puts his best contact hitters in as openers," George said. "Disciplined, technically sound batters are hard to get out because they're always very careful and selective in the way they play each pitch."

"So that's why you and Kinny often bat first?"

George nodded. "That's right. It's our job to take the shine off the ball. Number three batsman is usually the best all-round batter—the one you hope might single-handedly put your score out of the opposition's reach."

Arthur frowned. "So why is C. T. batting so far down the list?"

G. B. exhibited just a hint of brotherly pride. "Ah, because our Charlie is a genuine all-rounder—good batsman and bowler—this later batting slot gives him time to rest after bowling."

Play was just underway when a woman sitting three or four rows down to Hilda's right turned to speak to the lady behind her. Dora Sophia gasped. "Look, that's Lillie Langtry, the famous beauty."

Hilda stared at a wealth of auburn hair tucked under a deep

red velvet hat with two roses on the front, a high-necked gold dress with a single strand of garnet beads. Yes, she was very attractive, indeed, but Hilda would hardly have chosen her as one of the most beautiful women in England. Yet, even as she thought that, Hilda noticed the peachy pearlescent glow of Lillie Langtry's skin. Then the woman raised her enormous dark eyes, and Hilda knew the source of the Jersey Lillie's attraction.

Ida took one brief glance and then turned away. "Can you imagine, an actress out in respectable company?"

Hilda considered. Yes, a society woman becoming an actress was shocking, but by all accounts she had given a very competent performance as Rosalind in *As You Like It*. It was other aspects of Lillie Langtry's life, spoken of only in whispers, that made Hilda's eyebrows rise.

Then Hilda's attention was drawn back to the Oval as, with the score standing Australia 63, England 101, Australia began their second innings.

Australia's first batter was still at the wicket when G. B. leaned over to his brother and pointed to Hornby, the England captain, standing in the field. "Let's hope Australia doesn't put a ball there. Hornby's a brilliant captain and a good striker, but he's famous for not being able to throw."

The words had no more than left George's mouth than the Australian batter sent the ball right between Hornby and C. T. Hornby ran for it; C. T. followed.

The Australian batsmen ran back and forth between the wickets, adding 2 to their score. The Australian captain saw the ball in Hornby's hand. Apparently calculating that England's captain couldn't throw, he called for another run, and the Australians set off to exchange wickets again.

Instead of throwing the ball to the wicket-keeper, Hornby jerked it to C. T. Studd. The stands erupted with vigorous applause as the bright red ball landed squarely on the bail for the fall of an Australian wicket.

But even as Hilda applauded, she realized that there would be no chance of speaking to Kynaston amid the close quarters and activity of this enthusiastic throng, at least not for her. Ida, however, seemed to be doing quite well in her soft way, asking him to relay details to her that her shortsightedness left too fuzzy. Frowning, Hilda observed the two of them for a moment and then turned back to the field.

Hilda was following the play when she became aware of a movement at the edge of the field in front of the clubhouse. Again Dora was the first to identify the newcomers. "Oh, just look! The Prince of Wales and Princess Alexandra. Oh, isn't she lovely!"

Hilda looked. Prince Edward, clad in impeccable frock coat, gray gloves, and shining silk top hat above his perfectly trimmed beard, gave his arm to his wife. She wore a white lace gown, her fine red hair and exquisite complexion shaded by a lace parasol. Even from that distance Hilda was aware of the princess's long neck circled by multiple strands of a pearl choker.

Dora wrinkled her nose. "How interesting. Just see how intently Mrs. Langtry is not noticing."

Indeed, Lillie Langtry, engaged in seeming intimate conversation with the lady beside her, presented her full back to the spectacle of her "special friend" entering the Oval with his wife.

But Hilda could spare no more thought for the incident because W. G. Grace, the Gloucestershire doctor who had become the greatest cricketer in England, was batting. She leaned forward, finding George's commentary to Arthur helpful. "Grace played in the first test match against Australia two years ago."

They continued, George quoting statistics on runs amassed and number of wickets taken, but Hilda turned again to watch the tall bearded man in a gold and chili striped cap, colors of the Marylebone Cricket Club, stride toward the wicket with all the gusto that had made him so famous. Grace scored 32 runs, and English spirits were high when play stopped for the luncheon interval. They had only 85 runs left to make in the last innings to preserve England's unbroken record of superiority.

Along with a great many other spectators, the Studd party left the Oval and walked across the road to Kennington Park. Mrs. Studd, as careful about domestic details as her sons were about their athletic training, had instructed her servants to lay out a fine picnic for them there. Fortunately they had chosen a spot protected by shrubbery, as a cool breeze had arisen suddenly.

"What an excellent luncheon, Mrs. Studd." Hilda took a second helping of lobster mayonnaise and then turned to her hostess. "You must be so proud of your sons."

Hilda had obviously hit on the lady's favorite topic. "Oh, you can have no notion how true you speak, my dear Miss Beauchamp." Mrs. Studd set her plate of chicken salad and pickled onions aside. "Ever since my dear Edward was taken from me, my sons have been my entire support and stay." She smoothed the swag of the black silk skirt that draped to a high bustle behind her. "One should not say such a thing, I know, because our Lord is an ever-present help and comfort in time of trouble. But I do believe that one of the ways He has provided for me is by giving me such fine sons." She beamed at G. B. and Kynaston who were handing glasses of lemonade around to the party.

Hilda instantly recognized an ally. "You are fortunate, indeed, to have your sons so close to you. I understand that Mr. Studd made his fortune in India. How lucky that your sons aren't required to go out to India to see after family affairs." That was close enough to test the waters. A journey to see to family matters in India would be nothing compared to a lifetime of missionary work in inland China.

Mrs. Studd clasped the lace at her throat as if she were having palpitations. "Oh, my dear, don't say such a thing. I cannot bear even the thought. I'm sure it would kill me to lose one of my dear boys." Then she laughed and picked up a well-buttered slice of French bread. "But then I'm just being silly. My husband wisely sold his plantations before returning to England, so there's no need to think of such a thing."

Mrs. Studd drew a reinvigorating breath and continued. "The apprehension of losing my dear Kynaston especially gives me a turn. Much as I love the others, you understand, Kynaston is the most like his father—in looks and in ability. He has a fine head for business. I really can't understand this notion he has taken to study medicine—fine calling though it is. But I am quite certain God intended Kynaston to make his mark in London. Oh, my dear, I know you are of a family who never thinks of such things, and I suppose it's improper of me to speak to you of business, but I am so proud of his native abilities, and I don't think such things should be overlooked. God must have intended the gifts He gives all of us to be used for His purposes, or it would all come to such waste, wouldn't it?"

Hilda started to agree, but Mrs. Studd went on, "I mean, why would God have bothered to endow His children with special abilities if He didn't intend us to use them for His kingdom?"

"I'm sure you're quite right, ma'am. I can't think of any reason." Hilda's smug smile added emphasis to her words.

The ladies continued to chat throughout the meal, but although Hilda made one or two ventures to other topics, Mrs. Studd stayed very near to her theme of how important it was to her to have the support of her sons near at hand. Her elder sons, at any rate. Reginald and Herbert seemed to provide something less than support when they began a contest to see who could chomp their celery the loudest. Mrs. Studd did not have to deal with the situation, however, for Dora was quick to see to her brothers' manners.

Hilda held up her hand to refuse another sliver of Stilton cheese or slice of Bosc pear, but she readily accepted a cup of tea from water boiled over a spirit stove. "Yes, thank you. How clever of you to provide a hot drink, Mrs. Studd. How did you know it was going to turn so cold?"

"Experience, my dear. It's always cold in England the last of August."

"Perhaps you would be warmer moving about. Would you care to go for a walk?" Hilda was surprised at Kynaston's offer. She had no idea he was paying any attention to their conversation.

At that moment Ida was discussing Donne's *Meditations* with the scholarly Arthur, so there seemed no reason not to accept.

They stood at the divergence of a footpath across the green. "Which direction would you prefer? Over there by St. Mark's church is where the gallows stood last century—many famous rebels and highwaymen hung on that very spot." Hilda shivered, and not just from the cold. Kynaston went on quickly, "And it's also where George Whitefield preached some of his greatest sermons. John Wesley preached here, too, but his brother Charles had somewhat less success. He had to pay almost twenty pounds in fines for crossing an open field on his way to preach on the Common."

Hilda turned to her right. "What does this direction offer?"

"Ah." Kynaston began walking toward a cluster of lodges near the entrance. "These are very interesting—model cottages exhibited by the Prince Consort at the Great Exhibition of 1851 and moved here later."

Several other picnickers were gathered near the buildings. Hilda pulled her light shawl more closely around her shoulders. Why hadn't she considered the possibility of the day turning so cold? She looked at the woman in front of her wearing a gray cape. That woman had even thought to bring a muff to keep her hands warm. She seemed to be the only woman there wearing a cape.

Kynaston drew her attention back to the compact, well-designed buildings. "Considerably ahead of his time, Prince Albert was. Such a pity he didn't live to see his plans put into practice. Thirty years ago few factory workers had such sanitary lodgings as these for their families. You see, each unit contains four self-contained flats, two on each floor. Much of the prince's genius was in designing it so that the building could be multiplied horizontally or vertically to form a block of flats. Each unit cost £120 to build and was supposed to let for four shillings a week—which would be within the reach of most factory workers. Thus, you see, the builder could perform a much-needed social service while securing a return of about 7 percent on his investment."

Hilda laughed. "If you say so, I'll certainly take your word for it, Kynaston. Only minutes ago your mother was speaking enthusiastically of your acumen in such matters. Now I see what she meant."

Kynaston took a deep breath, and his features stiffened. "Yes. I heard her."

"Oh, I didn't think you did."

Kynaston turned his steps away from the exhibition toward a quieter area of the park. "It would have made little difference. I'm quite thoroughly acquainted with all her arguments."

"Kynaston, I know you disagree with her, but there was logic in her statements. God has given you the gifts she spoke of. Why would He have done so if He intended you to turn your back on them?"

"Sometimes it's difficult to know the difference between a gift and a temptation."

Hilda felt an exhilarating surge of triumph. "You mean you are tempted to abandon your notions of China?"

Kynaston shook his head. "If only I knew what was right. The more I read of *China's Millions,* the more enthralled I am with the work of Mr. Taylor's mission, the more aware I am of the need, and the more I long to be there carrying the light of the Gospel to the millions that sit in darkness. And yet the more I long to do so, the more tightly closed the door seems. Is God testing my resolution, or is He telling me I ought not to go in spite of all my desire? But why would He have planted such desire in my heart if I weren't to act on it?"

Hilda considered. For once she didn't rush in with an answer. "Kynaston, do you enjoy your medical studies? I mean, if it weren't for the notion of being another Harold Schofield, would you choose to study medicine?"

In spite of the seriousness of their discussion, Hilda couldn't suppress a giggle at the dumbfounded look that spread over her companion's face. "I never thought to ask such a question. I'm doing all right at my studies."

"I didn't ask if you were passing. I'm certain you could pass any course you set yourself to. I'm asking if you enjoy it. Would you choose a medical career for itself if you'd never heard of China?"

He removed his top hat and ran his fingers through his smooth, dark hair. "I—I don't think so. I don't know. I'll have to consider. But the thing is—China *does* exist. I *do* have the desire to go. So one can't really separate the two questions."

They walked on in silence for several moments. "I have been thinking of writing to Mr. Taylor... " Kynaston spoke softly, almost as if thinking aloud.

Hilda opened her mouth to tell him what she thought of that idea, but to her amazement a question emerged rather than an imperative. "So why haven't you?" As much as she did want him to think long before taking such action, inaction still surprised her. To her to think was to act. But, she admitted to herself, she often acted before she thought. She was trying, however, to correct that.

Kynaston stopped by an ornamental bush and fingered its shiny, dark green leaves abstractedly. "I'm not sure why I haven't written. That's what worries me more than any argument that my abilities may lie in some other direction. I *want* to write, but somehow it doesn't feel right. It's impossible to explain. It's like there's a barrier. The desire is there, but the door is shut. I know that sounds silly... "

"No, not at all." Now Hilda saw her way clearly. "Stanley Smith told me something of a similar dilemma. The Scripture given to him may serve as guidance for you as well." Her smile brightened. "Perhaps it was given to him particularly to serve as guidance for you." It was for just such an opportunity that Hilda had memorized the verse. "'For thou art not sent to a people of a strange speech and of a hard language, but to the house of Israel.' Did you know Mr. Smith had at one time considered foreign missions? When he found that Scripture, he knew God was telling him it was not to be." She held her breath.

He started to take her hands, then stopped, aware of the many people around them, who were now turning their steps back toward the Oval. Instead, he moved closer to her so their arms were almost touching. "Oh, Hilda, you are so good. I knew you would understand. You're always the one person who does."

"Indeed. I'm glad I could be of comfort."

"Comfort?" He jerked away from her. "Comfort? I can think

of nothing less comforting than the thought of being found unworthy for such great service." He shook his head. "Rejected by God."

"Surely that is nonsense. The fact that God has a different work for you hardly means you've been rejected."

"Oh, the Christian Union you mean? Well, that's scarcely equal to service in China, but I am most encouraged about the prospects of the Moody campaign in Cambridge in Octo—"

He broke off as a sharp cry rang out from the direction of the model dwellings.

Hilda and Kynaston set off at a run and arrived just as a tight circle was forming around a beautiful woman dressed in gold and deep red. "Seize that girl! I'm certain she took it!" Lillie Langtry pointed dramatically. "Pickpocket. Someone summon the police."

Hilda followed the direction of the actress's pointing finger. "Oh, no—it's Lizzie! Surely she couldn't have. We must help her." Hilda made her way through the throng, not so much pushing as simply striding forward as if the others weren't there. And people moved back for her.

Unfortunately, a policeman reached the terrified flower girl before Hilda could. "All right now. You come along with me, my girl. We'll have none of your kind troubling respectable people."

Lizzie set up a howl. "But I'm a good girl. I didn't do 'er no 'arm. Just wanted to sell a flower. I've got me living to make."

"Enough of that." The double row of brass buttons on the blue chest of the stalwart Metropolitan Policeman puffed out, and the black helmet strap between his chin and lower lip moved up and down. "You come along with me now."

Hilda saw Lizzie's desperate expression as the policeman marched her away.

"My purse! Recover my purse, officer," Lillie Langtry commanded.

"But I 'aven't got it. I didn't even see 'er purse." Lizzie began to cry.

Feeling desperate herself, Hilda now stopped barely short of shoving to get to Lizzie. She likely would have made it had she been watching where she stepped, but she wasn't. A small boy dragging a cricket bat crossed in front of her. Hilda's feet tangled with the bat. She pitched forward.

Hilda flung her arm out for support and grabbed the shoulder of the woman beside her. For an instant she thought she had her balance. Then, with a sharp ripping sound, the woman's cape tore from her shoulders.

Kynaston shot forward, but he did not pause to help Hilda. Rather he lunged at the woman whose gray cape now lay in a heap at Hilda's feet.

As Hilda regained her balance with the support of helping hands, she saw what she had not seen before. The woman's white satin muff appeared to be held firmly with two hands, while at the same time, her right arm and hand, stripped of their caped covering, hung fully unencumbered.

Now Hilda recognized the woman who had been sitting, likewise disguised, next to Ida the night her purse had disappeared. This time there was no mystery. The woman still held the Jersey Lillie's tapestry bag in her free hand.

"Oh, so you didn't have the purse, did you?" The constable's little black mustache twitched at Lizzie. "But yer lolly here did." Still clasping the sobbing Lizzie, his enormous hand closed around the pickpocket's wrist. He held her arm up like a prizefighter's, shaking it so the stolen purse dangled loosely.

Kynaston stepped forward, retrieved the bag, and presented it to the famous beauty with a flourish. Lillie Langtry curtsied over his outstretched hand before taking her bag. The assembled audience applauded. Never one to miss a cue, Lillie bowed to her audience and then extended her arm in indication that they should applaud for the restorer of her bag as well. Kynaston smiled, shook his head, and backed into the crowd.

Hilda stayed by the distraught flower girl. "I know you weren't working with her, Lizzie. Don't lose heart. We'll help you." As the constable marched Lizzie and the gray-clad woman off toward a police wagon parked along Kennington Park Road, Kynaston came alongside Hilda. She turned to him. "How dreadful. We must help Lizzie. What can we do?"

Kynaston shook his head. "We must try, of course. But it's

tricky. Fact of the matter is, Lizzie probably did distract Mrs. Langtry while her purse was being lifted, even though she acted in all innocence. Difficult thing to prove."

Hilda turned sharply and set out with the rest of the crowd toward the Oval. "Why couldn't you be studying something useful like law?"

Back in her seat at the Oval, Hilda ignored the situation behind her as Kynaston took his seat beside Ida and renewed his attentions to her. At the same time Hilda attempted to put both her own unsatisfactory discussion with Kynaston and Lizzie's problems out of her mind so as to enjoy fully England's victory. It soon seemed to be all over but the shouting. Thirty runs to make, with only two wickets down.

Then, inexplicably, the best English batsmen played over after over without making a run. Arthur looked sadly at his scorecard and shook his head as he counted. "Eighteen maidens! Howzat possible?"

G. B. was as lost for an explanation as anyone. It seemed the cold of the afternoon settled into the Oval. "Cricket's like life. Strange things happen. Cricket teaches courage, self-denial, endurance. We must endure."

Arthur took another look at his card and grinned. "Oh, it'll soon be put right. C. T. bats next."

"Mmm, I'm not so sure," G. B. mused as they all watched Hornby approach their brother. C. T. shrugged in compliance to whatever the captain said and turned back toward the club house. J. M. Read picked up his bat and approached the wicket.

"I say." Arthur frowned. "He changed the batting order. Can he do that?"

"Captain's job. Probably holding C. T. in reserve."

But the captain's new strategy was no help. A procession began. Hilda was shivering with cold and the fatigue of a stressful day by the time C. T. came to bat in the eighth place, pairing Steel.

The wicket went down, caught and bowled by the Australian Spofforth.

Now C. T. was joined by Peate. George groaned. "Peate's no

batsman. Let's hope Hornby warned him to be careful and leave the run-getting to Charlie."

But if he had been told, Peate didn't obey. He struck the ball off Boyle's delivery and called for a run. C. T. and Peate ran to the opposite wickets for two.

Hilda applauded vigorously, warming her hands as well as expressing her appreciation.

"We can do it yet!" Arthur bounced in his seat.

Such optimism, however, was short-lived. On the next delivery Peate lashed out at a straight one as the ball sped past him, hitting the wicket. England's hopes crashed with the ball. They had lost to Australia by seven runs.

The next morning Hilda, nursing a mild headache, didn't know whether she was more depressed over her failure to get through to Kynaston, Lizzie's arrest as a pickpocket's cover, or England's humiliating defeat. She sat at the breakfast table while the eggs and kedgeree congealed on her plate and the coffee cooled in her cup. She hardly looked up when Tottie strode in, dressed to go riding.

Tot ladled a generous scoop of marmalade on her toast and then picked up the *Sporting Times* Monty had left on his chair. "Pity about the match. Just as well I went riding. Mr. William Douglas Robinson-Douglas of Castle Douglas is a most amusing companion once one gets used to the way he talks."

"And such variety in his name. Helpful, I suppose, if you don't understand him the first time." In spite of her attempt at humor, Hilda's voice held no amusement.

Tot looked at her twin and frowned. "Never knew you to take a cricket match so to heart, Hilda." When Hilda didn't reply, Constance seized the moment to peruse the newspaper herself since there were no men in the room to read it to her as propriety dictated. A moment later she giggled. "Here now, Hilda. This will cheer you up. *Times* has a sense of humor about it." She held the page out and pointed.

In spite of herself, Hilda smiled. George had said that cricket was like life. It seemed that the *Sporting Times* was extending the metaphor:

In Affectionate Remembrance
of English Cricket
Which died at the Oval on
29th August, 1882,
Deeply lamented by a large circle
of Sorrowing Friends
and Acquaintances.
R.I.P.
N.B. The body will be cremated
and the ashes taken to Australia.

Hilda was just beginning to feel better when Ida sauntered in with a dreamy look on her face, poured herself a cup of tea at the sideboard, and settled into a chair across from Hilda. Ida took a sip and then set the cup down with a sigh. "Oh, Hilda, I can't thank you enough for pointing me to Kynaston. I'm sure I should never have taken my nose from a book long enough to look at him if you hadn't. Isn't he simply the most perfect gentleman?"

Fortunately Ida seemed too lost in her dream world even to notice that Hilda left the table without answering. Hilda really must see what could be done for Lizzie, but she had no idea where to begin. She did not know what to do about anything. It was a matter of record that England had lost yesterday. But had Hilda won or lost regarding Kynaston and China? For one of the first times in her life, Hilda had no idea what to tell anyone to do. Especially herself.

Eleven

Today the weather in Shansi was unseasonably warm for the northern China province. Elizabeth Schofield, clad in blue cotton pajamas like all the women around her, had chosen to leave two-year-old Harold, Jr., at the mission and accompany her husband on his joggling cart ride as he carried medicines and God's love to a neighboring village. From the dirt road that wound across the high plateau, she surveyed the valley before them with the yellow-brown river running slowly through it. "Oh, Harold, I can never get accustomed to the vastness of this place. It seems that China goes on forever. Its great size and age must explain why the people are so quiet and simple. The rhythms of patience are deep in the soul of their land."

"Quiet and simple until they flare with hatred of foreigners," Harold replied. Then his blue eyes crinkled as he smiled at his wife. "I'm so glad you find satisfaction here, Libby. I'm so aware of all you've given up to come to China with me." He shifted the reins to one hand so he could hold hers. "As much as I love it, I don't pretend there aren't hardships."

Libby thought of the days of traveling when the wind whipped up the yellowish-brown loam that covered the whole region and the dust obscured the whole sky. They quickly learned to tie handkerchiefs over their faces to protect their eyes. And the wind among the hills could be far keener than anything she knew at home—sometimes so cutting that she chilled in spite of her thickly padded clothing. But today the terraced hills were covered with soft green wheat several inches high, and sweet perfume from the flowers of bean and mustard plants filled the air.

She laughed, and it seemed to Harold that small bells rang in the air. "Hardships? Perhaps. But I am so honored to share all this with you. How many women in England have ever dreamed of such a place, let alone experienced it?"

Harold raised his blond eyebrows. "And count themselves lucky for it. You are a marvel, Libby. I thank God for you every day."

The road was very hilly. At one point Harold, forever the scientist, took out his aneroid and measured their elevation.

"It's 3,750 feet." He glanced at the steep ridge above them. "The hills themselves must be 5,000 or 6,000 feet high."

The path wound through a gully so deep that the view was completely obscured in every direction. Then, around another curve, the vista opened out to them. Harold stopped the cart and gazed. He had always delighted in the beauties of nature. As a child he had nowhere been so happy as in the wilds and beauties of the English countryside. He had loved to exercise his splendid physique in long tramps over open moors or in the Welsh mountains.

His special delight was running water, and in light and shade playing on water and on foliage. "Look, Libby." He pointed and watched, breathless, as the shadow of a cloud passed over the mountain. His face lit up brighter than the outburst of sunshine that followed the shade. "Has not God made everything splendidly?"

As they went down into the village, they met large numbers of men carrying loads of earthenware and iron jars slung from the ends of poles neatly balanced across their shoulders. They also passed donkeys, mules, and ponies—all laden with coal from the mines in the hills. There was even a string of seven or eight camels with deep-toned bells on their necks, whose sound contrasted agreeably with the tinklings of the mules' bells.

Then they passed through one of the T'ien-men, Heavenly Gates, where an old priest sat before the entrance to a temple. He was beating a gong and holding out a plate for contributions. From the road they could see over the vast plain of T'ai-yuen dotted with towns and villages. With the old priest's gong sounding behind them, Harold shook his head. "It is estimated that there are three million souls in that valley. And every one of them is God's child—a human being the Father loves. Yet there is not one solitary preacher of the Gospel, native or foreign, among them."

Libby pressed his arm silently. She knew the weight of the burden he carried. "I know, my love. It seems so hopeless. We help a few. But there are millions." After a moment she continued. "We must both remember what you have said more than once—all we have to do is to see that our light is burning, well supplied with oil and trimmed. Then it will shine out—God will take care of that."

They passed into their first village. Like many other villages on the upland plain, it was more than half-deserted. The empty houses, with broken roofs and crumbling walls—the silent streets gave sad evidence of the terrible famine two years earlier. Millions in the province of Shansi had died of hunger and disease.

The first people they saw were a band of blind beggars. The beggars passed by, one after the other, each with his begging bowl in his right hand, his left hand on the shoulder of the one in front of him. They were almost past when one near the end of the chain sank to the ground. Harold went to him instantly and cradled the man's head in his lap as he uncorked a brown bottle. He forced a few drops between the dry lips. "Nothing to do for him but make his last moments more comfortable."

"What is it?" Libby asked.

"Basically starvation." Harold placed his hand on the man's forehead and spoke to him in Chinese, telling him about the Jesus who loved him and would welcome him home to heaven if he opened his heart to Him.

The man gave a toothless smile and then closed his eyes. Harold rose and laid the body in a depression by the side of the road. He would tell the officials in the village, although it was doubtful that anyone would see to the matter with any speed. Libby took her husband's arm. "I think he heard you. I'm certain he sensed the love you expressed."

They walked on into the town of low houses built of mud and straw. Libby shook her head. "Not a single person is laughing. There's not even a flower in a pot or a bird anywhere."

Two tin pails stood outside every door. To catch rainwater

perhaps? Libby started to inquire and then hid her face, hot with embarrassment, as a pajama-clad man with graying pigtail came from the house and demonstrated the intended use of the pail. When he finished, he apparently judged the pails to be full enough. He hung them at the ends of a thick cane, hoisted the cane across his shoulders, and turned toward the wheat field.

"Harold?"

"Fertilizer. They are too poor to waste anything."

A few houses further, several men sprawled on a straw mat before a doorway. Brown smoke curled up from their pipes, and their eyes looked glazed. "They have reason to hate foreigners," Harold said. "British merchants bring opium from India to trade for tea and silk. We've forced this evil on them."

Libby frowned. "But surely the trade is illegal. Doesn't the Chinese government do anything?"

"That's why East India merchants farm the opium out to private traders—but it comes to the same thing. The money winds up in London. And now even London is dotted with dens of specimens as hopelessly lost as these."

"Oh, Harold, surely not hopeless?"

"Without Christ all they have is Buddha. And opium. The lowest level of initiation into the mysteries of Buddha is wine and opium—the quick escape into the dream world."

On the next corner Harold set up his temporary dispensary in the front of a small shop. The owner, who lived upstairs, had become a Christian on one of Harold's first visits to the village and now happily made space for the missionary among the baskets and bowls he sold. Harold began by fastening a cross to the wall by the door and then opened a case of ointments and bandages. Even before he was ready, a little boy with a running sore on his foot limped in behind a young mother holding a two-year-old girl who had been bruised by a fall. She now had large sores over her face and limbs where the native practitioner had cauterized her with a hot poker. Harold Schofield began immediately binding their wounds and talking to them of Jesus.

Libby went out into the street and called in Chinese to a cluster of half-naked, ragged children. "Come. Come here. Do you want to hear a story?" She held up a poster-sized picture. When she had finished telling them of the God who said, "Let the little children come unto me," she taught them to sing: "Tell me the story of Jesus, Write on my heart ev'ry word..."

As soon as the sun began to lower, the street filled with beggars looking for something to eat. Many seemed almost loaded down with the rags they wore, for whatever they owned, they wore. Others, who had no rags, tied clumps of straw around their waists with ropes and bits of string. Whatever they found they stuck in their belts—old socks, cucumbers, bottles.

Libby asked the children to join her in praying to the God who loves children. Then she sent them scampering to their homes, hoping that they had homes and bowls of vegetables and noodles awaiting them.

Sitting on straw mats at the back of Mr. Ho Chu's shop, Harold and Libby shared a pot of green tea and bowls of noodles while they told him more of the love of God.

As they jolted homeward in the red sunset glow, Libby's thoughts turned from the overwhelming need around them. "Harold, I know how you pray for God to speak to those in the universities in Britain. If you could speak to the varsity men, what would you say?"

He considered long before speaking. "I would tell them that the love of Jesus can do anything. Paul and Barnabas were mere men who hazarded their lives for Christ. I would present the gownsmen with a challenge, ask them, 'What have you hazarded for Him?' And I would warn them, 'You must be content to be considered peculiar—enthusiasts, if you will; for are not those who are enthusiastic over bad things enthusiastic enough about their own badness? What enthusiasm do you show for your Master?' I would ask, 'How do you commend Him if you do not show enthusiasm?'"

In Cambridge as the willows along the Cam turned golden and the ivy on the stone buildings glowed red, Kynaston Studd had enthusiastically prepared the way for God to speak to his fellow gownsmen. He had done all he could do. The campus was dotted with posters announcing the campaign with Messrs. Moody and Sankey. Kynaston had seen to it that every undergraduate received a personal invitation signed by J. E. K. Studd. There was nothing more to do but wait. And pray.

Unable to concentrate on his studies any longer, Kynaston pushed his books aside, shrugged his sleeveless, black academic gown on over his coat, and made his way across Trinity Street to the junior common room. He was not surprised that the sound of raucous laughter met him when he was barely halfway up the stairway, but as he went on up, he was surprised to hear his own name mentioned. "Always admired Studd for his cricket—all three of them, of course. Received my colors at Eton from C. T. But even then I thought it odd of them to hold Bible readings in their studies." He recognized the voice of Arthur Polhill-Turner.

"Even so, bet you never expected a personal invitation to an enthusiasts' meeting." The voice of Douglas Hooper rang with derisive laughter.

Someone whose voice Kynaston didn't know made a mocking remark about an illiterate Yankee from primitive America. "I hear he's been hired by P. T. Barnum."

"And that Sankey is here to sell organs." Hooper added. "What will Studd promote next? The Temperance Union?"

"Or Chinese missions? I hear he admires that Hudson Taylor fellow who goes around in pajamas and a pigtail like a Chinaman." That might be Gerald Lander. J. E. K. started to turn back down the stairs.

But he stopped as Monty Beauchamp and Willie Hoste bounded up the steps toward him. The banter continued upstairs. "Do you know why Chinamen wear pigtails?" Lander asked.

"No, why?"

"It's the law. Keeps them in order. When you catch them stealing and they start to run away, you can grab the pigtail. If you get one in each hand, you tie the pigtails together."

Hooper guffawed. "No wonder Taylor wears a detachable queue."

P.T. was laughing, but his answer held a ring of seriousness. "Surely, he wouldn't steal."

"You can never tell, old man. Can't ever be too careful. Never know who might be sneaking up on you." The laughing voices moved away.

Kynaston looked at his friends chagrined. "What have we gotten ourselves into? What have *I* gotten us into? Moule was right." He referred to the saintly principal of Ridley Hall. "He warned me that Cambridge undergraduates are the most intolerant and difficult audience in the world. 'They won't be reached,' he said." J. E. K. shook his head.

Monty clapped him on the back. "Did the right thing. Sure of it. Just need to pray more."

Willie Hoste, however, seemed less sure as they went on into the common room. "Hope you're right, Beauchamp. One does hear some odd reports of those American evangelists though." He surveyed the room filled with arrogant intellectuals and members of the breezily intolerant fast set.

Kynaston slid into the first empty chair inside the large room filled with men smoking, drinking, playing cards, and talking. "I might as well know the worst. What do you hear about Moody?"

"Uncivilized—to put the best face on it. Uncouth seems more to the point. They say he tosses out the Gospel as if hoping someone would get hit with it."

J. E. K. nodded. "So it's a matter of manners, not of his message?"

Hoste took a drink from a beaker of cider Monty set in front of him. "Hear he's a ranter. Bellows at his audience. Hellfire and brimstone—that sort of thing."

As if matters weren't bad enough, Arthur Polhill-Turner approached their table. Kynaston resisted the impulse to slide down in his chair. Christ had held firm before those who mocked Him. Kynaston could withstand a little razzing.

But Arthur had not come to mock. His real concern, thinly concealed under a veneer of amusement, was much harder to bear. "Have you thought about what you're doing?" he began without preamble.

"I hope to confront my fellows with Christ's claims on their lives. I want them to hear the truth of real Christianity. Surely you understand. You're studying for orders."

P.T. wrinkled his forehead beneath his wavy blond hair. "Feel that's what gives me the right to speak. Disorder. Emotion. Departure from the prayer book. Those things give Christianity a bad name. Make it a laughingstock. God brought order out of chaos when He created the world. Your enthusiastic evangelist replaces the order of worship with chaos."

"I know his manner is rough and his speech unpolished. But I do believe that if people give him a chance, they will see Christ rather than hearing bad grammar."

"Oh, from all accounts the manner and grammar are bad enough, but I'm talking about something more fundamental. Your Mr. Moody is not ordained. A shoe salesman, I'm told. Never studied theology, never had holy hands laid on him. A mere ranting layman. And Sankey is a tax collector."

Kynaston cringed. Was it really as bad as that? Then he squared his shoulders. No, his father had been transformed under such evangelism—their whole family brought to true faith as a result of Moody's thunderous preaching just five years ago. He started to speak, but Arthur continued. "Besides, it's unseemly."

"Unseemly?" Willie asked.

"All right for the lower classes, I suppose. But religion is a personal matter between a man and his God. This open propagation of religion by men of our class smacks of indecency."

Later, back in his room Kynaston sat, sunk deep in an upholstered chair, his legs extended toward the glowing coals of a dying fire. He had not even bothered to turn up the gaslights on the wall. It had seemed such a good idea months ago when Hilda's letter arrived. He had written a year ago to explore the idea of Moody coming to Cambridge. Then Hilda's letter had seemed an answer to prayer—a confirmation of the idea. Perhaps he had been more persuaded by his admiration for the lady making the suggestion than by his father's reports of the American evangelists. Whatever the case, he had moved full steam ahead, committing the full energies of the Christian Union and himself to this upcoming campaign.

Should he have considered more closely? Weighed the cost before plunging? He didn't relish being a laughingstock, and his mother would be horrified that he had held the family name up to ridicule. G. B. had supported the effort in an offhanded manner. But Kynaston's greatest disappointment was that Charlie would not be there to hear Mr. Moody. C. T. Studd had been chosen for the All-England cricket team that was to journey to Australia to regain their national honor. J. E. K. knew that his brother needed to hear Moody's message. If C. T.'s single-mindedness could ever be turned to God, there was no imagining what he could accomplish for the kingdom.

Kynaston turned his mind to a more serious question. What would his effort do to the faith in the eyes of those he wished to reach? He wanted more than anything to tell of the beauty and joy of the Christian life. And here he was, making it seem cheap and shoddy.

In spite of regular prayer times with Beauchamp and Hoste, Kynaston's worry persisted. His spirits got a lift, however, when Stanley Smith arrived from south London on leave from Newlands, his brother-in-law's school. "Got a long weekend off," S. P. S. announced. "What can I do to help? Saw the town and campus placarded with posters. Looks great."

Kynaston smiled but was less enthusiastic. "Hope so. What do you think of schoolmastering?"

"It's just the thing—earning my own living—beginning life in earnest. The work is light, and the boys seem to take to me. Think highly of athletes, you know. And Griffith gives me ample time off."

Kynaston nodded. "Apparently. Glad you're here now. How are things aside from the school?"

Smith grinned. "My spiritual temperament, you mean? Maybe I'm stabilizing at last. Plenty of opportunity for work at least. Every weekend at Aldershot or Windsor speaking at soldiers' or young men's meetings. Forever having to knock up the Newlands staff to open doors in the wee hours. Then I wonder if I'm being selfish. I have all the fun of speaking at the expense of their sleep." He suddenly bounded to his feet. "Speaking of fun—

promised myself a row on the river for old times' sake. Fun and doing good, that is. I'll invite the boat club to the campaign." He paused at the door. "Meeting Beauchamp and Hoste for prayer after hall? Right. I'll be there."

But Kynaston's niggling worry sank to despair the morning of the opening service when the believers from the town held a mass prayer service. Only the staunchest Christians from the university attended. The meeting got off to a good start with the opening hymn. J. E. K. was sure he had never sung "Rescue the Perishing" with more fervency. The enormous Ira Sankey waved his arms, urging the congregation to sing faster. The deep voice of Handley Moule beside Kynaston strengthened his resolve.

Then D. L. Moody sprang up the stairs to the pulpit and all but shouted the topic for his morning's address: "The Spirit's power for service." He thumped the sacred desk in front of him. "This here's a mighty fine-looking crowd this morning. If I were a betting man, I'd wager there's not many of you—maybe not any at all that wouldn't like to get in line right behind Elisha when he ran after the prophet Elijah and asked for a double portion of his spirit. Any Christian who don't want more of God's Spirit ain't much of a Christian.

"But do you know what Elijah told him? The same thing God says to you today: 'It's a hard thing you're asking.'" Moody swept the audience with his long, powerful arm. "Now hear me, brothers and sisters, God will honor such a request. Elisha received a double portion and did twice as many miracles as Elijah had done before him. But it cost him. Elisha broke his plow and sacrificed his ox. He gave up his livelihood, his security, his whole way of life."

The evangelist shook his thick, full beard as he surveyed individuals in the congregation. "How much are you willin' to pay?"

Sankey began pumping out the closing hymn on his harmonium. Handley Moule turned to Kynaston. "Very admirable. A most searching address, I thought."

But Kynaston couldn't answer. The ain'ts and flat a's rang in his ears far louder than the wheezing melodeon. It was true— the heart of Moody's address was excellent. It was apparent that the congregation of townies was much moved. But these were not varsity men. Moody's way of speaking was not their way; his accent was not their accent. What would undergraduates, full of spirits and ready to make fun of everything, do?

At that very moment three such varsity men sat over glasses of port in Gerald Lander's room.

"What? Go to an evangelistic campaign on Guy Fawkes's night?" Douglas Hooper set his glass down so hard some of its dark red contents sloshed on the table beside his chair. "What about the bonfire?"

"As today's Sunday, bonfires are tomorrow. Besides," Lander laughed, "they say this rustic American shoots sparks from his mouth better than any bonfire. Believe me, there promises to be more action at the Corn Exchange tonight than on the fen. Evans, Cowley, Sedgwick—they've got some good plans. Help get in shape for tomorrow's fights with the town lads."

Hooper picked his glass up again and raised it in Arthur's direction. "You going, Polhill?"

P.T. shrugged. "Thought I might. See what all the fuss is about. Wouldn't want to miss the fun."

"Well then, better have something to fortify us before we face the bearded lion." Lander brought out a bottle of his prize Scotch.

A few hours later the three undergraduates were in exceedingly high spirits. Church bells all over Cambridge tolled eight o'clock as they made their way toward the large new stone building at the end of Corn Exchange Street. As soon as they entered the cavernous hall, Arthur saw that they had come none too early. The crowded room rang with the rowdiness Lander had promised. They found seats near the back. Then Lander spotted some others of their set. "I say, Sedgie, this place wants a bit of livening up." Gerald leapt over the bench in front of him to join Sedgwick and the others.

"Come on, P.T. Don't want to miss out." Hooper started after their companion. "I say, fellows, save some for me." Lander had started piling up chairs in a pyramid against the wall.

"Go on," Arthur said. "I'll hold your seats."

"You call that a pyramid? And on bonfire night, too! I'd be ashamed to call myself a Trinity man if we couldn't double that." The group around Hooper laughed and applauded, cheering the pyramid builders on. Arthur laughed, too. But he was thoughtful as well. It would be interesting to see what the evening would bring. For all that he took issue with Studd, he didn't want the Christian Union to be completely humiliated. After all, the church was going to be his living.

Seventy undergraduates who had formed a choir took their places on the platform and began with determined voices: "'I will sing of my Redeemer, and His wondrous love to me...'"

A varsity man behind P.T. gave a loud, piercing catcall and then remarked to any who cared to hear his opinion, "I wouldn't join that lot for £200."

Just in front of Arthur a group linked arms and, swaying from side to side, sang loudly, "'She may have seen better days, When she was in her prime...'"

On the platform the choir members appeared to be sweating, but they struggled manfully on: "'Sing, O sing of my Redeemer, with His blood He purchased me...'"

While across the hall most of the 1,700 men in cap and gown took up the music hall refrain: "'Tho' by the wayside she fell, She may yet mend her ways. Some poor old mother is waiting for her, Who has seen better days.'"

"'...paid the debt and made me free.'" The choir labored to the end. A door at the side of the hall opened. Several dons and clergymen, including Handley Moule and John Barton, who filled the pulpit once occupied by Charles Simeon at Holy Trinity, led Moody and Sankey to the platform to the accompaniment of shouted cheers and raucous clapping.

The ruddy-faced Sankey strode to the side of the platform where his faithful harmonium stood. Pumping for all he was worth, he accompanied himself as he sang in his big baritone voice, "Jesus, Lover of My Soul."

Arthur couldn't fault his choice of a Wesley hymn, but he cringed at the idea of solo singing in what was ostensibly a church service, even though it was held in the Corn Exchange. This was not worship—it was a parade of human conceit. Distracting. Irreverent. He didn't actually condone his rowdy fellows' behavior, but neither could he condone the evangelists'.

The gownsmen remained relatively quiet during John Barton's prayer, but they broke into cries of "Hear! Hear!" at the end.

Then Sankey began his theme song, "The Ninety and Nine." The hall was strangely silent throughout the first verse: "'There were ninety and nine that safely lay In the shelter of the fold, But one was out on the hills away, Far off from the gates of gold— away on the mountains wild and bare, Away from the tender Shepherd's care...'" At the end of the verse the building vibrated with the thumps and bangs of umbrellas and canes beating against the floor.

Sankey's face grew redder as the story song unfolded. Each verse was greeted with cries of "Encore! Encore!" By the end of the hymn, Sankey appeared to be near to tears. Some of the dons in the audience ushered the most raucous men from the hall, but it had little effect on the others.

When a firecracker thrown outside exploded against a window near him, even Arthur started in his seat. Surely Moody wouldn't carry on in the face of all this. Best thing to do would be to admit his mistake like a man and return to preaching to the masses.

But Dwight L. Moody, his enormous chest and bull-like neck exhibiting enormous strength, approached the pulpit. "Gentlemen, may I remind you that this is not a political meeting. This service is God's. Such proceedings are irreverent."

For a moment it seemed as if his straightforward approach might reach his audience. Then he announced his topic: "Dan'l in the lions' den."

The response was immediate. "Dan'l! Dan'l!" The walls rang with it, but the preacher launched into his sermon anyway. Arthur had to admit that in spite of the speaker's pacing about, his loud voice, and uncultured vowel sounds, the content of the message with its emphasis on faith and manly courage was not inappropriate. But few in the hall heard it. Even with the evangelist's proclivity to shout, the audience was so unruly and the acoustics in the building so bad that those trying to listen heard little of it.

But what Arthur did hear was memorable. Daniel in his fine black frock coat, called before the feast of King Belshazzar and a thousand of his lords, called to read the writing on the wall because he was known as a man on whom the light and understanding and wisdom of God rested. "And Dan'l pulled his scroll from his hip pocket and pointed his finger at the king." Arthur cringed as Moody pointed. It seemed the evangelist was pointing directly at him. "You have not humbled your heart before God. You have set yourself up against the Lord of heaven." Arthur shifted in his seat. What did the man mean? He hadn't set himself against God. He was preparing to be a clergyman. What more could anyone ask?

The booming voice rolled on with colorful anecdotes supporting each pithy teaching. At least the rowdies followed the sermon closely enough to mark the speaker's most emphatic points with shouts of "Well done!"

How can anyone hold up in the face of such heckling, Arthur wondered? *Will Moody lose his temper? Surely even a man of his stamina must reach the end of his endurance at some point*. But an unconscious clearing of his throat to mark his most important points seemed to be the evangelist's only concession to nervousness. One had to admire the courage. Where did such strength come from?

The towering Sankey with his collar too tight and his coat sleeves too short returned to his harmonium for a final solo. "'Man of Sorrows, what a name For the Son of God who came…'" It was perhaps not the wisest choice. A more rousing tune might have given him a chance to outvoice at least some of the roisterers. "'Guilty, vile and helpless, we…'" brought forth such a roar the chandeliers seemed to sway.

Moody appeared ready to dismiss the crowd. A less stalwart man would have done so long before. But John Barton leaned over and said something to the evangelist. Moody spread his arms wide to the crowd and, incredibly, smiled. "Well now, unlikely as it may seem to some of you, I believe there are people here who would be happy for a chance to stay and pray a spell. For those who want to go, the meetin's over. But any who'd like to stay for a little prayer time, just sit a spell longer in your seats."

Arthur shrugged. He'd stayed this long. He might as well see it out. Only seemed like good sportsmanship. Arthur admired courage and stamina. No one could fault D. L. Moody on those points. Fair play demanded he be heard to the end.

When the echoing clatter of departure died, P.T. was amazed to see that some 400 remained, Gerald Lander among them. Moody's good humor continued unflagging. Now his audience was quiet, whether from shame at their recent behavior or simple fatigue. "Yes, sir, this prayer's a powerful thing. Dan'l understood all about it. When the King of Persia outlawed it, old Dan'l just went right on up to his open window and prayed right out to God, three times a day, just like he allus had.

"And what was the result of that? Well, now, you know the answer to that as well as I do. And I know old Dan'l must have been prayin' his heart out when he faced those hungry lions." Clasping the pulpit with both hands, the preacher shook his bushy beard and grinned. "'Pears I know something of how he musta' felt." The audience laughed, some sympathetically, some derisively.

After a time of prayer for the coming days of the campaign, Moody and Sankey left. Kynaston accompanied them, holding his head up in spite of the hoots several of his fellow varsity men directed at him. P.T. waited for Lander and Hooper, who had taken seats down front after their pyramid-building exploit.

"Well, some evening that was!" Hooper clutched the folds of his gown as a sharp wind caught it when they stepped out the door. "We went meaning to have fun. And, by Jove, we had it." He slapped his companions on the back and laughed.

"You didn't think it a bit unsporting?" Arthur ventured quietly.

Gerald Lander frowned, indignant at the suggestion. "If

uneducated men will come to teach the varsity, they deserve to be snubbed."

Arthur left his companions at the Great Gate of Trinity and continued on down the lane to his rooms. What he had heard of the sermon had interested him but left him unmoved. Perhaps he would go back, perhaps not.

Twelve

On Monday morning Kynaston made his way across the bustling market square to Moody's hotel room. Last night Sankey had been greatly upset, but Moody showed only courage and determination. Only his sweat-soaked collar gave testimony to what the evening had cost him. After a time praying on their knees, J. E. K. had promised to join the evangelists again the next day.

Sankey was still depressed. His usually tidy black hair hung limp. His dark eyes were surrounded with deep lines and purple shadows.

Moody's determination was grim. "I don't reckon more than fifty got the gist of what I was sayin' last night. And here I am for a whole week. I must go through with it somehow, but I don't hanker after that crowd, I can tell you."

"Like Daniel in the lions' den, sir?" Kynaston smiled at him.

Before Moody could reply, a knock came at the door. Studd was closest, so he opened it. The bellboy handed him a card. Kynaston's sharp, black eyebrows rose when he saw the name. "Mr. Gerald Lander. Trinity College," he said to the evangelist.

"Well, show him up. Show him up." Moody made a beckoning gesture.

Lander must have been waiting around the corner, because a moment later he was inside the room, his black gown hanging in precise folds over his blue jacket. He squared his shoulders. "I want to apologize, sir. And," he took a deep breath, "I've brought a letter of apology from the men."

Moody took the folded sheet of gray paper Lander held out. "Well now, that's right gentlemanly of you, sir."

"Er, that's what we thought. That is, we see now that as gentlemen, we overstepped the bounds of decency. I, um, was delegated to come to you."

"I do appreciate that, Mr. Lander. Won't you sit a spell?" Moody turned to a tray the maid had put on the sideboard a little earlier. "One of the finest things you have in England is your tea." He poured a cup for the newcomer. "Don't know why it never tastes this good at home." He took a sip from his own cup. "Ah, that's right fine. Now tell me something about yourself. How do you spend your free time?"

Lander looked abashed at the simple question. Then he shrugged. "The usual—card games, horse races, sport."

Moody looked at the rain blowing against the window. "Not such good weather for racing and sport just now."

Lander sipped his tea. "No, sir. Nothing doing at Newmarket right now."

"Well, that's fine then. Studies not too troublesome, are they?"

Gerald and Kynaston both laughed. Varsity men of their class didn't come to university to study.

Moody slapped his thigh. "So we can expect you at the meeting tonight. Seems the best way to prove your apology sincere. Not that I doubt it, you understand. But you wouldn't want to bet on a horse you knew nothing about, now would you?"

Lander was clearly surprised. "No, I wouldn't."

"And, sure's shootin', you couldn't have learned very much last night—except maybe about stacking chairs."

Lander had the grace to blush. He agreed that the sporting thing to do would be to return that evening.

Kynaston felt hopeful that the service would be quieter, if only because most of the fast set would be about their bonfires and fistfights with the townies and police. But when he entered the room where the meeting was being held, his heart fell. He had not wanted it that quiet.

Fewer than a hundred varsity men were scattered across the

room that would have held five hundred. And that included the seventy men of the choir. J. E. K. took a seat next to Handley Moule and began to pray for the service.

When he opened his eyes, he saw that, true to his promise, Gerald Lander sat listening attentively just a few rows over. This time there was no disturbance as Sankey played and sang, "'Lord, I care not for riches, Neither silver nor gold; I would make sure of Heaven, I would enter the fold...'" There was no disturbance, but neither was there any response. The one advantage to such a sparse crowd, besides the quiet—if stony silence was an advantage—was that Moody was able to speak to every man in the hall personally.

Five university men chose to follow Christ that night.

Tuesday afternoon the Corn Exchange was packed with town and country folk an hour before the meeting began. They nodded, smiled, and sang along with Sankey for a full half hour before the sermon. Even with all their good will, however, Sankey never could get them up to the tempo at which he preferred to sing. Moody welcomed the congregation with his full gusto and then asked them to pray for the university meetings. He shook his head. "In spite of the prayers of the faithful and our best human efforts, we've come up against a brick wall."

After the service an old woman, tiny and bent, gray hair wisping around the edges of her black hat, tapped Moody with her umbrella. "Young man." She looked up at the powerfully built preacher. "Why do you not call a prayer meeting of mothers?"

Moody ran a broad hand through his thick hair, "Well, now, ma'am, I often call on mothers to unite in prayer for their sons. I'll be glad to urge that tomorrow."

"No, you misunderstand me. Not for their own sons. We do that anyway. Who would have to remind a mother to pray for her own sons? I mean for these young men at the university."

Moody reared back, his brow wrinkling in thought. "Well, now, I'll admit that's an idea I never thought of. And would they do such a thing—band together to pray for other mothers' sons?"

The wrinkled face broke into a smile. "The Lord must love

those boys as much as we love our own sons. And it must be that some of their mothers don't know how to pray for them, or they wouldn't act as they do." She shook her head. "And if they *are* praying, their mothers' hearts must be breaking."

Kynaston slipped out the back of the Corn Exchange and turned toward his rooms, his step slow not from depression but from deep thought. At the sound of someone approaching him, he raised his head to speak. He didn't know the red-haired, freck-led Trinity freshman's name, but he had passed him more than once in hall and on the cricket field. Kynaston's mouth was open with a greeting when the man recognized him and turned abruptly to cross the street. J. E. K. stood blinking at the snub. It was hard to believe, yet it had happened. Kynaston had never put too much stock in his family's wealth or the admiration he received as a cricketer, but these were pleasant. He enjoyed being respected, and he always attempted to turn his position to good in his work with the Christian Union.

What was he to do now? If he had lost the respect of his fellows because he supported Moody, could it be regained? Was such ephemeral admiration worth regaining? Perhaps not but for the fact of his identification with Christian causes. The varsity men shunning J. E. K. Studd was one thing. Their shunning Christ was quite another.

He resumed walking, this time with an increased pace. By the time he reached his staircase, Kynaston was striding with his usual determination. He couldn't stick his neck out farther than he already had. He knew what he could do. He had nothing to lose. Without even bothering to close his door, he sat down at the writing desk and pulled out a sheet of his best paper.

At the end of the town meeting Wednesday afternoon, Moody walked to the very edge of the platform. With a gentleness in his voice that he seldom used when addressing such a vast audience, he spoke as if talking to his own mother in Northfield, Massachusetts. "Out in the desert the Shepherd heard the cry of the lamb, 'sick and helpless, and ready to die.'" He quoted Sankey's song. "I want to ask something very special of the mothers gathered here today. I want every one of you mothers red velvet hat with two roses on the front, a high-necked gold dress with a single strand of garnet beads. Yes, she was very attractive, indeed, but Hilda would hardly have chosen her as one of the most beautiful women in England. Yet, even as she thought that, Hilda noticed the peachy pearlescent glow of Lillie Langtry's skin. Then the woman raised her enormous dark eyes, and Hilda knew the source of the Jersey Lillie's attraction.

Ida took one brief glance and then turned away. "Can you imagine, an actress out in respectable company?"

Hilda considered. Yes, a society woman becoming an actress was shocking, but by all accounts she had given a very competent performance as Rosalind in *As You Like It*. It was other aspects of Lillie Langtry's life, spoken of only in whispers, that made Hilda's eyebrows rise.

Then Hilda's attention was drawn back to the Oval as, with the score standing Australia 63, England 101, Australia began their second innings.

Australia's first batter was still at the wicket when G. B. leaned over to his brother and pointed to Hornby, the England captain, standing in the field. "Let's hope Australia doesn't put a ball there. Hornby's a brilliant captain and a good striker, but he's famous for not being able to throw."

The words had no more than left George's mouth than the Australian batter sent the ball right between Hornby and C. T. Hornby ran for it; C. T. followed.

The Australian batsmen ran back and forth between the wickets, adding 2 to their score. The Australian captain saw the ball in Hornby's hand. Apparently calculating that England's captain couldn't throw, he called for another run, and the Australians set off to exchange wickets again.

Instead of throwing the ball to the wicket-keeper, Hornby jerked it to C. T. Studd. The stands erupted with vigorous applause as the bright red ball landed squarely on the bail for the fall of an Australian wicket.

But even as Hilda applauded, she realized that there would be no chance of speaking to Kynaston amid the close quarters and activity of this enthusiastic throng, at least not for her. Ida, however, seemed to be doing quite well in her soft way, asking him to relay details to her that her shortsightedness left too fuzzy. Frowning, Hilda observed the two of them for a moment and then turned back to the field.

Hilda was following the play when she became aware of a movement at the edge of the field in front of the clubhouse. Again Dora was the first to identify the newcomers. "Oh, just look! The Prince of Wales and Princess Alexandra. Oh, isn't she lovely!"

Hilda looked. Prince Edward, clad in impeccable frock coat, gray gloves, and shining silk top hat above his perfectly trimmed beard, gave his arm to his wife. She wore a white lace gown, her fine red hair and exquisite complexion shaded by a lace parasol. Even from that distance Hilda was aware of the princess's long neck circled by multiple strands of a pearl choker.

Dora wrinkled her nose. "How interesting. Just see how intently Mrs. Langtry is not noticing."

Indeed, Lillie Langtry, engaged in seeming intimate conversation with the lady beside her, presented her full back to the spectacle of her "special friend" entering the Oval with his wife.

But Hilda could spare no more thought for the incident because W. G. Grace, the Gloucestershire doctor who had become the greatest cricketer in England, was batting. She leaned forward, finding George's commentary to Arthur helpful. "Grace played in the first test match against Australia two years ago."

They continued, George quoting statistics on runs amassed and number of wickets taken, but Hilda turned again to watch the tall bearded man in a gold and chili striped cap, colors of the Marylebone Cricket Club, stride toward the wicket with all the gusto that had made him so famous. Grace scored 32 runs, and English spirits were high when play stopped for the luncheon interval. They had only 85 runs left to make in the last innings to preserve England's unbroken record of superiority.

Along with a great many other spectators, the Studd party left the Oval and walked across the road to Kennington Park. Mrs. Studd, as careful about domestic details as her sons were about their athletic training, had instructed her servants to lay out a to picture that lamb—lost, hungry, cold, and frightened—as a son. Not your own son, but some mother's son. Some mother who loves her son just as much as you love your own, just as the Shepherd loves every one of His sheep—even the blackest, most obstreperous, most arrogant among them.

"As a matter of fact, I want you to picture that lost, straying sheep for whom the Shepherd shed His blood as a black sheep—black in one of the gowns of a university man. I told you yesterday we've hit a brick wall in our university meetings. Only God can break that brick wall down. Only the Good Shepherd with 'His hands rent and torn' can remove the bricks from the hearts of these mother's sons. Will you stay now and pray with me for these boys?"

One hundred fifty mothers made their way to the front of the Corn Exchange to plead tearfully that God would move in the hearts of the young men of the university.

As Kynaston left the exchange where the others prayed, his prayer was for his mother—that she wouldn't suffer because of the action he had taken the day before. He would face what he must. He had never run from responsibility for his own actions, but he would not choose to hurt his family.

"J. E. K.!" He jerked to a stop at the sound of his brother's voice. He turned and saw G. B. with two of his cricketing friends. As he crossed the narrow street, he saw that they carried copies of the *Cambridge Review*. So it was off the press.

George slapped him on the back. "Well done. I'll be there tonight. Ashamed of my slacking off, but I've been busy. Tonight for certain though." G. B.'s companions were quiet, but they seemed congenial enough.

"Fine. See you there." Kynaston waved his brother off. Well, he would expect George to be supportive, but that was only a beginning. He might as well put it to the test. He turned his steps toward the common room. How would those gathered there feel about his reprimand to the varsity in the university paper?

Halfway across Trinity Great Court with its splashing Renaissance fountain, he met Beauchamp and Hoste. "Going up?" Monty rolled his heavy-lidded eyes toward the common room. "Better go with you. Set them by their ears, you have."

Then he saw that Monty, too, had the *Review*.

"Very proper set-down." Willie Hoste pointed to the front page where "An Open Rebuke to Varsity Men Regarding Their Manners" signed by J. E. K. Studd held center attention. "'I must remind my fellow undergraduates that Messrs. Moody and Sankey are here as the invited guests of the university. They deserve the respect usually extended guests...'" Willie stopped reading and grinned at Kynaston.

"We would have signed with you," Monty said as they started for the door. "Don't have to take the heat alone."

Kynaston shook his head. "My responsibility. I invited them."

Just before hall the room held only a few lounging men. Kynaston held his head up and tried to ignore the sidelong glances he felt from a group smoking in the corner. Then he saw a familiar four playing cards at a table near the center of the room. Gerald Lander did not smile, but he nodded in Studd's direction.

Arthur Polhill-Turner, however, laid his cards down and came to meet J. E. K. "Clever of you to warn us about Oxford. Don't think you'll find too many letting the side down. Couldn't have that Oxford lot saying we'd behaved worse than those far below us in the social scale. Useful hint, that."

Kynaston took a deep breath as P.T. returned to his cards.

It was with such encouragement that Kynaston returned to find the meeting room comfortably full that night. As usual he sat by the kindly Handley Moule from Ridley Hall. "Have you heard? A bedridden lady in the town sent out invitations Monday for others to join her in prayer for the undergraduates." He looked at the orderly crowd around them. "Their prayers must have burst right into heaven because the tide seems to have turned. Hope I'm not being premature, but I'd say the victory is ours."

Kynaston smiled. He hoped Moule was right. The atmosphere certainly felt warmer, although it seemed to him that Moody preached with less force than usual.

Moule, however, disagreed. He turned to Kynaston while Sankey sang his closing hymn. "Fine sermon. Moody spoke with great power. What a remarkable difference from that very discouraging occasion Sunday night."

Moody seemed to sense the turn of the tide and was apparently determined to prove it. He signaled for Sankey to stay at the melodeon as he approached the pulpit. "Gentlemen, I have not yet held an inquiry meeting for you. But I feel sure many of you are ready and yearning to know Christ. Now when you are in difficulties with mathematics or classics, what do you do? You do not hesitate to consult your tutors. Would it be unreasonable for you then to bring your soul-trouble to those who may be able to help you? Mr. Sankey and I will converse with any who will go up to the empty gallery yonder." And then instead of calling on his partner for a song, he said, "Let us have silent prayer."

Kynaston was too stunned to pray. The gallery Moody referred to was the fencing practice room. It was up a clattering iron staircase in the center of the hall in full view of all. No man would reach this inquiry room without a deliberate, noisy display before his friends. In a varsity that had proven so recently its quickness to ridicule eccentricity, where men hated to show their feelings, nothing could better serve to prevent shallow decisions. But would it also preclude inquiries that were honest but timid? Kynaston held his breath. Would anyone among these hundreds of undergraduates be willing to make such a stand? He closed his eyes in prayer.

No one moved.

"I know this may be new to you," encouraged Moody. "But if you have inquiries to make of us about the faith, or if you have inquiries to make of God about your soul, there's no better place than the inquiry room." The quiet in the hall was eerie.

Still no one moved.

Kynaston felt the tension in the room rising as Moody repeated his appeal a third time.

The silence echoed.

Moody made a fourth appeal.

The clattering sound of feet running up the iron stairway rang like a shot in the room. Kynaston jerked his head up to see a young Trinity man with bright red hair, half hiding his freck-led face in his gown, bound up the stairs two at a time. Another followed.

Now Moody nodded to Sankey, and the choir began, "'I gave My life for thee, My precious blood I shed, That thou might'st ransomed be...'" The room reverberated with the clatter of man after man charging up the stairs with his gown streaming behind him.

At the next clanging of iron, Kynaston caught his breath. His first reaction was one of guilt. He had not thought it possible. His faith had not extended to such power of the Spirit's moving. The man making his way up the noisy iron staircase to the inquiry room was Gerald Lander.

"You what?" Arthur Polhill-Turner blinked at the grinning, slightly abashed, ruddy face of Gerald Lander.

"I went to the inquiry room. Last night. Hooper, too."

"Douglas Hooper? Who lives for nothing but racing and Newmarket? In the inquiry room?"

Lander nodded. "There were more than fifty of us."

"Incredible."

"Yes, it is. Hooper has quit smoking. He's talking about going to Africa."

"Africa! Whatever for?"

"As a—well, you know—a missionary."

P.T. gave a shout of laughter.

But Lander continued. "Fact is, I'm thinking of—er, no—truth is, I've decided. I'm taking orders."

Arthur shook his head. The two leaders of the fast set. Changed men overnight?

"I, um—I'm thinking of offering for the foreign field, too."

Arthur was too amazed even to shake his head. But he did go to the meeting that night. Now there was none of the rowdyism that had marked the opening service nor of the coldness of the next two nights. When Sankey came to his little harmonium standing at the very edge of the platform—so near to the edge Arthur thought both man and instrument must surely topple into the audience—the musician was greeted with an expectant hush. Arthur wondered if he were the only undergraduate in the room who resisted Sankey's unctuous gestures and eye-rolling expressions.

Then Sankey touched a few simple chords. It was as if they reverberated in Arthur's heart. "'There were ninety and nine...'" His voice was sweet and powerful. As the silence deepened in the room, Arthur was amazed and alarmed to find his own eyes damp. "'Rejoice, for the Lord brings back His own.'"

And then Moody took the pulpit to preach on the prodigal son. "And so he took his inheritance—all the wealth, all the blessings that the Father so freely bestowed on him. He bought the fastest horse and the finest carriage, and he went to London and gathered all his friends around him and began to live the life he had always thought himself suited for...."

Arthur saw that young man as clearly as if he were looking in a mirror. He could even see the fair, wavy hair, the carefully tended luxurious mustache, the exquisitely cut suit his tailor had just sent down from London. And he knew the life—the hollow drifting, the feeble mundane ambitions, the selfishness. Giving no service, making no sacrifice, gliding along on the surface of everything. Every word seemed to probe to his own heart. How did this American evangelist know his lifestyle? His attitudes? His thoughts? Arthur Polhill-Turner shifted in his seat.

He remembered his old nanny. Nanny Redshaw had spent many an hour telling Bible stories to the Polhill-Turner children. And Arthur and Cecil had pulled their sisters' braids and tossed toys about the nursery. But Alice had listened. Alice who had made so many attempts to talk to him seriously during the long vacation. Now he saw what an ungrateful wretch he had been.

"And the prodigal son returned home, broken in purse and in spirit, and threw himself at his father's feet and begged to be taken back as a swineherd. The father reached down and threw his arms around his son, clasped him in love, and lifted him to his feet. Just so Jesus calls us to come to Him. We are invited to come to the feet of the crucified Savior, to see His bleeding hand and dimmed eye, and the heart of infinite love."

Moody held out his arms as if he would clasp each person in that room in his own arms. "Just accept Him. In a moment, in the twinkling of an eye, you may be His—nestling in His arms—with the burden of sin and selfishness resting at His feet."

Arthur was overwhelmed with contrition. Moody began the invitation, and Sankey sang. The clattering sound on iron steps announced that many were making their way to the inquiry room. But Arthur felt no impulse to go up those stairs with them. Instead, he wanted to be alone. He must think. Arthur Polhill-Turner went out into the black of a November night.

In his room in Trinity Hall he faced the fact that his plan to enter the ministry as an easy livelihood was gross hypocrisy. To do so would be to mock God. And yet what was the alternative? He counted the cost. If he were to become an out-and-out Christian, like Douglas Hooper and Gerald Lander—the thought still boggled his mind—his life would have to be a good deal readjusted. And he liked his easy life very much.

He could never accept Christ unless he meant to make a wholehearted decision. There could be no half measures. Christ had given all for him. He would have to give all to Christ. Or nothing.

He would not ask Christ to forgive his sins and then go about living life as usual. To be sincerely sorry for his sins would mean to turn his back on them completely. He would say, "Whatever You want me to do, Lord; wherever You want me to go." Or he would say, "No thank You, Jesus."

He would have Christ for his Lord as well as his Savior, or he would not have Him at all. It was a momentous decision. He could make no mistakes about this. Once taken, there would be no going back.

Arthur returned to the services Friday night and Saturday night. Each night the iron steps rang as men clambered up to meet their Savior. All over the university men clustered in black-gowned groups to hear their friends tell of the changes that had come into their lives. And Arthur listened. The weight of decision was so heavy he sometimes thought he couldn't breathe. But he would not rush. He had to be certain.

Sunday was murky and cold. Two thousand university men

crowded into the Corn Exchange for the closing meeting of the campaign. Arthur Polhill-Turner sat intent. This was the night. He must decide. Christ called every person. Everyone must decide. Arthur was not fighting. He was not rebellious. But he was afraid.

"I bring you good tidings of great joy!" Moody announced. "Rejoice! This is the best news ever come from heaven to earth. And I bring it to you. 'Unto you is born a Savior.'" The sermon continued with the evangelist explaining the meaning of the Cross and the fact of the Resurrection. "And with His resurrection, Christ conquered all enemies. All of mankind's enemies, all of your enemies—death and sin, judgment and fear.

"Remember, the angels said, 'Fear not.' And the prophet Isaiah said, 'Behold, God is my salvation: I will trust and not be afraid; for the Lord Jehovah is my strength; He also is become my salvation.'"

The words rang in Arthur's mind. *I will trust and not be afraid.* Suddenly he saw how groundless his fears were. If Christ had died to save, He lived to keep. There was nothing to fear; the Lord would prove a strength and a song.

Arthur blinked as he returned from the depths of his own thoughts to the close of the service. "If you will take my advice," Moody was saying, "you will decide the question, and decide this night. Believe the Gospel and make room for God in your hearts."

Sankey began pumping on the harmonium. "'Just as I am without one plea...'" Arthur found himself on his feet singing with all his might. "'...I come, I come.'" Yes, he did come. He would choose Christ. With all his heart and all his mind. "'Because Thy promise I believe, O Lamb of God, I come! I come!'"

All across the exchange gownsmen sat or knelt with bowed heads while Moody prayed. Then, as a great silence held the hall, Moody raised his head. "Now I want to ask one more thing. I want all who have received a blessing during this week to stand up in token of their faith." More than 200 stood.

Arthur Polhill-Turner stood, free of doubt, free of fear.

Thirteen

M ust come. Mama expects you." Monty Beauchamp leapt the three marble steps to the portico of 3 Cromwell Road at a single bound.

Kynaston gritted his teeth. Of course he must do his duty. But he was so anxious to get on to Mildmay.

"Mama likes you. Can't imagine why. Not to mention Ida and old Hilda." His next strides carried him halfway across the hall toward Lady Beauchamp's drawing room under the pained gaze of the butler who found the front door flung wide open without his services.

Lady Beauchamp, in a velvet afternoon dress of a deep enough shade to be deemed appropriate for a widow, greeted her boisterous son. As she handed him a delicately flowered teacup, she warned, "Do try not to spill it, Monty." She turned to his guests. "Mr. Hoste and Mr. Studd, how charming of you to call on me. You knew nothing could give me more pleasure than a firsthand account of the mission at Cambridge. We've heard such wonderful reports."

Kynaston took a thick slice of fruitcake from the three-tier tray and settled into a deep plush chair by the fire. "I don't think it would be an overstatement to say that there is not one man at Cambridge who has not been influenced in some way by the campaign. I sent out a notice to say that any who had reason to be thankful for the visit of Mr. Moody might have the opportunity of writing their names in a book in my room at a time when I was not there." He shook his head, still amazed. "There have been hundreds sign. Many, I'm sure, will make their mark in the future of the church."

Willie Hoste agreed. "Unprecedented in Cambridge life. Could easily be the most momentous week in the religious history of England in our lifetime."

Lady Beauchamp put her hand to her mouth, and her eyes filled with tears. "Oh, I am so thankful. So thankful that it should have been while you all were there."

Kynaston turned at the sound of the drawing room door opening. He came to his feet as Hilda and Ida entered—Hilda in a dark, rich green, Ida in glowing amber. He had never seen them look better. Lady Beauchamp quickly gave her daughters the background of the conversation.

"Oh, that is wonderful." Hilda beamed with satisfaction. "I knew it would not fail."

Kynaston smiled, recalling how very nearly it had failed and how extremely worried he had been before all had turned around in response to the prayers of the faithful.

"And was Mr. Smith able to be there?" Hilda asked.

Kynaston nodded. "For the weekend. He brought his friends from the boat along. Worked in the prayer room. Declared it to be one of the best weekends of his life." Kynaston was puzzled at the lack of enthusiasm in his voice.

Hilda was quick to pick it up. "So? You sound troubled."

"No, not troubled. And disappointed would be too strong a word. Yet… I can't help feeling that there should be something more for Smith." He shook his head. "I don't know—can't express it—just feel he's still searching." Kynaston took refuge in a long sip of tea. Perhaps he was judging his friend by his own feelings. For all of J. E. K.'s public leadership of Christian affairs at Cambridge, he knew that he, too, was still searching.

And he couldn't help thinking he might find some answers at the China Inland Mission. If only he could make his escape from this admittedly charming company and get on to Mildmay.

"P.T.'s a new man. Joined Christian Union. Came to prayers this morning." Monty took three sandwiches off the tray his sister offered him.

Ida all but bounced on the sofa. "Polhill-Turner? Arthur? Oh, Alice will be so happy! She has prayed for so long. Oh!" She clasped her hands with a sigh. "This will give her strength to keep praying for Cecil and the others. I must write to her." Kynaston was certain he had never seen Ida more animated.

He smiled. "Alice will have a strong ally now. I spoke to P.T. after the prayer meeting. Says he had no notion it was possible to feel so happy. He's laying his plans for term end. Cecil will have winter leave from his regiment. Arthur's determined to talk to him straight. You might tell his sister so she can pray for that."

"And, Mr. Hoste, what of the week for you?" Lady Beauchamp inquired as she refilled his cup and added two lumps of sugar.

"Wonderful week. Much renewed—encouraged. Rather like P.T. in a way. Determined to win my brother. Dixon's the best of fellows but can't think of anything except military promotion. I must make him see there's more to life than that." He continued as he stirred his tea. "I feel confident God's ahead of me anyway. Moody goes to Brighton when he finishes at Oxford. I got a letter from Dick yesterday. His regiment will be back from the Isle of Wight in December. I'll get him to those meetings if it's at the point of his own sword."

Kynaston bit his lip. He felt guilty at his own depression. There was so much to praise God for, so many answered prayers. Yet he couldn't help feeling an ache for his own brother. What might have happened in his brother's life last week if C. T. hadn't been in Australia with the England Eleven?

He glanced at the clock on the mantel. There was just time to get around to Mildmay. He had sent a note to Mr. Broomhall requesting an interview. The reply was that Friday afternoon or Saturday morning would be most convenient.

"Thank you for a most delightful tea, Lady Beauchamp." Kynaston stood and set his cup on the side table.

"Yes, Mama." Hilda stood also. "We must be going now. We've just time to get to the Old Bailey."

Lady Beauchamp frowned. "Hilda, I know you see this as your duty, and I wouldn't want to fault that. But I don't like your going there alone even if you take your maid."

"I have no intention of taking Daisy away from her duties, Mama. Mr. Studd will provide far more suitable escort." She turned to Kynaston. "Nothing could be more providential. After all, you were there when she was arrested."

Kynaston's eyebrows rose. "Old Bailey? Arrested?"

"Yes. Surely you recall Lizzie who was accused of covering for the pickpocket. She is to appear before the magistrate this afternoon."

"Oh, the flower girl." He glanced at the clock again with a sinking feeling. Well, Broomhall had said this afternoon or tomorrow morning. Perhaps he could even call round this evening.

"We must be there to support her. And then we shall help Ida prepare tea and sandwiches for her policemen."

"Thank you." Ida gave Kynaston one of her sweet smiles. "That would be most appreciated. It is so cold on the streets now. The mission's tea run does much good. We take trolleys to the policemen and to the poor people sleeping on the street."

"I would be honored to assist." Kynaston offered his arm to Hilda.

As the Beauchamp carriage horses trotted smartly up the Strand, Hilda wasted no time on maidenly blushes as she openly watched well-dressed young women strolling along the street nodding and smiling at every passing man. "Oh, Kynaston, you see why we must rescue Lizzie. If she can't keep herself fed selling flowers, the inevitable next step for her is much worse."

Kynaston felt her shudder on the seat beside him. They both watched as a young blade nodded to a girl who didn't appear to be above sixteen. Together they turned to one of the houses lining the Strand.

"And appalling as this is, Lizzie wouldn't even be able to work in an establishment of this quality or in the coffeehouses in Covent Garden." Hilda's large, dark eyes grew wide with horror. "I can't even think how awful her life would be. We must do everything we can."

Kynaston agreed. And he admired Hilda for her determination to face facts. He refused to be shocked at her forthrightness. Ladies of her class should not know of the existence of houses of accommodation in the Strand or coffeehouse rooms in Covent Garden—should not know or should pretend they didn't.

But Hilda knew and was unwavering in her work to help the unfortunate. He must help her, whatever chaos it played with his personal plans.

At the end of Old Bailey Street was the Central Criminal Court. Kynaston alighted and held his hand out to Hilda. They entered a heavy iron gate and went up a walk to the front of the Justice Hall, which had been rebuilt since the Gordon Riots a hundred years before. Court had been held on this spot since before the time of Queen Elizabeth, and here Milton's books were burned by the hangman two hundred years earlier. Kynaston put his hand under Hilda's elbow, and they ascended the stone steps to the courtroom.

His grip tightened protectively as they passed the enclosed dock where prisoners awaiting their trial were kept. One could not tell by the angry, defiant or hopeless, despairing faces what each one's crime was, but Kynaston knew the likely list—pimps and whores' bullies; bug-hunters, who made a practice of robbing drunks; shofulmen, who were expert in passing counterfeit money; sneaksmen, who dipped their nimble fingers into carriage windows… He sighed. The list was endless. He shook his head over the depths that sin, poverty, and despair could lead people into. People who had been created in the image of God. It seemed so hopeless, yet he must do something. He must find a way to help.

The Police Court was crowded and hot. The smell of human bodies hung like a cloud. Kynaston pulled Hilda closer to him and found seats next to a respectable-looking woman. They had to wait only through three other matters before Lizzie was ushered into the dock. She stood there in a plain long-sleeved gray dress, her hair pulled severely back, her eyes frightened in her pale face. The surprising effect was to make her look much younger than her eighteen years.

The bewigged black-robed magistrate sitting before the bench fingered the white bands at his neck and peered grimly over the silver rims of his spectacles at Lizzie. Lillie Langtry, who had departed for a tour of America with her acting company, was not there to testify, but her statement was read out by counsel for the Crown.

"And what do you have to say for yourself, gel?" The judge glared at Lizzie.

Her answer was inaudible.

"Eh? Speak up, gel. Might as well admit it. What do you say?"

"I'm ever so sorry, m'lord. I never done it before. But she said she'd give my brother over to Binney if I didn't 'elp 'er."

"Binney? What are you nattering about? Speak up. Stop sniveling."

Lizzie wiped her nose on her sleeve. "Binney, 'im wot whips 'is boys with the strap from his wooden leg."

The courtroom erupted in guffaws at the picture of an underworld taskmaster who kept his petty criminals under his control by beating them with the strap that held his artificial leg. The judge gaveled sharply. "That's enough. The court doesn't have time for your prattle, gel. You did it and that's that. Two months in Pentonville." He slammed the gavel again and signaled the bailiff to bring in the next prisoner.

Hilda grabbed Kynaston's arm with both hands. "Do something. Can't you stop them? She'll come out a hardened criminal."

Kynaston shook his head. "Nothing can be done. At least Pentonville is the newest prison. Run on very modern lines, I'm told."

Hilda jumped to her feet and pushed past Kynaston. "I must speak to her. I can't let her think she's been abandoned."

Outside the courtroom Hilda paused, unsure of where to go. Kynaston, close behind her, pointed toward the bail dock enclosed with rails and banisters where the prisoners waited. A heavy, dark-coated bailiff stood spraddle-legged before the gate, his hands behind him. Kynaston approached the man, wondering what argument he could give or how high a bribe he must pay to be allowed to speak to a prisoner,

He cleared his throat, still not sure what to say, when the man drew himself to attention and all but saluted. "Blimey, aren't you one of those Studds? I saw you and your brothers play last year. Finest match I ever saw."

J. E. K. tried to reply, but the man rushed on. "Tell me now, how do you bowl those balls that change direction? I've a nipper

I'd like to teach that to. He'd think mighty high of his pa if I could tell 'im I learned from the great C. T. Studd himself."

J. E. K. started to correct the man and then thought better of it. "It's really nothing but an off break bowled with a motion to make the batter think it's a leg break." Kynaston stepped back and rotated his arm counterclockwise as he would when bowling a leg break, which would make the ball bounce away from the batter. Then at the last moment before releasing the pretend ball, he turned his wrist over in a way that would have made the ball bounce into the batter, as if he had rotated his arm clockwise.

The bailiff gave an enormous guffaw and slapped his thigh. He rotated his arm, stiffened his elbow, and twisted his wrist in imitation of Kynaston. "Well, now, who would ever have thought it? What will my nipper think of his old pa, eh?" He beamed and repeated the action.

"Yes, that's right. Needs a lot of practice though. Now I wonder if—"

The man drew himself up with a sharp jerk as if suddenly recalling where he was. "Er, I'm much obliged, sir. And what can I do for you?"

Kynaston explained their errand. The bailiff's turning of the key was more quickly done than Kynaston's wrist pivot. Lizzie sat slumped on a backless wooden bench, her hands clasped in her lap. A severe-looking matron stood over her. "'S all right, Stella. These gentlefolk just want a word," the bailiff called from his post at the door. The matron looked them up and down, glowering, and then moved back a few steps to stand against the wall.

Lizzie jumped to her feet with a cry. "Oh, miss, I'm so sorry. Please don't scold. After you and the mission folk were so kind to me. I wouldn't 'ave done it—I knew it were wrong—but Jackie, I couldn't see 'im given over to Binney. 'E just started out as a sob boy, no 'arm really. Earned a penny a day to keep bread in 'is stomach. No 'arm." She shook her head and sobbed.

Hilda blinked. "A sob boy?"

Lizzie sniffed deeply. "Beggar's assistant. 'E followed behind an old sailor who'd been shipwrecked. Pretendin' to be his son, like. Big, sorrowful eyes, Jackie 'as. Could cry something pitiful.

But now 'e's twelve. Too big for the orphan act. 'Course 'e is an orphan, but you know what I mean."

"So he has to go to work for this Binney?" Hilda's voice showed that she clearly didn't understand.

Lizzie explained patiently, seeming to lose some of her distress over her own situation in talking about her brother. "Jackie picks men's silk pocket handkerchiefs. Them at the mission explained that aren't right, but there's those that do lots worse. Mab Brown—she wot lifts ladies' purses—she fences 'em for a fine price. But if she goes off a boy, she turns 'im over to Binney. Binney's something fierce—especially when he's in a rage with the blue ruin."

"Gin," Kynaston translated at Hilda's obvious bewilderment.

Lizzie slumped back onto the bench. "Now Mab and me are both for it. There's nothing for Jackie but Binney." She started suddenly to cry again. "I landed us both in it."

Hilda started to commiserate with Lizzie, but Kynaston stepped forward. "No. It isn't hopeless, Lizzie. You were wrong to help a pickpocket, and I'm afraid there's nothing for that but that you go to Pentonville. But we won't desert you. You can have visitors, and there is a good chaplain there—you won't be without spiritual comfort."

Lizzie sniffed loudly. "I'll be a'right. It's Jackie."

"Yes," Kynaston agreed. "Something must be done for him."

"Where can we find your brother?" Hilda asked. "We'll take him to Mr. Groom at the mission. He can help him get honest employment—perhaps minding a cabby's horse or selling baked potatoes… " She paused. "Or a clerk's apprentice—that could be a very fine position."

Lizzie shook her head. "'E'd 'ave to read for that, miss."

"He should be in school," Kynaston began, then realized the impracticability of the suggestion. There were the Earl of Shaftesbury's ragged schools, but children living on the street like Jackie would most often attend for a while and then return to the street to live by pilfering and begging. Or work most of the night and then be too tired to stay awake in class. Something should be done. A school where boys like Jackie could be taught a practical trade a few hours a day... He came back from his drifting thoughts to hear Lizzie giving Hilda directions for finding Jackie.

"'E dosses with Taff Lewes in Windmill Street."

"Yes, we'll find him." Hilda's assurances were interrupted by the matron's large red hand clamping down on Lizzie's shoulder and propelling her to her feet.

"All right, off you go now. And see you mind yourself in Penton, girl. Don't you be picking up no evil ways from those around you, or you'll be back in there quicker 'n you can say Jack Spratt." She pushed Lizzie into a long, dark corridor.

"Don't worry, Lizzie—we'll find him tonight," Hilda called after her.

"We'll do no such thing." Kynaston took Hilda's arm and moved her toward the door. They had been far too long in the overheated, malodorous air of the Old Bailey.

Hilda squared her shoulders and raised her chin. "Of course we will. At least I will. I promised."

Kynaston smiled and shook his head at her. "My dear Hilda, no one could possibly fault your determination to do good. Your good sense, however, leaves much to be desired at times."

Hilda's dark eyebrows knitted in a frown. "How dare you, sir. And you call yourself a gentleman."

Kynaston opened the door, and they stepped out into the blessedly fresh air. The gaslights had been lit while they were indoors, and the fog surrounded the lamps in golden clouds. The mist hung in drops almost as if it were raining, so all-pervading that an umbrella would be useless. Kynaston took a deep breath to clear his lungs and then turned back to Hilda. "It is precisely because I call myself a gentleman that I would take no lady into the warren of disease and crime to which Lizzie directed you."

"But—" Hilda's protest was interrupted by the arrival of the Beauchamp carriage. The driver had parked just down the street and had been watching for them. Once settled on the seat with the calesh top up and a heavy wool rug around her legs, Hilda tried again. "I gave my word."

"And you will be far better able to carry it out if you remain alive and well."

"Surely you exaggerate. My sisters and I are acquainted with the poorer parts of the city. As a matter of fact, we should be in one of them right now helping Ida prepare tea and sandwiches."

Kynaston checked his pocket watch in the glow of a streetlight as they passed. "I believe we are rather late for that. I am certain you will find your sister sensibly back in Cromwell Road by now."

"This is no matter for you, sir. Please instruct Fennell where you would like him to put you down, and I shall see to my own affairs."

Kynaston felt his mustache twitch as he tried to control his amusement. It would not do to let Hilda think he was laughing at her. Indeed, one had to admire her resolution. "Cromwell Road will do very well for me, thank you." If she remained obdurate when they arrived at the Beauchamp home, he could lift her off the seat bodily and carry her into the house.

However, he would make one more appeal. "Hilda, please listen to me. Why do you think I know Jackie's area so well?"

"I'm sure I have no notion of your activities in such an area, sir. I can only hope they were in the nature of mission work and not for the more common reason young men frequent such places." She drew herself into the far corner of the carriage away from him.

Now he couldn't resist laughing at her. "Really, Hilda, you are too much." Then he turned serious. "But I must tell you this for your own protection. Last summer a mission worker at the soldiers' home where I sometimes speak was foolhardy enough to enter the kitchen of a lodging house in that part of Bloomsbury where Jackie lives. A gang of women knocked him down and stripped him almost naked. Their menfolk dragged him outside, stuffed his mouth with mustard, and plunged him headfirst into a water butt. That was done for sport. What they would have done if they had meant him ill, I shudder to think. And I could tell you much worse, but your imagination is lively enough without my prompting."

"And that, sir, is precisely why I cannot leave a twelve-year-old orphan boy there. I can far too clearly imagine what his life must be like."

"There is no question of leaving him there. Of course, something must be done for Jackie. But you are not going there. I shall go tomorrow afternoon."

"Morning. It must be morning."

Kynaston sighed. If he didn't agree to morning, Hilda was likely to go there herself while he was at Mildmay drinking tea, discussing the needs of China's millions and his desire to help them. Indeed, it seemed that charity must begin at home. "Tomorrow morning," he agreed. It was too dark to see Hilda's smile, but he was certain it was there as she relaxed from her stiff position in the corner.

The next morning, with a deep sigh of resignation, Kynaston sent a messenger boy to the China Inland Mission secretary explaining that he had been delayed and that if he were unable to complete his business before noon, he would call upon Mr. Broomhall at his earliest convenience. He shook his head. It was the best he could do.

Then he smoothed his hair with a final dab of macassar and walked across Hyde Park from the Studd home in Hyde Park Gardens to the Beauchamp home. The butler ushered him into the drawing room where the family and servants were assembled for morning prayers. With grim determination to do his duty as the eldest male family member present, Monty was charging his way through the lesson. The gospel reading for the day was Zacharias's Benedictus: "'Blessed be the Lord God of Israel; for he hath visited and redeemed his people… that we, being delivered out of the hand of our enemies, might serve him without fear, in holiness and righteousness before him, all the days of our life.… To give knowledge of salvation unto his people.… To give light to them that sit in darkness and in the shadow of death, to guide our feet into the way of peace.'"

"Glory be to the Father, and to the Son, and to the Holy Ghost; as it was in the beginning, is now, and ever shall be, world without end. Amen."

Then, drawing a deep breath that left his cheeks puffed out, Monty charged at the collect for Grace, "'O Lord, our heavenly Father, almighty and everlasting God, who hast safely brought us to the beginning of this day, defend us in the same with thy mighty power; and grant that this day we fall into no sin, neither run into any kind of danger; but that all our doings may be ordered by thy governance, to do always what is righteous in thy sight; through Jesus Christ our Lord. Amen.'"

The fact that Monty got the whole thing out in a single breath did nothing to mar the beauty of the words or the sincerity with which Kynaston asked for safety and guidance for that day. He took his own deep breath and squared his shoulders for battle when he saw Hilda approaching with the expression he knew so well.

"Mr. Studd, I've quite made up my mind."

"No, Hilda. I will not take you into the rookeries even in the daytime. It is not safe. Lady Beauchamp would never allow it, and—"

"You are quite right."

"Hilda, you must listen to reason… " He blinked. "What did you say?"

"I said you are quite right. I see that I was being foolhardy and headstrong last night, and I could have led us both into danger that would have benefited no one, least of all Lizzie or Jackie."

Her announcement—it could hardly have been called an apology—left him breathless. And she looked so fine this morning, the brightness of her flashing eyes and flushed cheeks set off by the dark burgundy dress she wore. Her tall figure and narrow waist were emphasized by its swagged skirt and bustle. He started to tell her so, but she hurried on in her single-minded way.

"Monty shall go with you. And I have ordered Fennell to take two extra men." Suddenly she softened. "And do be careful. I would never forgive myself if my rash promise caused you harm. I thought I knew—I have done so much mission work. I had no idea of the conditions you described last night. I shall pray for your safety and success."

"Thank you." He would have said more, but he was too surprised.

Fourteen

Dixon Hoste lowered his newspaper with a quiet laugh that was not quite a sneer and not quite a triumph. The soft-spoken lieutenant home on leave from his Royal Artillery regiment was too much a gentleman to treat his brother's Christian gossip with open disdain. Besides, the children of Major-General Hoste had been taught to take pride in their Flemish Protestant ancestors who had fled from religious persecution in the sixteenth century and the ancestress who had been burned at the stake for her faith. Dixon, though, had taken far less interest in their religious roots than in the family's military heritage. He rather fancied himself carrying on in the tradition of his great-uncle who had gone to sea under Nelson and been made a baronet for his brilliant services in the Napoleonic wars. Besides, Willie's new fervor since he came down from Cambridge for Christmas vacation was beginning to grate on his brother.

The fact that Willie had chosen to go to the evangelical-leaning Ridley Hall to prepare for holy orders was quite his own affair, but that was no reason to be forever at a fellow about this American revivalist. Dixon shifted his feet on the plush footstool in front of the fire before he launched into his reply. "Just see here, Willie, *The Gazette* says it perfectly: 'Cultured society will blush to know anything about Messrs. Moody and Sankey and others of their crowd. Revivalism in religion, and American revivalism in particular, is desperately vulgar.'"

William regarded him from across the room, a small smile curling his lips. Dick had to admit that religious enthusiasm had not soured Willie's temperament. "But then you must admit the same might be said of every popular movement—religious or irreligious," William pointed out.

Dixon rattled the paper in his lap. "That says little to the matter, brother, for one is not being asked to encounter any other popular movement. Now just listen to this—I'm sure they're right: 'Almost every religion has its origins among men of low degree, and the sons of fishermen and carpenters who create or revive the faiths and superstitions are, as a rule, very objectionable persons in the estimation of men of light and learning of their time.'"

"It's certainly true that Christianity was brought to us by fishermen and carpenters."

Dixon was mild-mannered enough himself. Some would even describe him as taciturn or shy, but his brother's calm was simply too much. It would be much easier to dismiss his arguments if Willie would react with temper. "I don't understand you. You're the university man. How can you place so much confidence in someone who is little better than an itinerant preacher?"

Willie heaved himself out of the deep chair he had sprawled in and crossed to Dixon. He held out his hand for the paper. "Allow me." He took a turn reading to Dick. "'Moody and Sankey are not, it is true, graduates of any university. They are men of the people, speaking the language and using the methods not of the refined, but of the generality. Yet they have probably left a deeper impress of their individuality upon a greater section of Englishmen and Englishwomen than any other persons who could be named. Whatever we may think of them, however much their methods may grate upon the sensibilities of those who have at length succeeded in living up to their blue china, these men are factors of considerable potency in the complex sum of influences which make up contemporary English life.'

"Don't you think you should at least go to the Dome and see what it's all about?" Willie set the paper aside.

"I know very well what it's all about. It's about ruining my chances for promotion. The garrison church is quite sufficient for my needs. Further devotion would be detrimental to my career."

For Dixon that would have ended the argument even if Willie had not left the room. Anything that stood in the way of climbing the ladder of success was not to be considered. His education at Clifton College and the Royal Military Academy, Woolwich, had provided sufficient head knowledge and all the public school churchmanship one should need, no matter how uncompromising one's family was in their Christianity.

Recently commissioned lieutenant, Dixon was already calculating how soon he could hope for his captaincy. Nothing could block advancement in the military more quickly than religious fanaticism. His thoughts drifted back to pleasant days these past months with his battery at Sandown Fort in the Isle of Wight—mornings spent on immaculate drill, afternoons of polo, long evenings of camaraderie in the officers' mess, sipping excellent port at long tables set with gleaming silver and crystal, followed by a game of cards. A fellow would be insane to jeopardize such a life.

"Dixon, dear, you aren't ready. We must leave soon, or the Dome will be full. Mr. Moody always draws enormous crowds."

Dick started at his mother's voice and then drew himself from his relaxed position to full military stance. "Thank you, Mama, but I shall spend the evening here. I'm certain Willie intends to escort you and the girls."

"Oh, Dick, please come with us. Everyone says Mr. Sankey's music is most amazing."

Dick shook his head at his elder sister, an accomplished musician herself. "Not as amazing as you, Aggie, I'm sure. And don't you let any of his revivalist tricks spoil your elegant style on the pianoforte."

Alexa, his next to youngest sister, gave him a quick hug. "I'm so sorry you won't come, Dick. I shall miss you dreadfully. We see so little of you."

Surely he imagined the tear in her eye. He sank back into his chair as the women left the room. He liked to think how neatly their family was arranged, four girls and six boys in two sets of five with a sister at the head and tail of each group of three brothers. Dixon himself was the middle of the first set of brothers, William just younger than himself.

Dick returned to his newspaper. With a sense of relief, he heard the front door bang. There would be no more badgering him tonight. And yet it wasn't the print on the page he saw in front of him, but rather the disappointment on his mother's face when he refused her invitation. He was sorry to have hurt his mother and sisters for the sake of his own comfort. Spending an evening at the Dome would hardly do violence to his chances for early advancement.

He pushed a vague sense of guilt aside and forced his concentration on the paper. A few minutes later the door banged again. Had someone forgotten something?

He looked up in surprise as William strode into the room. "Come on, Dick. Put on your wraps and go with me."

Dick blinked. "Oh, all right. I'll get my ulster." He was halfway down the hall, shrugging on his heavy, loose overcoat before he even realized he had given in.

Although it was dark, it was a pleasant walk from Haverlock Lodge in Waterloo Place past the Victoria Gardens to the Old Steine dominated by George IV's grandiose Royal Pavilion. The fantastic pleasure palace was now sadly fallen from its former glory. Queen Victoria, who had no use for such a conceit, had sold it to the town of Brighton thirty years ago. Now it was used for concerts and private parties. Indeed, Dick had accepted an invitation for a holiday ball there tomorrow evening.

Dick shook his head as he observed the pale shape of the pavilion's minarets and onion-shaped domes in gaslit illumination. "It always reminds me of something that should be made out of marzipan."

Willie laughed and agreed as the two brothers followed the crowd going into the Dome theater, which had formerly been the royal stables. The great glass dome of the circular hall was hidden by a false ceiling, but the room retained its mosquelike effect in its fan-shaped windows and the rows of scalloped arches supporting the balcony. Dixon quickly sank into the first empty seat he could find, thankful for its velour padding in case this brash

American should choose to preach for the full hour or two most British enthusiasts were known to spend on a sermon.

Dick listened without interest to the singing of the choir and congregation. He did not care much for the strange "gospel songs" the portly Yankee in black side whiskers worked so hard to introduce. This was decidedly not what one would find at the garrison church.

Dick became even more alarmed when a stocky man with a wavy bush of a beard, wearing ordinary laymen's clothes, approached the pulpit. Yet in spite of himself, Dick watched with considerable interest. The preacher held his Bible in his left hand like a bow as he gestured backward with his right, as if he would shoot his text straight to the heart of his hearers. "'Come unto me, all ye that labour and are heavy laden, and I will give you rest....He that cometh unto me, I will in no wise cast out.'"

The preacher developed his text with homely aphorisms and quaint humor, telling Bible stories as though he were personally acquainted with the people or had witnessed the events in his travels. But the thing that most appealed to the man of military training was Moody's common sense and emphasis on action. He spoke in simple sentences with no flowery phrases. He hammered out his stories with concrete nouns and strong verbs in good, plain Anglo-Saxon.

And, unlike the niceties of popular Victorian conversation, he called a spade a spade. He drove straight ahead, convincing his audience of their need. Then he laid out the remedy and called for action on the dotted line. And he was intensely personal. He focused on individuals. Even Dixon, sitting near the back of the hall, felt the pull as Moody singled him out with his eye, his voice, his forefinger with a force that simply would not tolerate indifference.

Moody spoke at a great speed, worthy of a military drill, Dick thought, and yet his articulation was so distinct that his husky voice was clear to every listener.

And he minced no words. You were bound for hell, but Jesus could save you, providing you came to Him. Now. "God will judge the impenitent and ungodly. You must flee, flee from the wrath to come."

And then the preacher quit. Dick drew out his pocket watch. Twenty-five minutes. Moody had preached less than half an hour. Incredible. None of the great preachers of the day spoke for less than an hour. Spurgeon always held his audiences for at least two.

When Moody prayed, Dick was amazed. He had never before heard a man talk to God as a friend who was present beside him, and yet with utter reverence and humility. As the prayer continued, a deep sense of his own sinful and perilous state laid hold of Dick's soul. His pride and indifference crumbled as if the minarets had tumbled from the Royal Pavilion. He saw with clarity that, in spite of his promotion, he had been dissatisfied for months. He had sensed this vaguely before and assumed that the answer lay in gaining more advancement. But could the solution be in quite another direction?

Surely not. He was well begun upon his course. He did not want to think of changing. The cost would be too great.

When Dick entered the breakfast room the next morning, he hoped to avoid discussing last night's service. Willie, however, was up already and reading the account of the meeting from the *Brighton Gazette* to his sisters.

Dick made an unnecessary clatter pouring coffee and buttering his toast as Willie recounted Moody's text for the little sister who had been too young to attend. Then Willie continued: "'Mr. Moody earnestly impressed upon his hearers the necessity of seeking rest in God, offered up a powerful prayer, and invited those who wished to find rest in God to remain behind for a second prayer meeting.'

"'Meetings continue at 3:00 and 8:00.'"

Dick dropped the toast onto his plate and pushed away from the table with a scraping of his chair.

"Dick, you haven't eaten a bite."

He didn't bother replying to Alexa, nor did he stop to take his ulster from the hall tree. He must get some fresh air.

The weather was mild for mid-December. A breeze blew in from the sea, and the sky, while overcast, was still bright. Beyond the Marine Parade, whitecapped waves lapped the pale sand where a few sturdy souls walked on the beach, keeping their coats tucked well around them. Dick wanted to think, and yet he didn't want to think. He strolled for some time, paying little attention to where he was going. Then he heard a band standing on the open deck at the entrance to the Chain Pier strike up a lively marching tune. Dick turned his steps in that direction.

"Would you like a tract, sir?" Dick turned at the compelling but not unpleasant voice of a young woman. He started to refuse. The last thing he wanted was to have more religion thrust at him. Yet something about the girl attracted him. She was dressed expensively in the best of taste. She was not beautiful, but the blue-eyed girl beside her was—with her fetchingly beribboned hat on her softly curled hair. The tall girl's features were too strong, her eyebrows too dark, her mouth too wide. And yet there was a look of compassion in her eyes, a sweetness to her smile that he could not dismiss. Belatedly he held out his hand. "Come unto Me." He couldn't believe it. The tract had the same text Moody had used. He thrust it in his pocket.

"May I help you with anything?" The taller woman asked. Dick was embarrassed that she had seen his confusion.

"No. No thank you." He started to back away and then stopped. He knew her. He blinked. Where could they have met? "Excuse me, ma'am, but—"

Apparently it clicked with her at the same moment. "Oh! You're Mr. Hoste's brother, aren't you? We met at the park last summer—when the pickpocket took my sister's purse." Before he could reply, she turned to a lanky young man giving out tracts at the top of the stairs. "Monty, come see whom I've found."

In a few minutes Dick found himself being propelled down the balustraded steps to the ornate clock tower-topped entrance to the aquarium where the Beauchamp party was meeting for lunch. At the linen-draped table tucked discreetly behind a potted palm, Dick was presented to Lady Beauchamp and Mrs. Studd.

"You were at the meeting last night, Mr. Hoste?" Hilda

Beauchamp asked as soon as the white-jacketed waiter had taken their orders.

"Yes."

"It was splendid, wasn't it?" Miss Beauchamp's question met with general agreement from the party. "I simply had to hear Mr. Moody after the wonderful reports of the Cambridge meetings."

"These meetings are certainly getting off to a better start than they did in Cambridge," J. E. K. Studd, sitting across from Hilda, commented. "Of course, there are none of the barriers to be broken down here."

"Barriers? What are you talking about, Kynaston?" Mrs. Studd looked handsome in her high-necked black dress.

"Mr. Moody's grammar, for example. Here an occasional 'ain't' makes no difference to the crowd. I will admit I cringed the first time or two I heard him preach. But then one ceases to notice. The man's spirit speaks more loudly than his grammar."

Kynaston's brother G. B., sitting on the other side of his mother, paused midway in buttering his roll. "I think Moody's Americanisms are one of his best qualities. Fresh air, energy—just what we need. I'm to meet with him before the three o'clock service. Want to come with me, Monty? In Cambridge I asked him for some information on evangelistic missions in California. He said he would get some for me."

Mrs. Studd's hand shook on the long-stemmed water goblet. "Whatever can you want that for, George?"

"G. B.'s always been interested in cowboys and Indians. You know that, Mother," Kynaston said.

"But surely you've outgrown that, George." Her fine, dark eyes filled with fear. "Missions? What can you be thinking of?"

George shrugged. "Just interested, Mama. Aren't we supposed to care about souls everywhere? 'All the world,' Christ said."

"Yes, of course. But wild Indians, bears..." She shuddered. "C. T. going off to Australia is bad enough. I've heard some terrible tales about the aborigines."

J. E. K. smiled. "I think Charlie will be quite safe enough, Mama. The Hon. Ivo Bligh is a reliable leader for the cricket team."

Mrs. Studd relaxed with a smile. "Yes, dear, I'm certain

you're right. After all, cricket is a most civilized sport. And I understand Ivo Bligh is in line to become Lord Darnley."

"Saint Ivo, *Punch* called him," G. B. added. "Said he was setting out on a pilgrimage to Australia to recover the ashes."

"Yes, that's all very well." A worried crease crept back onto Mrs. Studd's forehead. "But C. T. forgot to take his best silk hat, and I discovered he only took three pair of flannels. Of course, I immediately instructed his tailor to send him two more pair. But now it's turning so cold. I should have sent him a topcoat, too."

"It's summer in Australia, Mama." G. B. smiled at her.

"How very strange. Are you quite certain?"

"Quite certain." Kynaston patted her hand. "Charlie will be fine."

"I do hope so. Perhaps I should just send him a couple of pairs of socks."

Dixon found the casual family banter relaxing. When the luncheon was over and some of the group went off to watch the skaters in the rink, he accepted Kynaston's invitation to view the aquarium. "Probably old hat to you since you live here, but quite a wonder to the rest of the world, you know."

Dick shook his head and held Hilda Beauchamp's chair for her to rise. "By no means. I've never been here myself. A favorite of my younger brothers and sisters though. They love the monkeys."

"I understand Brighton has quite set a world fashion. I believe several places here and abroad are beginning to build aquariums now that your city has shown them how," Hilda said.

"Oh, but I'm certain their shark tanks couldn't be as good as ours are," Dick boasted. "You won't be alarmed by them, will you, Miss Beauchamp?"

Her brother, who was just leaving with G. B., stopped in the middle of his long-legged stride and laughed. "Old Hilda's never been afraid of anything in her life. Don't worry about her."

Hilda raised her chin defiantly. "I'm sure I shall find all the scientific exhibits most interesting."

For some time they wandered through the elegantly arched building. It resembled the undercroft of a great cathedral, except for the glass-fronted tanks full of marine life lining the walls, the live monkeys running free among branches of potted trees, and the three-piece band playing in the corner. They observed with special interest the vivid display of flowerlike anemones and then went on to the bright blue splendors of the shark tanks exhibiting every kind of shark living in the waters around Great Britain.

Light banter punctuated the scientific discussion until Hilda Beauchamp turned to Dick. "Oh, we must be getting to the Dome. We wouldn't want to make you late, Mr. Hoste." When he didn't reply, she looked at him levelly. "You aren't going this afternoon?"

"I hadn't planned to, no." He hadn't meant his reply to sound so stiffly formal. Her question had been innocent enough.

She blinked. "Oh, I see. Pardon me. I had assumed... " Then with apparent determination she finished her sentence. "I had assumed you were a believer."

"I believe that the Bible is true."

"You believe, but you do not accept its truths for yourself."

As her statement was not phrased as a question, he was not required to reply. At the top of the stairs he took leave of his companions, thanking them sincerely for a delightful time. He continued back to Havelock Lodge with no break in his military stride, but inside he continued to replay his conversation with Hilda Beauchamp. He believed the Bible to be true. He knew he needed to do more than that. But the price of changing was too great.

Fifteen

As Dick dressed for the evening festivities, he felt the weight of his decision not to make a commitment to God. But he easily shed all heaviness as he focused on the evening ahead. The invitation to the annual holiday ball had come to all officers of the regiment—and to town commissioners, among others. That meant that Miss Cecilia Lansdown would certainly be there with her parents.

Dick thought of Miss Lansdown's considerable charms, picturing her small but elegant person, a vision in lace and silk roses, her golden hair a cascade of curls. He could not hope to ask for anything of her beyond the pleasure of dancing and taking supper with her for the present. And it was doubtful that a captain's rank would be high enough, but when he made major... With a flourish worthy of the regiment, he tossed his red and white cape over his shoulders, set his shiny, high-crowned black hat on his head at just the right angle, and picked up his spotless white gloves. He paused only once before the glass go make certain that his boots held their gleaming polish. Then he strode out into the crisp December night whistling "Rule Britannia."

As the ball was to begin at ten o'clock, many of those who had stayed for the second prayer gathering at the Dome were just leaving when Dixon arrived at the Old Steine. He glanced over the departing carriages and pedestrians to see if any of his family or acquaintances were there. For just an instant he felt an inner tug to be among the group departing with gentle chatter and happy calls to one another.

Then he recalled himself and made for the entrance to the pavilion. Even with the hubbub of coaches arriving, entering the cool green and gray hall was like taking a deep breath of fresh air between the outside world and the fantasy to come. The pavilion was in less pristine condition than when it had been the personal pleasure palace of the Prince Regent, frequented by the most glittering of the nation's society and artists. But the town commissioners had seen to an enthusiastic, if somewhat heavy-handed, refurbishing of the building some twenty years before. And now, although the succeeding layers of varnish over wood and wallpaper alike had yellowed blue to green, turned pink to amber, and silver to gold, the effect when seen by candlelight was still stunning. Dixon handed his engraved invitation to the liveried footman at the door and then gave his hat and cape to the next servant.

As Dixon went through the small side door to the grand corridor, he took in the 162-foot gallery draped with blue and white curtains and lavishly decorated with plants, flowers, and palms, alternating with the costly chinoiserie cabinets. As in the day of the Prince Regent, the guests assembled in the corridor, strolling, sitting, and conversing until the arrival of the host and guest of honor.

Hands behind his back, Dixon slowly strolled the length of the gallery, bowing to the ladies, greeting fellow officers and old friends, and admiring the elegance of the bamboo cabinets and porcelains. But, while appearing casual, he was most intent on locating one certain lady. Almost at the end of the corridor, he gave a relieved smile and bowed over the hand of Mrs. Lansdown who sat resplendent in a purple satin gown swagged with wide gold ribbons and garlands of gilt roses. He likewise greeted Councilman Lansdown before turning to the daughter.

"Miss Lansdown, how is it possible? You are even lovelier than I remembered from last summer." And this was no mere flattery. The rosy blush of lace framing the low-cut neckline of Cecilia Lansdown's emerald crepe de chine gown emphasized the creaminess of her skin, and the lace flounces peeking from under the swags of her skirt that swept back to a flower-decked bustle displayed the delicacy of her figure. Dick Hoste caught his breath.

He offered his arm. "Would you do me the honor of a stroll?"

She placed a small, lace-gloved hand on his arm and fluttered her drooping eyelashes charmingly. It was difficult to converse as they moved slowly up the crowded room, but the soft-spoken Dixon managed to secure her promise for the supper dance.

Then there was a break in the crush, and Cecilia tossed her curls and laughed. "Did you see all those people leaving the Dome? I do believe there were more there than at the ball—of course, it's open to simply *anyone*. But still—can you imagine? Choosing to spend an evening being harangued by a preacher?"

To avoid answering, Dick paused before an intricately inlaid cabinet of simulated bamboo with tufted red silk insets. "Exquisite, isn't it? Seems a pity though that so few of the pieces are actually of Chinese workmanship."

"But surely, sir, this is much prettier than anything a foreigner could make. Authenticity seems a much overrated quality."

Dixon thought it odd to imitate bamboo out of beech or satinwood rather than using the real item, but he didn't argue. And further discussion was forestalled as the guest of honor and the Chevalier du Poitiers and his lady were announced. According to the custom established by the Prince Regent, they strolled the length of the corridor, smiling at each guest and talking briefly with some. Then they led the company into the music room, which tonight was to be used for dancing.

The strains of a string orchestra welcomed them into the magnificent room. The dancing flames of candles and of the lotus-shaped gasoliers that seemed to float in the air above their heads lent a feeling of fairy-tale enchantment. Dixon felt Cecilia's hand tighten on his arm as she caught her breath. "Oh, it's too beautiful to be real."

Dixon had for some time been working with disciplined determination to overcome his shyness. This seemed an opportune time to press his luck and ask Miss Lansdown for the first dance as well as the later one. It was proper to dance three times with the same partner even if one were not engaged to be married, but he would not want to push to that extreme.

Before he could open his mouth, however, a dashing Lancer made his bow and bore the lovely Cecilia off. Mr. Hoste took a position by one of the handsome mirrors draped with white lace curtains and surveyed the dancers swirling and dipping to a Strauss waltz. The musicians' platform was decorated with plants and draped in white satin fringed with bullion gold. It was elegant, but Dixon felt it a shame to have obscured the original decor. Behind the added finery, he could see crimson and gold landscape murals framed by gigantic painted serpents and flying dragons. Even fantastic as it was, the Chinese theme gripped his imagination. He would like to know more of the culture that produced such art as this.

Puzzled by this strange turn of thought, Dixon wandered into the south drawing room where those who did ot choose to dance, such as Mr. and Mrs. Lansdown, were playing cards or chess or indulging in conversation and sherry. The outstanding features of the room were the row of support columns down the center, which were sculpted as replicas of palm trees, and the recently painted ceiling in an arabesque design not quite in keeping with the rest of the decor. Dixon began to look around for a chess partner. Just then a table of military men invited him to join their card game.

Although Dixon often played a hand or two in the officers' mess, cards were not his favorite way to spend an evening. But it would seem unfriendly not to accept their invitation. The cards were barely dealt when Jackson, a fellow gunner, asked, "Any of you been to hear the vulgar Americans yet?"

The question was taken for the witticism it was intended to be and met with a hoot of guffaws, although Dick remained silent. "No, but I watched the Punch and Judy show on the pier last night—comes to the same thing."

"I hear the singing one is really here to sell organs."

"Well, he is an American. What would one expect?"

"I hear he started with a minstrel show but found evangelism paid better."

"They'll soon be back to the land of the everlasting dollar, gazing on their cozy homesteads purchased with good English gold."

Jackson laughed in agreement and then shrugged. "Serves 'em right—the thrill-seekers silly enough to fall for that ranting."

Dixon worried lest his fellows would notice his silence, but his reputation for being untalkative was well enough established. Besides, he unintentionally kept the others happy by losing a considerable sum of money, although actually playing for money at the holiday ball had to be done discreetly.

It was with considerable relief that Dick finally heard the Master of Ceremonies announce the supper dance. He jumped to his feet.

"Getting up a party for the pier Monday," Jackson said as Dick left the table. The gunner gave him a broad wink. "Little different class of clientele from this." He waved his hand around the room. "But should be worth an evening's amusement. Got to have all the fun we can before it's back to drill duty."

Dick gave a noncommittal smile and hurried off to the glowing red and gold music room to find Miss Lansdown. Cecilia tipped her head up and smiled at him in her charmingly dimpled manner and then floated through the steps of the waltz as effortlessly as one of the gasoliers suspended above them.

As a senior commissioner, Mr. Lansdown was to present his party to the Chevalier at supper. "Hoste?" The master of ceremonies looked Dick up and down. "Ah, son of the major-general? Yes, yes, fine family. See you're following in your father's footsteps. Well done. You'll go far, lad. Just play your cards right— you'll go far."

"Thank you, sir." Dick bowed smartly and smiled. As he savored the scallops of veal de marchand and the timbale of macaroni, Dixon admired the panels of Indian wallpaper. They were still exquisite even though partially obscured by the yellowing varnish and sumptuous ormolu cabinets.

Then he turned his attention back to Cecilia. She gave him her dimpled smile. At that moment Dixon thought his goals had never been clearer. Cecilia, society, recognition—this was what he wanted. How could he have given a thought to the goings-on at the Dome? He had his foot firmly on the first rung of the ladder. He would be crazy to turn his back on all this now.

Yet by the next morning the glow had faded. Dixon saw the evening for its true worth: A pleasant enough amusement; a few hours' enjoyment of beauty and splendor—albeit a fading, often imitation beauty—harmless enough in its own way, unless one let it take the place of things of lasting value.

During his few hours of pleasure, he had managed to shake off the weight of decision he had carried since Friday night. But now it descended again in full force. *Repent. Turn your life to Christ.* The message was nothing he hadn't heard hundreds of times before. But never before had he faced it personally with such immediate intensity. He must decide, if only to free himself of the torture of indecision.

He knew that the question of what place he would give Jesus Christ in his life—if any—was a question for eternity. But Dixon Hoste was only twenty-one. Eternity should be considered, but before that there was this life—a long one, he hoped. How could it be best spent? He thrust himself to his feet and paced the floor in his room. What did he really want? Society balls? Military honors? Service to queen and country? Whatever he decided, the commitment had to be total. He did not want to live an imitation in-between life. He smiled at the thought: *If I owned a bamboo cabinet, I would not want it simulated.*

He heard the downstairs door close and the voices and footsteps of his large family returning from church. A few moments later there was a tap at his door. "Come."

Alexa stood there, still in her cape and muff, her Sunday bonnet framing her face. "Dick," she began and then bit her full pink lower lip. She lowered her gaze and swallowed.

He crossed the room to her. "What is it, Poppet?"

"Nothing. I just wanted you to know I missed you this morning."

With a rush of brotherly affection, he picked her up and

whirled her around in a complete circle. "How about an early Christmas treat, Poppet?" He set her down on her feet. "I'll take you to the Punch and Judy show on the pier tomorrow. Would you like that?"

"Oh, yes, Dick!" She clapped her hands. "You're the best of brothers. But—" She bit her lip again. "Could it be next week? Mama said I could go hear Mr. Moody tomorrow as it's the last service."

"Yes, of course. Whenever you like." How could the values of his ten-year-old sister make him feel guilty? "Then I shall go to hear Mr. Moody with you."

"Oooo!" Alexa squealed and hugged him, then skipped off to her room, apparently forgetting that such behavior was not appropriate for the Sabbath.

A short time later the family gathered at the long table in the dark oak wainscoted dining room, watching their father carve the Sunday joint. The Hoste family always ate a cold roast on Sundays so the servants could have the day to worship. General Hoste placed the slices of meat on each plate and handed it to his wife. She served the potatoes, carrots, brussels sprouts, and beans from bowls in front of her and passed the plate around the table. "Would you like another potato, Dixon, dear?"

It was a question she asked each of her sons every time she served them, but something about the tenderness in her voice or the look of concern that accompanied it struck a special chord with Dick. He declined the potato and looked at William sitting so quietly across from him. Somehow he knew, without anything being voiced, that his mother and brother, perhaps some of the others as well, were praying fervently for him.

That certain knowledge added to the weight of the decision he must make. Which would be worse, ridicule in the officers' mess or hurting his family? Yet even as he asked the question, he knew it was unworthy. This was not a decision to be made for the sake of friends or family. It was entirely between himself and Jesus Christ.

That night he went to the Dome. He listened carefully, thought hard, and came away depressed. He had gone hoping the weight would lift, hoping to find an easy decision—or better—a way to avoid making the choice. Life had been so easy, so pleasant. There seemed to be no reason it couldn't go on so forever. Why should things have to change?

Monday at lunch Alexa's smile was radiant. Her adored big brother had promised to take her to the meeting. Dixon lay his napkin aside and pushed his chair away from the table. "I'll be back, Poppet. Promised to see a fellow from the regiment first."

He hadn't actually promised Jackson he would meet him at the pier, but he might as well walk down to the beach. Activity seemed to be the only escape from the weight inside. He took a deep breath of invigorating salt air as he approached the West Pier. Built almost twenty years earlier, it was the most elegant pier in existence, featuring ornamental gaslighting, an observation deck over the ocean, and a magnificent glass pavilion for refreshments and amusements.

Dixon saw the flags flying in the sea breeze, heard the band playing, and smelled the gingerbread. A nanny, walking erectly in black cape and bonnet, held tightly to the hands of two little girls clad in white coats and fur caps. Three young ladies, escorted by a man who appeared to be their father or uncle, strolled past Dixon. "Isn't this marvelous? Imagine, experiencing all the novelty of strolling safely over the sea without any of the dangers of sailing on it!" They moved on toward the entrance arcade, which was resplendent with ornamental ironwork, banners, and arches of colored glass.

Halfway along the pier, Dixon spotted his fellow officers attending on two fashionable young ladies. He walked toward them. The sound of water lapping the pylons below and the cries of gulls circling overhead mingled with the laughter and happy chatter of the merrymakers.

When he reached his friends, his rather solemn face lit with pleasure. "Ah, Miss Lansdown, I didn't realize you would be honoring us with your company today." He bowed over her hand.

"Is that your excuse for failing to wear your uniform, sir?"

He hesitated to explain that his reason for wearing mufti was that he intended to go to the Moody campaign later.

"Never mind. Mr. Hoste is very handsome just as he is." The red-haired Pamela Arneson took his arm. "Although you are rather severe-looking, sir." She gave him a smile that would be considered coquettish in a woman of a lower class. "Come," she said to the group in general. "I have heard that the juggling show is most amusing. It will be just the thing to cheer Mr. Hoste up."

The December air was damp and chill, but under the arching glass roof of the arcade all was exhilarating warmth. Children on a pre-Christmas outing clapped for the trained bird act and laughed at the clowns. Jackson and Wyatt exhibited their skill with a rifle at the shooting gallery, but Hoste hung back, feeling such exhibition was unprofessional. They drank tall cups of cocoa topped with cream and shaved chocolate. Then they moved on to watch a thin man in a yellow and orange checkered suit spin plates on a pole while riding a bicycle.

The performance over, they meandered toward the ring-toss games. Jackson and Cecilia walked just ahead of Dixon. The red-coated officer made a casual remark to Cecilia, and she looked up at him, laughing and dimpling. Although perfectly proper, there was an air of intimacy in the exchange that made Dixon stop. He realized then that, since her initial greeting, Cecilia Lansdown had hardly spoken to him. Her eyes had been only for the men in uniform.

Could their relationship have been that shallow? She was as pretty and charming as ever. But watching her with his friend, he could see that the dimples and blonde curls were the major sum of her charms. And she had admired him merely as a fine figure in a uniform. Yet how many people built their lives on nothing more substantial than that?

"Let us walk to the end of the pier and observe the sea," Miss Arneson suggested.

Dixon looked around, startled, as they exited the south door of the arcade. The gaslights were on. It was dark. What time was it? He pulled his watch from his pocket. How could the time have passed so quickly? How could he have forgotten his promise to his sister? He shook his head, hoping to rid himself of the image of the hurt look in her eyes.

He turned so abruptly he almost trod on the hem of Pamela Arneson's skirt. "I'm sorry. Must take my leave. Prior engagement." He nodded a bow and spun on his heel, not bothering to answer the surprised replies of his companions. He strode around the deck that circled the amusement arcade, his footsteps ringing on the boardwalk.

It was too late to go home for Alexa. The service would already have started. He could only hope there would be a seat left in the Dome.

The congregation was singing the "Old Hundredth" as Dixon sank into a seat at the back of the hall. He looked around but could see his family nowhere. Across the aisle and toward the front, however, he did recognize the Studd and Beauchamp parties. Somehow the weight he carried like a huge stone in his chest seemed lifted as he watched them singing with such radiance.

Dixon felt a great longing to be able to rejoice with them. He recalled how he had felt touched with light and kindness when Hilda Beauchamp offered him a tract on Marine Drive. Her depth and sincerity sprang from a solid foundation, so unlike the shallow values of women like Cecilia Lansdown. And he thought of J. E. K. Studd. Dick had met him only twice and knew him slightly by reputation. They had not directly discussed the Christian faith in their time together, and yet the silent power of the inner man had spoken to Dixon Hoste. Kynaston Studd's life also stood for sterling value.

Then in his simple, direct way Moody stood in the pulpit and began telling Bible stories. There were none that Dixon Hoste had not heard time and again since childhood, but this time the preacher made it clear that Christianity is not mere understanding nor mere feeling, but a total surrender of the whole nature to a personal, living Christ. This truth burned in Dick's mind.

"The Lord Jesus is not interested in mealy-mouthed, weak-kneed sentimentality. He can find plenty of that on every street corner." The preacher pointed, and Dick knew it was straight at him. "Jesus Christ calls you to become an out-and-out Christian with your heart on fire for Him. He wants you ready to use your every power and every opportunity for service."

When the congregation stood to sing a song of invitation, Dick was amazed that the weight inside him did not pull him through the floor. How could he have thought he was happy living so selfishly?

"Now is the accepted time. Now is the time of salvation. Christ died to bear your sin. Do not vacillate longer. Kneel with me now in prayer."

Dick dropped to his knees right at his seat. Victory was his. He gave himself unreservedly to Christ. His whole being was at his Lord's disposal to do with as He saw fit.

To Dick's amazement a great sense of peace washed over him. Days, weeks of struggle were wiped out in a moment. He was flooded with a consciousness of forgiveness and an awareness of God's graciousness. The weight of fear and indecision was replaced with an incredible lightness of joy.

"Now all you who have responded to the call of the Master need to confess your faith. Do it openly by coming on down here to the front for another prayer."

Moody had not finished the invitation before Dick was in the aisle, striding forward, head up, shoulders square, his face and whole bearing exultant.

"Oh, Dick!" Alexa was the first member of the Hoste family to greet him when he entered Havelock Lodge. She came running, her skirts flying. "I was so worried when you didn't come. I prayed and prayed."

Dick caught her under the arms and spun her around. "Thank you, Poppet, thank you. I'm so sorry to have let you down."

She hugged him around the shoulders and buried her face in his chest. "Oh, no. It's fine—now. I was so happy when I saw you walking down the aisle. It was just like you were marching to battle. Only better."

"Yes, it was better, Poppet, because the battle was won." His laughter rang with freedom and joy.

It was a few days later, on Christmas Eve, with the house full of the scent of pine and spices and the cheery sounds of Mrs. Hoste and her daughters making mince pies in the kitchen when

Dick sought out his father for a quiet word. "Sir, I've come to a decision. I hope this won't be a disappointment to you. You know how I've hoped to carry on the family tradition and emulate your success in the army." He paused for a breath before rushing ahead. "But I've decided. I wish to resign my commission."

General Hoste put his book aside and stood to look his son directly in the eye. Dick always felt that looking at his father was like looking in a mirror that had simply turned the clock ahead twenty-five years. Both men had the same sharp cheekbones, steady gaze, and long, full sideburns and mustache. General Hoste's skin was more weathered and lined, his hair and side whiskers touched with gray, but his eyes were no less piercing, his bearing no less erect. "It's a fine step you've taken, son. I can ask no more than to see each of my children make the same decision to follow Christ. There's no question of disappointing me." He indicated that they should both sit before the fire. "But why do you want to leave the regiment?"

Dick leaned forward in his chair, alight with the new flame burning inside him. "I want to offer myself for the foreign field."

General Hoste nodded. "Yes, I see. A fine ambition. And quite natural, I should think, as a military career normally entails overseas duty as well." He nodded. "Perhaps that would be just the thing in time."

"In time?" Dick raised his sharp, dark eyebrows. "I meant now, sir."

General Hoste's mustache twitched. "Yes, I thought perhaps you did. Best not to rush into battle before your gun's primed though."

"I—I don't understand, sir. Are you refusing permission?"

"I am advising you to avoid haste. Return to your regiment. If this is the call of God, it will remain. If merely over-enthusiasm, you will have avoided a costly mistake."

"There can be no mistake, Father. My commitment is total. I would offer God nothing less."

General Hoste shook his head. "There is no questioning your commitment, Dick. One has only to look at you. I've seldom seen a man so changed. But what did our Lord tell the Gadarene demoniac who wanted to follow Jesus after his healing?"

Dick sat back in his chair. "To go home and tell his friends." He took in the full meaning. It was one thing to turn his back on his old life and embrace a whole new future serving Christ. It was quite another thing to take Christ back into his old life.

All those days he had struggled and resisted, fearing the ridicule of the officers' mess. Now the shouts of laughter and jeers rang in his ears. He must face what he had feared most. But even as he quailed, he knew such trials could be nothing compared to what Christ had faced from the mob on his way to Calvary. "Yes, thank you, Father. I will return to Sandown."

Sixteen

January 1883 in northern China was even colder than normal. Harold Schofield usually shunned all concessions to convenience and comfort. Even at its most modest, the small study beside his surgery at the mission station was luxury compared to the conditions countless millions of his beloved Chinese lived in. Tonight, however, Harold did not reject the little charcoal burner Libby insisted on lighting.

"Please don't argue with me, Harold. The ink will congeal on your nib if you refuse all warmth, and then you'll never finish writing that letter, and you'll never come to bed."

In spite of his fatigue, he dropped his pen and opened his arms to his wife. "Then by all means, light your brazier. And come sit on my lap while we wait for the room to warm."

In a moment she was nestling in his arms. "Harold, you work too hard."

"But there is so much to do. Our Lord never spared Himself. How can I find excuse to stint my duty?"

"But have you no duty to yourself? I won't press your duty to your wife and *children*." She moved his hand from her shoulder to her abdomen.

"*Children*, Libby?" He felt no roundness under his hand, but surely he did not mistake her meaning. "You did say *children?*"

She raised her head to kiss his cheek. "Yes, my darling. Little Harold will have that playmate we have wished for him."

"Oh, my dear." He wrapped her tightly in his arms, his cheek against her soft hair. "I am so happy. When?"

"Early next summer."

He started to tell her again how happy he was, to ask how she was feeling, to thank God. But she kissed him once more and jumped lightly from his lap. "Now back to work for you. I'll not keep you up any later even for such good news."

He shook his head. "How can I concentrate on my correspondence now?"

"Tell them how good God is, how beautiful life is." She blew him a kiss and left the room.

Harold looked back over his notes. He was writing home, trying to express the call strongest on his heart—next to his own desire to serve God and China—his longing that God would move in the universities of Britain. Always it was before him, the longing to see the best, the brightest catch the vision of serving God with complete consecration—that they would find the beauty and the joy in Christ that he had found. Libby did not have to tell him to speak of the goodness of life. Its reality was always before him.

He dipped his pen and wrote: "Be all that you have in your power to be. You can with God's help become almost anything as a Christian. Open your heart and keep it open to the love of the Lord Jesus, to the love of others, and to everything beautiful, letting it send His pleasure through your heart, and thanking your Father who gives you both the pleasure and the power to enjoy it."

Hilda, in a momentarily languid mood, looked through the lace curtains of the front parlor at the snow falling softly on the square across Cromwell Road. The lilting melody of "Sleepers Awake" filled the room at Ida's touch on the piano. She knew she should stir herself to action while she waited for Monty. She should be helping her mother with her correspondence. She should be giving a hand with the poor baskets she had instructed the kitchen staff to prepare. She should...

She gave an irritated thump on the silk-fringed tapestry cushions, knocking one of them to the floor. Then she jumped to her feet. "Oh, what can be keeping him?" She turned to her placid sister. "How can you sit there hour after hour playing Bach? Don't you long to be outside, feeling the flakes on your face, breathing the crisp air? Don't you want to *do* something?"

The final trills and chords faded under Ida's fingers. She looked up, blinking. "Did you say something, Hilda?"

Hilda sighed. "No, Ida. I didn't say anything."

Ida took out a new sheet of music and began "Sheep May Safely Graze." Hilda plucked the fallen pillow off the floor with an irritated gesture, flung it toward the sofa, and then winced as she heard the Royal Doulton ornament on the side table fall over with a crack.

Finally came the sound she had been waiting for. "Monty— what took you so long?" She hurried toward the entrance hall. Now she would have an escort to help take the baskets to the Watercress and Flower Girls Mission. "We mustn't delay. You know those poor girls struggle so in this weather when fruit and flowers are out of season."

But it was not Monty who answered. "I do apologize. I fear I'm the one who insisted we call in at Berkeley Square to collect Smith."

Hilda stopped at the sound of Kynaston Studd's voice. She had not expected her brother to bring visitors. And especially not Mr. Studd whom she hadn't seen since Brighton and who always aroused such confused emotions in her. Now she made no serious attempt to hide her irritation. Lady Beauchamp was occupied, so Hilda would have to see to ordering refreshment for their guests and serving them. More delays. Of course, it should have been Ida's job to deputize for their mother, but she was hopeless.

Leaving the three young men to sort themselves out, she turned to the fireplace where a warm fire of sea coal blazed on the hearth. She gave three sharp tugs to the bell pull hanging there. "Please don't bother the servants on our account. Mrs. Smith gave us tea." Hilda started at Kynaston's voice so close behind her. She had not realized he had followed her into the parlor.

She turned so abruptly she all but slammed into him. He put a hand on each of her shoulders to steady them both. "I can see we've come at an inopportune time." She started to offer a polite denial, but Kynaston laughed. "Don't try, Hilda. You're hopeless at prevaricating." Then he became serious again. "Really, though S. P. S. has the most remarkable account to give. Thrilling, I'd even say. I want you—" He looked at Ida still at the piano. "—you all to hear this."

"Very well." Hilda chose the stiffest chair in the room and sat with her back straight, her hands folded in her lap. When the parlor maid appeared in the doorway, Hilda dismissed her. She supposed Stanley Smith had discovered a new area of Christian service, although what could possibly be left to add to his list she couldn't imagine.

Smith seemed to follow her line of thought. "As you know, I've been much involved in Christian service." He stood half-leaning against the high marble mantel, his refined good looks accented by the smooth cut of his dark brown jacket. "Doing good for people made me feel good. But the good feeling never lasted." He turned away and ran a hand through his smooth blond hair. "At bottom I was ashamed. Oh, I really wanted to bring people to the Lord, but I was doing it for selfish reasons. It made me look creditable."

Hilda sat forward, her stiffness and frustration forgotten. She suddenly realized how changed he was. For all his outstandingly attractive qualities, she could never have said that humility was one of them. Now as he sought for the right words, she felt warmed by more than the fire beside him. She saw a beauty of spirit in this man that before had exhibited only a surface charm. What could have brought about this transformation? It wasn't salvation, for he had long been a Christian—albeit a mercurial one.

Smith shook his head and gave a little half smile. "It really is the most amazing thing. Almost as amazing as salvation. You see, I had no idea there was anything else—that there was more to being a Christian than forgiveness for sins and good works. And I had all that—" He gave another self-deprecating smile. "Sorry, I'm rambling. The thing is, it's so simple I don't really know how to tell it.

"I stayed the weekend with an acquaintance—old Mr. Price

at Pakefield—and he showed me that one needs to be redeemed as well as forgiven. One must make a definite consecration of the whole self to God—not just give Him one's sins for forgiveness, but one's whole life to direct as He sees fit. And when one makes this total commitment, the Holy Spirit comes into one's life in an entirely new way to guide and direct and comfort."

Hilda frowned. It was evident that Stanley was different. And yet she couldn't grasp the difference. "Yes, that's very nice. But what are you telling us? What are you going to do differently?"

Stanley spread his hands in an open-palmed gesture. "Nothing that I know of—outwardly. I shall continue teaching the boys at Newlands and speaking at missions and open-airs. But inside the change is radical—the difference between day and night. The struggle is gone. The direction for everything is given over to the Holy Spirit. The freedom is inexpressible."

"Freedom? It sounds like slavery." Hilda bit her lip. As usual, she had spoken without thinking.

But Stanley turned his full smile on her. The sweetness of it caught at her throat. "Before, I was a slave to my own plans and desires—even though they were plans to do things for God. Now I'm free to live every moment in His holiness. I wish I could explain it better, but once you see it, the Bible is full of the teaching: From the beginning God wasn't satisfied just to forgive sins; He wanted people wholly committed. There's Romans 12 and—"

He stopped as the butler knocked and then entered with the afternoon post on a silver tray. Hilda breathed a sigh of relief. "Thank you, Talley." She was in no mood to listen to a sermon on submission.

Hilda's irritation grew as Kynaston and Monty continued discussing Stanley Smith's experience of holiness with him. She had waited hours for her brother to return so she could be about her work, and yet they talked on. At a slight pause in the conversation she turned to her sister. "What has the postman brought you, Ida? Have you news to share?"

In her quiet corner Ida had been glancing over a pale blue letter written in a feminine hand. "Oh, yes. It's quite wonderful."

She smiled at Stanley. "And quite in keeping with what you were saying, Mr. Smith. Do you mind?"

"Oh, please, proceed. I've held forth for far too long." He settled on a plush ottoman.

"It's from Alice Polhill-Turner. She says Arthur is quite a new man. 'It's such a delight to watch him with our younger brothers and sisters—so patient and always laughing with them. I don't think he knew they existed before. I commented I had never seen him like that before.'

"'He replied he had never been like this before, never realized the world was so beautiful, life so good. "Strange, isn't it?" he said. "When I lived for pleasure, I worried all the time that I was missing something—not having enough fun. Now I never think of it, and I've never been so happy."'"

Ida looked up. "Shall I go on? It's rather long."

Hilda started to cut in with a suggestion that they hear the rest later—after she had seen to her flower girls—but Monty replied, "Carry on, Ida. Wondered how P.T. was making out. Best of fellows. Never missed prayers since Moody."

Ida smiled at her brother and continued in her soft voice. "'Cecil received the greatest shock of all though—did I tell you he's on winter's leave from his regiment in Ireland? He had commented once or twice upon Arthur's lack of interest in dancing, racing, and cards, and when they were walking to the parish church last Sunday, he remarked how pleasant it would be for Arthur when he succeeded to the family living there. Cecil was totally unprepared for Arthur's reply. Arthur said he probably will not take the living because he is thinking of *going to preach in China.*'

"'You can't imagine what a stir that has caused in Howbury Hall. Cecil was horrified. He misses no chance to try to dissuade Arthur of what he calls his "wild scheme." Of course, our mother is prostrate. But I am happy to report that Arthur holds firm.'"

The room was silent when she lowered the letter. Hilda looked at Kynaston. His face was white, his fine, sharp features rigid.

Monty broke the silence. "What did I tell you? Best of fellows, Arthur. *China* though." He shook his head. "Hope I'm not to blame. Gave him some literature from Taylor. Only meant for him to pray, give money—that sort of thing. Not go overboard."

In the shocked silence that followed, Hilda stood and smoothed her skirt with a single swish. "Well, this has been most instructive. How very gratifying that Mr. Moody's campaign has produced lasting results. But I fear that the Maiden Lane poor will suffer needlessly if I fail in my duty to deliver their baskets." She turned to her brother. "Montague, you promised to accompany me."

"Getting dark now, Hilda." Monty glanced out the window. "Still snowing, too. Take them in the morning."

"Allow me." Kynaston Studd stood.

To Kynaston the carriage seemed held in a cocoon of quiet white as the horses crunched softly through the evening snow. All the carriage wheels in Piccadilly rolled over the enveloping carpet, and street lamps illuminated the shop windows as the last of the shoppers and clerks hurried homeward, wrapped in coats, hats, and mufflers. An almost idyllic scene, and yet Kynaston felt it hard to let the peace of the surroundings into his heart. P. T. had announced his desire to go to China and had let the matter take its consequences with his family, while Kynaston still had not spoken. Was he being cowardly or thoughtful?

J. E. K. agreed fully with all that Smith had said. There was no doubt that he acknowledged Christ as Lord as well as Savior. But that was the trouble. "It's not a matter of submitting to His will; it's a matter of knowing it."

Only when Hilda turned to him did he realize he had spoken aloud. "You must find Mr. Polhill-Turner's announcement freeing."

"Freeing?"

"Certainly. If he's to go to China, you can remain with the work here."

Kynaston smiled in spite of himself. "China is a very large

place, Hilda. There are millions who have never heard the Gospel. They can use more than one worker."

"Certainly China is vast. But the China Inland Mission is a very small affair. How many workers of university quality can they handle? Surely not many or the work would be overwhelmed."

Kynaston laughed. "At least your argument is unique, Hilda. But I fear it would be impossible to overwhelm China's need for workers. I was just reading in *China's Millions* that one of the largest of China's seven provinces has a total of fifty-five missionaries while Great Britain has 35,000 ministers. That single province has 17,500,000 souls." He turned to her on the carriage seat. "Think of the need, Hilda. Think of the opportunity."

"I do. But I think of the need and opportunity right here. I have heard it calculated that even with the enormous success of Mr. Moody, it would take twelve years of constant campaigns at the same intensity at which he labors, preaching to crowds of 5,000 people in several services a day, to reach all of London alone. The task here is great."

The carriage stopped before the tenement houses beyond Covent Garden. Kynaston continued the argument as he helped her out of the carriage and began unloading the baskets of bread, preserves, and baked meats. "And, besides, think how much easier the task is here: The inhabitants of London are almost all nominal Christians; most can read; they have the Bible; they have some knowledge, however defective, of its contents, and Moody speaks and Sankey sings to men and women in their own tongue—"

A group of boys ran down the street throwing snowballs at one another.

Hilda seized the opportunity. "I fail to see how the fact that God has prepared the way for the work here can make it less important." Exasperated, she took a basket from his hands and turned toward the door.

"Hilda, be careful. The snow—" His warning came too late. Hilda turned to avoid a snowball carefully aimed at the clump of small black feathers on her hat. Her feet slipped from under her. She landed in the snow, loaves of bread rolling every direction.

Kynaston dumped his own armful and knelt to help her.

The urchins scattered, but one came to own up to his behavior. "Sorry, ma'am—er, miss. Fearful sorry."

"Jackie!" Kynaston turned from Hilda as he recognized the young scoundrel. "What do you mean by throwing snowballs at Miss Beauchamp who has been so kind to your sister and is bringing food to your neighborhood?"

"I'm sorry, I said."

"That's all very well, young man, but—"

"Kynaston." Hilda's exasperated voice made him turn to where she still sat in the snow, her hat crooked, loaves of bread spread over the snow. "Would it be too much to ask you to help me to my feet before you see to this young man's moral improvement?"

"Oh!" Horrified at his lapse of manners, Kynaston turned back to her. He grasped her hand and placed his arm under her elbow to lift her. At that moment he stepped on a patch of ice under the snow. His legs shot out in front of him. Still holding Hilda's arm, he pulled her down on top of him. Kynaston was too horrified to apologize. He could feel her shaking. From pain or anger? "Hilda—"

And then her laughter broke, full and rippling. Jackie, who had been looking on in frozen horror, grinned from ear to ear and then began chuckling with her.

Kynaston gave up the struggle to right himself and leaned back on his elbows. By the time any of them had regained enough control to speak, a crowd had gathered. Most were staring in amazement at the fine lady and gentleman in such a predicament, but some were eyeing the loaves of bread.

A small girl, her legs bare, with only rags around her feet, stooped and grabbed a loaf. "'Ere now, that ain't yers." Jackie made a grab at her, but she eluded him.

Hilda waved her arm at the crusty loaves. "Take them. I brought them for you all. I hope they haven't gotten too soggy." Then she was laughing again.

"Hilda." Kynaston's voice came out in a breathless pleading. "Forgive my mentioning it, but I can't breathe."

"Oh!" Hilda grabbed Jackie's hand for support as she scrambled to her feet, blushing hotly that she had been sitting on top of a man in a public street.

At last the food was distributed and decorum restored, except for the occasional snicker that still burst from Hilda.

But Kynaston turned to Jackie. "Now, young man, I think you owe us an explanation."

"I didn't know—"

"No, I don't mean about the snowball. Why aren't you in school? Evening classes at the ragged school started an hour ago."

Jackie hung his head. "Yessir, well, I meant to go—but there was the snow…and all they do is read—and preach an' stuff. Wot good's that?"

"Don't you do sums?"

"Oh, yes. I'm right good at sums. But we don't *do* anything. Nuthin' useful like blacking boots or repairin' 'arness or such."

"Well, however that may be, see that you are in class tomorrow without fail. What will Lizzie say when she comes back if you've spoiled your chance for advancement?"

Jackie's face clouded. "When is she comin' back?"

"It should be soon. Three or four weeks, I think."

"Have you had no word from her?" Hilda turned to the small boy in concern.

Jackie frowned. "Naw. 'Ow could I?"

Hilda looked at Kynaston. "We must see what we can do. I hadn't realized—she will think she's been abandoned. I had hoped Mr. Groom might have visited…"

Kynaston shook his head. "I'm certain he must have his hands full with the mission here. I will go tomorrow."

"Yes. You may call for me at ten o'clock. We will have word for you soon, Jackie."

"Mr. Groom can let you know when you see him *after school*," Kynaston emphasized.

Hilda was in high spirits all the way back to Cromwell Road. "See, what did I tell you? There is more than enough to be done here—and I'm certain it can be quite as exhilarating as tramping through China."

Kynaston was quiet. If he was looking for exhilaration, it

was certain that he would never need to look beyond the handsome, outspoken young lady beside him. He knew no one whose courage and determination he admired more. Or who amused him more. And yet there was Ida. Her sweetness was alluring, and there was a vulnerability in her eyes when she offered him her shy smile. He was certain she cared for him. And he could not bear to think of bringing pain to such a dear creature.

When they arrived at Cromwell Road, Kynaston made one more attempt to dissuade Hilda from going to Pentonville with him. But as he expected, he might as well have saved his breath.

Even as Hilda sat beside him once again in the carriage the next morning, Kynaston was still arguing with himself over the propriety of taking a young woman of gentle breeding into a prison—even a model one such as Pentonville. Yet he knew that if Hilda Beauchamp had determined on visiting Lizzie, there was little he could do to prevent it. And Lady Beauchamp herself subscribed to several charities that did work in such institutions. Ladies even served on the boards of governors of hospitals and prisons—both equally unsavory places—so he could hardly argue social impropriety for such a charitable visit.

Still, he did not want to expose Hilda to an atmosphere that might be upsetting. For all her apparent strength, he knew that much of her determination sprang from the depth of her caring about the social problems around them. Through the window of the carriage he observed the soot-blackened, overcrowded, broken buildings lining Tottenham Court Road and the hungry, ragged creatures who lived there. It was bad enough to be accompanying a lady through such streets without contemplating what lay ahead. He relaxed a bit as they turned onto Euston Road.

"What's to be done for Jackie?" Hilda asked.

Kynaston looked at her. "Oh, I'm certain he'll go back to school. And the mission will feed him until Lizzie gets out of prison." He looked out the window as they passed the Gothic St. Pancras train station. "I always think St. Pancras looks rather like a cathedral, don't—"

But Hilda would not be interrupted. "The ragged school is fine as far as it goes. But it doesn't prepare boys adequately for a place in the industrialized world. England is quite a different country from what it was when the Earl of Shaftesbury began his schools forty years or so ago."

"Yes, I suppose you're right." Kynaston considered further. "Yes, and the apprentice system is outmoded. Something new needs to be done for those among the lower and artisan classes… "

"Something practical to teach them a trade, like Jackie said." Hilda nodded encouragingly.

All of a sudden the idea gripped Kynaston. He turned and grasped Hilda's gloved hands. "Yes, that's it—practical training for useful work, physical development, religious teaching—"

The carriage stopped before the high stone wall surrounding the prison, and the conversation ended. Kynaston knew it was useless to suggest that Hilda remain wrapped in warm blankets inside the carriage, but he shivered as he looked at the forbidding coldness of the massive stone building. Inside it was even colder, as the chill was held and echoed by the stones. And the smell. It seemed the icy air had solidified the odors of clogged drains and exhausted bodies shut in closed rooms.

He gripped Hilda's arm, as much from his own need for human warmth as from his desire to support her. The heavy wooden doors closed behind them with a hollow clang. A blue-suited warden led them to a small, bare, gray stone room. Since Kynaston had sent a message ahead requesting this visit, Lizzie was awaiting them. She sat with her hands folded on a plain wooden table, a heavy, scowling matron looming behind her. Kynaston and Hilda sat in stiff wooden chairs on the other side of the table.

"How are you, Lizzie?" Hilda began.

"I'm fine. Right fine. It's ever so good of you to come see me. Is Jackie a'right?"

"He's fine," Hilda assured her. "We saw him just yesterday." Then she gasped and started to reach for Lizzie's hands. The matron made a warning motion, and Hilda pulled back. "But, Lizzie, your fingers. What's happened?"

Lizzie's hands, which were always soiled and rough, were

now red and raw with bleeding broken blisters between new-formed calluses.

Lizzie spread her fingers and looked at them in surprise as if she hadn't noticed before. She shrugged. "Pickin' oakum. It does that."

Hilda jumped to her feet and looked the matron squarely in the eye. "What is this? I thought Pentonville was a model prison. What are you doing to her?"

The matron gave a bellow of laughter. "Ooh and 'ose the fine lady? All the prisoners pick oakum—none 'ere too good fer 'onest work. Keeps 'em outer trouble. Wouldn't be 'ere if they'd kept outer trouble afore, would they?" She laughed again.

Kynaston placed a hand on Hilda's shoulder to ease her back to her seat. "They unravel bits of old rope. The fiber is used in caulking ships' seams to stop up leaks." He paused. "That is, it was. Not sure what it's used for now that they're building iron-clads." He looked at the matron, but she only sneered at him.

"It's a'right," Lizzie insisted. "Much better than the treadmill."

"What?" Hilda asked.

Lizzie shrugged. "Everyone starts out on it 'ere. To get us broken in, they said. Steps what turn. You just keep treading. Only trouble is, you can't get no firm tread, as the steps allus sink away from under yer feet." She shrugged again. "Made me very tired, so I 'adn't any trouble sleepin'."

Hilda gave a brave, if forced-looking, smile. "Well, Lizzie, only a few more weeks now, and you'll be out of here."

Lizzie hung her head. "I suppose I 'avter go?"

Hilda's mouth gaped open. Kynaston was the one who asked, "What? Do you mean to say you don't want out of here?"

"Well." Lizzie stared at the table. "The food's a'right. They give us cocoa and bread for breakfast, meat and potatoes for dinner, and gruel and bread for supper. I'd never 'ave that much outside... 'Course, I know it's wrong o' me. I should be out seein' to Jackie."

"But don't you miss your work?" Hilda asked.

Lizzie raised her head and smiled. "Oh, I like sellin' flowers right fine in the summer. They smell so sweet, and allus such pretty colors. But there'll be no flowers to sell for three months yet. And now that I've quit 'elpin' those that lift things—" She bit her lower lip.

"Well, there's the mission…," Hilda began.

But Kynaston had a better suggestion. "Lizzie, do you know about the Emily Loan Fund?"

From the blank look on her face it was clear she didn't.

"The Earl of Shaftesbury started it in memory of his wife—"

Hilda clapped her hands. "Oh, yes! Why didn't I think of that? They do wonderful work. Lizzie, you could make application for the loan of a baked-potato oven, a coffee-stall, a barrow and board for the sale of whelks—anything you might see as a reasonable prospect of earning a living."

Lizzie's face lit up. "Baked potatoes? Garn. If I sold enough, me and Jackie could eat one every day—nice and 'ot." She looked at her inflamed hands. "And no oakum picking."

For a moment Lizzie's smile went soft and dreamy. Then it faded suddenly with a shake of her head. "Oh, no. It would take a very large sum for a baked-potato oven."

"How much?" Hilda asked.

"Oh, very large. I should think not a penny less than two pounds."

Hilda blinked. "Well, then—" She started to reach for her reticule.

But Kynaston put a hand over hers to stop her. "I'm certain such a sum could be arranged. I myself would stand security for you. You would be required to pay the loan fund back at something like six pence a week. But when the actual value is repaid, it would be your own property. I frequently buy coffee from a stall owned by a former watercress girl. In the summer she sells watercress as well."

"I'd like that right well." Lizzie rose obediently at the matron's signal that the time was up. "I won't mind pickin' oakum near so much when I can think of givin' my Jackie a nice 'ot potato every day."

"You can give him two," Hilda said.

They were just signing out at the warden's office when a

slightly built, vigorous man entered with a companion. Kynaston had a feeling he had seen that smooth, round forehead beneath thinning brown hair and those level, intelligent eyes somewhere before.

The warden hurried out from the inner office, his hand extended in greeting. "Mr. Hogg, welcome to Pentonville. I am so pleased that you could address our board of governors today. We are much interested in your excellent work."

Then Kynaston remembered. Of course, this was Quinten Hogg, one of the great merchants of London. His father was once a chairman of the East India Company. And Q. H. owned vast sugar plantations in Demarrara, but he gave all his time and resources to philanthropy. Hogg had been at Eton fifteen years before Kynaston and was still known as an old boy.

J. E. K. approached. "Excuse me, Mr. Hogg, but we met once at a Young Men's Christian Association meeting—"

Hogg gave a cry of recognition. "J. E. K. Studd—the cricketer! Pleased to see you again, sir."

With a glance at his pocket watch, the warden invited Mr. Studd and Miss Beauchamp to join his other guests at the chapel service that was just beginning. The warden, a portly man in a gray suit, led the way down a clean but chilly stone corridor. The chapel was a long wood-paneled room. Its walls, as most others in the prison, were hung with mottoes: "The Eyes of the Lord Are Everywhere." "Be Sure Your Sins Will Find You Out." "Thou, God, Seest Me." At the front of the room was a low platform with a large, dark wood cross behind a bare pulpit.

The rows of seats in which the prisoners sat looked at first glance like choir stalls filled with hooded monks. Then it became clear that the high-sided boxes in which each prisoner sat made it impossible for a prisoner to communicate with his neighbor and yet kept his head visible to the blue-uniformed wardens standing at the back. And the monks' hoods were actually masks of brown cloth through which only the prisoners eyes shone—like the sockets of a skull.

"We allow no communication of any kind between prisoners," the warden explained to his visitors. "Any such attempt is severely punished."

"And how is that done?" Quinten Hogg asked.

"Refractory cells—keep them in total darkness. A few days of that makes 'em glad enough to obey our rules. Won't have any passing on of evil tricks here. First offenders kept strictly to themselves, too. Run on the most advanced lines, we are. No coddling, but every prisoner is allowed letters and visitors. No one spends more than six hours a day on the treadmill. No one begins work before six o'clock in the morning and always quits by seven. We turn them loose better men and women than they come in here, yes siree."

Quinten Hogg nodded politely. "I can see you're doing an efficient job, Warden. But are there any measures to teach your inmates to read?" The warden's bushy eyebrows shot up at the suggestion. "Or to learn a useful trade? Something by which they can support themselves and their families when they're released?" Hogg pressed.

The warden was saved from having to answer by the chaplain beginning the service. After reading the lessons and delivering an earnest exhortation to all to repent and let the Lord Jesus make them better, the chaplain led them in a hearty, if off-key, singing of "I Lay My Sins on Jesus." Then he dismissed his captive audience.

Kynaston turned to Quinten Hogg. "It was a great pleasure to see you again, sir. Are you still working with the YMCA?"

Hogg shook his head. "Fine organization, fine. As far as it goes. But it does nothing to reach the apprentices and lower classes."

"So you're supporting the ragged schools?"

Again Hogg shook his well-trimmed beard. "No. No, tried that, too, but it's not quite the thing. Doesn't meet the needs of the lads I want to help. Working on something better suited to their nature. Religion and the three R's are excellent things, but don't provide the poor lad with sufficient equipment. He needs skills, practical knowledge. School and club—develop the whole man—low fees, morning and evening classes so they can work—sports teams, outings. Come see us. Come see us anytime."

The warden was looking at his watch again, indicating that they needed to be moving on to his board meeting, but Hogg's enthusiasm for his new work was not to be curbed. "You know the Polytechnic Institution on Regent Street? Purchased it a while back. Moving my school there from Drury Lane—room for thousands of students. Come see us." He grasped Kynaston's hand and began shaking it. "Come play cricket with my lads. We have three teams. They're not bad, not bad at all."

"You come, too, Miss Beauchamp. It's exciting work. Making a real difference in lives."

Kynaston was quiet as the carriage made its way back through the soot-blackened, slushy snow. For a moment the force of Quinten Hogg's personality had held him. Kynaston felt the man's enthusiasm for the work lighting a spark within himself. "Making a real difference in lives" was something one could give oneself to wholeheartedly. Without distressing one's mother. Without turning one's back on family responsibilities. Without giving up the company of charming young women. He glanced at Hilda beside him.

But no. Such thoughts were clearly sent as temptations to steer him from his course. Arthur Polhill-Turner had set the right course when he announced his intention to go to China. And P.T. would go as an ordained minister. Kynaston would go as a medical missionary. What a team they would make.

But close on the exhilaration of the thought, the weight of guilt struck him. He had not yet made his way to Pyrland Road to present himself to the China Inland Mission. What was he waiting for?

Seventeen

April in Cambridge. Daffodils blazed yellow along the Backs. Downy newly hatched ducks swam in obedient lines behind their mothers on the Cam. Birds chirped from trees just turning to full-leafed green. Silvery drops from the morning's rain glistened as the midday sun broke into a patch of soft blue. But Kynaston Studd missed most of the beauty of the world around him as he tugged at the open front of the short sleeveless black gown over his tweed suit and stepped onto the mud-covered bricks of King's Parade.

He really mustn't be late. Wouldn't do to come in late for Bible reading and prayers—especially when they were meeting in his rooms. Especially when he so needed the support.

A few minutes later when he slipped into the chair at the front of the room and looked at the friendly, earnest faces of these men who had shared so many struggles and victories together, he knew he was in the right place. Before he could even inquire if anyone had any reports or requests, Willie Hoste pulled out a letter from his brother.

"Excellent word from Dick. Couldn't be better. 'Still feel an almost ecstatic sense of the presence and joy of Christ,' he writes. 'Amazing to find the Bible transformed from a dreary compilation to a revelation which is a privilege and delight to study. I'm still determined to devote my life to the Gospel. Nothing else seems worthy.'"

Hoste looked up with a shy grin at his friends. "You don't mind, do you—if I just read a bit more? He's very enthusiastic."

Everyone encouraged Willie to continue. "'The Gospel changed my life; I want to make it known where Christ is not known. There are many people in other lands who have never heard the good news, and the Lord wants them to hear it. *I want to give my life to this.*'"

"Resigned his commission, has he?" Monty asked.

"No. Father still hasn't given his permission."

"How's the regiment taking it?" Arthur Polhill-Turner asked.

Willie grinned and shook his head. "That's the most amazing thing of all." He turned the closely written ivory sheet over. "'My first step on returning to Sandown was to inform my commander of my decision for Christ. I don't mind telling you I approached him with considerable trepidation. He's known for being irascible and fault-finding, but he received the news calmly. Probably thought it would wear off in a few days. My fellow officers have been amazingly accepting. I try harder than ever to keep my work up to snuff, knowing they're all watching me. But to tell the truth, my heart isn't in it. I never think of anything but my desire to serve Christ. I spend all my spare time studying the Bible and have found many opportunities to teach and preach on the beach.'"

Arthur Polhill-Turner ran his fingers through his blond waves and raised his head. "Awfully happy for you, Hoste. I don't know whether to be encouraged or depressed myself. You can't imagine how I long for such a letter from my brother."

"Any news from Cecil?" Monty asked.

Arthur shrugged. "Enjoying regiment life to the full. Plenty of opportunities to enjoy oneself in Ireland, I take it." He quit speaking, then added. "Oh, our uncle in Germany has decided to make Cecil his heir."

The talk in the room became general for a few minutes while Kynaston reflected that Polhill-Turner wasn't the only one deeply concerned for a brother. It had been six months since C. T. had left to play cricket in Australia. Kynaston smiled at George, appreciative of his quiet steadiness. G. B. could be relied on whether leading a Bible reading or captaining a cricket team.

He nodded, and G. B. opened his Bible and began the day's reading. But Kynaston found it hard to follow it or to take comfort in the story of the good shepherd who gave his life for his sheep. Kynaston had to ask himself what he would be willing to give to see C. T. a strong, committed Christian. The team would soon return. Reports of cricketing success were already preceding the all-England Eleven, but what effect would all this have on Charlie?

J. E. K.'s attention came back to the room as he realized Monty was requesting prayer for Stanley Smith. "Saw him last week at Newlands."

"He isn't wavering again, is he?" Hoste asked. "I thought he'd found solid ground at last."

"Oh, he has. He has." Monty nodded his head vigorously. "Said to me, 'I know to *whom* I'm committed, but not to *what*.' Meant he's not sure what to do. Plenty of opportunities in teaching, but his heart's not in it. Thinking of joining the Church Army. Said he'd like to go to the foreign field but feels bound by a command of Scripture—not sent to a people of strange speech." Monty grinned. "Guess you don't get much stranger than Chinese."

That jogged Kynaston's memory. "Oh, yes. Glad you mentioned that, Beauchamp. Wanted to read something to you all." He crossed the room and began rummaging through a stack of papers on his desk. At last he pulled out Hudson Taylor's booklet. He rifled a few pages and then read: "'Three hundred and eighty-five millions in China are utterly and hopelessly beyond the reach of the Gospel. The imperative is clear, "Go ye into all the world, and preach the gospel to every creature." Can the Christians of England sit still with folded arms while these multitudes are perishing?'"

The call never failed to stir Kynaston's heart. There was nothing he wanted more than to give himself wholeheartedly to it. So what was holding him back? He felt choked with desire and frustration. It was as if there were a great brick wall in front of him, and he did not know whether he was to scale it or to submit.

"Oh, yes, that's grand. The very thing!" There was no doubt that Arthur still had the vision of the call he had divulged to his brother on that snowy January afternoon on the way to Evensong. "Three hundred and eighty-five millions." He shook his head. "I can't begin to conceive of such numbers. I can't wait to start."

"Have you contacted anyone yet? The China Inland Mission? The Church Missionary Society?" Kynaston asked. When P. T. shook his head, Kynaston continued. "Cassels is thinking of the Church Missionary Society. They do fine work—only in the treaty ports though. C.I.M. missionaries are the only ones who go to the interior."

But Willie Hoste seemed the most taken with the article. "Say, could I borrow that, Studd? I'd like to send it to Dick. Don't know if he's ever heard of Taylor's work. He talks about the foreign field, but I don't think he knows anything about it. He's never mentioned China specifically."

Kynaston handed the booklet to his friend. "Well, are we ready to pray?" He looked around the room, thinking of the needs that had been mentioned: Smith looking for guidance, Cassels looking for guidance, Dick Hoste looking for guidance, Arthur P-T concerned for his brother. Kynaston hadn't even mentioned his own concerns.

Then Monty spoke up. "Better pray for me, too. Thinking of quitting. Not sure ordination's the right thing."

Kynaston bowed his head. How could they ever hope to make an impact on their own families and friends, much less on China's millions, when they couldn't get their own lives sorted out?

Three weeks later Kynaston and George Studd and Willie Hoste sat in the front room of Mrs. Studd's London home in Hyde Park Gardens. In half an hour they would to go Waterloo Station to join in the welcome for England's triumphant Test Team. With a rustle of newsprint, Kynaston folded *The Times* and handed it to G. B. "*Times* has kind words for our brother."

A slow grin spread over George's face as he read the article. "Willie, listen to this." He read aloud: "'Among the returning victors is Mr. C. T. Studd, who will captain Cambridge in his last year there. His career can only be described as one long blaze of cricketing glory.

"'Mr. Studd must, for the second year in succession, be accorded the premier position as an all-round cricketer. And some years have elapsed since the post has been filled by a player so excellent in all the three departments of the game. His batting especially has been of the highest class.'"

G. B.'s pleasure showed in his face and his voice. "Well, that's all right, isn't it? Certainly shows what single-minded dedication can accomplish."

Kynaston agreed wholeheartedly, and yet he worried.

Before George returned to the paper, he offhandedly offered a packet to Kynaston. "Here, Kinny. Want to take a peek at the information Mr. Moody sent me on missionary work in California?"

Kynaston took the pamphlets but shook his head. "Can't believe you, George. How can you think of going to the Wild West? They don't play cricket there. That's what makes it wild, you know."

G. B. peered at him over the top of *The Times*. "Don't think it's quite as wild as China. Although there are a number of Chinamen there, too—went out to work on the railroad and in the mines, I take it."

Kynaston started. What was George saying? How did he know of Kynaston's desire to go to China? Surely he had told only Hilda. He looked across the room, but Hoste seemed thoroughly involved in his own reading. "How—," he began, realizing his face must have drained white.

His brother was still looking at him. "Don't worry, Kinny. I won't say anything in front of Mama."

"But how did you know?"

George's gentle, concerned expression turned to amusement. "Transparent, you are. I've known for months—see it in your eyes every time someone mentions C.I.M. Suppose I recognize it because I feel the same way about California."

Kynaston was still too shocked to speak. "George—"

G. B.'s hand rested briefly on his shoulder. "Not easy being the oldest. Duty to be done and all that. I pray for you." He returned to his paper.

Kynaston shook his head. George was the best of brothers. The quiet one. The steady one. Always caring, always gently humorous. Trouble was, one tended to forget he was there except on the cricket field. It seemed that the boyhood interest they had all shared of reading cowboy and Indian books had grown into a spiritual call, and George had said nothing... And all this time G. B. had seen Kynaston's own struggles...and had been praying for him...

His thoughts were interrupted when the butler opened the door. "Mr. Hoste, sir."

William, sitting on the sofa before the window, jumped to his feet. "Yes?"

Then it was apparent that Jameson wasn't addressing Mr. William Hoste. He was announcing the arrival of Mr. Dixon Hoste.

Dick strode in, his head up, his face glowing. He crossed the room in three strides and clasped his brother's hand. "Father gave his permission."

Willie blinked. "Dick? What are you doing here? How did you find me?"

Dick grinned from ear to ear and pumped his brother's hand up and down. "Went to Cambridge first. Chased you all the way here. Had to tell you in person."

William shook his head. "I've never seen anything like it, Dick. You were always so shy and retiring. You—you're on fire with this."

Dick Hoste gave a shout of laughter and threw up his hands. "I've never seen anything like it either. Never even imagined such a thing was possible. And it gets better all the time. Every morning I wake up, and life—the world—God—everything is brighter than the day before. I keep thinking the bubble will burst, that I'll go back to being my old dissatisfied self, but I don't."

Still shaking his head, Willie returned his smile. "So what now?" He looked at his brother's civilian clothing. "You haven't resigned yet, have you?"

"No. Just took two days' leave. Must get back—drills, inspections, all that. Spit-spot and shipshape, so to speak. But I am thinking most seriously about that China Inland Mission material you sent." He raised one curving eyebrow and cocked his head. "Send more along anytime."

Mrs. Studd came in with a rustle of her crisp, black taffeta dress, the ruffles around neck and wrists edged in white to emphasize her perfect grooming, her small-brimmed, high-crowned black hat in the up-to-the-minute fashion. "Come along now. We must leave this minute. It wouldn't do for dear Charles to think his family slacking in their support."

G. B. greeted his mother with a peck on her cheek. "Don't worry, Mama. No one could possibly accuse you of being less than attentive to your brood."

"I should think not." Mrs. Studd pulled on her lace gloves. Then she sighed. "But I do hope Charles has remembered to get a haircut. I wouldn't want him looking like he's gone native. I trust he had the proper things to eat in Australia. Do you think they have good roast beef there? I'm certain they wouldn't have Yorkshire pudding to the standard he's used to. It's so important that the batter be beaten until all the flour lumps are rubbed down." She turned to the butler holding the door for her. "Jameson, be certain Cook has the pudding baked as soon as the roast is done so it can go directly on top of it. So much better when the pudding can absorb all the juices."

She exited with a swish of her skirts, her sons and their friends following her.

Even with Mrs. Studd's best efforts, however, Waterloo Station was already crowded with enthusiastic welcomers by the time they arrived. A small but loud brass band played energetically, its notes echoing from the metal railings, high glass ceiling, and concrete platforms. Kynaston escorted his mother nearer to the bunting-draped rostrum where the welcoming speeches would be given—no easy task in the happy, milling throng.

They had no sooner found a place than the train steamed in with a rush of power, exhaling a great cloud of white vapor. The band boomed louder, the crowd cheered, and the eleven greatest cricketers in the world, wearing white flannels and striped blazers and caps, made their way, waving and smiling, to the platform. Kynaston felt his face stretching with the width of his smile and his hands stinging with the fervor of his applause.

The Hon. Ivo Bligh, team leader, stepped forward after the politicians and cricket officials had offered their public congratulations for the success of the tour, and most especially for soundly beating Australia in two matches out of three. In reply to the crowd's cheers, he raised his arm, revealing that he held a small silver urn.

Ivo Bligh's sleek blond mustache curled upward as he smiled, waiting for the cheers to subside. At last there was relative calm. "Perhaps there may be one or two of you present here who will remember a certain article in the *Sporting Times* last year." Laughter and calls of agreement met him. "It wasn't so much an article as an epitaph memorializing the death of English cricket." The band played three bars of a dirge, and the crowd booed good-naturedly.

The speaker grinned. "And then, more optimistically, *Punch* suggested we were setting out on a pilgrimage to recover the ashes." Now the crowd applauded.

"Well, we have done it!" Bligh brandished the silver urn. "Honor is avenged!"

When the cheers died down, Bligh continued. "After the third match—the outcome of which you know," he grinned, "some Melbourne ladies put some ashes into this urn and gave them to us. I'll read the inscription to you."

> *"When Ivo goes back with the Urn, the Urn,*
> *Studds, Steel, Read, and Tylecote return, return!*
> *The welkin will ring loud,*
> *The great crowd will feel proud*
> *Seeing Barlow and Bates with the Urn, the Urn,*
> *And the rest coming home with the Urn."*

"We thank our Australian friends."

Ivo Bligh bowed, and indeed the welkin did ring loud.

Young women dressed in charming white frocks with red and blue sashes hurried forward with flowers for each of the players. Kynaston noted that the one who presented C. T.'s bouquet was especially pretty. And he could see that the fact did not go unnoticed by C. T.

It was considerably later that the Studd party could gather outside the station in enough peace to speak to each other. Mrs. Studd hugged her son and chose not to let go of his arm. "My dear Charles, my dear, dear boy. We are so proud. But we have missed you so dreadfully. You must never go so far away from home again." She scrutinized his face. "I can see that you're dreadfully tired. I'm persuaded you haven't slept or eaten properly since you left home. You must come straight down to Tedworth with me, and we'll get you back to yourself again."

"No, Mother, I'm fine. Great. Never better."

"Oh, I'm certain you think that's true. But no one understands these things like a mother. You don't know how I've longed to have you back again." Still holding his arm, she leaned back to observe his attire. "What can you have been thinking of, Charles? These are your oldest flannels. I sent three new pair after you."

"Yes, Mama, but these are the most comfortable. Really, I had plenty. More than enough."

"Well, you must call in at your tailor before we go on to Tedworth. And shoes. You'll need several new pair, I know."

C. T. clapped a long, strong arm around his mother's shoulders and gently propelled her toward the gleaming Studd carriage. Before C. T. could get in himself, however, Kynaston caught his arm. "Charlie, I don't think you've met Willie's brother—Dixon Hoste."

C. T. offered his hand. "Oh yes, military, aren't you? What regiment?"

"Royal Artillery. For a few more months."

"Oh?"

The excited smile that Dick simply couldn't suppress lit his face. "Yes. Plan to resign soon. Going to the foreign field."

C. T. blinked as if not certain he'd heard him properly. "Oh. Well, best of good luck."

William stayed behind to see his brother off on the next train to Portsmouth and the Isle of Wight. When the family was alone in the carriage, C. T. shook his head. "Did he say foreign field? A Royal Artillery officer be a missionary? What a daft notion."

The usually quiet George spoke up. "Daft? I think it's the finest thing I've ever heard." He took a deep breath and then plunged. "Thinking of it myself."

Mrs. Studd cried out George's name in a strangled voice. Then she remained silent.

Kynaston held his breath. George had spoken the words he had long wanted to. And G. B. was right. Matters had gone on far too long. At first he was merely being thoughtful. But he was beginning to see his delay as cowardice. Surely he had overestimated the strength of his mother's reaction anyway. He would let George have his moment. Then Kynaston would speak out as well.

In the space of time it took the carriage to lurch over three ruts in the road approaching Waterloo Bridge, Mrs. Studd turned frozen white, then an alarming red. The choked words came out in jerks. "No. I shan't hear of it. I won't have any of my children going off to foreign parts." She gasped for breath, her hand on her chest as if she were having palpitations. "Having my dear Charlie in Australia was nearly more than I could bear. It would kill me to have to go through that again."

C. T. laughed and hugged her again. "Glad to know I was missed, Mama. But you needn't worry. Georgie is just kidding. He wouldn't do anything so nonsensical. And playing cricket is quite enough missionary effort for me."

He began outlining the prospects for his captaincy of the Cambridge Eleven for the coming season. But Kynaston couldn't give it his attention. So much for his idea of speaking of his own future. He would thoroughly upset his mother if he attempted such a thing right now. But what could he possibly do if she couldn't be brought around to the prospect of her sons going to the foreign field? The future seemed a locked door. Only one thing was certain. He must hold his tongue for the present.

Dixon Hoste, however, felt no such restrictions. Back on the Isle of Wight, he saw to it that he had the cleanest rifle, the whitest belt, the shiniest boots for every inspection. He kept his shooting to the highest mark and his men in sharpest order on parade. Now he had a far stronger motive to succeed than his own desire for advancement. Everyone in the regiment knew of his stand. With Jesus Christ as Captain and Leader, he could do no less than his best, for any slacking would be to let down far more than his own reputation.

And in every free moment he worked tirelessly, talking to his fellow officers, preaching to crowds of holidayers who gathered on the beach below the fort, and studying his Bible. And reading the material his brother continued to send him on the China Inland Mission. The more he read, the more his certainty grew. As did his admiration for the mission built almost single-handedly by the vision and devotion of one man against overwhelming odds. James Hudson Taylor, a Yorkshire lad of obscure origins, indifferent education, and miserable health, had dared the impossible for a purpose his contemporaries considered mad. And little by little, he and his coworkers were winning the respect of both Orientals and Westerners as they traveled throughout that vast, exotic land taking hardship and privation in their stride as they shared the love of Jesus.

Dick Hoste smiled. Here was his life's work.

At least his desire grew. At times he was certain. At others, doubts flooded in. Would he be right for the enormous task? Would the mission accept him, especially since he was such a new Christian? Should he take time to study for orders as William was doing? Or should he offer straight away?

At last, in his room after a particularly tiring day of leading his men in parade drill, rifle practice, and guard duty, he lit a lamp, fastened a new nib on his pen, and dipped it deeply.

Dear Sir:
I have for some time been thinking about offering myself for the China Inland Mission...

His carefully formed letters looked boyish on the stiff ivory paper.

In his reading and study during the past months, he had been impressed by the demanding standard of the apostle Peter's injunction: "If any man speak, let him speak as the oracles of God." The weight of such responsibility bore in upon Dick now as he sat in the wavering light, his pen poised above the ink pot. He had firmly resolved to pray and wait on God until he was sure of his leading before he took any action, whether preaching or letter-writing. Was he being so led now?

Surely the urgency he felt within himself, his enormous desire to follow this path, the joy he felt at the very thought of becoming a missionary—surely these were leadings of the Spirit.

He dipped his pen.

My time is just now very taken up with my duties. This must be my apology for asking whether I can see you on Friday or Saturday next. I have the honor to be, sir, your obedient servant, D E Hoste, Lieut. R A.

Willie's last letter had informed Dick that Hudson Taylor was back in England, holding conferences and recruiting new workers for the China mission. But Dick had no idea where Mr. Taylor was at present. His only option was to post his letter to the headquarters in London and await a response.

All week he fretted. How would his letter be received? Would Mr. Taylor even see it? Would Dixon be able to get leave to go to London? He spent much time pacing his room.

He stopped mid-pace and ran his fingers through his hair at the sound of a knock on his door. "Yes?" He regretted the impatience in his voice when his batsman entered. Dixon had concentrated much on reflecting kindness and Christian love to those around him. Especially his underlings.

"Er, sorry, sir. Daily orders. And post arrived late. Thought I should bring it right around." His orderly held out three letters.

"Yes, Friesen. Well done." Dick gave him a smile.

He turned first to the orders. Then groaned. Inspection of troops next weekend. All leave canceled. So much for following up on his letter this week.

He flung himself on his cot and tore open the top letter on his stack. He jerked to an upright position when he saw the letterhead: "China Inland Mission, Pyrland Road, Mildmay, North London." Then he settled back, deflated, as he skimmed to the signature: "Benjamin Broomhall." Mr. Taylor was in the north. He would read Mr. Hoste's letter on his return. Would Mr. Hoste care to inquire early in August?

All Dick's earlier shyness returned. Did the stiff formality of the letter imply his inquiry had been unacceptable? Was he being put off for a more final rejection by Hudson Taylor? Had he been above himself in thinking that an artillery officer would be a fine addition to the China mission's forces? Would he ever learn to wait properly on God's guidance?

Eighteen

T'ai-yuen Fu, Shansi, July 1883
"What the Lord blesses everywhere is not great knowledge, but great devotedness of heart to Himself." Harold Schofield lay his pen aside and rubbed his eyes. Even with the physical strength and ability to endure fatigue God had given him, Harold had to admit that he was working beyond his limits. That day, in addition to his regular duties, he had performed four very demanding operations. One man in particular he was deeply concerned about. He prayed that the Lord would add His healing touch, for Harold had done all he could do.

In nearly three years he had treated some 10,000 patients and performed almost 300 operations, but it was a drop of water in the ocean of need around him. *Please, Lord, let my appeal for more workers fall on willing ears.* He picked up his pen. "There are already eight American lady doctors in China. One American mission alone has five such ladies..."

What did he hear? Was that Libby with two-month-old Timothy? He crept to the door of the bedroom and peeked in. The pale light fell across the face of his wife and infant son. A lump rose in Harold's throat. They were so precious. And two-year-old Harold, Jr., on the cot beside them. *Thank You, God, for such richness of blessings.*

Harold returned to his desk. "The Christian life is a pouring out of ourselves as Christ poured Himself out for us. Prayer is a pouring out of our deepest desires before Jesus..."

He dropped his pen and bowed his head. *Oh, Lord, let me be poured out for China. And let my prayers be poured before You for revival in the universities of England and Scotland.*

Once more he wrote to the young people of Great Britain: "Be all that you have in your power to be. You can, with God's help, become almost anything as a Christian."

There it was again. Downstairs. Was someone trying to break into the house? Then quiet. *It must have been someone in the street.* Now what had he intended to write? Oh, yes. A line of personal testimony. "My health, my time, my all is a sacred trust from God to be used and improved for Him."

This time the knocking below was distinct. Harold hastily closed his appeal. "That God may speedily call some who read this appeal to work for China is my earnest prayer."

He picked up his candle and made his way down the narrow stairs, hurrying so that the increasingly insistent knocking wouldn't waken his wife and children. It must be an emergency or the porter would never admit anyone at this hour.

In the light of the wavering candle, Harold recognized Pao-ting Fu, who had accepted Christ at a street meeting only a few weeks before. The man leaned against the wall for support. "Cannot breathe. Cannot swallow."

Harold saw the thick bluish-white membrane in the man's throat. Diphtheria. He gave Pao-ting Fu his best medicines.

Pao-ting shook his head, his black queue bobbing from side to side. "No, Doctor, I stay here. You give medicines."

Harold was kind but firm. "No, I cannot let you stay here. Diphtheria is highly infectious. I cannot risk the lives of my other patients." Harold walked the man to the door and shut it behind him before going upstairs to his bed.

"Doctor Harold, Doctor Harold."

Harold jumped out of bed and groped for his slippers. He had slept later than he meant to. Apparently his assistant had already made the morning rounds of their inpatients.

Before the door was fully open, Miss Lancaster broke the

news. "Please come. We have had a death in the hospital." His assistant was pale and shaking.

"Oh, no." Harold pulled his blue Makwa jacket over his head. "That poor man with the abscess I operated on yesterday." He shook his head. "I was much afraid for him."

Even from outside the room, he noticed a foul smell from the stove-bed on which the body was lying. But as he approached the k'ang, he realized it was not his surgery patient. It was Pao-ting Fu. He must have sneaked back into the clinic after Harold sent him away.

Anxious to prevent infection of his other patients lying on the same stove-bed, Harold grasped the man's jacket and tugged him off the k'ang. As he did so, a cloud of body lice from Pao-ting Fu's clothing made Harold sneeze and choke.

One week later Harold Schofield could no longer ignore the fever, aches, and weakness he had struggled against for days. The doctor took to his own bed. His eyes were bleary, his circulation sluggish, his fingers spotted with gangrene. He had contracted a severe case of typhus from Pao-ting Fu.

Libby came in, barely able to control her concern. It had been years since Harold had been ill. He was noted for his robust physique and unflagging energy. It was Harold who took care of all others. "Tell me what to do for you, my dear. How can we nurse you?"

She carefully wrote down his directions—cold packs to the torso, elixir of aconite and quinine for fever... "And, Libby, I would like to see our little boy. Libby, lead them—the children—to Jesus *early*, for that is far above all. The highest of all knowledge is to know the love of Jesus."

Too choked to speak, she nodded as he continued. "And tell Mr. Taylor and the Council that these years in China have been the happiest of my life."

Elizabeth sent for Timothy Richard of the Baptist Missionary Society. Together they nursed Harold for six days. Thursday evening Timothy read the thermometer. "It's 106 degrees." He shook his head.

Libby reviewed her notes, although she knew them by heart. "Ten towels, wetted with ice water, for forty-five minutes." She set to work.

But the fever did not abate. "Surely we aren't going to give up hope?" Libby's eyes were wide, her throat hot and dry.

Richard spooned a mixture of brandy and milk into Harold's mouth. But the fever rose. 107 degrees. 108 degrees.

At 2:15 A.M. Harold Schofield opened his eyes. "Heaven at last. It is so beautiful." He closed his eyes.

In London Dixon Hoste mopped his brow in the muggy early August heat. At last Hudson Taylor had returned from the Keswick convention, and Dick had been able to get leave from his regiment. The meeting he had been anticipating and dreading for so long would finally take place.

"Mr. Taylor will be with you shortly, sir." Benjamin Broomhall ushered him in. "Would you care to take a seat in the parlor?" The secretary pushed open a heavy oak door. "Oh, Gertrude, my dear, I didn't realize you were in here."

Dixon, fresh from the dazzle of the London street, blinked as he stepped into the gentle light of the lace-curtained parlor. Then he blinked again at the sweetness of the smile from the petite girl on the piano bench. At first glance he thought her a child, but when Benjamin Broomhall presented his daughter to Dixon, he realized that, although no more than out of the schoolroom, Gertrude was a young lady.

"Would you think me terribly rude if I continued with my practice, Mr. Hoste?"

Her lips were so pink...her blue eyes so round...the way her blonde hair curled around her face... "Oh, I'm sorry. No, no. Please continue. It would give me great pleasure to hear you play. My sisters often do so." Feeling himself babbling, Dick took a chair that gave him the best view of the pianist.

"I wouldn't, but you see, we have a prayer gathering here

every Saturday evening, and I must play for them tonight." She turned to the keys. "Thy life was given for me; what can I give for thee?" The gentle musical question filled the air.

But Dixon Hoste wasn't following the music. One thought filled his mind as he looked at the vision before him. "I shall marry her one day."

He tried to argue with himself. It was nonsensical. He was just overwrought coming into such gentle sanctuary from the heat and traffic outside. Yet the thought remained. *One day...*

"Mr. Taylor will see you now."

Dick jumped at the secretary's entrance as if a call to arms had sounded in the middle of the night.

But once in Hudson Taylor's office there was no question of distractions. The fifty-one-year-old missionary came from behind a deeply cluttered desk to greet the prospective candidate. As they shook hands, Dick was aware of a steel-hardened firmness beneath the kind manner. Humor, intelligence, and assurance blended to exude a sense of the presence of Christ. Dick had thought himself perfectly prepared for this interview. He had awaited it for months. But now he was painfully aware of his youth, his impatience, his shyness.

"So you are interested in learning about service in China, Mr. Hoste?" Taylor sat in a chair across from Dick, a small man with deep-set eyes. His naturally sandy hair still showed streaks of the black dye he used in China, the front just grown out from having been shaved in native style.

"Yes, sir. I—" Dick didn't know what else to say.

"Then let me tell you that in all honesty I don't know of a more demanding life than that in inland China. It involves isolation, privation, exposure to the hostility of the people there, combined with the contempt of our own countrymen. If you have told others of your inquiry today, I'm sure you've experienced some of that already—shock if not outright mockery."

Dick smiled and nodded. "Yes, sir. But I still want—"

"And you know that we require Chinese dress and hairstyles of all our inland missionaries. To become Chinese to the Chinese is essential."

Dick suddenly felt out of place in his well-cut coat and fashionable sideburns and mustache. "I—er, yes, I know."

"How long have you been a Christian?"

"It will be a year this December. But I was raised in a Christian home." And at last Dick found his tongue as he told Hudson Taylor of his commitment at the Moody campaign, of his almost immediate desire to go to the foreign field and of his father's restraint.

"And you have your father's permission now?"

"Oh, yes. I would not be here if I hadn't."

Taylor nodded. "Yes, quite right. Without obedience to our earthly parents, we cannot practice obedience to our heavenly Father." Dick tried not to squirm as he felt Hudson Taylor observing him. But not observing the outward man. He felt Taylor looked inward to his heart.

"Yes." Taylor nodded at last. "I see you are deeply sincere. And your enthusiasm is much to be prized. But you are not yet ready for foreign service. Especially not in inland China. You must mature as a Christian first. Seek opportunities to gain experience in evangelism. Your beach services are a fine thing. Perhaps you could organize a Bible class to teach. When you are in London, come along to Pyrland Road and join our prayer meetings."

A grim shadow suddenly covered Taylor's face. He dropped his head momentarily, then looked up, white with hard-won control. "You must forgive me. We have recently received word... Perhaps you would care to come along Saturday next. It will be a memorial service. We have suffered a grievous loss—perhaps the finest man of his generation... "

It was several moments before Hudson Taylor was able to conclude the meeting. He gave some parting advice: "Give the new wine of the Spirit time to ripen."

Dick agreed to all Hudson Taylor said, but he could not help feeling abashed. He knew he was much in need of maturing, yet he had so much energy, such great desire for service. The silvery notes of the piano followed him out to the street.

All the way across London in the hansom cab, he relived every aspect of the interview. Much to his surprise, when he reached the station, he alighted with a bound, his heart light. Yes, he hated to wait, but one thing was overwhelmingly clear to him. He was more conscious than ever of the depth of his desire to go to China. It would all come about in God's time.

The Mildmay conference room was packed to overflowing for the memorial service for Harold Schofield. It would be many weeks, even months, before the full accounts could arrive by post, but the brief accounts sent from China by telegram told of the shock and grief Schofield's fellow missionaries felt and the enormous void his passing left on the field.

Benjamin Broomhall stood before the room of black-clad mourners and read the memorials. "'It was a privilege to witness the bright face, the joy and peace of his countenance, and the childlike trust in his Savior. He has reached the shining land, but we miss him sorely, and pray that the Divine Master will send someone filled with a like earnest spirit to carry on the work here.'" Broomhall lowered the small sheet of yellow paper. "That from Miss Lancaster who helped with his nursing at the last."

He picked up another. "This from a fellow-laborer in the field: 'We cannot realize he has really gone, that we shall never again hear his voice pleading so lovingly and earnestly with the Chinese.'"

"And Mrs. Schofield herself writes, 'His soul was filled with joy and peace, and his smile for the last day and a half was heavenly. It was a brightness not of earth, but a reflection of the Lord Himself. My husband lived much in the spirit of prayer.'"

And then Hudson Taylor, his diminutive form seeming stooped under the weight of loss, stood by the pulpit and opened his Bible. "A seed must fall into the ground and die before it can bear fruit. Dark though the way seems to us now, we must trust that Harold Schofield's death will bear much fruit.

"Upon whom shall his mantle fall? Surely there are others who stand in full view of earthly honors and emoluments, and are glad to make them a sacrifice to Christ for the extension of His kingdom.

"We pray that this life, so early terminated, may, by the blessing of God, prove to be His call to many, that not only the present breach may be filled, but that this work may be extended into other needy fields."

Dixon Hoste stood with the others and sang the song that had been sung a few weeks earlier at Harold Schofield's funeral in Shansi, China. "'Safe in the arms of Jesus...'" Dick followed the words, singing of the golden shore where night was o'er, but his mind was seeing clearly the very solid earthly shore of China where he knew his work would be.

Nineteen

C. T. smiled with satisfaction as the hansom cab from King's Cross Station rolled down Oxford Street toward Hyde Park Gardens. A shimmer of crystal frost lay over the park to his left, edging trees and bushes with silver as a December sun shone without warming. His mind skimmed back over the good times of parties and sports that had marked the beginning term of his last year at Cambridge. It couldn't have been better. And now Christmas at Tedworth—tomorrow the family would travel down to their Wiltshire home together.

He took a deep breath, filling his lungs with the invigorating frosty air. Life really couldn't be much better. Pity it couldn't go on like this forever. But he had no idea what he would do after he took his degree next June—other than playing cricket, of course. He supposed he might read for the bar. He didn't feel particularly motivated to be a barrister, but it would be something to do. However, there was really no need to do anything. Kinny would do all that needed doing about the family firm, and Tedworth offered all a fellow could want in the way of comfort, sport, and social position.

He thought of the great house now ready for Christmas—decked with garlands and bows, the smells of baking pies and steaming puddings. And balls at the other great homes in the neighborhood. He smiled at the remembered sound of swirling waltzes and clinking punch glasses. There had been some fine times in Australia. Of course, he would never be able to convince Kinny to indulge, but he might get Georgie to go with him.

As the cab turned up Cavendish Place, C. T. thought of the many Christmases when he and his brothers had gone home to Tedworth together from Eton. They held a contest to see who could catch the first glimpse of the house's palatial lines through the almost-bare branches of the copper beeches lining the lane. In his memory the mellow gray stone glowed softly; tall, symmetrical windows gleamed in their stately double rows running from the two-story pedimented columns in front, around the curving side wings, to the glassed-in loggia in the back. Yes, it would be good to be home.

His mind came back to his London surroundings as the rattling cab wheels were suddenly muffled by straw laid down thickly over the street. Someone must be sick. Probably old Mrs. Gerrard across the square. Ninety-five if she was a day.

The carriage had come to a full stop before the front portico, but there was no sign of life from the house. Then the door opened, and Jameson hurried down the front steps, his heavy eyebrows frowning in a forbidding look.

C. T. sprang down from the seat. "Where is everyone, Jameson? What's all this litter?" C. T. disliked having his plans disrupted.

"Doctor's orders, sir. So as not to disturb Mr. George."

"*George?* What's going on?" In irritation he rushed past the butler and bounded up the steps.

Inside, however, his irritation quickly changed to concern when he saw the frightened look on his mother's face as she came to meet him. "Charles, I'm so glad you're here. You can't imagine how it's been. There wasn't time to send a message."

He had never seen her handsome dark eyes look so hollow or so ringed with dark circles. "What is it? What's this about George?"

She shook her head. "We don't know for sure. Two days ago he didn't come down for breakfast. Russell found him in a stupor, soaked with sweat. Dr. Altman says—" She choked and her voice dropped. "He offers very little hope."

C. T. was too stunned to speak. Georgie? Taken by a fever?

So suddenly? What did "little hope" mean? Impossible. He had played cricket with G. B. less than a week ago.

"It's such a relief to have you home." His mother took his arm. "Such a comfort. I don't know what I'd do without you."

He gave her a quick hug. "Yes, Mama. I'll take care of everything." He looked at her maid standing nearby. "See that she rests, Ellen."

Frowning deeply, C. T. strode to his brother's room. Surely his mother exaggerated. She was always an over-careful parent, and more so since their father died. But C. T. had never found her to be given to actual hysteria.

At the end of the corridor, he saw Dr. Altman just entering G. B.'s room. Russell, George's man, stood at the foot of the bed, looking helpless.

Charles felt equally helpless as he stood by, watching the doctor examine his brother. It took only one look to see that their mother hadn't exaggerated. G. B. was seriously ill. His normally lively features were sunken in grayish skin that had been smooth and ruddy only a few days ago. The smallest of the three brothers, George now barely made a lump under the bedclothes. And he lay so still. Surely Charles wasn't too late?

Dr. Altman stood up, shaking his head. He turned to C. T. and took him to the side of the room. "Your brother is gravely ill. I've never seen a more virulent fever."

"But he will recover?" C. T. could not keep the question out of his voice. "He was always so healthy."

"We are doing all we can." The doctor opened his bag and took out a brown bottle stoppered with a tall cork. "I've prepared a new draught. See that he has one teaspoon of this every hour. Give him drops of water on his tongue—all he'll take." He turned to Russell. "Continue with the compresses of vinegar water on his forehead when he's hot, warm bricks at his feet when he chills as he is now."

"I'll stay with him." C. T. felt choked.

Dr. Altman nodded. "It is vital that he be nursed constantly. Do not let him throw his covers off. A chill would certainly be fatal. There are ropes by the bed. If he thrashes about in delirium, he may have to be restrained."

"You can count on me."

The doctor started toward the door, then turned back. "I know this is a praying household. I can commend nothing better." Dr. Altman left.

Apparently Russell saw C. T.'s knees go weak, for he pushed a chair under him before he crumpled. By the time the valet returned with fresh spoons, basin, and cloths, Charlie was himself again. "Thank you, Russell. Please tell my mother that George is resting and that I'm staying with him. Assure her she may rest easy."

"Very good, sir. Shall I relieve you later?"

"No. I'll stay the night." C. T. pulled the cork from the bottle and began the tricky business of forcing a few drops of the elixir between his brother's blue lips.

With all the traffic sounds muffled, the quiet in the room seemed eerily ominous as the hours dragged by. At first there was little time to think about anything but keeping the bricks warm, wringing out fresh cloths, and trying the best way to get his brother to take some water. But then the nursing became routine, and Charles had time to worry. It was unimaginable that George might not pull through this. And yet Dr. Altman had hardly been optimistic.

One heard of virulent fevers striking down vigorous people in the prime of life, but such accounts never seemed real. Death was something that happened at the end of a long, happy life— not to an athletic varsity man. Not to one's brother. The brother closest to him in age and affection.

George's gray, drawn face flushed with hot red spots on the cheeks, and he began moaning and thrashing about. C. T. removed the bricks, applied cold compresses, and fought to keep his brother covered. C. T. Studd was famous for his athletic prowess, but George's fevered strength nearly outdid him. Even if ordered by the doctor, however, Charlie could not imagine tying his brother down with ropes. He would hold him with his own arms as long as he could. *Please, God, let it be enough.*

And with that simple phrase C. T. Studd realized how long it had been since he had prayed about anything from his heart. Certainly he was regular enough at church services, never failed to repeat the entire liturgy with the congregation. But a prayer he really meant was a different matter.

Through the long, dark hours, C. T. Studd did the most serious thinking of his life. As all of life narrowed to the four walls of his brother's sickroom where George fought for his life, C. T. began to see life in its true perspective. What was the world really worth? What did all the honor, all the pleasure, all the riches he had so enjoyed really mean? What good was any of that to George now?

On the third day George was peaceful when Kynaston walked quietly into the room. He gave C. T. a questioning look. C. T. shook his head, then moved to the bench at the end of the bed so Kynaston could have the chair closer to George. Kynaston opened the Bible he carried. "'The Lord is my shepherd. I shall not want...'"

George opened his eyes. A shadow of a smile flickered across his face. Kynaston read on to the end of the psalm, then bowed his head, and prayed quietly. And C. T. saw so clearly he almost gasped. That was it. That was all that was really important. All George cared about was the Bible and the Lord Jesus Christ. That was all that mattered.

C. T. looked at Kynaston and compared their two lives at university. C. T. knew that he was recognized as a Christian, but he had never led another to Christ. His religion was effete, mincing, cold. In contrast, he had often heard their cricketing friends call Kynaston "the austere man" because his life was true to God. And Kynaston was faithful to their friends in speaking to them about their souls.

Charlie had experienced that himself. It was only by the influence of Kynaston's courage and loyalty to the Lord Jesus Christ that C. T. had been kept from utter betrayal of his convictions. But he could not live forever on his brothers' spiritual strength. He had always been convinced of the truth of the Scriptures. Now it was time he acted on them.

Charlie left his brothers together and went to his own room. The fire had gone out, and the floor was winter-chilled as he slipped to his knees. But a short time later he rose, glowing with warmth.

Ten days later when the church bells across London rang in the new year, George sat up, as pale as the cushions that propped him, but smiling. Mrs. Studd bustled in, followed by her younger children, their faces rosy from walking through the frosty air after midnight service. Mrs. Studd engulfed George in a hug. "My dear boy, my dear, dear boy. God has restored you to life."

Across the room Kynaston turned to C. T. and clasped his hand. "And you, too, I think."

As he gripped his brother's hand and the bells pealed, C. T. knew that his life had changed. He had always been intensely single-minded. And now he would be as single-minded for Christ as he had been for cricket. He felt an exhilaration at the very thought. All the energy that he had formerly put into sport for a fleeting moment of glory, he would now put into things that would last for eternity.

He couldn't wait to start. Moody was returning to England and would be starting his London campaign in a few weeks. C. T. would take all his friends. He would go into the cricket field and help the men there to know the Lord Jesus. Yes, he would begin now. What better time? He spun around and took two long strides toward the door, then stopped, grinning foolishly. There would be no one on the cricket field at 12:30 on New Year's Eve.

Twenty

The Earl of Shaftesbury will sit to Lady Beauchamp's right. See to it that the candles are arranged so they will not glare in his eyes and be certain Cook does not put too much pepper in the soup." Hilda walked around the long mahogany table, checking the gleam of the china and crystal, touching each place card with the tip of her finger as she mentally checked the arrangement.

At the head of the table she paused. Talley, following her, obediently waited while she considered. Monty, of course, would serve as host. If she put Ida, as the next ranking lady, to his right, that would put her sister next to Kynaston Studd. But if she put Ida to the right of the earl, then she herself could sit next to Kynaston. But all would know—at least suspect—she had set the cards. And she could not bear the thought that anyone would think she was throwing herself at Mr. Studd.

She handed the card to the butler. "Miss Ida between my brother and Mr. Kynaston Studd. You may see to the rest."

She reached out with an impetuous gesture to straighten a taper in one of the branched candelabra lining the table. The candle slipped from her fingers and fell to the table, knocking over a long-stemmed crystal goblet. "Oh, see to it, Talley."

She turned so fast, the navy blue fringe edging the bustle of her ivory silk gown swished against her wrist as she hurried from the room. Hilda hadn't seen Kynaston Studd for months, and yet she found he was rarely far from her thoughts no matter what her activity. Working at the flower girl mission she thought of Lizzie and cricket—with Kynaston. Seeing a policeman while walking down a London street would bring back memories of visiting Pentonville— with Kynaston. Every mention of Mr. Moody, and his name seemed to be on every tongue in London, put her mentally on Marine Parade or in the Dome at Brighton—with Kynaston.

Hilda was halfway up the broad, dark-banistered stairway when Tottie blew in through the front door with a gust of March wind. "Oh, Hilda, you can have no notion what an invigorating ride I've had." She pulled off her white gloves and handed them with her crop to Talley who had emerged hurriedly from the din- ing room. "Mr. Robinson-Douglas is by far the finest rider of my acquaintance."

Hilda laughed, her own confused emotions soothed by her twin's radiance. "And I'm sure there could be no higher recom- mendation from you, Tot. I'm glad you've had such a pleasant afternoon. But do you know where Ida is? I haven't seen her all day, and we must dress for dinner. I hope she remembers we're dining early tonight so we can get good seats at St. Pancras to hear Mr. Moody. You didn't forget, did you, Tot? Is Mr. Robinson-Douglas coming to the campaign?"

Tottie hurried up the stairs to take Hilda's arm. Laughing, she ticked off her answers on her fingers. "Yes, I could recommend no one higher than Mr. R-D—for riding or for anything else I can think of. Yes, I remembered about our dinner, or I shouldn't be home now. Yes, Mr. Robinson-Douglas and his sisters will all be at St. Pancras. They heard Mr. Moody in Edinburgh and are most anxious to hear him again. Er—what else did you ask?"

"Ida. Where can she be?"

"Oh, yes, I wondered, too. We met Captain Lowe on Rotten Row, and he inquired after her. Perhaps you can persuade her to go riding with me tomorrow. She always listens to you. I'm cer- tain the dashing captain will be there again in all his gold braid, and Ida looks very fine on a horse."

Hilda crossed the room and picked up an ornate silver mir- ror to check the flowers and ribbons adorning the back of her upswept hair. "I shall certainly mention it to her, but I've no faith in my powers of persuasion with Ida."

Constance laughed and pulled the bell cord for their maid. "What are you talking about, Hilda? Ida does everything you tell her."

Hilda was not certain that she found that thought comforting. "Well, I shall tell her to go riding tomorrow if I see her. Where could she possibly have gone?"

At that moment Daisy entered with a curtsy. "Miss Ida? She said I was to tell you if anyone asked for her. She is helping Mr. Studd with a meeting in Hyde Park."

Hilda dropped to her dressing table bench as if she'd been hit in the stomach. Ida had been out with Kynaston all day? Working at an open-air? And no one had invited her? Or even told her about it?

With a stiff force of will, she straightened her back and lifted her chin. Of course, there was no reason Ida shouldn't help at all the street meetings she chose to. And Mr. Kynaston Studd could certainly hold as many open-airs with whomever he chose…. But the pain was so intense Hilda could hardly breathe.

At that moment Ida came in, her cheeks flushed, her soft curls shining, her pale green and yellow dress looking like daffodils scattered across a park. Hilda had never seen her sister look happier.

"Oh, it was lovely. So many strollers by Marble Arch. And so many stopped to listen. Stanley Smith can really hold a crowd. And Algernon Dudley Ryder was there. He is so direct on calling people to come out—" She looked up as their mother entered the room.

"Oh, were you with the Earl of Harrowby's son this afternoon, Ida? I remember his father when he was Lord Sandon. Very active in carrying on the work of William Wilberforce, their family was—but that was before my time. Very gratifying to know the family is still working for good." She looked through the clutter of ribbons and lace bows on the dresser and then picked up the fan she had come for. "Constance, dear, come help me choose which dress I should wear tonight. I believe the earl would like my dark purple silk, but perhaps black would be best for going on to the campaign."

When they were gone, Ida continued as Daisy readied her for dinner. "We sang three hymns while the crowd gathered. There were so many because it was such a lovely day. One lady, very finely dressed, gave her name and address. Mr. Ryder invited her to attend his chapel in Brunswick Mews. And another gentleman...Hilda, are you listening?"

"Yes, of course I am. It is most gratifying to hear that Stanley Smith is so courageous for the faith."

"Oh, yes, he's simply radiant. And so vigorous. It seems strange now to recall how weak he used to be—in body and in spirit." Ida sighed. "Oh, but you really should have seen Kynaston. So handsome standing beneath the Achilles statue in his tall silk hat and tight frock coat. You really should have come, Hilda."

Hilda tossed her hand mirror on the dressing table, knocking the silver stopper out of a perfume bottle. "Oh, that's a fine thing for you to say. And who would see to matters here if I went off gallivanting as you did?"

Ida looked hurt. "I thought you'd be pleased, Hilda. You always told me I should get out more...and pay more attention to Kynaston Studd." She ducked her head and smiled shyly. "And he *is* terribly nice, isn't he?"

Hilda's voice was tight. "Yes. He is."

"And so very handsome." The comment was almost swallowed by the sigh that followed. "I do hope—"

"Ida, stop acting like a schoolgirl." This time Hilda made no attempt to keep the irritation out of her voice.

"Is Reginald at Langley?"

Hilda blinked at her sister's non sequitur. "Yes, I believe Violet is quite near her time. The heir must, of course, be born at Langley." She turned to her sister with a frown. "But why should you ask about our brother's whereabouts?"

Ida fiddled with a lace-edged handkerchief as the maid expertly arranged her hair with intertwined lace and pearls. "You may add the silk rosebuds, too, Daisy." Then she looked at Hilda. "Kynaston asked me where Reggie is. Three times. As if he wanted to make very certain. He must have something most particular to speak to our brother about."

Daisy finished Ida's hair and handed her a crystal atomizer. Ida squeezed the silk-covered bulb three times and then drifted from the room smelling like the spring air.

But Hilda stood frozen. "Leave it," she ordered Daisy, who had begun picking up the clutter in the room. Even when she was alone, Hilda continued to stand like a statue. She could think of only one reason a young man would wish to speak to the head of the family of a marriageable young woman.

Kynaston Studd wanted permission to ask for Ida's hand in marriage—an offer Ida would obviously accept. And Hilda had virtually thrown them together. In so doing she had thrown away her own happiness.

Vaguely, in the back of her mind, Hilda knew she should be downstairs. Their guests would be arriving any moment—probably were right now. But she couldn't move. She who once thought she could manage anything, could do nothing.

She glanced toward the tall pier glass in the corner, but it stood at such an angle that she couldn't see her own reflection. What a perfect image. She was nothing. All her efforts were futile. She was incapable of achieving anything by her own power. She felt completely empty.

At last she moved woodenly toward the door. As she descended the stairs, she was concerned to find no guests gathering in the hall. With considerable embarrassment Hilda discovered everyone already seated at the table. She slipped in as unobtrusively as possible and made her apology to her mother and their honored guest.

"That is quite all right, my dear. I told Talley he might serve the soup." Lady Beauchamp signaled a footman to bring Hilda's plate. "The earl was just telling me of Mr. Moody's first campaign in London."

Hilda smiled at the tall, gauntly thin man who was often referred to as "the poor man's earl." His entire fortune and energy had been dedicated to helping England's unfortunate poor in the name of Jesus Christ. He was well into his eighties now, but his voice was still firm.

"Yes, almost ten years ago that was." Shaftesbury picked up the strain of his story. "I had been very surprised not to be asked to serve on a committee or to lend my support, and I was much concerned at first, because judging from the newspaper accounts, I did not believe Mr. Moody preached Christ crucified, but only some shallow, popular form of Christianity."

The first course was removed, and a delicate sole in fennel sauce was set before them. The earl took a bite, then continued. "I went for the first time on Good Friday and found that, indeed, they preached the whole Gospel, and very forcefully. Most forceful, I believe I could say, because of the imperfection of the whole thing. Sankey's song was so simple. Moody's voice was bad and his language colloquial. And his anecdotes..." The earl shook his head. "I don't wish to discomfort you, Lady Beauchamp, but I must say that some bordered on the humorous almost to the extent of provoking laughter."

"And yet the result was effective, I believe, sir."

"Oh, strikingly so. I have often said since that England has little idea what she owes to Mr. Moody, both in the standard his campaigns set of *reality* in religion and in the men and women whom they influenced." He paused, his eyes down, as if looking inward. "The Holy Spirit can work out of feeble materials, indeed. I never cease to be amazed at what He can do out of a life wholly yielded to Him. The longer I live, the more I believe that submission is all."

As the next course of roast lamb with mint sauce, tiny boiled potatoes, asparagus Hollandaise, potatoes rissoles, and stewed compote was served, Hilda realized she had rested quite long enough on her mother's conversation. She turned to C. T. Studd. "And is your brother quite recovered, Mr. Studd?"

Hilda had always known Charlie to be charming and enthusiastic for whatever he was giving his mind to, but she was quite bowled over at the warmth of his reply. "George has made a remarkable—I can only say miraculous—recovery. And I must tell you, Miss Hilda, the most wonderful thing has come about. I've been having the most marvelous time since then."

Hilda smiled. "Oh, forgive me. I didn't realize the cricket season had started yet."

C. T.'s smile widened even more. "No, even better than cricket. The greatest joy I guess a person can have—the Lord allowed me to lead a fellow to Him just yesterday." He paused and took a sip of lemoned water. "First time. I never knew such a thrill was possible. I want to spend my whole life doing nothing else. And George is talking of going to the foreign field—that is, if you call California foreign."

A debate ensued over the question. In the end, Lady Beauchamp concluded in her soft voice, with a little shake of her head, "What an honor it would be to have a child of one's own called to be a missionary."

In the silence that followed, Hilda turned back to C. T. "And now you're helping with the Moody campaign?"

"Good thing it's the Easter vacation. I couldn't stay away from Moody, and my tutor wouldn't think much of my missing too many lectures. I've talked to most of the England Eleven. Bligh has promised to come. Webbe and Steel, too. Tonight, I hope."

Ida looked up from across the table. Hilda had carefully avoided looking that way as she did not want to encounter Kynaston Studd's eyes. "Oh, yes, we must get there early. Did I tell you I had a letter from Alice Polhill-Turner? She and her brothers will be there tonight as well."

Kynaston turned to Ida with such obvious delight that Hilda jabbed her fork at her plate, shattering the meringue. "Both brothers? *Cecil* is coming to hear Moody, too? That's wonderful."

Ida nodded. "Yes, isn't it! Alice said that Cecil spent his Christmas holiday in Germany with his uncle, Baron somebody-or-other. He's British Resident at the court of Württemberg. Something like that."

"One who made Cecil his heir?" Monty was leaning back in his chair, his arms slack, his eyes half-closed, but he came to attention at Ida's news.

"Alice said the uncle went all out to show Cecil a good

time—the opera, balls, dinners, but all the time what he really had on his mind was what Arthur had said to him about Jesus Christ. Cecil always argued hotly with Arthur when he would try to talk to him about matters of faith. But now he admits he knew Arthur was right all along."

"You mean he's accepted Christ?" Now Montague was leaning forward.

Ida smiled. "He said he made up his mind by the time he got off the train at Bedford. Of course, his uncle will probably disown him—quite a vast fortune, I take it—but it doesn't make the least difference to him."

"Quite right." C. T. nodded vigorously.

Lady Beauchamp signaled Talley to remove the cheese board. A footman stepped forward and helped her with her chair. "I am sorry to rush us, but I do think we should be going. There's always such a crush of carriages around St. Pancras."

Hilda couldn't help but note the alacrity with which Kynaston rose and helped Ida with her chair, offering his arm to escort her to the carriage.

Had C. T. not been holding the back of Hilda's chair for her, she would not have risen. She had mechanically placed her hand on the arm he offered and started to follow the others into the hall when she heard Monty say, "You going to Langley tomorrow, Kinny? Go with you if you like."

Hilda didn't wait to hear Kynaston's reply. She had no desire to see the warm look that would pass between him and Ida. "Excuse me," she mumbled and dropped C. T.'s arm. "Dreadfully sorry to miss Mr. Moody, but I seem to have the most severe headache." She turned and fled from the room.

"Ida, close that curtain." Hilda sat up in bed with a scowl the next morning and looked at her sister, who stood by the open window. Fresh air, sunshine, and birdsong were flooding into the room. "Whatever are you thinking of? We'll all catch our death of cold."

Ida spun around and held her arms out, looking delicate

and lovely in her smocked white nightdress. "Oh, Hilda, aren't you feeling better? I'm so sorry you missed the service last night. The most remarkable thing happened. Some old vicar who was sitting on the platform—no one ever did get his name—started to pray after the choir sang. And he prayed and he prayed and he prayed. I quite thought I'd drop, as we were all standing up. You can't believe how long he went on—hours it seemed. We were all suffocating. I even saw a young man who had come in late start to leave.

"Mr. Moody must have seen it, too, because he spoke out in his loud American voice—right while the man was praying—and said, 'Let us sing a hymn while our brother finishes praying.'

"We were well into the second verse before the man ended his prayer," she finished with a peal of laughter.

"And the young man—did he leave?"

"No, he stayed. And a good thing, too. He seemed much moved."

Tottie, who had already finished her breakfast, came in. "Ida, aren't you dressed yet? Captain Lowe will have finished his ride if you don't hurry. He really is most striking in his red and black Guards uniform."

Hilda burrowed deeper under her covers. "Ida, close the window."

During the next few days, Hilda saw steadfastly to her duties at home and at the mission and attempted to hold the rest of the world at bay. But isolation was impossible. Activity whirled around her. Monty came back the next day from Langley with a fine report of their brother and the nearing arrival of his first child. Then he and Stanley Smith were off with Arthur Polhill-Turner to visit Cecil at his regiment, now moved to Aldershot just southwest of London, and help him invite his fellow officers to hear Moody. She heard reports of the success of the London campaign and of the auxiliary meetings that C. T., G. B., and J. E. K. Studd were holding. And Ida's chatter rang constantly in her ears. What had happened to the mousy sister that would do nothing but hide in her room and read sermons? Now it seemed Hilda was the one hiding in her room.

But Ida always sought her out. If she wasn't talking about Captain Lowe, she was talking about Kynaston Studd. "And then after a most moving address, Kynaston asked all those who intended following Christ to stand up. It seemed a very sensible question, but nobody stood.

"Then one boy way down front—a sailor, I think—stood up. Then that young man I told you about who almost left when the old vicar prayed so long—you remember, the night you had your headache?"

Hilda nodded. Her head was aching again.

"Well, that same one stood up. Monty talked to him afterwards. His name's Wilfred Grenfell. He's a medical student, and now he's thinking of becoming a missionary." Ida spun round and round, hugging herself. "Oh, Hilda, isn't life beautiful!"

Twenty-one

B y mid-May most of the daffodils had faded in Langley Park. Lady Violet had been delivered of a beautiful baby girl whom they christened Sheila Ginevra Hilda Mary. Then Reggie accompanied his wife to the home of the Earl of Roden so that the exquisite Sheila Ginevra might get properly acquainted with her maternal grandparents.

Once again Hilda was awaiting the arrival of Monty and his friends—but not with any of the anticipation she had felt three years earlier. This time the tables were turned, and Ida was pushing her.

"But it's a perfect day for tea on the lawn, Hilda. There won't be enough for croquet without you. And it will look so unfriendly if you don't come down." Hilda blanched at Ida's words. Had she used an almost identical argument on her sister? Had Ida felt as unhappy at being pushed and maneuvered as she felt now? If she had understood, surely she would have been less demanding on those around her. But Ida's reclusive inclinations had sprung from opposite motives. At that time Ida had felt too little for Kynaston Studd. Now Hilda felt too much. If only the situations could be reversed.

The sound of carriage wheels crunching on the gravel below came in through their open second-story window. Ida looked out. "Oh, they're here. I'll greet them, Hilda. But you must take over when Captain Lowe arrives. He has a new hunter he's most anxious for Tottie and me to see."

Hilda followed her sister into the hallway. "Captain Lowe? Whatever is he doing here?"

Ida called over her shoulder without slowing her pace, "I told you last week his regiment was being moved to Wymondham. Really, Hilda, you are becoming much too absentminded."

"But Kynaston—Ida, you can't—" Her sister disappeared down the stairs. Hilda heard voices in the hall below and turned slowly back to her room. What could Ida be thinking of? Kynaston would be deeply wounded. Surely Ida was aware he had come to ask her to be his bride. After all, Ida was the one who had told Hilda he had come to Langley some time ago to ask Reginald's permission. She sat on the tufted window seat overlooking the park as she thought.

Knowing that facing facts would be less painful than the uncertainty, Hilda herself had asked Reginald if Mr. Studd had spoken to him. She closed her eyes against the memory. She had been holding her tiny namesake, clad in the same long white gown in which Hilda herself had been christened. Reggie's answer had been abstractedly offhand. "What? Oh, Studd? Oh, yes, yes, he was here. Fine fellow."

"Reginald! What did you answer him?"

Reggie had looked startled that she could ask. As he doubtless was. "Gave my blessing, of course. What did you think?" Then the vicar had arrived, and they went in for the service.

Now she drew a deep breath to steady herself. She must not think of her own pain. She must think of Kynaston's if Ida's unthinking departure with Tottie's friend should spoil his careful plans. She couldn't let that happen.

She glanced casually out her window. Then she gave the scene in the park her full attention. Was that a flash of red? The red of a Grenadier Guard's jacket?

Yes. There was no mistaking the rider approaching below on the high-spirited horse. She must do something. She must soften the blow somehow. Kynaston must not be left thinking Ida preferred the company of a dashing officer to that of the man who had come to ask for her hand in marriage. But what could she do? At the very least she could distract Kynaston by talking to him.

And then she knew. She turned and fled down the hall as

the plan formed in her mind. She would prevent Lowe from getting to Ida. She felt the sweet pain of her own love for Kynaston and knew he felt the same for Ida. Hilda also knew her own strength. She knew she could endure the pain of losing Kynaston far better than she could bear seeing his pain.

She must reach Lowe before he reached Ida. She would flirt with him outrageously. Her feet found the stairs, and she sped downward, the smooth satin of the banister slipping under her hand. No, she wouldn't flirt with Lowe. She would tell him her own horse was ill—lame—something—that he must come at once to advise her. She stumbled on a step. Yes, then she would feign a sprained ankle. Common courtesy would require him to help her to the house. Or perhaps it would be better to wheedle Lowe into going riding with her—a long ride through the park. No—across the countryside. Kynaston would likely invite Ida to walk in the park to make his proposal. The pain of the thought was so sharp Hilda couldn't breathe, and yet she hurried forward.

Pity she couldn't reach Lowe by going around the back, but that would take far too long. To have any hope of reaching him first, she must go the most direct route—straight across the lawn. Past the three sitting there over tea and cakes in the May sunshine.

She fully realized she would be making a spectacle of herself. And yet she was perfectly willing to do so. She had never been so aware of her love for Kynaston as at this moment when all her half-formed dreams were about to be taken from her forever. And yet it was not her own unhappiness she thought of, but his.

As she followed the gravel walk toward the group sitting around the linen-draped table on the lawn, she saw the red-coated rider out of the corner of her eye. He dismounted at the stable and gave his reins to the groom. He was walking this way. It would be a race to the finish. She lifted her skirt and stepped onto the grass, all but breaking into a run.

"Hullo, Hilda," Monty called.

Kynaston stood to greet her. She saw the light in his eyes, his sweet smile. She could not bear to see that quenched in pain.

But at the same moment, Ida turned in her seat to extend her hand to the officer. Hilda was too late.

In confusion she turned toward Kynaston and held her hand out to him—and felt herself flying through the air as her foot caught in a croquet wicket.

Kynaston caught her before she reached the ground. Even as she turned in his arms, she saw Captain Lowe bowing over Ida's hand. Well, there was nothing like making a fool of herself. But at least she had succeeded in distracting Kynaston.

She made a confused apology and was glad Kynaston stayed by her while Lowe chatted with Monty, refused a cup of tea, and took Ida off to see his horse. "Like to see it myself." Monty jumped up, leaving a half-eaten Florentine on his plate—which Hilda knew to be his favorite sweet. She frowned at his disappearing back. What was Monty's rush?

"Are you all right, Hilda?" She turned at Kynaston's voice, soft with concern beside her.

"Oh, yes—quite."

"Ankle all right?"

"Yes. Yes, fine. Er—" She took the seat vacated by Ida. "Um, may I warm your tea?" This was ridiculous. She had never had trouble talking to Kynaston. And he was so quiet. She must have failed in her attempt to spare him pain. She looked now and saw the shadow of worry in his eyes.

She offered him her most cheerful, if forced, smile with his tea. But he didn't even see the cup as he leaned toward her. "I'm glad they're gone, Hilda. I had hoped for a chance to talk to you alone."

"You did?" She was so surprised, the tea sloshed into the saucer. She set it down in front of him with a clatter.

But he was quiet, as if he didn't know what to say. Surely he didn't mean to talk to her about proposing to Ida? What could she suggest as a topic of conversation? Cricket? University? Open-airs? Lady Beauchamp had schooled her daughters well in the social arts. Hilda couldn't believe her training had deserted her. "Er—what do you hear of Mr. Moody?"

"Wonderful results in London. C. T. has seen almost all his

cricket friends accept Christ there. The London campaign will end next month, and Moody will return to America. He has invited me to go to America to work with him there—speak at some of their universities and conferences...."

"Oh, Kynaston, that's wonderful!" But as soon as the words were out of her mouth, she bit her lip. Was it wonderful? Ida might have refused to go to China. She wouldn't refuse America.

And with the thought, Hilda realized the true strength of her feelings. For all she had argued against his going to China, she knew now that her feelings for him were strong enough that she would go anywhere—even to China with him.

And then she saw that her outburst had made Kynaston look more confused. "I don't know. I would like to go, of course. But—"

"It's still China?"

He shook his head despairingly. She had never seen him look more miserable. He took a paper from his pocket. "Read this—it's Harold Schofield's 'Appeal for Medical Missionaries.' He wrote it just before he died. And with his death the need is greater than ever. And yet—" He paused. "I don't know. There are so many obstacles. Why doesn't the way open if it's the right thing?"

"Have you talked to Mr. Taylor?" She pushed her own problems aside to focus on his.

Kynaston nodded. "I've been to several Saturday night prayer meetings at Mildmay with Dick Hoste. He has resigned his commission in the Gunners and is spending all the time he can helping Moody. He is absolutely determined on China."

Hilda nodded, happy to hear him talk, although she could see that recounting the progress he found all around him did little to lighten Kynaston's load. "William Cassels is talking about going to China. He's been to the Church Missionary Society, but they only work in the treaty ports. Cassels feels more interest in inland work." He paused.

"And Smith?"

"Smith has been interviewed by the C.I.M. council and accepted."

"Stanley Smith? But I thought he felt direct leading that he was not to go to the foreign field."

Now Kynaston lost much of his own discouragement in talking about his friend. "Hasn't Monty told you? The Lord gave Smith Isaiah 49:6, 'I will also give thee for a light to the Gentiles, that thou mayest be my salvation unto the end of the earth,' as a release from the earlier Scripture.

"In March Mrs. Smith invited Taylor to dinner in John Street. Taylor even led in family prayers. Smith interviewed with the China Inland Mission Council last month and was accepted."

Hilda clasped her hands to her chest. "Oh, that's wonderful! So Hoste and Smith will both be going to China—with their families' approval." She saw the hurt in his eyes and had to grip the edge of the table to keep from reaching out to him. "Oh, Kynaston—" She swallowed to cover the fact that she had almost called him dear. "Kynaston, do not lose heart. The way will open for you. It must. You would be superb. Surely this is just a testing of your faith. The way will open for you as it has for Stanley Smith."

Now he was the one who reached across and grasped her hands. "Hilda? Do you mean—is it possible? Are you in agreement with me?"

How did she feel about China? In the face of more pressing concerns, she had put the question out of her mind for some time. She knew little about China. But she did know that her overwhelming desire—her call if one wished to name it so—was to help Kynaston. *Even if in China?* her mind pressed her.

Did she love even Kynaston enough for that—to abandon all? Did she trust God enough? Even as she asked such questions, she knew there was only one answer. Her heart cried with Ruth, 'Whither thou goest, I will go.' And wherever that was, Hilda would help him with every ounce of strength within her. If only she were given the chance.

She took a deep breath and tried to make her answer detached...to sound as if her only concern was spiritual...sisterly even. "Of course. Your steadfastness and generosity, readiness to sacrifice self—" She might have succeeded had she not looked up at him, his furrowed brow, his intense eyes, his fine mouth.

She opened her mouth to continue, but no words would come out. She tried to nod, but the motion made the tears spill from her eyes.

And suddenly Kynaston was on his knees at her feet, offering her his handkerchief. "Hilda. My dear, dear Hilda." She accepted the linen square and dabbed at her eyes.

"And do I dare to hope you would accept my heart as well?" His hand covered hers that lay trembling in her lap.

Again all she could do was nod.

"Hilda, I have no right to ask you that when my future is so uncertain. You have no idea what you might be saying yes to. On reflection if you should find it more than you can face—"

"No!" At last she found her voice. She gripped his hand as if her life depended on it—as, indeed, it did. "The only thing I couldn't face would be going on without you."

He kissed her hand, then her lips. Then realizing how exposed they were to view, he pulled a chair over and sat very close beside her. They were sitting thus and talking when Ida and Monty returned. Hilda started. Ida. She had not once considered her sister's feelings. Her own joy told her how intense her pain would be were their positions reversed.

But it was too late. Ida stood there, observing them sitting side by side, Hilda's hand in Kynaston's. "Ida, I—" Hilda began.

"Oh!" Ida's face lit with delight. "Oh! How marvelous. How perfectly marvelous."

Hilda rose, embraced her sister, and moved just beyond the men's hearing. "Ida, such generosity is so like you. Thank you."

Ida looked confused. "Generosity? Oh, Hilda, you thought I wanted Mr. Studd for *myself?*"

"Of course. We talked so often… That is, you said…"

Ida smiled. "Well, I knew it was your idea at first that Kynaston and I should make a match. But it was so obvious when your own affection moved to him. So I thought I should get to know him better—to make him feel welcome in the family. It was perfectly obvious he never cared for anyone but you."

Hilda sank back onto her chair. "It wasn't obvious to me."

At last Montague bore Kynaston off just in time to catch the last train to Cambridge. And only when he was gone did Hilda's bliss waver. What did the future hold? She felt a prickle of fear. But no. They had each other. They had God. It would be all right. It had to be. She was determined.

Twenty-two

In spite of his joy over his betrothal to Hilda and their approaching December wedding, Kynaston became increasingly depressed during the summer of 1884.

And he was not alone in his feeling that the heavens were closed and all channels of divine guidance blocked. C. T., with his easy athletic grace, entered the morning room of the Studd home at 2 Hyde Park Gardens. He looked even more disheartened than Kynaston, who sat at the small writing desk making little progress on the matters his man of business had presented to him. And even C. T.'s natural elegance deserted him as he flung his long form into a chair and groaned. "I don't understand this. I was so happy in Christian work, speaking to my friends, bringing them to hear Moody. Now it's all over, and I have nothing to do with myself.

"I've been reading—God led the children of Israel through the desert with a pillar of cloud by day and a pillar of fire by night. I'm not even getting a spark." He bent over and put his head in his powerful hands. "Here it's just all desert. I feel so guilty to be in such a funk. Bligh, Webbe, Steel—they're all so happy in their newfound faith....I suppose I shouldn't be so focused on myself. But all my life I've known what I wanted to do, where I wanted to go. Now I've walked into a great void."

C. T. paused, and Kynaston realized his brother was waiting for him to offer help. The trouble was, all he could do was agree with Charlie.

The silence grew heavy in the room. C. T. leaned back in the floral upholstered chair again. "I know this sounds vain, but I do believe I have some small influence. Surely I could put it to work for the kingdom. What am I to do for the rest of my life?"

The demand was flung out with all the force of Charlie's frustration, and he emphasized it by hitting the arm of the chair. He thrust himself to his feet and began pacing the room, coming within inches of knocking a pair of china figurines from a shawl-draped drum table.

Suddenly C. T.'s face drained as ashen as his pale flannel lounge jacket. He half staggered to the hearth and leaned against the mantel for support.

Kynaston sprang to his feet, alarmed. "Charlie!" He grabbed his brother's elbow and helped him to the sofa. "You've worn yourself out over this. And little wonder. You never rested during the Moody campaign. Early morning prayer meetings, open-airs, two services a day, late every night in the inquiry room. I've heard you pacing the floor in the middle of the nights since then." On top of that he now realized how little he'd seen Charlie eat lately. "You've worn yourself out with work and worry."

"I don't mind the work—that's what I want. If God would just give me something to do. He made me strong. What's the good of it if I can't use it for Him?"

Kynaston shook his head. "You're asking the wrong person. Go to Tedworth. Walk in the fields, breathe the country air, read your Bible. Get your balance back."

Even as he spoke the words, and especially as C. T. grasped his hand in gratitude and acceptance of his advice, Kynaston felt like a hypocrite. How could he tell anyone what to do when he had no answers for himself? "Come on, I'll help you pack your bags. And take Russell with you. I don't think you should travel down alone." Kynaston picked up a book from his desk. "Here, take this. George got it from one of his American friends. Very popular there, they say." He handed Charlie a copy of *The Christian's Secret of a Happy Life.*

The activity of helping his brother and making arrangements with his manservant helped Kynaston through the next hours, but when C. T. was gone, his own darkness closed in on him. 'Not even a spark,' C. T. had said. Kynaston, back at his accounts, nodded at the memory. But one who *was* on fire was Stanley Smith. He had continued to blaze with a steady, hot flame ever since totally committing himself to God a year and a half ago. Kynaston felt warmed just being around him. Smith's final term of teaching would close in a few days. In the meantime he was holding missions in South Lambeth with William Cassels.

By all reports, Cassels's curacy in his working-class church was flourishing. Every Sunday pews, aisles, even chancel and pulpit steps overflowed with people. Three thousand children filled six Sunday schools. Kynaston toyed abstractedly with his pen for a few moments. Then he closed his ledger with a snap. He would join Smith at his mission. Perhaps he would find an answer there.

As soon as he emerged from the underground station, the heat and grime of a South Lambeth summer struck Kynaston. But Stanley Smith was as trim, fresh, and dynamic as ever. "Great you could join us, Studd. Always use another hand in the Lord's work." He set out along the crowded street at a pace even the athletic Kynaston had difficulty keeping up with.

Stanley's clear, perfectly modulated voice rang crisply above the clash of fishmongers, pie-sellers, and knife-sharpeners hawking their wares. "Holding an open-air on Clapham Common. Wonderful time last week at Aldershot. Met P.T.'s brother Cecil—he's there with his regiment. He gave us warm support. Arthur's still thinking of China. Wouldn't be surprised to see Cecil do the same, as much as he talked about it." He shook his sleek blond head. "Poor fellows though. Only support at home is their sister. Arthur said he tried to talk to their mother—unsatisfactory."

Stanley Smith led on toward the assigned meeting place for the mission workers, talking about his own plans to go to China. "C.I.M. Council has decided I should delay going out for a month or two. Want me to hold a series of farewells in the varsities. Start in Edinburgh as soon as I'm through at Newlands.

"Ah, there's Cassels." He waved to the stalwart, silent man in the clerical collar. "He's making great progress toward China.

Wouldn't be at all surprised if we go out together. Amazing how the Lord works, isn't it?"

Kynaston muttered agreement and turned to greet the other workers, but already he could see that his idea in coming here had not been a good one. His own blindness seemed the darker when with friends who were walking in blazing light.

At least his dejection didn't dampen the mission. By the time they began their second hymn, a large crowd was gathered around. Smith preached an animated message, enlivened with his inner spirit. Some nine or ten made commitments to Christ there on the common.

When the seekers and other workers were gone, the three walked across the common toward Cassels's rooms. And now "William the Silent" was doing all the talking.

"I guess I've thought about service overseas ever since I decided to be ordained. Natural, I suppose, since I was born in Portugal. But I've been focusing on China more and more steadily since February. Had to give up idea of going out with Church Missionary Society though." Cassels shook his head. "They definitely will not consider operating beyond the treaty ports. So I've written to Hudson Taylor."

Spoken in Cassels's soft voice, the words took a moment to register with Smith. When they did, he stopped dead in his tracks and turned with almost a shout. "Praise God! What did I tell you, Studd?" He slapped Cassels on the back. "That will be three of us! Hoste is all but confirmed."

Cassels gave his shy grin and shook his head. "Whoa. Matters here are far from certain."

"You mean you aren't certain?"

"I'm certain. But the decision isn't mine. Shortly after I wrote, my mother called on Mr. Taylor. She's set against it."

Smith frowned. "Naturally a parent's feelings are to be regarded, but aren't there something like thirteen children in your family—six or seven sons?"

William nodded, his pale blue eyes still focused downward. "I'm sixth of seven sons. That's the problem. I'm the only one

still in England. Shippers in Edinburgh, merchants in Lisbon—
family spread all over."

"Yes, but mission work is different. I thought your mother
was very devout."

Cassels smiled. "She is. But she's also a mother. Anyway,
Taylor assured her he held a parent's wishes sacred. He will not
accept me if she remains opposed." He sighed. "Taylor and I are
much in prayer."

Smith clasped his hand. "As I will be, too."

Kynaston left them and turned toward the station. If that was
Hudson Taylor's position, there was no use in his even thinking
about China. And yet he could think of little else. Besides Hilda.

With thought of her, his heart soared. He increased his pace
to reach the train, which he heard rumbling along the track
deeper on down in the tube.

At 3 Cromwell Road the gaslights glowed warmly, and Talley
opened the door with a welcoming smile to one who would soon
be a son of the family. Hilda met him in the hall with a ready handclasp, but her smile was tight and her eyes red-rimmed. "Hilda,
what is it? Are you ill?" He put his arm around her protectively.

For a moment she rested her head on his shoulder. Then she
pulled away. "No, I'm perfectly well, but I'm so glad you've come,
Kynaston. It's Monty."

"Monty's ill?"

She shook her head. "Not physically. I don't know—I've
never seen him like this. He came down from Ridley Hall two
days ago. I was about to send you a note, but I was sure you'd
come soon."

"Yes, but you should have sent for me the minute you
needed anything." To his surprise Hilda led toward the morning
room instead of the front parlor where they usually sat.

"Monty and Ida are in there." She pointed to the closed
door across the hall. "It seems she's the only one he can talk to."
They sat on the black and rose tapestry sofa in the pleasant room.
"He's withdrawn from Ridley Hall, given up all plans for ordination. I think he doubts his very salvation." Hilda's dark eyes were
wide with something very near to fear.

When Kynaston made no comment, she went on, as if arguing with herself. "He was always so steady. He was the first of the whole group to make a stable decision." She gave Kynaston a small smile. "Except you, my dear, dear stout-heart." But the smile faded quickly. "That Christmas we spent in Normandy, Stanley Smith was wavering terribly—had begun smoking again. Monty was the one who brought him back."

Kynaston nodded. "And he was always the one who gave others C.I.M. materials. The strongest supporter of China missions I know of."

His words, meant to encourage, had the opposite effect. A single tear spilled over and started down Hilda's cheek before she caught it with a lace-edged handkerchief. "And now look—everyone is talking about going out to China: Stanley Smith, Mr. Cassels, Willie Hoste's brother, both of Alice Polhill-Turner's brothers even. And our dear Monty is so—so lost."

Before another tear could spill, Kynaston gathered her into his arms and held her. "I know. Hilda, I shouldn't speak of more discouragement at such a time, but if it's any help to you, I do know how you feel." His own doubts and struggles he would not burden her with, but he shared his deep concerns for his brother.

The park at Tedworth ran lush and green down to a meandering stream bordered with low-hanging willows. C. T. smiled at the chorusing birdsong overhead as he strode through alternating patches of sun and shadow toward his favorite spot on the stream bank. As had become his pattern in the soothing days since he left London in turmoil, he carried a hamper containing crumbly sharp cheese, slabs of well-buttered fresh bread, and tart, juicy apples—and two books: his Bible and *The Christian's Secret of a Happy Life*. The things he had been reading in Hannah Smith's book were a revelation that both excited and confused him.

He spread a plaid wool rug under a tree, sat with his long legs stretched out in front of him, and opened the volume. He had read the book twice. Now he went back to parts he had underlined:

The greatest burden we have to carry in life is self.... In laying off your burdens, therefore, the first one you must get rid of is yourself. You must hand yourself, with your temptations, your temperament, your frames and feelings, and all your inward and outward experiences, over into the care and keeping of your God, and leave it all there.... And here you must rest....

Next you must lay off every other burden—your health, your reputation, your Christian work, your houses, your children, your business, your servants—everything, in short, that concerns you, whether inward or outward.

C. T. looked up, half watching two gray squirrels chase along a tree branch as he thought on those words. He took two snapping bites of apple and then, still chewing, turned back to his book:

It is a very simple secret.... 'Be careful for nothing, but in everything by prayer and supplication, with thanksgiving, let your requests be made known unto God...and the peace of God which passeth all understanding shall keep your hearts and minds through Christ Jesus.'

He tossed his apple core out and watched, smiling, as the quicker of his bushy-tailed friends scampered off with it. Then he turned the page:

Let your souls lie down upon the couch of His sweet will, as your bodies lie down in their beds at night. Relax every strain, and lay off every burden.... Since He holds you up, you are perfectly safe. Your part is simply to rest. His part is to sustain you; and He cannot fail.

C. T. shook his head at the words. Such a life sounded so wonderful. If only it could be that simple. Just reading of the concept had relaxed him immeasurably. He ate a portion of the bread and cheese from the hamper, tossing his crusts to the squirrels.

The sound of the water swishing through the long grass of the banks was so soporific he closed his eyes...

At first he thought it was the squirrels rustling in the grass, but when C. T. opened his drowsy eyes and saw two very ancient ladies—one tall and thin, the other short and round, both dressed in black with their gray hair tucked into trim straw hats—tiptoeing along the stream bank, he decided he was still dreaming. He raised himself to one elbow and gave them the lazy smile that came so readily to his lips of late. "Don't let me disturb your walk, ladies."

"Oh, Mr. Studd," the shorter one fluttered her wrinkled white hands at her throat, "we didn't want to disturb you. So sorry. You looked so sweetly peaceful. Oh, my—" Now the hands fluttered around her waist.

"No, no." He swept his arm in an arc. "The park is open to all. My father would never hear of fencing."

The tall one, who was very erect but whose head wobbled alarmingly when she talked, took a step toward him. "Fine man, your father. We were well acquainted. I remember as if it were yesterday how things changed at the manor when Edward Studd became a Christian."

Suddenly C. T. remembered his manners and leapt to his feet. "Er—could I offer you ladies a seat? I mean, I've only the rug, but—er—Miss..."

"Watson, Miss Emily Watson." The round, fluttery one bobbed and then indicated her sister. "And Miss Sophia Watson. We would never have taken the liberty, but now as we're talking, I've longed to tell you. Sophia and I undertook to pray for you when you came back from Australia and your name was in all the papers."

C. T. blinked. "Indeed? How extraordinary. What a fine thing. And why did you do that?"

Sophia Watson tapped her walking stick on the narrow path. "Knew your father half his life. Watched you boys grow up. The Lord told me to pray. Told me you needed to make a complete dedication of yourself, young man."

"Extraordinary." C. T. shook his head. "Well, the Lord was right. Thank you. Er—keep praying."

Miss Emily gave a twitter of a laugh. "Oh, you needn't worry about that one bit. First thing every morning and again right after afternoon tea. As long as we have breath. As if you were our own boy."

C. T. could think of no reply, so he made them a bow. When he straightened up, they were gone. If he couldn't have still seen their black skirts disappearing down the path, he would have thought he had dreamed the encounter. Even so, he wasn't certain.

Was it possible that there were three works of grace? He had heard it said that John Wesley believed it so. If that was the case, it explained much. First, as a young boy he had become convinced of the truth of the Gospel. But that had produced only a cold, outward obedience. When George was so ill, he had acted on that belief, asking forgiveness for his sins and inviting Christ into his heart—like in that picture in Smith's room. But now he saw the need for a more complete dedication, a complete giving of himself to God with an empowering by the Holy Spirit. He trembled at the awesome step.

But one thing he was certain of. It was time to return to London. His vigorous health had fully returned and with it his usual energy. He must do something. So, lacking any other guidance, he would read for the bar. Hannah Smith talked much in her book about God opening doors. Surely He could open a door for Christian service through the legal profession.

But even as C. T. made his decision, the choice seemed shallow—a distraction from the thing he cared most about. Single-minded as Charlie was, he knew that nothing less than full-time dedication to soul-winning would satisfy him.

He had no need to work for money, so how could he spend the most fruitful years of his life working for the honor and pleasures of this world while thousands upon thousands of souls were perishing every day without the Lord Jesus Christ? The vision of countless souls going down to hopeless, Christless graves haunted him. And yet he didn't know what to do about it. The book he had read had convinced him that he must wait on God to show His way. C. T. had not found the complete childlike rest of *The Christian's Secret*, but he believed it existed.

Back in his room in Hyde Park Gardens two days later, he turned again to Hannah Smith's book.

> *...perhaps the word* abandonment *might express this idea better than the word* consecration. *But whatever word we use, we mean an entire surrender of the whole being to God—spirit, soul, and body placed under His absolute control, for Him to do with just what He pleases. We mean that the language of our hearts, under all circumstances and in view of every act, is to be "Thy will be done." We mean that giving up of all liberty of choice. We mean a life of inevitable obedience.*

And as the words jumped from the page at him, C. T. Studd knew that this was the answer. His life was to be one of simple, childlike faith. He was to trust in God to work His good pleasure. He saw that God was his loving Father, that He would guide and keep His child, and that He was well able to do it.

C. T. was ready for the complete, happy Christian life. As he prayed, "Take my life and let it be consecrated, Lord, to Thee," suddenly he knew that his future lay in China.

"China!" Mrs. Studd clasped her chest and started forward in her chair as if having a seizure.

"I can't tell you what pain it causes me to distress you, Mama. I would never do it if I weren't absolutely certain it is God leading me. You see, I've come to an entirely new understanding—"

"Dora, my smelling salts."

C. T. held his tongue as his little sister rushed from the room. As soon as she returned and a few sharp whiffs of the acrid vinaigrette had settled Mrs. Studd's breathing, he tried again, holding her hand and speaking very gently. "Mama, you know I love you—"

"And this is how you repay me—by deserting me? You've always been such a good boy."

He had known his mother would be heartbroken, but this

246

was worse than he had imagined. He patted her hand and tried again. "Please believe me, I would consider this for nothing less than the will of God. Obedience to Him is the only thing I place before obedience to you, Mama."

"But you've been a Christian since you were a little boy. I don't understand—" Her voice strangled to a halt. She dabbed at her eyes with an embroidered silk square.

C. T. prayed for the right words. "Yes, I knew about Jesus dying for me, Mama. I believed He died to save sinners. But I had never understood that if He died for me, then I didn't belong to myself."

"Or to your mother?" The words were muffled by sobs, but they were clear enough to C. T.

And the matter was clear enough to Kynaston who sat quietly at the end of the breakfast table, his coffee cooling in its cup. There was no way he could add to his mother's distress by mentioning his own long-standing desires. When Hilda had accepted him and declared her willingness to go to China—had even encouraged and supported him—he had thought the way was opening. But now he had never seen a more tightly shut door. Shut and barred.

Nor was he at all certain C. T. was doing the right thing. Quite apart from Kynaston's own desires in the matter, it didn't seem possible that Charlie could be right to cause such pain to another.

A shudder passed over Mrs. Studd. She sniffed softly and then tried again. "Charlie, I beg you, don't go to Mr. Taylor yet. Give the matter just one week. Is that too much to ask? One week?"

"Would you have me disobey God, Mother?"

"You're breaking my heart." Mrs. Studd turned from C. T. "Dora, ring for Ellen." A few minutes later she left the room supported by her daughter and her maid.

C. T. turned to Kynaston. "Hardest thing I've ever had to do. Thank you for being here. Seems you're always the one we all rely on."

Kynaston swallowed hard. "Sorry, Charlie, but I must say this. I'm not at all sure you're right in this. You're still an infant in your life in Christ. A step like this needs tremendous maturity."

C. T. looked as if Kynaston had struck him in the face. "I thought you'd be the one person who would understand. Your help and advice have always meant so much."

"Have you searched the Scriptures? They seem clear to me: 'Children, obey your parents in the Lord, for this is right.' Honor your mother and father. How can you go against that, Charlie?"

C. T. shook his head. "It's so hard to have *you*—of all people—think I'm making a mistake, Kinny." He was quiet a moment. "I don't want to be pigheaded and go out to China of my own accord. I just want to do God's will."

"Let's put the matter in God's hands," Kynaston said.

Together the two brothers slipped to their knees.

Kynaston remained on his knees after Charlie had gone out. He fully realized that in taking his mother's side, he was arguing against his own desires as well as Charlie's. Kynaston searched his heart, examined his own motives. His goal was to reflect Christ in all his life. But how could he do that if he were not to be allowed to serve?

And why did everything keep getting worse? When he first identified his desire to go to China, he had anticipated difficulties—perhaps even hardships—along the way. But he expected to make progress.

After all, he only wanted to serve God. How could a desire to spread the Gospel possibly be outside God's will? Christ Himself had commanded, "Go ye into all the world." And Kynaston longed to do just that. So why did he feel more hampered the longer he worked toward that goal?

He did believe God was in control of the world. His own setbacks did not mean that God had suddenly dropped the reins. Yet nothing seemed to be going right.

How much longer must he hold on until the way opened?

Twenty-three

It wasn't until Kynaston stepped out the door and saw the thick cloud of steam his breath raised that he recalled that it was the first of November and a heavy frost covered Hyde Park. He had been so preoccupied with his family's turmoil that he had lost all sense of time and place. He turned back for his overcoat. Then, white puffs of breath preceding him in the equally white air and the frozen grass snapping under his feet, Kynaston crossed Hyde Park and went on to Cromwell Road. Thank God for Hilda. Apart from his own salvation, she was the only thing in his life he was certain of right now. Perhaps she would have good news for him.

When he joined Hilda, Lady Beauchamp, and Montague in the morning room a few minutes later, however, it was apparent that matters stood little better there. Monty's basset-hound expression was more forlorn than ever. And the effect of Lady Beauchamp's kind welcome and brave smile was vitiated by the stray locks that had slipped from the small fashionable bun atop her head.

Not wanting to add to their concerns, but knowing no way to conceal the matter, as close as their two families were, Kynaston took a deep breath and launched into his account. He saw that his news about C. T., however, was far from depressing to Lady Beauchamp. Her soft eyes took on a sudden light; her pale skin lost its tired look. "Oh, how thrilling! How did his call come about? Tell me."

Hilda, sitting next to J. E. K. on the sofa, placed her hand on his arm with a gentle pressure. That communication of her understanding meant everything to Kynaston. Hilda knew how hard this situation was for him. Hilda was at one with him—whatever happened. He gave her a small smile and then turned to his hostess. "Charlie went to a C.I.M. meeting with Stanley Smith—a farewell for a returning missionary. He says when he heard of the vastness of the spiritual need, he knew God was leading him to China. Apparently he would have stood and offered himself right then, but he didn't want to be thought rash."

"Just imagine what this will do for the kingdom." Lady Beauchamp clasped her hands. "C. T. Studd giving up cricket and a legal career for China—it will cause a sensation. Does he worry over the disapproval of his worldly friends? He may have some severe testing."

Kynaston shook his head. "I don't think he cares for anything. You know how Charlie is about heading straight for the mark."

"But he's had every luxury. How does he feel about physical hardships?"

"I think he welcomes them. Charlie always liked a challenge." Kynaston paused. "Only thing that worries him—and of course it's an enormous obstacle—is the suffering he's causing our mother."

Lady Beauchamp looked at him wide-eyed. "Surely not. How could a Christian mother not be thrilled to have a son called to the foreign field?"

They all started at the sound of the closing door. Kynaston looked up and saw Monty's empty chair. He had forgotten Montague. Had his report added to his friend's turmoil? That was the last thing he wanted.

And that night, pacing the floor in his room, a similar thought was uppermost in C. T.'s mind. Kindness was one of the virtues he prized most. He would never knowingly be unkind to anyone. The very idea of hurting his own mother struck him so hard he could hardly breathe.

But the thought of turning his back on the call of God left him knowing he could not live.

Over and over as he rambled from window to fireplace to bedside, he heard the same words inside his head, as clearly as if the speaker were beside him in the room: "Ask of me, and I shall give thee the heathen for thine inheritance, and the uttermost parts of the earth for thy possession."

He picked up his Bible and read on through the second Psalm: "...Serve the Lord with fear, and rejoice with trembling.... Blessed are all they that put their trust in him." His mind cleared. He could sleep now.

After less than two hours in bed, he rose and dressed while it was still dark. C. T. had never felt surer, never been more his old charge-toward-the-goal self than he was that morning. There was no hansom cab in sight, so he all but ran the two-thirds of a mile to Bayswater Underground Station. At King's Cross he caught a horse-bus to take him on to Pyrland Road, Mildmay. Never once did it enter his mind that Hudson Taylor might not be at home or that Taylor might not accept him. Dick Hoste had gone through months of inquiries and interviews; Cassels's decision had hung in the balance for weeks until his mother embraced her son's call. But C. T. Studd was determined. This was the day.

And so it was. Benjamin Broomhall ushered him into the comfortable well-worn parlor. "I'll just ask you to wait in here while I tell Mr. Taylor." He poked at a fire burning very low on the grate. "I apologize for the chill in the room. We always kept it warm because my daughter Gertrude played the piano in here, but she went out to China in September."

In a few minutes Hudson Taylor himself came to welcome C. T. The cricket player was easily double the missionary's weight and strength, but Hudson Taylor's energy for the China mission and his zeal for serving God made him seem to have twice the power of the all-England cricketer. And each man recognized the other's strengths and their oneness in spirit. There was little need for an interview. It was more a sharing of excitement for the vision of saving souls.

Hudson Taylor was a man who could run as straight for a mark as C. T. Studd. By the time Charlie left Pyrland Road late that cold, foggy afternoon, his application for China was confirmed, and he was scheduled to begin his farewells the next week.

It wasn't until C. T. was settled in the horse-bus returning toward King's Cross that the euphoria began to fade. The conflict was not over. God had spoken to him. Hudson Taylor had welcomed him. But his mother was still grieving, his brother doubting. His mother's entreaties and Kynaston's arguments now sounded louder in his ears than the word of Scripture had in his room just hours ago. Had he been driving his own carriage, he would have turned around there in the dimly lit Essex Road and withdrawn his offer to the mission.

At the underground station he stood on the platform. The train was late. Did that mean he should yet return? He had come so far. But going far in the wrong direction was no progress. *Oh, God, I need a word of guidance. A sure word to cling to. This must be of You, not of my own enthusiasm.*

He drew out his little pocket Bible and moved so that the light of the gas lamp would shine on its pages. Who was right? His inner leading, or his family? His Bible opened at Matthew 10—the mission statement of Jesus' disciples and their relationship to their families. C. T. read: "A man's foes shall be they of his own household."

Now he knew what to say to his mother.

An hour later he put it to the test. Ellen ushered him into his mother's room. He had never seen her look so tired and drawn. Dorothy Sophia Studd was the sturdy mother of sporting sons, the matriarch of a large, active family. She did not often droop. But it was clear that facing the loss of her Charles had nearly overset her.

"Mama?"

Her smile was weak, her eyes still clouded with worry, but her hands rested calmly in her lap, her chin up. "I have missed you today, Charlie."

"I have been to Mildmay. I offered myself to the China Inland Mission and was accepted."

She drew her breath in sharply, but there was no hysteria. "And you are certain?"

"Never more certain of anything in my life. Our Lord said, 'He that loveth father or mother more than me is not worthy of me.' I want nothing so much as to be worthy of Him."

Her eyes filled with tears. "Your father would be so proud of you." For a moment she couldn't speak. Then she rose and took both his hands. "But, Charlie, you must promise me—"

"Yes, Mama?"

"You must take plenty of warm clothes."

Kynaston had been across the park at Cromwell Road when Charlie returned. It was the next morning that C. T., with the renewed vigor of a good night of sleep and with a mind at peace, told him the news.

Kynaston knew the rightness of it all. He had never heard a man surer of his call. He walked across the morning room and clasped his brother's hand. There were no words for all he was feeling.

But Kynaston was not the only one with feelings to be considered. Last night he had left Monty Beauchamp in a state of dreadful depression. He couldn't predict what effect Charlie's story would have on Beauchamp, but Monty must be told.

Later that morning Kynaston and C. T. stood on the black and white marble under the Corinthian-pillared portico of the Beauchamp home. Kynaston opened his mouth to ask Talley to announce them to Miss Hilda and then closed it in surprise at finding the door opened by Montague—a Montague looking like a basset hound who had just eaten a sirloin.

Kynaston couldn't wait to hear what had wrought such a change, but he accepted the offer of coffee and toast in the breakfast room in the hope that he would find Hilda there. He was not disappointed. And he knew that her radiant glow was for more than the entrance of her betrothed. Something had happened in the Beauchamp household.

But Monty was not so changed as to have become a

Demosthenes. "Oh, for goodness sake, Monty. Tell them," Hilda burst out in the quiet that followed the general greetings and coffee pouring.

"Read my Bible and prayed. Most of the night." His eyes sparkled under his drooping eyelids. "The Lord was there. Realized His presence in a way I've never done before." The ends of his long mustache curled up as he smiled. "Going to China. I'm to go and induce others to go as well. Sure of it."

In the wake of the general hubbub that followed his announcement, Monty and C. T. compared careful notes on their experiences. It seemed that only a few hours after God had spoken to C. T. at King's Cross Station, He had spoken to Monty in his bedroom—with almost exactly the same message.

"And what does your mother say to this?" Charlie asked.

Monty leaned back in his chair. "Upstairs packing my kit now. Glad to see me go."

"Monty, that sounds awful!" Hilda protested with a gurgle of laughter.

"You know what I mean. Always said she wanted a missionary son." He grinned again. "Now she's got one." Then he looked at C. T. seriously. "Felt guilty though. Knew what you were going through with the *mater*. Asked myself how could I hold back when I had a mother who would encourage me."

Kynaston looked up at the sound of Talley's entrance. "Mr. Stanley Smith," the butler announced, then withdrew.

Monty sprang to his feet, crossed the room in two strides, and grasped Smith's hand. "Decided! Going into all the world— as the Scripture says."

Even the silver-tongued Stanley Smith was speechless as both Monty Beauchamp and C. T. Studd poured out the details of their calls to China. But at last he found his voice. "Tell you what. We're going to Cambridge next week. Cassels, Hoste, myself—farewell meetings and mission. You must come, too. What a grand thing— five of us all for China. We'll set a blaze they won't soon forget. Christian Union is all ready for us. Hudson Taylor coming, too— a full week for China Inland Mission and the whole foreign field."

Then he grinned. "Might get some time for a quick scull on the river, too. May not be much rowing in China."

A short time later Stanley Smith bore the two new intended missionaries off to see William Cassels, who was packing after having preached his farewell sermon in his parish church. In the nearly deserted room, Kynaston and Hilda looked at each other across the table.

"Would you care for more coffee?" Hilda offered.

Kynaston shook his head.

Hilda rose and came around the table to sit by him. "I know it must be terribly hard for you when it's what you've wanted to do for so long."

Kynaston shook his head. "I shouldn't be thinking of myself at all when there's so much cause for rejoicing. I want to enter into it all a hundred percent. The fact that I can't makes me feel so self-centered."

"Never." Hilda gripped his arm and shook it. "James Edward Kynaston Studd, you are the least selfish, least self-centered person I have ever known. There is nothing wrong with an overwhelming desire to do more for God."

He hated to give voice to the doubts that crowded his mind. But maybe if he got them out, Hilda could help him deal with them. His voice was barely above a whisper. "Why did the way open for them and not for me? In spite of all my work and preparation, has God found me unworthy? I don't know what I can do, Hilda. I can work no harder. I can pray no more."

"And yet the way remains closed for you."

He nodded without meeting her eyes.

"Well, then, that's your answer. You must accept it."

He looked at her in amazement.

"You have to accept the fact that God is in control of the world. He knows best."

"Oh, Hilda, I don't doubt that. But what am I to do with my life if I'm not to be a medical missionary to China?"

Twenty-four

S even days later, 12 November, Kynaston sat near the back of Alexandra Hall in Cambridge, watching the stir of undergraduates around him. The announcement that C. T. Studd had abandoned cricket at the height of his fame and was going to China had caused immense excitement. Kynaston smiled as he heard his brother's name again and again in the buzz that whirled around him.

At least Kynaston's talk with Hilda had enabled him to accept fully his brother's decision and enter wholeheartedly into supporting the missionary band. It did not diminish his own desire to be part of it or his own longing for a place of service, but now he could share the others' joy.

And there was plenty of joy in Alexandra Hall. The rafters fairly rang with enthusiasm as Kynaston's old friend Handley Moule, principal of Ridley Hall, took the chair and led them in "Christ for the World We Sing."

They had just started on the last verse when Kynaston saw Willie Hoste enter. He got Willie's attention and moved back a row where they could sit together.

They congratulated each other on their brothers, and Kynaston realized the similarities of their positions. Each had urged his brother forward, yet each would be staying behind. Then Kynaston gave his attention to Hudson Taylor, who spoke of the joy of surrendering to a divine Master who more than satisfies His servants' hearts. Kynaston's mind agreed to every word of the message, even though his heart was sore.

He saw one other whose joy was not yet full. Monty Beauchamp, who had not yet been accepted by the mission, sat to the side. He, like Kynaston, was there to support the others, but his desire to have his own application official showed in the lines of his face.

But then Kynaston's attention returned to the front of the hall where the intended missionaries stood to give their testimonies. Stanley Smith charmed his audience with his brilliance and shook them with the fervor of his call. Then C. T., looking taller than ever on the platform, spoke in the clipped, direct phrases of a cricket captain. "I guess I've tasted most of the pleasures of the world." The crowd cheered, recalling the honors he had won for Cambridge and for England. C. T. looked down and shook his head. "I don't suppose there are any I haven't tasted— any that I cared about, that is. But I can tell you that none of them compared in the smallest drop to the thrill of leading a soul to Christ." He looked at the varsity men filling the hall. "Try it, and you won't want any other."

Then there was a surprise addition to the program. Arthur Polhill-Turner took the platform. "This is my anniversary. Two years ago to this very day I surrendered my life to Jesus Christ during the Moody campaign at the Corn Exchange right around the corner here." The audience, many of whom had been there at the time, applauded.

When the meeting concluded, Kynaston sat for a moment, listening to the comments of two men in front of him: "Easy enough for them—they're millionaires, they are."

The other one tugged at his gown. "Spiritual millionaires, I'd say. What they have makes anything else look paltry."

They were joined by a third, wearing a blue varsity blazer. "These fellows turn everything upside down. One feels that *not* making an all-out commitment would be a sacrifice."

"Nothing less seems worth having." The three walked out, still talking.

Kynaston felt at a loss. The hall emptied around him, the men all going out in small groups, talking excitedly. He stayed in his seat. "Coming, Studd? We're going up to P.T.'s rooms." At first he thought Willie Hoste was speaking to C. T. Then he realized the invitation was for him.

By the time they made their way across Queen's Road to Ridley Hall, the others were already deep in conversation.

"Amazing thing," Polhill-Turner was saying, "the social round at Howbury suddenly seemed so hollow and unreal. Best thing there was visiting the villagers with my sister Alice. The vicar thought us terrible fanatics. Wouldn't have anything to do with our teaching conversion. So we held cottage meetings. And you know what else is amazing—I met these little old ladies who told me they'd been praying for me *for years*." Arthur shook his head. "Can you imagine? I remember some of Nanny Redshaw's Bible stories—vaguely—but Old Mrs. Symons, I'd never seen her—yet she had spent *hours* praying for me."

"That is amazing," C. T. said.

Arthur ducked his head. "Yes, isn't it? God bless her. It makes one feel so humble."

"But that's not what I mean." C. T. launched into the story of the two little old ladies he had never heard of before who had prayed for him likewise. Then he went on to tell of his deeper experience of total commitment to the will of God.

When he finished, Arthur was staring. "Amazing!" He stopped and rubbed his luxuriant blond mustache. "Been saying that a lot, haven't I? But it's the only word I can think of for it. Just two weeks ago I took Alice to Edinburgh for a holiness convention. First time I'd heard of complete consecration and constant abiding in the power of the Holy Spirit. The blessing—it's... unspeakable."

And then Stanley Smith told of his experience under the guidance of old Mr. Price at Pakefield. And Monty Beauchamp of his experience in London so very recently.

It was well past midnight when Dick Hoste, who had been listening quietly to the conversation for some time, interrupted with a laugh. "*Amazing* seems to be the key word tonight—but these stories astonish me because my experience was so different. Probably comes from my mother's strict teaching that if one is truly sorry, he is ready for complete obedience. I haven't given much credence to a lot of this second-blessing holiness teaching because when I submitted to God at the Dome in Brighton, I was saying, 'I'm sorry for my sins and here—take all of me. I'll do whatever you want me to do.' I wouldn't go forward until I could say it all at once. I hadn't realized there's more than one step to it for many people." He was quiet for a moment. "Makes sense though."

"Yes," Kynaston said more to himself than to the room at large, "God does deal with each of us as individuals—with different plans for each life as well." Somehow he didn't find that thought as comforting as it should have been.

Then his attention turned to the other side where Monty Beauchamp was recounting in detail his visit to the China Inland Mission. "Definitely found what I wanted—something worth giving my whole life to. Can't think of anything better—nothing I'd rather do." He turned abruptly to the quiet man beside him. "But what are your plans, P.T.?"

The little crease between Arthur's brows deepened. "Well, I don't know. Read all the material you sent, Beauchamp. But it's a tremendous step to take. Thought about it, of course, ever since I became a Christian." He laughed. "I remember when I first mentioned C.I.M. to Cecil. *Fanatic* would have been far too nice a word for what he thought of me then. Now he's been around to Mildmay calling on Hudson Taylor himself."

Arthur paused again, then concluded, "Guess a fellow never knows what will happen when little old ladies start praying for him."

Dick Hoste turned to Arthur. "How is your brother getting along in the Mess?" He shook his head. "I well remember my trepidation there as a new Christian."

Arthur nodded. "Cecil said his brother officers were remarkably considerate—occasionally indulged in a quiet laugh at his expense, but he had hardly any ragging to put up with. Although I daresay he would have borne it well."

Hoste smiled. "I'm sure he's shown himself too good an officer to be treated with disrespect."

Arthur agreed. "He's grown in grace remarkably in a very

short time. I shouldn't be surprised to see him declaring for China eventually. Although the Bays are shortly to go out to India, and he's been advised the missionary value of Christian officers there is incalculable."

Monty, who hadn't received an answer to his question the first time, persisted. "But what do you plan to do, P.T.?"

Arthur shrugged. "I've been seeking a curacy since the vicar at Howbury won't have anything to do with my fanaticism. Nothing opened up though. No decision made yet." He sighed and sat back, deep in thought.

Sometime later Kynaston trudged back to his rooms. C. T. and Smith walked just ahead, talking softly, puffs of white breath illuminated in the gaslights along King's Parade. Even in the dark and cold, Kynaston could sense the tide of excitement rising around him. This first meeting had been only the beginning. Arthur Polhill-Turner and he seemed to be the only ones not swept along on the wave. It was well enough for P.T. to be feeling his way slowly to a place of service. Arthur had only been a Christian for two years, and he wasn't getting married in less than a month. But it was quite a different matter for Kynaston.

He filled his lungs with the frosty night air and then let out a long, slow breath. Perhaps he would yet find the answers he had come to Cambridge seeking before the week was out.

On Friday night Smith and C. T. held a watch night—praying from eleven o'clock until six-thirty the next morning, taking only forty-five minutes to rest. Kynaston endeavored to lend them support by praying in his own room. He felt too depressed to wrestle with his own needs but strove to bolster the others. The next morning, however, he had a grinding headache while his brother and Smith were energized.

On Sunday night Hudson Taylor and Stanley Smith spoke to a hall filled with enthusiastic varsity men. At the close of the meeting, Taylor asked all who would be willing to serve abroad to stand. Kynaston was among the fifty who stood, but it was simply a matter of a straightforward answer to a simple question. Would he be willing to serve? Of course, he would be willing to do anything God asked of him. No strong feeling accompanied the gesture.

Tuesday night, however, at the closing meeting with Alexandra Hall packed wall-to-wall, all Christians seeking God's leading for their lives, the question Smith put was more pointed. "All who intend to become missionaries stay for a time of prayer."

Kynaston would have loved to stay, to have been part of that band of forty-five men praying about their own distinct calls. But a general desire and willingness to serve God could hardly be called a distinct call. Until God revealed a specific place of service, Kynaston could not join that happy band. As he moved toward the back of the hall, however, he saw a radiant Arthur Polhill-Turner moving toward the front. It was evident that Arthur's time of waiting was over. From his first enthusiastic announcement to his brother, through two years of quietly testing his call and counting the cost, Arthur had emerged triumphant.

The last days of November melted away as rapidly as the languid flakes of snow that fell from gray skies to be trampled under cart and carriage wheels on London's streets. Word spread of the remarkable group of young men of wealth, position, and athletic prowess who were abandoning all to bury themselves in China working with an obscure mission. Requests poured in from all over England and Scotland for them to hold meetings. The captain of the Cambridge Eleven and the stroke oar of the Cambridge boat were in special demand, and Montague Beauchamp, though his acceptance was not official yet, spoke often in support of the others. Monty surprised everyone by developing into a fluent speaker.

Monty and C. T. had never been known as orators, but now they discovered the power in simply standing before an audience and telling in straightforward terms the story of their commitments to Christ and drive to take Him to a lost world. They made an impact on hundreds, especially on young men like themselves. But thrilling though this rising tide of national attention was, it did not smooth the way for the wedding plans of Hilda and Kynaston.

"Yes, Ida, I know you wanted to greet Monty at the station,

but you simply must work in time for a fitting at the dressmaker's." Hilda sorted through a pile of lace swatches on the table in the front parlor. "Now, Tot, please tell me which pattern you prefer. The Nottingham is exquisite—much the finer, but the Brussels is very elegant."

Constance tossed an issue of *Sporting Life* onto the table and took a small cake from the tea tray. "Hilda, if you could just wait a few hours—after the London farewell, this missionary fervor will settle down, and we can all concentrate on your wedding."

Hilda held the lace at arms' length, still considering. "I'm not asking you to give up attending Monty's farewell. I'm just asking for five minutes of your time for your opinion."

Hilda's twin sister laughed. "I can't believe you're asking our opinion, Hilda. You've always known far more about such things than Ida or I."

"But I can't see how it hangs down the back."

Ida looked up from Monty's copy of the latest issue of *China's Millions*. "I would choose the Nottingham. The rose pattern is lovely against your dark hair."

Hilda appreciated Ida's attempt to help, even if her enthusiasm did sound forced. She barely suppressed a sigh as she replaced the samples. She did not want to seem impatient. And she certainly was in full support of Monty's missionary commitment. But she and Kynaston had had no idea they would be competing with such a whirlwind when they set their wedding date for 10 December. Once all the fervor of farewell meetings was behind them, they could have their wedding, and the families could have a nice quiet Christmas with their missionary sons. She smiled as her mind raced ahead. The missionary band would depart for China the first of January. And in the peace and quiet that would follow, she and Kynaston would take their honeymoon trip on the continent. She closed her eyes as she pictured the joy of being alone with Kynaston for long, peaceful days.

There, in the solace of her dearly held vision of departing quietly on the boat train and sailing off alone with Kynaston, Hilda's equilibrium returned. She had been silly to be thrown momentarily off balance by the hubbub around her.

After the meeting tonight at Eccleston Hall, they could all put the China Inland Mission out of mind for a few days. She smiled as she pictured the calm and beauty of a time of quiet with her family—and then beginning her life with her dear Kynaston.

"Kynaston Studd, miss."

She gave a startled cry at the butler's voice and rushed across the room to hide the lengths of lace before the bridegroom could see them. She would have had ample time for the maneuver, but as she swirled the swatches away, the tail of one caught on the arrangement of dried flowers in the center of the table, bringing it over with a crash.

Kynaston entered to find his bride-to-be on her hands and knees, gathering shattered roses and heather with one hand as she held a bundle of fabric behind her with the other. "Have I come at a bad time?"

"No." She jumped up to greet him and thrust the lace at Tottie, who stood there laughing helplessly. "No, it's never a bad time to see you." She lifted her skirt and stepped over the broken stems and baby's breath. "As a matter of fact, I was just thinking how lovely it will be after tonight when all we'll have to think about is the wedding."

"That's what I came to tell you—"

Before he could go on, Monty bounded into the room, followed by Smith and C. T. "Monty, what are you doing here? I thought you were with Mr. Taylor," Hilda asked.

"Was. Just home to tell Mama good-bye. Won't be time after the meeting. Hoste and Cassels have a full slate—I'm going along for support. Sure my application will be final soon." He showed only the slightest indication of covering his worry with bravado. "Going to Scotland."

"*Scotland?* But you can't. Our wedding." She looked from one to the other of the young men before her. Their eyes were bright; their faces glowed; they were obviously impervious to the sleety weather they had just walked through. By simply being in the same room with them, one could feel their energy, could tell their minds were focused on distant rhythms.

Stanley Smith responded to her cry with a sweet smile.

"Don't worry. We didn't forget. It isn't until afternoon, is it? We'll take the night train down from Edinburgh. It gets in before breakfast."

Kynaston turned to his brother. "What's this? Tonight was supposed to be your last meeting."

C. T. grinned. "Taylor got a plea from a friend of his. Christian students at Edinburgh have been praying earnestly for something special for their unconverted fellows. Seems we're to be the answer to their prayers. Taking the night train to Glasgow."

"But this was to be your last meeting. You'll have no time—" Hilda stopped. She could see it was useless.

"Glasgow, Dundee, Aberdeen, Edinburgh." Smith began reciting their itinerary. He blazed with the excitement of the challenge. "What an opportunity! Edinburgh University—all scientists and rational philosophers. They think Christianity is only good for psalm-singing and glowering."

"They haven't seen real Christianity if that's what they think. Never had such a time in my life." C. T. suddenly spotted the tea tray on the sideboard and began wolfing down sandwiches.

"We'll show them. Let them see real love and joy." Smith picked up a slice of spice cake. "Too much flat selfishness passing for Christian service. We'll lift up Christ crucified—show them the power of a personal Savior."

"Yes, that's wonderful, but—" Already the men were moving toward the door. Hilda stood there shaking her head.

Monty turned back to engulf Hilda in a brotherly bear hug, almost smothering her against his broad shoulders. "Don't worry, old Hilda. Wouldn't miss your wedding for all the tea in China."

Everyone laughed. Then he continued. "Besides, plenty of time. Talking of delaying our departure. Time for more meetings."

If Kynaston hadn't been close beside her, she would have staggered when Monty released her and charged up the stairs toward his room. *Our wedding. Christmas. Our honeymoon,* buzzed round and round in her head. But she could see she could not hold back a tidal wave. Instead she leaned quietly into the comfort of Kynaston's arm.

And later that night after the farewell—which was to be only temporary as already another farewell was being planned for 30 January to accommodate the revised schedule—Hilda missed Kynaston's supporting arm. Although he was nearby, he had to give his full attention to his mother.

The families had walked the short distance from Eccleston Hall to Victoria Station to see the missionaries off. The train had just pulled out, chugging its way to Euston where C. T. and Smith would catch the night train to Glasgow. Hudson Taylor turned to Mrs. Studd and asked her if she could post a parcel to C. T. in Scotland. It seemed that he had left for a two-week's speaking tour with only the clothes he wore.

Mrs. Studd wrung her hands. "I can't think what Charlie will do in China if he can't manage to go to Scotland properly." She took a deep wavering breath. "Of course I will send him a parcel. But what's a mother to do?" She dabbed at her eyes and then raised her chin bravely. "I cannot understand these erratic movements. Going off to Scotland without clothes. Why would he wear one shirt night and day from now until the ninth of December? He has a more than ample supply. And he has always been taught that cleanliness is next to godliness. I simply don't know what to expect next."

Twenty-five

I n spite of her worry over the narrow margin for the return of the brother who would be walking her down the aisle, and the brother who would be standing up with Kynaston, Hilda was relieved to find the Cromwell Road house much quieter and her sisters more ready to help her during the next few days.

At least she was happy until the day before the wedding when Constance came into the breakfast room fresh from her early morning canter in the park. "Oh, it's brisk out there."

Ida looked up from her reading and laughed. "Only Tottie could call these temperatures brisk. Frigid would be much more accurate. I do hope there isn't enough snow in Scotland to stop the trains."

"Snow in Scotland? Now? How deep?" Hilda lowered her cup, missing her saucer and sloshing coffee on the tablecloth.

Tottie began removing the covers from the dishes on the sideboard and filling her plate with eggs, sausage, and bacon. "Don't borrow trouble, Ida. Mr. Douglas says it almost never snows enough to stop the trains in Dumfries. Of course, further north—" She shrugged. "Well, we must hope for the best."

"But who will stand up with Kynaston? Who will give me away? With Reginald and Violet on the continent, and—"

For one with so many brothers, she had a sudden shortage: Reggie on the continent, Pelham ill, Horace serving in Suakin with his regiment... Hilda stopped. Monty was her favorite brother. No one else would do. And she knew Kynaston felt the same about C. T. At least he could turn to George, but it wouldn't be the same.

Well, that worry would just have to wait until tomorrow

morning. There was more than enough to see to today. And the first item would be a delight. Boxes of greenery for the wedding had arrived from Langley Park yesterday—luxuriant ivy garlands and sprigs of dark, shiny holly laden with plump red berries. She and her sisters had spent much of the day tying their arrangements with red velvet bows. Now they only needed the fresh white blossoms of the greenhouse flowers to make everything perfect. She couldn't wait for Kynaston to arrive so they could drive down to Richmond and select their wedding flowers.

An hour later, however, Hilda questioned the wisdom of her decision to choose the flowers themselves. She shivered under the pile of rugs Kynaston had wrapped around her inside the closed carriage. "Perhaps I should have let them send the flowers up in a hamper."

"My dear, are the bricks cooling? Shall we stop and have them warmed? Or shall I instruct the driver to turn around? You mustn't take a chill."

She smiled at Kynaston. The warmth of his caring would keep her cozy even if the bricks under her feet were not holding the heat so well. "No, my love. I was just thinking of all there is to do. But I did want us to have this time alone together. Tomorrow is sure to be such a rush." She thought of bringing up her concern over the report of bad weather in Scotland, but she could tell by the deep quiet behind his solicitude for her that Kynaston had worries of his own. "I thought this would be an excellent chance for us to talk." She left it at that, knowing he would open to her when he was ready. She took his gloved hand and drew it inside her muff.

She didn't have long to wait. "I had a letter from C. T. yesterday," he began.

"Oh, good. How are they?"

He shook his head wonderingly. "It's absolutely incredible—the outpouring of the Holy Spirit. We all say we believe God can do miracles, but when He does one—through a member of one's own family especially—it's very hard to comprehend."

"Miracle?" She turned in the seat to face him more squarely. "What are you talking about?"

"The reports from Scotland are astounding." He withdrew

his hand from her muff and reached inside his overcoat. "Here, let me read from Charlie's letter:

> "*When we went to Edinburgh, we were in a mortal funk about meeting the students because we had never done anything like this, and we had heard the students were very resistant to any religion. We were told on one hand that no one would come, and on the other, that if they did come, there would be a row. We stayed all night by the fire on the mat, sometimes praying and sometimes sleeping.*"

He paused as the carriage lurched at uneven cobbles in the road and then continued:

> "*The organizers had taken, on faith, a hall that held a thousand, circulated printed notices, and sent sandwichmen tramping the neighborhood. I praise God to tell you the hall was filled to overflowing...*"

He stopped suddenly and put the letter down.

"Kynaston—don't stop. What happened?" Now she felt no chill in the carriage. The story had completely warmed her.

"Yes, he says more, but he's very modest." Her companion drew another letter from his pocket. "Let me read to you what Professor Henry Drummond from the university wrote to our mother:

> "*As soon as the speakers entered, they were loudly cheered. We had made it plain on our notices that they were going to China as missionaries, and our men had come to hear what Studd, who had made the biggest score at cricket in Cambridge, had to say about religion. The students admired the missionary athlete's consecration. Again and again during their addresses, they were cheered. Stanley Smith was eloquent, but Studd spoke hardly at all. It was the fact of his devotion to Christ which told, and he made the greatest impression.*
>
> "*When C. T. Studd, a name to the students as familiar as a household word, and perhaps the greatest gentle-*

man bowler in England, supplemented his fellow athlete's words by quiet but intense and burning utterances of personal testimony to the love and power of a personal Savior, opposition and criticism were disarmed. Professors and students together were seen in tears."

Kynaston looked up just as Hilda dashed a tear from her own eyes. He smiled at her and then went on:

"When the speeches were over, the chair announced that if any would like to shake hands with these Christian athletes who were on their way to preach Christ to the Chinese, they could come forward as soon as the benediction had been pronounced. We doubted any would have the courage to do so, but it seemed a good idea to offer the opportunity. I hasten to tell you there was a stampede for the platform. I wish you could have seen the deep earnestness on the faces of our students. All is so evidently the work of the Holy Spirit of God."

Hilda squeezed his arm as he folded the paper. "Oh, Kynaston. That's so wonderful. I can't believe it. God is doing a miracle."

"Yes, He is. It makes one humble just to read about it." He picked up his brother's letter again.

"Charlie concludes his letter by telling of their last afternoon in Edinburgh.

"All day long men came to us for interviews—which we had to restrict to a quarter of an hour. The interviews consisted of: "Well, are you a Christian?" "No." "Would you like to be one?" "Yes." "Well, let us pray." And the fellow would get up full of joy—he'd got salvation. We believe these fellows will now form hands under good leaders and that the fire will spread over all the universities of England, Scotland, and Ireland."

Laughing, Hilda wiped her eyes. "It's so wonderful, I can't take it in. It's what Harold Schofield prayed for—like they said at the memorial service. Oh, Kynaston, doesn't that do wonders to boost your own faith?"

He paused just a fraction too long before answering. "Yes, certainly, of course it does." Apparently he heard the forced sound of his enthusiasm because he threw his head back with a groan. "Oh, Hilda, I feel such a dog in the manger. Of course I rejoice over this—it's the kind of outpouring we pray for but never expect to see in our own lifetime. It's far more than I could even have thought to ask… "

Hilda took his hand. "And yet you feel—" she searched for the right word, "—shut out."

"Thank you for saying that, Hilda." He raised her hand to his lips and kissed it through her glove. "That's exactly how I feel. Shut out and useless. God seems to have made it perfectly clear to me that I'm not to go to China. I'm not struggling with Him over that. But there must be something I can do for the kingdom."

"You do believe God is working?"

"Yes. Of course. It would be impossible to read such letters and not believe it. There is power in just hearing the words."

"Yes, God is working in Scotland, in the universities, in the China mission. But do you believe He is working in your life—in our lives?"

Now his answer was less enthusiastic but not less fervent. "Yes. I do believe that, Hilda. I can't see His hand at work, but I do believe it's there."

"And do you believe our marriage is the right step?"

"Yes!" He clasped her hands tightly. "How could you ask that? You mustn't think—because I seem to question everything—you mustn't think I doubt us."

She smiled at him. "Right. This is the right step. So—" She wanted him to finish it for himself.

"Yes. I see. One step at a time. And my first step is meeting you at the altar of All Souls' tomorrow." He leaned over and kissed the tip of her nose as the carriage rolled to a stop.

Hilda had forgotten about the cold until she stepped out of the carriage. "Oh, brrr." She held her coat more tightly around her throat as she walked toward the great glass hothouse standing in the center of a garden surrounded by trees. The winter sun sparkled coldly on the glass, making it look as if it were built of blocks of ice. Hilda shivered, and Kynaston put his arm around her for added warmth.

"Oh, the warmth of that building will feel delicious. Hurry. I do hope they have well-heated liners for their hampers, or the flowers will be damaged before we can get them into the carriage." She could see tall bushes and vining plants hanging against the interior of the greenhouse. What a marvel steam heat had produced. They could even grow oranges in winter now.

Kynaston opened the door, and she stepped inside to take a deep breath of the hot, humid air. She coughed in surprise. The air inside was as icy as that outside. A harried-looking man in a tweed jacket and cloth cap, a muffler wrapped high around his throat, hurried toward them. "Miss Beauchamp? You're the lady about the flowers? I'm that sorry, but our main boiler blew last night. We may be able to rescue the hardier specimens if they can get the steam going again soon, but the flowers went fast."

Hilda looked at the bank of plants he indicated. The star-shaped white blossoms of the windflowers stood drooping and brown, their points curling under. "But is that all you have? Orange blossoms? Crocus? Hyacinths? Surely some bulbs? In another greenhouse?"

He shook his head and belatedly removed his cap. "I'm sorry, miss. It took them all."

Hilda raised her head. Now she needed all the brave words she had spoken to Kynaston in the carriage. Certainly they would be just as married in the sight of God without flowers. The really important things were their love for each other, the approval of their families, and God's blessing on their union—those they had in abundance, and she was thankful. But she had so wanted lovely, fresh white flowers to add to the purity and the radiance of the occasion.

Somehow it seemed that having their wedding be exquisite in every detail might help Kynaston feel less shut out. She swallowed hard and raised her head. "Never mind then. We won't detain you from rescuing what you can of your plants. We'll think of something."

All the way back to Cromwell Road, she kept up a cheerful banter about substituting crystal ornaments or silver bells or white beading. She would contrive something, perhaps flowers fashioned of paper or feathers. But she did recoil from the thought of walking down the aisle of their beautiful white and gold church carrying paper flowers. She could have perhaps rearranged the dried flowers from the morning room had she not smashed them.

When they entered the hall of the Beauchamp residence, the butler met them. "There is a person—a young woman to see you, miss." Talley's voice was perfectly correct, but the rigidity of his bearing told much. "I took the liberty of putting her in the morning room, as Lady Beauchamp was not here to consult. I do hope I did right."

"Thank you, Talley. A young woman? I wonder who—" Hilda pushed open the door. "Lizzie!" She crossed the room to welcome her guest. "What a pleasant surprise."

Lizzie tugged at the sleeves of her plain coat. "Thank you, miss. I do hope you don't mind my comin' 'ere. Awful liberty I took, but I didn't dare trust 'em to no delivery man. And I'd 'ave 'ad to pay 'im. I'm saving every farthing to repay the fund."

"Lizzie, do sit down. Of course I don't mind." Hilda indicated the bell pull. "Kynaston, order some tea, please. I'm certain we're all famished." Hilda took a chair near Lizzie. "You must tell me all about yourself and Jackie. How is he doing at school?"

"That's what I come about, miss. I 'eard at the mission that it was your wedding tomorrow. Nothing would do for Jackie but that I bring you these. 'E grew 'em at the Poly." She indicated a large hamper in the corner.

"What do you mean? Grew what at the Poly?" Hilda crossed the room and lifted the lid on the hamper. A spicy, sweet scent filled the air as if she had opened a bottle of fine perfume. She blinked, unable to believe the sight. "Lizzie, how can this be?"

Hilda reached into the basket and drew out an armful of the most perfect white lilies she had ever seen.

"The Poly—Jackie wasn't getting nowhere at the ragged school, so Mr. Groom at the mission talked to Mr. Hogg who runs his new sort of school to teach boys a trade. He wouldn't of took Jackie—it's more for the workin' poor, and we're not quite that high, as all I have is my potato oven—but since Mr. Groom spoke for him... Well, anyway, Jackie took right on to growing flowers in their 'othouse. What with my selling flowers in the summer, I suppose Jackie felt right at home."

Hilda was so overcome she could only shake her head. Kynaston carried on, asking Lizzie about Quinten Hogg's school until the tea arrived.

The next morning Hilda jumped out of bed even before Daisy could get to her with her morning tea. This was her wedding day. And no matter what happened—even if her worst fears came true and the Aberdeen Express down from Edinburgh failed to bring Charlie Studd and Stanley Smith in time, and Monty missed his train from the meetings he was holding with Cassels and Hoste, it wouldn't really matter. She and Kynaston Studd would be married. She could ask for no greater happiness.

Then Ida and Tottie burst in singing, their hands full of lace and ribbons. And she realized that for once she would not be badgering her sisters about their attire. Today they would dress her. Since the last few years had taught her a little of the pleasure that could come from not always having to be in charge, she gladly submitted to their ministrations. "But I must have breakfast first," she protested. "Then you may do for me to your hearts' content."

Only when her mother came in later to clasp the family pearls around her neck did Hilda's concerns nudge her. "Has Monty come yet, Mama?"

Lady Beauchamp kissed her daughter's cheek. "Not yet, my dear, but your Uncle Radstock just arrived. And Granville, too." The tiniest frown shadowed her forehead. "If our dear Montague is prevented, one of them will be more than happy to serve."

"Yes, Mama, we will soon have to do without Monty at all—" She stopped. That was not a line of reasoning that would lead to cheer. It was because Monty would soon be so far away from them that she had especially wanted him.

"Look, my dear." Her mother turned her toward the looking glass. "See how lovely the second Lady Beauchamp's pearls look on you."

Ida, dressed in rich green lace over gold satin, her bustle pulled back with a cluster of gold roses, came in with the bouquet of lilies that had been kept overnight in the cool pantry. Hilda buried her face in their scented loveliness. Then she looked up and smiled. She would not ask about the train from Scotland. God was doing miracles in Edinburgh. Getting a train down to London should be the merest routine to Him, no matter what the weather.

As the carriage rolled up Regent Street to All Souls' Place, however, Hilda had to admit to feeling disappointment. Ever the optimist, their mother had sent Monty's best silk hat and tailed coat on to the church with his man—just in case he arrived at the eleventh hour. But as Hilda surveyed those standing around the circular pillared portico under the needle-pointed spire of the church, she could see that her brother's tall, lanky form was not among them. She must make a hurried decision. Should she ask her uncle or cousin to escort her? Cousin, she supposed. It seemed a fitting choice since Granville Waldegrave had been such an influence on Montague's spiritual life.

Inside the vestry she scanned the overflowing church. The golden simulated marble columns and walls, the crimson hangings, the supremely serene Christ portrayed above the altar—all glowed in the flickering light of a winter afternoon. All was perfect. Except... She turned to her twin. "Tottie, ask one of the ushers to find Granville Waldegrave. He must escort me."

Tot gave her hand a quick squeeze. "Brave girl. Only thing to do."

"Granville? What's this? Won't I do?"

"Monty!" Hilda flung herself at the tall form of her beloved brother, remembering just in time to hold her bouquet to the side.

The congregation had already begun singing, "Love divine, all loves excelling, Joy of heav'n, to earth come down; Fix in us Thy humble dwelling..."

Hilda put her hand on Monty's elbow. She stood on tiptoe and whispered in his ear, "The train from Edinburgh?"

For answer he nodded toward the front of the church. She looked down the wide center aisle. For a moment her eyes locked on Kynaston, standing so handsome, so perfectly tailored. Then her gaze shifted to the man beside him.

Her heart leapt at the sight of C. T., standing three inches taller than his brother. She smiled, thinking of Kynaston's happiness. Then her joy turned to mirth. It was all she could do to stifle an outburst of giggles. "What happened to C. T.'s pants?"

Monty grinned. "Liverpool, London slums—Charlie saw the poor. Was horrified at the way he'd been living. 'So many suits, clothes of all sorts,' he wrote home. 'Thousands are starving and perishing of cold. All must be sold.'"

"C. T. ordered *all* his clothes sold for the poor?"

Monty nodded and leaned closer to her ear so she could hear over the congregational singing. "Appears George took his orders up rather too literally. He's wearing Kynaston's trousers."

The "Trumpet Voluntary" called Hilda and Monty forward. In all her imaginings of this moment, all the things she had worried about, the one fear that had never crossed her mind was that she would be bursting with giggles as she walked down the aisle. She bit her lip and forced her gaze straight ahead.

She had almost gained control when her eyes met Kynaston's. The lively laughter she saw there would have been her undoing had she not suddenly been choked by a far deeper emotion. To live her life beside this man. To bear his children. To share his burdens. To support him in all his work as together they built a home and worked for the kingdom. It did not seem possible that earthly life could hold so much. Surely there could be no finer metaphor for God's grace, no brighter reflection of the life to come.

The rich Scottish burr of the Reverend Douglas Campbell Douglas pronounced the blessing: "Almighty God, who at the beginning did create our first parents, Adam and Eve, and did sanctify and join them together in marriage; pour upon you the riches of His grace, sanctify and bless you, that ye may please Him both in body and soul, and live together in holy love unto your lives' end."

Hilda and Kynaston joined their voices with the minister's "Amen."

Twenty-six

I shall be back in time for Christmas dinner." C. T. kissed his mother's cheek. "And if I'm not, save me a bit of the plum pudding."

"Charlie!" He turned back. "Your scarf." She wound a warm muffler around his neck. "Why you must speak at the YMCA on Christmas day, I don't understand. Wouldn't Boxing Day do as well?"

"Could there be a better day to proclaim Jesus than on His birthday, Mama?" He started toward the door and then paused midstride. "Oh, I almost forgot to tell you—our departure's postponed until late January."

Mrs. Studd clapped her hands. "Oh, Charlie! That's wonderful! Then we will have some time with you before you sail."

"'Fraid not, Mother. We're to go to Scotland again." This time he made it out the door.

Mrs. Studd turned to her Chippendale writing desk and took out a gold-embossed diary. "Oh, dear. He didn't tell me the dates." She sank onto the chair. "How am I to enter all this in my diary if he doesn't tell me the dates? My own dear son, and I don't even know when he's sailing to China." She took out a delicate handkerchief. "China. I still can't believe it." A tear fell on the page. "Oh, my. Now look what I've done. I can't even read this entry."

Hilda crossed to her new mother-in-law, took the leather volume, and blotted the stain. "There. I believe it says: '27 December, Windsor; 29 Brighton—'" She turned the page over. "'2 January,

277

Bedford; 8 Exeter Hall.' I heard C. T. telling Kynaston about the schedule changes. I believe they are to go to Liverpool on the ninth and then on to Scotland. Shall I make the entry for you?"

Mrs. Studd nodded. "But what's to come of all this? It's all so—so foreign. Everything seems out of control—like a wildfire. It frightens me."

Hilda kissed her mother-in-law. "Out of our control, but not out of God's, Mother Studd." She looked around for something to cheer Mrs. Studd up before Christmas dinner. Already the scent of roast goose with rosemary and thyme stuffing filled the room. "Would you like me to help you with some correspondence?"

"Oh, my dear, you are so good. I am losing a son, but God has given me such a good daughter. You are right. All is in His hands. Still—perhaps we can help matters on just a bit. I would be most grateful for your help. If you would just send a letter to Mr. Taylor." She moved to the gold brocade chaise lounge, and Hilda sat at the writing desk. "Tell him that I am most grateful for his giving advice to my dear Charles on the wearing of proper clothing and that I trust it will be heeded."

Hilda began writing, distilling the essence of Mrs. Studd's monologue: "Dear fellow! He is very erratic and needs to be with older and more consistent Christians. Just compose a few lines asking Mr. Taylor to continue to impress on him the necessity of taking what is necessary to be comfortable. He does seem inclined to take so very little—hardly enough to last him, to say nothing about cleanliness." She paused. "Or do you think such a letter would be best sent to Mrs. Taylor? Perhaps a woman's heart would understand best."

Hilda smiled. "I'm sure anyone of feeling could understand the concern of a mother's heart and appreciate how very tender yours is. But perhaps I could just send a short note to Mr. and Mrs. Taylor each?"

"Yes! An excellent plan. You are very wise, my dear. My dear Kynaston is so fortunate. If only Charles could find such a one as you for a companion. But where one might be found in China, I can't imagine." A look of horror struck her. "You don't think he might marry someone Chinese, do you?"

Hilda crossed to the sofa and took Mrs. Studd's hand. "I believe there are some quite lovely lady missionaries. Refined women from good families. You must ask the Lord to choose one for C. T."

Mrs. Studd brightened. "Yes. That's the very thing. A good wife would see that Charlie dressed properly and ate adequately. I have heard that a gentleman is sending a Stilton cheese out for each of the Cambridge band. That will make a nice treat for them. Now we must make a list." Mrs. Studd went to the desk and began jotting notes. "Curtains, knives and forks, table napkins, China teapot, tea... What else should I include in a hamper? I will send it on ahead to Hanzhong to be unpacked before Charlie arrives so that he will find a room prepared."

Hilda bit her lip. C. T. was the most ascetic person she knew. If silver cutlery reached him in China, he would certainly dispose of it at once. "Er, well—I don't think it should be necessary to send tea to China, Mother Studd."

The final days of 1884 and the opening ones of 1885 offered anything but the peaceful family time to prepare for the Kynaston Studds' honeymoon trip. Hilda's life seemed to be circumscribed by a triangle. In Hyde Park Gardens she attempted to support Kynaston's mother. In Cromwell Road she (of all people to be preaching patience) did her best to soothe Monty, who was awaiting Hudson Taylor's final decision on his application. And in Cavendish Place, practically across the street from All Souls' Church, she directed the settling into their charming residence while striving to boost Kynaston's spirits.

Ever the man of action—having served as captain of the cricket team, chairman of the Christian Union, organizer of the Moody campaign—her new husband was not taking easily to his enforced period of waiting on the Lord.

Today they drove through the mid-January cold to Cromwell Road to be greeted by a warm fire on the drawing-room hearth and the family drawn around a sumptuously laden tea table. "Come in, my dears." Lady Beauchamp, radiant in black taffeta with pearls, kissed them both. "You've come at the perfect moment. Celebrate with us."

"Celebrating?" Hilda looked around the room. Had one of her sisters become engaged? The attentions of Captain Lowe to Ida and Mr. Robinson-Douglas to Constance had become more pronounced of late, but she did not think matters had advanced so far. Then she looked at her brother. His tall, lanky form seemed to have grown and filled out several inches. His long face and drooping eyelids and mustache all turned upward in a smile that sprang from deep inside him.

Hilda hurled herself into her brother's arms. "Monty! It's official? You're a China missionary?"

He ducked his head but couldn't hide his pleasure. "That's it. The committee accepted me this morning." He held out a copy of the China Inland Mission's *Principles and Practice,* which outlined in detail the requirements for their missionaries—of which the most strict and innovative was the wearing of native dress. "Read and signed this—turn it in tomorrow. That's it."

Hilda looked at his sleek black hair shining in the firelight. "It's perfect. You won't even have to dye your hair." She paused. "Pity about having to shave the top of your forehead though. You're so handsome."

Tottie laughed. "Better stop, Hilda. Vanity's not so good a quality in a missionary, I'm sure."

When they were settled in comfortable chairs with thick slices of fruitcake to accompany their cups of tea, Ida picked up a letter from the side table. "There's more to celebrate. It looks as though Monty isn't the only addition to the Cambridge contingent."

Hilda recognized the stationery of Ida's faithful correspondent. "Oh, one of the Polhill-Turners? I knew they had arranged farewells in Bedford for C. T. and Stanley Smith."

"Yes." Ida glanced at her letter. "Then they held a drawing room for some thirty-five of the county families. Alice says their mother gave her consent for the occasion but was stiff with disapproval at her son's enthusiasm for two eccentric athletes. As soon as the meeting was over, Cecil sat down and wrote to

Hudson Taylor requesting an interview for himself and his brother."

Hilda gasped. "*Both* of them? Arthur and Cecil are both intending to be missionaries? But what about Cecil's commission?"

"Alice says he hasn't resigned it yet, but he certainly will as soon as all is official."

Hilda set her cup down and counted on her fingers. "Stanley Smith, C. T. Studd, Dixon Hoste, William Cassels, our own dear Monty, and two Polhill-Turners. *Seven.* Seven China missionaries. Who would ever have thought... Has there ever been anything like it?"

And it seemed as if those questions were on everyone's lips in the coming days as members of the remarkable band crossed Great Britain from one end to the other, holding meetings from Brighton to Aberdeen. Letters, newspaper accounts, word-of-mouth reports poured in at such a pace that Hilda felt quite dizzy. She abandoned all attempts to keep Mrs. Studd's diary in order for her.

There must have been similar outpourings of the Spirit of God at other times, but the only analogy Hilda could think of was Pentecost where hundreds were added daily to the church. At times, listening to the thrilling accounts, she could even visualize tongues of flame on the heads of the throngs.

As Hilda directed Daisy in the packing of her steamer trunks for their long-awaited honeymoon, her mind lingered for a moment on the warm knot of tender, breathless excitement deep inside her over the wedding trip. Then her thoughts moved outward to the wider blazing miracle that could only be described in terms of a spiritual fire.

Just a few days ago Kynaston had received a letter from Stanley Smith in Liverpool: "A most remarkable meeting. Twelve hundred there—such a time of power. Many received Jesus—seventy or more."

Then *The Record* had reported that in Edinburgh seekers packed the largest hall in the city. Two thousand students greeted Smith and Studd in the largest meeting of students ever held in Edinburgh. Smith had lifted up Christ crucified, and C. T. gave his testimony to the love and power of a personal Savior. More than half the hall responded to the fervent appeal for men to consecrate themselves to the service of God.

Then the fire spread to Glasgow where God came down in power. This was a true religious revival. Men converted one day sought out their friends and brought them in to find Christ the next.

Newcastle, Manchester, Leeds... "In Manchester a most glorious meeting, fully a thousand stayed to the after-meeting. It was like a charge of dynamite had exploded among them," C. T. wrote to his mother.

"No, Daisy, put the watered silk in the larger trunk." Hilda forced herself to attend to the matter at hand. Then her mind drifted back to the letter Mrs. Studd had received from her son only that morning.

I cannot tell you how very much the Lord has blessed us. And we grow daily in the knowledge of Jesus and His wonderful love. What a different life from my former one. Why, cricket and racquets and shooting are nothing to this overwhelming joy.

And Hilda felt again the cramp at her throat, just as she had that morning when Mrs. Studd read the letter to them. Hilda had seen Kynaston's very real thrill for his brother's experience and for the kingdom, and yet his frustration seemed to increase at his own directionless state. If only she could help him.

Well, tonight was to be the final London farewell for the missionary band. Then she and Kynaston would be off, just the two of them. Surely they could work through their future together in the peace that would follow. Hilda smiled at the thought.

"Yes, that's right." She nodded at her maid. "The gold for the green velvet, the aquamarines for the blue silk. We're to dine at the captain's table the first night. I'm not certain which gown I'll wear."

That night the Beauchamp and Studd families were carried along with the throng working its way into Eccleston Hall where all seven of the Cambridge Band would be together for the first time. "I'm sure this is a very fine thing." Mrs. Studd looked around her at the crowd overflowing the room. "I know I wouldn't want to be the one to say otherwise. But one does wonder how many farewell services there must be."

Hilda patted her mother-in-law's kid-gloved hand. "You're holding up remarkably well, Mother Studd. Just this last one for your nerves to endure. Then I believe they're to hold brief meetings in Cambridge and at Oxford, and they'll set sail." *And Kynaston and I will be on our honeymoon,* she added under her breath. She counted the days on her fingers.

"Not quite, my love." Her husband's voice broke in on her daydream.

"What? What do you mean?"

"There's been an urgent request from the YMCA for them to postpone their departure just a little longer so there can be one more final London farewell."

Postpone? Again? More delay? But they've already postponed twice. Hilda bit her tongue against protest. It was evident the hand of God was directing all—as she had so often reminded Kynaston. And through the last three years, she had slowly come to understand the blessedness of saying, "Not my will, but Thine." But this was their honeymoon. Even delaying one more day would mean changing all their plans. Would they ever get off?

She was so certain their life together was God's will. She had to believe He was directing their plans, even if the goal was not in sight yet. So why did it all have to go wrong now? Would all the work of packing have to be redone?

Or should they go ahead and leave tomorrow? There would be hundreds, thousands at the final, final, last farewell. No one would notice if she and Kynaston were not there. Or if they did notice, who would blame a newly married couple for going on their wedding trip? And yet she knew that even to suggest such a thing would be unspeakably selfish. Their brothers and friends were giving their lives to this. They must support them through the final step.

The next morning, at the hour they had planned to be departing for Victoria Station, Hilda sat in her peach satin wrap trimmed with deep rows of ivory lace, sipping tea at the small table before the fire in the bedroom of their new home at 2 Cavendish Place while Kynaston, his slippered feet on a stool, read the morning paper. "My love, after only seven weeks we quite resemble an old married couple. But at least if one must delay one's wedding trip, we couldn't have more pleasant surroundings."

Kynaston looked at her over the top of his paper. "I'm sorry, my dear. Did you say something?"

She smiled at him. "No, nothing important."

"There is a most remarkable account of last night's meeting. Shall I read it out to you?"

"By all means."

"Very nice prose, I think." He raised the paper and read:

"When before were the stroke of a university eight, the captain of a university eleven, an officer of the Royal Artillery, an officer of the Dragoon Guards, the son of a baronet and a clergyman footballer—in all, five B.A.s and two officers, seen standing side by side renouncing the careers in which they had already gained no small distinction, putting aside the splendid prizes of earthly ambition and plunging into that warfare whose splendours are seen only by faith and whose rewards seem so shadowy to the unopened vision of ordinary men?"

He stopped, gasping for breath. "That fellow does write long sentences." Then he continued reading.

"Yet the crowds did not come to flatter or gape. Spirituality marked most emphatically the densely crowded meeting. The speakers told, modestly and yet fearlessly, of the Lord's goodness to them, and of the joy of serving Him, and they appealed to young men, not for their mission, but for their Master. The Cambridge Seven demonstrated in an unforgettable fashion hearts which have truly laid all at the Lord's feet, and whose delight is the most open confession of His name and its power upon themselves."

"Oh, Kynaston." Hilda blinked hard and swallowed. "That's wonderful."

"Yes, it is."

And again she saw the hurt in his eyes. The pain of being rejected by his Master was intensified by the joy over the Lord's working he felt at the same time.

She tried to pray, but her own pain, born of feeling his, was too sharp. It was like ripping the bandage off an open sore. Why couldn't she see a way to help Kynaston? A way for them? Why must she be so blind? Why must blindness be the lot of fallen mankind? They would rush forth gladly to do anything God asked of them. But the stifling darkness held them captive.

She thought of the long struggle she had had over China, her initial abhorrence that Kynaston should be preparing to go out. Then her own gradual turning and final triumphant embracing of the vision. And with the remembered joy of that moment, the pain came again. All those dreams. All the souls to be won. All the prayers—for nothing?

When all they longed to do was to win souls, why didn't God make a way? Why were the heavens shut? How could one pray when the heavens were shut? And now she knew more truly than ever before the weight Kynaston had lived with these past months.

A flood of love for him washed over her. And with that she felt her aching soul lift, and the prayer came to her, *Take all my own desires away, Lord. All my plans, all my dreams. Take it all away and put back anything You want. Take it and put back only what is pure in Your sight.*

And then she knew what to say to Kynaston. She leaned forward and grabbed his arm urgently. "Now I understand. You see—your work for China is done!"

"Done? I didn't do any."

"Yes, you did." She almost shook him in her insistence. "You did all this." She gestured toward the newspaper. "You prepared the way. You were the first to respond to the call. You organized the Christian Union. You arranged for Moody to go to Cambridge. You held strong when the others wavered. You did more than any other person to prepare for the others to become established so the Lord could use them. Your work for China is done." She paused for breath. "Now there will be a new work for you."

"Yes, I see…. And I don't doubt He has a new work for me. But what?"

Hilda was quiet. It had all come to her as a blinding vision. But here she was again without an answer.

A knock at the door broke the silence. "Yes, Daisy, you may take the tray," Hilda responded.

Hilda did not look up until she smelled the heavy sweetness. "Daisy, are you wearing scent?"

"A young man at the door, miss, er—ma'am. He brought these. To welcome you to the neighborhood, he said."

Hilda looked at the clay pot bursting with tall oval stalks of purple hyacinths. "Did he give his name? Is he still here?" She jumped up.

"Said he's Jackie, mi—ma'am."

"Ask him to wait. Then come help me." She hurried into her dressing room.

Daisy returned to report that the lad had already left. But it didn't matter. Hilda knew where he had gone. And she knew where she and Kynaston must go. The answer had been there all along. From Cavendish Place, 390 Regent Street was barely a brisk walk. Two years ago Quinten Hogg had told them of his remarkable work and invited them to visit him. But Kynaston had been too full of his ideas of China, and she was always too focused on her own plans. All the time God had been standing there holding the door open, and neither of them had seen it.

"Come for a walk with me, Kynaston."

"Walk? Hilda, have you looked at the sky? I've never seen heavier rain clouds hanging over London."

"Yes, yes. Never mind. We won't go far." It was all she could do to keep her voice level. But she wanted him to discover it for himself.

They strolled along the pavement to a splendid stone building with pedimented windows. Royal Polytechnic Institution was engraved large over the door. Hilda led the way under the Egyptian portico capped with an enthroned marble statue of wisdom. They were met by the energetic figure of Q. H. himself. He was even kinder and more gracious than Hilda remembered. His perky sandy beard was set off by a well-tailored gray suit and silk tie beneath his crisp high collar. "My dear Studd and Mrs. Studd, I understand heartiest congratulations are in order. What a great honor to have you call on me, and so soon after your nuptials. I thought you had forgotten my invitation to visit our busy institution here—but you see that I had not forgotten you.

"Matter of fact, I plan to attend your brother's farewell tonight. Fine thing he's doing. You must be very proud. Hope the rain holds off for the big event. Darkest clouds I've ever seen."

As he talked, he led the way toward a large room off the central hall. "This is our social and refreshment room. It is the general lounging and rallying room for our members." Hilda looked at a room she judged to be fifty feet by sixty feet filled with clean but cheaply dressed men and boys. Ranging in age from late childhood to early adulthood, they were reading, talking, or taking refreshment. "You understand, we operate on the basis of membership. We provide recreation, classes, sport, social development, and most of all, spiritual training—all for a single low fee. And, of course, we have scholarships for many who can't afford to pay."

Hilda caught a glimpse of newspapers, chess games, and bulletin boards before their host swept them onward. He pushed open a tall, dark door. "Our club room. Committees meet here to plan rowing events, football matches," he looked at Kynaston, "and cricket matches, of course."

They crossed the hall. "And here is our lending library. Several thousand volumes—reference works, periodicals." Hilda was beginning to feel dizzy as she hurried to keep up with their guide, weaving his way between groups of students dressed for sport, work, or study. "I know you'll be interested to see our gymnasium—one of our most popular features. Nearly 2,000 members avail themselves of it regularly. We charge a small locker rent of eighteen pence for half a year. The swimming-bath is one of the finest in England... "

They continued through the classrooms, the lecture hall,

band-practice room, and barber's shop while Mr. Hogg listed their activities: choral society, military band, German Society, French Society, literary club, debating club, cycling club, tennis club, rambling club...

"And our courses of study are quite complete. Mostly night and early morning classes so the members can work. We teach all the trades—with cooperation of the unions, of course—carpentry, brickwork, plumbing, boot-making, printing, photography—"

"And gardening, I believe," Hilda added. "We've had occasion to be most grateful for your greenhouse." And she told him of her wedding flowers and the hyacinths that precipitated their visit that morning.

"Yes, yes. That's excellent. And we offer arithmetic, grammar, elocution, shorthand, pharmacy. Did I tell you about our music department? And savings bank and sick fund?"

Even the athletic Kynaston sounded just a little out of breath as he asked, "It's all perfectly astounding. But what of religious training?"

"But, my dear Studd, that's the basis of the whole thing. What would it profit a man to gain all this but lose his own soul? Devotions at ten o'clock every morning, 700 men in our Bible class, some 1,500 regularly at Sunday evening service, Christian Workers Union, strong Total Abstinence Society. There's more, of course, but that gives you an idea."

"This is perhaps the most splendid work I've ever seen, Mr. Hogg." Hilda bit her lip. She didn't want to offend their host. And yet— "But there are no opportunities for girls and women. It seems that in London females need, even more than men, the advantages you offer."

"Oh, my dear Mrs. Studd, how remiss of me not to mention—from the first women have been admitted to the educational facilities of the Institute. Bible classes for women are conducted on Sunday afternoons and weekday evenings by Mrs. Hogg. We would do more—but there is much need for workers." He paused. "The sporting and the religious work of the Poly is much in need of strong assistance by a muscular Christian."

Just then a familiar small figure ran down the hall toward them. "Jackie, how fine you look." Hilda held her hand out to him. "Thank you so much for the splendid flowers."

Jackie beamed. "It were my pleasure, ma'am."

Mr. Hogg gave an amused grimace. "We're still working on the grammar." He turned to Jackie. "Did you wish to see me, son?"

"Yes sir, Mr. Hogg. That is, not me, sir. But there's a fellow from a magazine. Says he has an appointment fer a interview."

"Oh, I forgot." Q. H. rubbed his high, round forehead. "Do forgive me—Mr. Studd, Mrs. Studd. Please look around all you'd like. Have a cup of tea in the social room. I insist on its always being fresh." He nodded a bow to Hilda and hurried toward his office.

"Wanna come to my class? Making cabinets. It's swell!" Hilda was pleased to note the whiteness of the teeth Jackie's grin revealed.

"Maybe just a bit later," Kynaston said. "And I'll expect to see you at the Cricket Club when the season starts."

"Right-o!"

As soon as they were alone, Kynaston pulled Hilda into an empty meeting room. She held her breath for him to speak, and yet there was no need for him to. The animation that had been absent for so long was back in his face, his dark eyes brilliant. He had the look she had seen so often on the cricket pitch just before he took a wicket. "This is it. Plenty to do and a lifelong work."

"Yes."

"Thank God. Oh, thank God."

Hilda nodded, her eyes misty, her throat choked with her great love for this man and for God. They had come through deep waters together. And now, standing on the brink of the other shore with the winds stilled around them, she could see how everything fit together so perfectly that it could only have been crafted by the hand of God.

Kynaston took her hand and drew her closer to him. "Now I realize, Smith's verse was for me. 'Thou art not sent to a people of a strange speech.'"

Just then the door burst open, and a young man wearing a

bright green sack coat burst in. He took one look at the elegant visitors standing so close together and blushed as bright a red as his carrot-colored hair. "Awrr, ret sawry ahm, guv'nr, ma'am." He backed out.

Hilda laughed. "Not sent to a people of a strange speech, you said?"

Kynaston engulfed her in a hearty hug as he laughed with a freedom she hadn't heard for many, many months.

Twenty-seven

"Oh, just look at the rain." Mrs. Studd pulled back the lace curtain of her drawing room two hours later, and Hilda gasped. The sheet of rain was so heavy she could not even see the gardens across the street.

Mrs. Studd dropped the curtain and wrung her hands. "Oh my, do you suppose the YMCA leaders who wished to back out of the farewell were right? I heard that one of the officers threatened to resign. What a disappointment for the last meeting to be a failure after all."

Hilda sighed. For all of Mother Studd's propensity to dramatize every situation, there was truth to what she said. After the initial excitement of postponing everything for one more day for a final London farewell, there had been controversy among the organizers over the decision. It had looked as if it might not go ahead until Benjamin Broomhall of the C.I.M. took the matter in hand. The meeting had been widely publicized. But no one could blame even the most stout-hearted for staying home on such a night.

Still, one must go on. And no matter what the results of tonight's meeting, this would be a beginning, not an end for Hilda and Kynaston. They were finally to set out on their honeymoon. The next morning they would take the boat train from Victoria Station and travel as far as Calais with the Cambridge band.

Hilda was determined that it would be glorious whatever the circumstances. But deep in her heart she admitted that it would be far more glorious if tonight's meeting were a success.

Please, Lord. You've done everything in such amazing perfection. Please let Your blessing continue.

A short time later water sprayed from the wheels of the Studd carriage, lashed against the windows, and thumped on the roof. Lady Beauchamp, whom they had collected in Cromwell Road, sat across from Hilda and Kynaston, soothing Mrs. Studd. But Hilda could tell that even her composed mother was tense.

"Oh, why are we stopping? We can't be there yet," Mrs. Studd cried as they jolted to a stop.

Hilda cleared a peephole through the steamy window and peered out. "This is incredible!" Even though they were still some distance from Exeter Hall, the Strand was clogged solid with carriages. A throng of people hurried, almost shoulder to shoulder, along the sidewalk, most not even bothering with umbrellas in their rush to get a seat inside.

"Perhaps we should alight here if you don't mind walking a bit. We'll be lucky to get seats," Kynaston suggested.

"But surely they'll be reserved for us," Mrs. Studd began. "If I should miss seeing my own dear boy on his last evening at home..."

They were finally inside the vast hall that had been the scene of so many memorable evangelical and civic gatherings. Here Lord Shaftesbury had presided at meetings of the Ragged School Union, Prince Albert had made his first public appearance—that for the extinction of the slave trade, Mendelssohn had played the great organ and conducted the first performance of *Elijah*. But never before had so many thousands crowded into Exeter Hall. As Hilda surveyed the living sea of humanity, she saw that Mrs. Studd's fears about seating were valid.

"Can you help us find seats?" Kynaston hailed a harried usher.

"Well, there's an overflow room downstairs..." Then the man recognized the mothers of two of the missionaries. "Mmm, we must do something. Lady Beauchamp, I believe your daughter is playing the organ. We could make room for you on the bench beside her. If Your Ladyship would agree—"

"I would be most honored to sit at the organ Mendelssohn

played." She followed the usher to join Ida while Kynaston found a seat for the remaining three by asking some cricketing friends to squeeze even closer together.

In the row ahead of them Hilda spotted Alice Polhill-Turner with her mother. Hilda leaned forward and spoke to them. Alice radiated a quiet joy, her smile soft, her light blue eyes misty. "The answer to all my prayers," she whispered. "It makes one feel so humble."

"I don't know what you're talking about, Alice." Mrs. Polhill-Turner, a dark, sharp-featured woman, turned from her daughter to Hilda. "You understand, my sons are not formally connected with this mission. They will merely be traveling in China to see the work." She waved her hand airily.

Hilda muttered a confused reply and sank back in her seat, shaking her head with sorrow that the lady should count it a disgrace to be the mother of missionaries. But then the excitement in the room claimed all of Hilda's attention. Across the front hung a vast map of China. Beneath it were forty Cambridge undergraduates, all dedicated to become missionaries.

And then the seven filed in, led by George Williams, the founder of the YMCA. The hall rang with cheers and clapping. The fire God had set ablaze across Britain shone in each of the seven men and set the hall alight.

Under Ida's touch the great organ pealed forth, and 3,000 or more voices sang, "Tell it out among the heathen that the Lord is King..." George Williams presented each of the seven with a Chinese New Testament from the British and Foreign Bible Society. In place of Hudson Taylor, who had already set sail, Benjamin Broomhall spoke briefly on the work of the China Inland Mission.

Then the part everyone had come for—each of the seven, representative of the strongest, finest, most noble of English youth, spoke of his love for Jesus Christ. Stanley Smith was first, vibrant, brilliant, burning with the power of his vision. "We do not go to that far distant field to speak of doctrine or theory, but of a living, bright, present and rejoicing Savior."

He was interrupted with a roaring chorus of amens. "We go

to tell those who have not heard what a blessed thing it is to have the love of the Lord Jesus Christ reigning in their hearts. We go to say, 'My brother, I bring you an almighty Savior.'

"'Whosoever loveth the Lord keepeth His commandments.' And what does He command?" Smith paused as the question rang in every heart. He spread his long arms, stretching out the hands that had formerly earned such fame holding an oar and would now hold the nail-pierced hands of his Savior. "He commands, 'Go ye into all the world and preach the gospel to every creature.'"

Hilda thought she would burst with the fervor in the room and inside herself. But how was Kynaston taking this? He who had so recently abdicated his desire to go into all the world? Surely, his new vision—only a few hours old—could have no more severe test than this. She dared not look. Instead she applauded as Smith left the platform to go down to those in the overflow room, and Monty rose to speak, calling for many more right there in that room and those they would influence to put themselves at Christ's disposal.

Dixon Hoste, erect and polished with his precise officer's bearing, told how in the army he had been blind until Christ opened his eyes to see Him. He appealed to the audience, "Pray that God may keep us faithful. We cannot do this in our own strength. There will be times when the need is too great, our strength too small to pray for all that is needful. You can have a part in our work—the most vital part—by keeping us and all missionaries ever before the throne in prayer."

Hilda squeezed Kynaston's arm and breathed her own prayer for her husband, for his faith and strength in all that he must do, too. Then William Cassels stepped forward. Hilda smiled, recalling the day at Henley when he had sat so quietly, unable to row for Cambridge because of a broken foot, listening to her cousin talk of missionary work. The William before them tonight was no longer silent. He spoke with elegant, quiet maturity for his Lord and for the need for more heroism in Christians. "Oh, for shame that He who gave His own life on the cross should still be crying for helpers. The field is white unto harvest. Where are the laborers to bring the sheaves into the storehouse?"

Cecil Polhill-Turner's resignation from the Dragoon Guards had not yet been published, so he stood before them as a serving officer of his crack cavalry regiment to tell how his own life had been transformed and redirected when he met Jesus Christ. "I found the greatest peace and happiness by resting my soul on the Lord. I recommend all of you to do the same." He spoke only five sentences.

And Arthur, the youngest of the seven, just three days short of his twenty-third birthday, was as brief as his brother. He declared that leaving home to go to the unknown was not hard but glorious—"Like a bird when let out of a cage." Again Hilda saw the elation on the face of the sister who, in spite of ridicule and resistance, had prayed so faithfully for these brothers. She could not see their mother's face.

Hilda was not looking toward the platform when C. T. got up, but she could feel the stir in the audience. The greatest cricketer in England—going to China. He told openly about his conversion, slow progress, and backsliding before his brother's near-fatal illness. "I had formerly as much love for cricket as any man could have. But after I yielded to Jesus Christ as Lord, my heart was no longer in the game."

And then he told how he came to the secret of total commitment. "I gave Him an iron ring, the iron ring of my will, with all the keys of my life on it, except one little key that I kept back. And the Master said, 'Are they all here?' I said, 'They are all there but one, the key of a tiny closet of my heart of which I must keep control.' He said, 'If you don't trust Me in all, you don't trust Me at all.' I tried to make terms; I said, 'Lord, I will be so devoted in everything else, but I can't live without the contents of that closet.'"

Hilda felt every breath in the room being held as they relived the story of a life hovering in the balance. "If I had kept the key of that closet and mistrusted Christ, He never would have trusted me with the ministry of His blessed Word. He seemed to be receding from me."

There was a gasp as C. T. leaned across the pulpit as if grasping for a lifeline. "I called Him back and said, 'I am not willing. But I am willing to be made willing.'"

A sigh of released tension filled the hall. "That was enough. He came near and took that key out of my hand and went straight for the closet. I knew what He would find there, and He knew, too." C. T. shook his head. "What a fool I was! He wanted to take away the sham jewels, to give me the real ones. He took away the thing that was eating out my life and gave me Himself."

Two hours had passed. Hilda felt as if she had been there perhaps twenty minutes. She could readily have stayed all night and gone straight from there to Victoria Station. Her only concern was for the man beside her. *Don't let him feel left out,* she prayed.

A noted preacher closed the service by calling all to "submit to Christ. Offer yourself to God as a living sacrifice. There is enough power in this meeting to stir the whole world."

The organ pealed, and Hilda was on her feet with all the gathering. "Take my life and let it be consecrated, Lord, to Thee...'" Hilda sang so hard she thought her heart would burst as she applied the words to the lives of the men before her.

"'Take my lips and let them be filled with messages from Thee...'" Stanley Smith, the captivating orator.

"'Take my silver and my gold...'" Cecil Polhill-Turner giving up a large inheritance.

"'Take my intellect and use, Every pow'r as Thou shalt choose...'" William Cassels, the most scholarly.

"'Take my will and make it Thine—It shall be no longer mine...'" C. T. giving Him the iron ring of his will.

"'Take myself—and I will be ever, only, all for Thee. Ever, only, all for Thee.'"

The service ended, but Hilda moved with reluctance.

She went out feeling she should have removed her shoes, for surely she had been on holy ground. Only heaven itself could match this experience. But Kynaston was silent.

At 9:30 the next morning they all gathered at the station, still wrapped in the cocoon of God's presence, talking in hushed tones of the night before. All except Kynaston. He had said almost nothing since the meeting, and Hilda had not gathered the nerve to pry. She dared not tread on ground that might bring him pain. She held gently to his arm, letting him know she was there and praying for him. Several of the Marylebone Cricket Club members had come to see C. T. off. Monty helped his mother settle in her compartment, as Lady Beauchamp was going with them as far as Calais also.

"Booooard!" The call was accented with a great puff of white steam released from the engine.

As they left the shelter of Victoria Station, Hilda realized how long she had waited for this moment. Alone in their compartment with her husband, she turned to Kynaston. "My love..." How could she frame the question?

Kynaston flung his arms out, hitting both sides of the compartment. "Hilda, Hilda! I am so thankful. All last night and this morning, I felt the most awful guilt at being so *thankful* that I wasn't up there with those others. What a terrible mistake that would have been. How well He knows us. How perfect His plan is for each life. Now I'm embarrassed that I was in such a funk thinking He'd refused me. Hilda, what will you ever do with such a husband?"

She flung herself into his arms with such force that he staggered backward. They landed in a pile on the seat. "I will love him and have his children and serve beside him." She paused as Kynaston settled her more comfortably on his lap. "And knock him off his feet occasionally."

Afterword

The thrill of serving Christ in soul-winning lasted a lifetime for all the Cambridge Seven, and they had as profound an effect on China as they had on Britain.

William Cassels became Bishop of Western China in 1895. He remained there until his death in 1925, the first of the seven to die.

Stanley Smith spent his life in north China where he became as fluent a preacher in Chinese as in English. He died in 1931. His son became a medical missionary to Rwanda.

C. T. Studd determined to live by faith alone and gave his whole fortune to missions. (His family educated his four beautiful daughters, three of whom married missionaries.) His health failed in 1894, and he and his wife left China. He became known as a missionary pioneer, working for six years in India, and then in the depths of tropical Africa. From his work grew the Heart of Africa Mission. He died in the Belgian Congo in 1931 with over 1,000 Africans seeing him to his grave.

Arthur Polhill (they dropped the Turner) completed his ordination in China. He was one of the few missionaries to remain in China throughout the Boxer Rebellion and Revolution of 1911. He retired at the age of 65 to become a country vicar in Britain. He died in 1935.

Cecil Polhill had a special work in Tibet where he made great friends with the people and made contact with the Dalai

Lama. He was invalided home in 1900 and inherited Howbury Hall in 1903, but his heart was in China, to which he made seven prolonged missionary visits. He died at Howbury Hall in 1938 at the age of eighty.

Montague Beauchamp was the itinerant member of the band. He loved long, difficult evangelistic journeys and once traveled 1,000 miles in intense heat with Hudson Taylor. On such treks Monty carried a large palm leaf fan inscribed in Chinese characters, "Repent, the Kingdom of Heaven is at hand."

Evacuated from China during the Boxer Rebellion, he became a chaplain and served the armed forces in Egypt and Greece during the Great War. When his next elder brother was killed in action, he inherited the baronetcy. He gave the money he inherited to build the C.I.M. headquarters and missionary residences in Shanghai. He was founder of World Evangelism. In 1939 Sir Montague died at his son's mission station in Paoning, China.

The current baronet, Sir Christopher Proctor-Beauchamp, writes, "I have always been told that my grandfather was a most intrepid man who went in for tough route marches all over China, walking great distances and never sparing himself physically."

D. E. Hoste most directly fulfilled Harold Schofield's prayers by working in Shansi and becoming a great man of prayer. In 1894 he married the diminutive Gertrude Broomhall, whom he had seen at the piano in Pyrland Road in 1883. They had three sons. He succeeded Hudson Taylor as head of the China Inland Mission in 1903. He was interned by the Japanese when they overran China, and he left China in 1945, more than sixty years after his arrival. He died in London in 1945, the last of the Cambridge Seven. Retired C.I.M. missionaries today remember him fondly as "Old Hoste" and say that he would always take time to pray with anyone who came to him.

All of the seven married, and many of their children became missionaries.

George B. Studd also went to China for a time and then later to the "Wild West" mission nearest his heart. He died in California in 1945.

Gerald Lander, one-time leader of the Cambridge "fast set," became a missionary bishop in south China. And the young man who almost walked out on Moody's London campaign when the prayer became too long was Wilfred Grenfell, knighted by King George V for twenty years of service as a medical missionary to Labrador.

By the early 1950s China was closed to all missionary activity on the part of Westerners. The China Inland Mission was renamed Overseas Missionary Fellowship. Today OMF International works in sixteen Asian countries. They have 1,000 members of twenty-seven nationalities from twenty-one countries.

The Polytechnic Institute became the life work of Kynaston and Hilda Studd. On Quinten Hogg's death in 1903, J. E. K. became president. He was knighted in 1923, elected Lord Mayor of London in 1928, made a baronet and awarded an honorary LL.D. from Cambridge University in 1929.

The Dictionary of National Biography records that Kynaston Studd's career is "a conspicuous example of how a man, devoid of personal ambition, can be raised by his fellow citizens to the highest post they have to bestow, by their esteem for (his) generosity in judgment as well as his gifts, high Christian example, great modesty, and unobtrusive but constant devotion to the service of mankind."

The biography of Kynaston Studd records that "the unity in aim and outlook (shared by Hilda and Kynaston) lasted unhindered and undimmed" throughout their married life. In the summer of 1885, they went to America at the invitation of D. L. Moody where Kynaston spoke at Yale, Harvard, and other universities. Hilda had many speaking engagements at women's colleges.

They had a close, happy family of four sons and one daughter. Eric, the eldest son and heir, served in the family firm until he retired in 1938, when he became governor of the Polytechnic. Ronald Studd served seventeen years in the Royal Navy and then became managing director of the Polytechnic Touring Association.

The third son, Lionel, became ordained to the ministry of the Church of England, but in 1914 he chose to go to the Western Front as a combatant rather than as a chaplain. He was killed near Ypres in February of that year. Bernard Studd, the fourth son, fulfilled long business commitments in India and then was elected to the Polytechnic presidency his father had held. Vera, the only daughter, became a missionary in 1925.

Hilda died in 1921. Four years later Kynaston married Princess Alexandra Lieven, daughter of Prince Paul Lieven, grand master of ceremonies at the imperial court of Russia to which Baron Radstock and Granville Waldegrave had gone as missionaries. She fully shared in his evangelistic and civic endeavors.

On Thursday, January 13, 1944, Kynaston Studd did a full day of work, which included presiding on the bench at the Guildhall. He went to bed, and early the next morning was found to have passed peacefully away. A moving memorial service was held in St. Paul's Cathedral. He was described as "a great Christian gentleman" by those who knew him. "Everything he touched was lifted up." "You could not be with J. E. K. and hear him speak without realizing the Spirit of the living Christ whom he served."

The service ended with the singing of one of Kynaston Studd's favorite hymns: "And Can it Be?"

> *No condemnation now I dread:*
> *Jesus, and all in Him, is mine...*
> *Bold I approach th'eternal throne,*
> *And claim the crown, through Christ my own.*

AUTHOR'S COMMENTS

My favorite story is always the one I'm currently writing, but I found the story of the Cambridge Seven to be exceptionally exciting because it shows so explicitly the power of prayer and what God can accomplish through lives completely yielded to Him. God does have perfect control over individuals and over nations. He will bring revival when enough people are yielded to Him in prayer.

I also thoroughly enjoyed writing a novel for which almost nothing had be to invented. So much has been recorded by and about these remarkable people that the task was almost entirely one of research rather than invention. Time and again I was amazed at how God arranged events far better than any novelist's imagination could.

If you have been moved by the account of what God did through these people a hundred years ago, please join me in praying that our generation would see a similar outpouring of the work of the Holy Spirit.

GLOSSARY OF SPORTING TERMS

Croquet

Balk line:	Portion of yard line from which player starts his ball.
Roquet:	To drive one's ball against another.
To take croquet:	To place one's ball in contact with roqueted ball and strike one's own ball so as to move both balls.
Peel:	To score by knocking partner's ball through a hoop in order.
Rover:	The final loop from the last wicket played back to the peg in the center of the field.
To make a break:	Skillful alternation of making points and roqueting balls resulting in point after point being made.

Rowing

Blue (or varsity blue):	Blue blazer indicating wearer chosen to represent his school in rowing, cricket, etc.
The Mays or Eights:	University boat races held during summer term.
Trial Eight:	Eight-oared boat's provisional crew, from among whom some members of the final eight may be chosen.
Stroke:	Rower who sets the pace for a crew.
Single scull:	Boat rowed by one person.
Rowlocks:	Device for holding an oar in place.

Cricket

XI:	Team of eleven members
On-drive:	Straight bat stroke used to hit delivery bounced close to the batter.
Innings:	A team's or individual's turn at bat (always plural).
Popping crease:	Line in front of wicket over which batter must touch bat or part of his body to be safe or to score.
Delivery:	Pitch (as a verb).
Bowled out:	Bowler gets delivery past the batter, hits his wicket, knocks off bail.
Bowler:	Pitcher
Wicket:	Set of three wooden poles that function like bases in American baseball.
Bails:	Small pegs that rest in grooves on top of the wicket. Knocking bail off results in an out. Referred to as "wicket went down" or "fall of the wicket."
Shooter:	Ball delivered fast and low.
Captain's innings:	Outstanding performance under difficult circumstances by team's captain.
Over:	A set of six deliveries.
Maiden:	An over in which no runs are scored.
Caught:	Out from fielder catching fly ball.
Off break:	Slow delivery that causes ball to bounce into the batter.
Leg break:	Slow delivery that causes ball to bounce away from the batter.

REFERENCES

Broomhall, Benjamin. *The Evangelisation of the World, A Missionary Band: A Recording of Consecration*. London: Morgan and Scott, 1887.

Curtis, Richard K. *They Called Him Mister Moody*. Garden City, N.Y.: Doubleday & Co., Inc., 1962.

Grubb, Norman. *C. T. Studd, Cricketer & Pioneer*. Ft. Washington, Penn.: Christian Literature Crusade, 1982.

Hamilton, Alys L. Douglas. *Kynaston Studd*. London: The London Polytechnic Institute, 1953.

Melville, Tom. *Cricket for Americans: Playing and Understanding the Game*. Bowling Green, Ohio: Bowling Green State U. Popular Press, 1993.

Pollock, John C. *Moody: A Biographical Portrait*. New York: Macmillan Company, 1963.

_____. *Shaftesbury, The Poor Man's Earl*. London: Hodder and Stoughton, 1985.

_____. *The Cambridge Seven, Centenary Edition 1885-1985*. Basingstoke: Marshall Pickering Ltd., 1985.

Schofield, A. T. *Memorials of R. Harold A. Schofield*. London: Hodder and Stoughton, 1898.

Shaw, Albert. "London Polytechnics and People's Palaces." *The Century Magazine*, vol. 40, no. 2, June 1890.

Smith, Hanna Whitall. *The Christian's Secret of a Happy Life*. Chicago: Fleming H. Revell, 1888.

Taylor, J. Hudson. *China's Spiritual Need and Claims*, 7th ed. London: Morgan and Scott, 1887.